Cyrus Cort, Bouquet Memorial Committee

Col. Henry Bouquet and his Campaigns of 1763 and 1764

Cyrus Cort, Bouquet Memorial Committee

Col. Henry Bouquet and his Campaigns of 1763 and 1764

ISBN/EAN: 9783337423377

Printed in Europe, USA, Canada, Australia, Japan

Cover: Foto ©Andreas Hilbeck / pixelio.de

More available books at **www.hansebooks.com**

COL. HENRY BOUQUET

AND

HIS CAMPAIGNS

OF

1763 AND 1764.

By REV. CYRUS CORT,

OF GREENCASTLE, FRANKLIN COUNTY, PA.

LANCASTER, PA.
STEINMAN & HENSEL, PRINTERS.
1883.

TO THE PRECIOUS MEMORY OF

BEATRICE BYERLY,

WHO ESCAPED PONTIAC'S CONFEDERATES AND BORE HER TENDER
BABES THROUGH THE WILDERNESS FROM BUSHY RUN TO FORT
LIGONIER, IN 1763; WHO ORGANIZED AND CONDUCTED A SUN-
DAY SCHOOL AT FORT WALTHOUR, IN WESTMORELAND COUNTY,
PENNSYLVANIA, DURING THE DARK AND DANGEROUS DAYS OF
THE REVOLUTION, AND WHO WAS A BLESSING TO HUNDREDS OF
PIONEER SETTLERS BY HER DEEDS OF CHRISTIAN CHARITY AND
PATRIOTIC DEVOTION DURING A LONG AND EVENTFUL LIFE ON
THE FRONTIERS, THIS LITTLE VOLUME IS DEDICATED BY ONE
OF HER GRATEFUL DESCENDANTS.

"THOUGH HEAVEN ALONE RECORDS THE TEAR,
AND FAME SHALL NEVER KNOW HER STORY,
HER HEART HAS SHED A DROP AS DEAR
AS E'ER BEDEWED THE FIELD OF GLORY."

TABLE OF CONTENTS.

COL. HENRY BOUQUET

AND

HIS CAMPAIGNS OF 1763 AND 1764.

●

INTRODUCTION.

On the 26th of April 1883, a meeting was held in the arbitration room of the court house at Greensburg, Westmoreland county, Pa., to consider the propriety of celebrating the 120th anniversary of the victory of Col. Henry Bouquet at Bushy Run, August 5 and 6, 1763, over the Confederates of Pontiac.

Ex-Lieut.-Gov. John Latta was called to the chair, and Gen'l Richard Coulter and Hon. Jacob Turney were elected Vice Presidents ; Maj. Jas. M. Laird, Frank Vogle and Curtis Gregg were chosen as Secretaries.

By request of the meeting Rev. Cyrus Cort, a resident of Greencastle, Pa., but a native of Greensburg, Pa., was called upon to address the meeting, which he did for over half an hour, eulogizing the character and achievements of Bouquet and showing the far-reaching results of his decisive victory at Bushy Run. Rev. Cort read a letter from Hon. Joseph H. Kuhns, regretting his inability to be present and heartily approving the object of the meeting in its efforts to honor the memory of Bouquet, whose march and victory in 1763 were wonderful military achievements and did much to promote the rapid settlement of the west.

On motion, Revs. J. W. Love, W. W. Moorehead, Lucien Cort and Philip Kuhns, Dr. Kline and A. M. Sloan, Esq.,

A

were appointed a committee to draft resolutions expressive of the sense of the meeting. The following were reported:

Resolved, That in the judgment of this meeting, it is eminently right and proper to commemorate the 120th anniversary of the victory of Col. Henry Bouquet over Pontiac's confederates at Bushy Run, August 5th and 6th, 1763.

Resolved, That inasmuch as August 5th comes on Sunday this year, and inasmuch as all the interests of humanity and Christian civilization were promoted by the decisive victory of Bouquet, we would respectfully suggest to the pastors of all of our churches in the town and county, the propriety of making such special reference to the anniversary, in their regular religious services, as in their judgment may be right and proper.

Resolved, That the victory of Bouquet be commemorated August 6th, in the grove of the old Bushy Run battle-field, by a public celebration, embracing addresses, a poem, a military display, pic-nic, dinner, &c.

Resolved, That a committee of arrangements, to secure and prepare the grounds; a committe on finance, to raise funds to defray necessary expenses of the celebration, and a committee to invite speakers, distinguished guests, military organizations, &c., be appointed.

The resolutions were adopted and committees in accordance appointed, as follows:

Commitee of Arrangements to Secure and Prepare Grounds for the Celebration.—Amos B. Kline, J. B. Laux, Lewis Wannamaker, E. F. Houseman, Lewis Gongaware, William Moore, Mr. Shadwick, Jos. Clark, Robert Byerly, Wm. G. Shuster, Abner Cort.

Committee on Finance.—Jas. Gregg, Esq., Geo. F. Huff, Capt. J. J. Wirsing, Dr. Sowash, Wm. B. Skelly, Paul Lauffer, David Snyder, John Rankin, Sebastian Baer, Esq., Hon. N. M. Marker, H. F. Ludwick, Esq., Hon. John Hugus, and George Plumer Smith of Philadelphia.

Committee on Invitation.—General R. Coulter, Hon. Jos. H. Kuhns, Hon. Jacob Turney, Hon. John Latta, Maj. James M. Laird, G. D. Albert, Esq., John A. Marchand, Esq., Dr. Frank Cowan.

The annexed resolution was likewise adopted:

Resolved, That the chairmen of the three committees aforesaid be an executive committee to fill all vacancies and have a general oversight of the celebration.

A discussion then took place in regard to the advisability of issuing a pamphlet for popular circulation, giving a sketch of Col. Bouquet and his campaigns. It was felt that such a work would form a very important factor in the celebration, and the sentiment of the meeting was that it should be issued without delay. Next day Rev. C. Cort received a letter from Gen. Richard Coulter, A. B. Kline, Esq., and James Gregg, Esq., stating that it was the sense of the meeting that a pamphlet, consisting of one hundred pages, should be prepared as soon as possible, containing a historical sketch of Bouquet and all matters of colonial interest bearing especially on his campaign against the Confederates of Pontiac. These gentlemen, forming the Executive Committee of the celebration, also stated further that it was their wish that he (Rev. C.) should prepare the aforesaid pamphlet. This task was accepted as a labor of love, with the understanding that the writer would assume all pecuniary responsibilities, and that if any profits resulted from the sale of the book or pamphlet above necessary cost of publication, the proceeds should be devoted to a fund for a monument to Bouquet

As the time was limited, and the duties of a large and laborious pastoral charge devolved upon the writer, the work has been prepared in great haste, but with conscientious care and fidelity to the facts of history and reliable traditions. I would gratefully acknowledge my obligations to writings of Francis Parkman, Geo. Harrison Fisher, C. W. Butterfield and the Penn'a Historical Society for valuable assistance in preparing this imperfect sketch of the best military man and one of the finest gentlemen and scholars of colonial times. May it help to rescue from oblivion the memory of a truly good and great man, whose heroic efforts saved our colonial ancestors from the tomahawk and scalping knife and established the supremacy of the Anglo-Saxon race in the valley of the Mississippi.

Dr. Wm Smith's publication in 1765, and Dumas' sketch in 1769, form the basis of this present effort to present the facts of his life for general circulaton.

At a meeting of the executive committee and committee on invitation, at which Rev. Cort was present, June
19th, it was decided to issue special invitations to the
governors of Pennsylvania, Ohio and West Virginia, to
the British Minister, Swiss Consul, Gen. R. C. Drum, &c.
Also that Rev. Samuel Wilson, D.D., Gen. James A. Beaver, Hon. W. S. Stenger and W. U. Hensel, Esq., be invited to deliver addresses at the celebration on the battle-
field, Aug. 6 ; Dr. Frank Cowan to read a poem, and Dr.
Wm. H. Egle to read a paper.

May the skies be bright and all things propitious.

BOUQUET'S BIRTH-PLACE.

HENRY BOUQUET, the subject of our sketch, was born
at Rolle, a small Swiss town on the northern shore of Lake
Geneva in 1719. This town at that time belonged to the
Canton of Berne, one of the largest and most influential Cantons of the Swiss Confederation. It now belongs to the
Canton of Vaud, which is a part of French Switzerland, the
dialect spoken being the Vaudois. The inhabitants since
Reformation days have been chiefly members of the Reformed church, and always ardent lovers of civil and religious liberty. They are noted for industry and intelligence.

From this part of Switzerland comes a large proportion
of the Swiss teachers and governesses to be met with in all
parts of the world.

Lansanne, the capital of the Canton Vaud, is pictur-
esquely situated on the southern slope of the Jura mountains and near the northern shore of Lake Geneva. It is
distinguished for its religious, educational and scientific
institutions. The beautiful Gothic Cathedral, begun in
the 10th and completed in the 13th century, adorns the
city and helps to attract vast crowds of visitors from all
parts of the world. Here Gibbon, the historian resided
many years, and here he wrote the greater part of his
great work on the " Decline and Fall of the Roman Empire." Here, in the western corner of Switzerland, between
the Jura and the Bernese Alps, near the French borders,
Henry Bouquet first saw the light. Amid the most beau-

tiful scenery on the northern shores of the celebrated Lake
Geneva which is fifty miles long and eight wide, amid or-
chards, vineyards and fertile farming and pasture lands, in
full view of Mount Blanc and the most inspiring Alpine
scenery he spent the formative days of childhood and
youth. All these left their impress upon his soul and
aided greatly in forming the noble and heroic character
which shone forth resplendantly in his future eventful
career, both in the old world and the new.

Little is known of the family of Bouquet. The Deutsche
Pioneer of Cincinnati has contended that his family name
was originally *Strauss* from which it was changed into
Bouquet, its French equivalent, when our hero had fairly
begun his military career.

This is certainly a mistake founded on mere conjecture
based on the analogy of such changes as Schoenberg to
Belmont, &c. There is no reliable evidence to show that
Bouquet ever changed his family name, much less to show
that he had any special predilection for France or the
French. The Vaudois people amongst whom he was born
and reared have always spoken a French dialect, and in
that language particularly he doubtless received his education. But it is a noteworthy fact that Bouquet always
fought against France. He seemed to regard her as the
representative of civil and religious despotism, and he gallantly fought against her under the banner of the government which for the time being best represented the cause
and principles of constitutional liberty.

I have before me a copy of Bouquet's last Will and
Testament made June 5, 1765, from which I transcribe a
clause, viz : " I give and bequeath to my father, if then
living, or after him to Colonel Lewis Bouquet and heirs
all the effects of any nature whatsoever which I may die
possessed of in the Continent of Europe without exception." This would indicate that Bouquet was the original
and genuine family name, and not merely the result of a
capricious predilection for foreign terms. It would indicate also that the family was not so obscure as some have
supposed. Mr. Koradi, the Swiss consul, has undertaken
to gather data on this point which we hope will be on
hand at an early day.

The war of American Independence which was loom-
ing up at the time of Bouquet's death in 1765, and the
fact that Col. Frederick Haldimand, his executor, and to
a large extent the legatee of his American possessions remained loyal to King George III. in that struggle, prevented proper examination of these matters by those most
interested in Bouquet's career over a hundred years ago.
This accounts in a measure also for the obscurity and comparative injustice connected with the treatment of Bouquet by writers of Colonial history.

A hundred and twenty years ago his name was a household word in America, and the memory of his heroic
deeds was cherished for a generation with fond affection,
by descendants of pioneer settlers whom he- had rescued
from the tomahawk of the red savages.   Perhaps because
he was a Swiss and gained his greatest distinction in the
British service on Pennsylvania soil in Colonial times the
muse of history and poetry has failed to embalm and perpetuate his name and achievements in a more worthy and
grateful manner.

Be this as it may, the time has come when the grateful
and intelligent descendants of pioneer Colonial settlers,
and all public spirited citizens are called upon to remedy
the defect and rectify the wrongs or omissions of a century, as regards the memory of one of the very best men
that trod this continent before our country became a free
and independent republic.   To this end I have begun this
narrative as an aid to the forthcoming celebration of the
one hundred and twentieth anniversary of the victory of
Bouquet over the confederates of Pontiac at Bushy Run,
Aug. 6, 1763.

BOUQUET LEAVES HOME.

Growing up amid the inspiring scenery of liberty loving
Switzerland, Bouquet sought a theatre more commensurate
with his talents and aspirations than the narrow confines
bounded by his native Alps.   In 1736 at the age of seventeen he made his way along the historic Rhine to the Lowlands of Holland and entered the service of the Dutch
Republic, as a cadet in the Regiment of Constant.   In

1738 he obtained the commission of an ensign in the same regiment. He thus began his career under the government that long had championed the cause of civil and religious liberty, and which was the forerunner of our own great Republic. The King of Sardinia, whose country borders on Switzerland near the home of Bouquet, became involved in a war with the combined forces of France and Spain, then leading powers of Europe. Bouquet entered the Sardinian service and distinguished himself greatly first as lieutenant, and afterwards as adjutant in several memorable and ably conducted campaigns. At the battle of Cony especially did he display great presence of mind and strategic talent in occupying a perilous position in such a way that his men were not aware of the imminent risk to which they were exposed. His very accurate and interesting accounts of these campaigns sent to Holland, attracted the attention of the Prince of Orange, and induced him to secure the services of Bouquet in the army of the Dutch Republic. He entered it in 1748 as captain commandant with the rank of lieutenant colonel of the Swiss guards, a regiment lately formed at the Hague.

He was sent at once with Generals Burmannia and Cornabe to receive from the French the posts in the Low Countries about to be evacuated, and the prisoners of war given up to the Republic by France at the close of the war, according to the terms of the treaty of Aix-la-Chapelle. A few months later he accepted an invitation to accompany Lord Middleton in a tour through France and Italy. It is supposed that in his intimate associations with this nobleman, Bouquet gained his surprising knowledge of the English language which he wrote better than the great majority of English officers.

HOW BOUQUET SPENT LEISURE TIME.

On his return to the Hague, Bouquet devoted every moment not needed in the discharge of regimental duties, to the careful study of matters pertaining to military art and tactics, especially of the higher mathematics which forms their basis. At the Hague he always moved in the

best society and cultivated the friendship of the learned
Professors Hemsterhius, Kœning and Allamand and other
leading men in every department of science.

Instead of gambling and carousing as many military
men are wont to do when off active duty, Bouquet always
improved his leisure moments, by enlarging his acquisi-
tions of knowledge.   At Philadelphia he was a great favorite in the most intelligent circles and enjoyed the confiden-
tial friendship of Chief Justice Allen, Benj. Chew, the
Attorney General, Dr. Wm. Smith Provost of the University and Bertram the Botanist.   His tastes, like his talents,
were of a high order.

ENTERS BRITISH SERVICE.   ROYAL AMERICANS.

In 1754 war broke out between France and England on
a scale that involved two continents.   It was resolved to
raise a corps under the name of Royal Americans consisting of four battallions each containing one thousand
men.   It was proposed to fill the ranks of this regiment
by enlisting Protestant German and Swiss settlers in Pennsylvania and Maryland, who for the most part were unable to speak or understand the English language.

About $400,000 was voted for this purpose by Parlia-
ment.   Smollet, in speaking of these German and Swiss
settlers says : " As they were all zealous Protestants and
in general strong, hardy men accustomed to the climate, it
was judged that a regiment of good and faithful soldiers
might be raised out of them, particularly proper to oppose
the French ; but to this end it was necessary to appoint
some officers, especially subalterns, who understood military discipline and could speak the German language ; and
as a sufficient number of such could not be found among
the English officers it was necessary to bring over and
grant commissions to several German and Swiss officers
and engineers.   But as this step by the Act of Settlement
could not be taken without the authority of Parliament, an
act was now passed for enabling his majesty to grant commissions to a certain number of foreign Protestants who
had served abroad as officers or engineers to act and rank
as officers or engineers in America only."

Henry Bouquet and his intimate friend and countryman Frederick Haldiman were appointed lieutenant colonels of this Royal American Brigade, and as colonels commandant each of a thousand men were placed on an equality with the colonel-in-chief. They were allowed to select subordinate officers especially for the artillery and engineer departments, and these were chosen with rare judgment, for the most part from the lately disbanded armies of the Dutch Republic. Hence it was that such gallant soldiers and good scholars as Ecuyer, a countryman of Bouquet, obtained command in this famous regiment.

Sir Joseph Yorke major general and English minister to the Dutch Republic was mainly instrumental in the creation of this body of troops and also in securing the services of such able continental commanders as Haldimand and Bouquet. Fifty of the officers might be foreign Protestants according to the Act of Parliament, while the enlisted men were to be raised principally among the German settlers in America.

Bouquet sailed for America in the summer of 1756, the year after Braddock's disastrous defeat. Lord Loudoun was colonel of the Royal American corps and commander-in-chief of the British army in America. Like some other British officers of Colonial days he was haughty and blustering in peaceful communities, but very slow in facing the foe where actual danger and military duty called. As remarked by a friend of Franklin, Loudoun was like the figure of St. George, painted on the sign boards—always on horseback but never riding on.

BOUQUET GOES TO PHILADELPHIA.

Under the orders of Londoun Bouquet first appears in Philadelphia late in the Fall of 1756, in command of 550 officers and men, consisting of a battallion of Royal Americans and two independent companies. A demand for comfortable quarters for the troops did not meet the re· sponse from the Assembly which the Governor and British officers deemed proper, and considerable bad blood was stirred up, which, under a less judicious officer than

A*

Bouquet might have resulted disastrously to all concerned.
The breach of faith on the part of the sheriff in laying the
warrant for lodgings in private houses prematurely before
the Assembly, almost led to a collision between the civil
and military authorities.   Had Londoun himself been
present at Philadelphia it is probable that the sack and
pillage of part of the city would have been the outcome of
this dispute.   During the remainder of the winter matters
moved along smoóthly, and Bouquet mingled in the best
intellectual and social circles of the city. He was particularly intimate with the Shippen family, and formed a very
tender attachment for a Miss Anne Willing, whose mother
was a Shippen.   He carried on a very interesting correspondence with this young lady, even amid the cares and
turmoils of the camp, verifying in a measure the sentiment
of the old Castillian song.
    "'Tis the spirit most gallant in war
    That is fondest and truest in love."
    In May, 1757, Bouquet was ordered to South Carolina
with a detachment of Royal Americans.   In September he
wrote that his men were fast dying of the fever, and he
seemed anxious for a more healthy location.   In a quarrel
that arose between Governor Lyttleton and the Assembly
of South Carolina, Bancroft tells us that Bouquet successfully acted the part of a conciliator.

FORBES' EXPEDITION AND DISPUTE WITH WASHINGTON.

    Military matters were in a very lethargic state in America
during 1756 and 1757, until William Pitt took the reins
with a master hand and a giant's grasp.   A change soon
came over the face of affairs.   New Jersey, New York and
New England were to assist in Northern campaigns against
the French.   Pennsylvania and the more Southern colonies were to aid in the conquest of the West, and finish
the work in which Braddock so miserably failed three
years previous.   England was to provide arms, ammunition
and tents, and even in the end, reimburse the colonies for
all other expenses.   With this expectation Pennsylvania
went into the the campaign of 1758 with great earnestness

and furnished 2,700 men for the expedition against Fort Duquesne.

General John Forbes, a brave and meritorious Scotch officer, was placed in command.

Bouquet was re-called from South Carolina with his Royal Americans and given charge of the First Division, while Colonel George Washington had command of the Second Division, Virginia having furnished 2,600 troops for the campaign. Bouquet was at Fort Bedford early in July, with a part of the forces in advance of the main army. Washington was at Fort Cumberland, 30 or 40 miles south of Bedford. July 25, he wrote Bouquet, earnestly advising that the expedition should advance at once by the Braddock road from Cumberland, instead of delaying to cut a aoad through the wilderness of Pennsylvania to Fort Duquesne. But Bouquet did not see it in that light. He thought that a new road was demanded by the exigencies of the situation. As a military necessity, and on account of other important considerations, he proposed to cut one by as short and direct a route as possible to the Loyalhannah creek. Washington bitterly opposed this, and some very sharp correspondence ensued on the subject. Bouquet's motives have been impugned by some writers, and it has been asserted by Hildreth that the choice was made in the interest of Pennsylvania land speculators. But he adduces no evidence to prove his assertion. It is enough to know that Bouquet's route was nearly fifty miles shorter from Bedford to Duquesne than the Cumberland route. This would commend it in a military point of view, and the subsequent course of events fully vindicated the wisdom of Bouquet in selecting it in spite of the strenuous opposition of the Father of our Country. Great and good as Washington was, or afterwards became, he was still human, and, as an ardent Virginian, looked with a jealous eye upon any project that would tend to rob Virginia of her wonted prestige. His two older brothers were members of the Ohio Land Company, whose interests were at stake in this affair. Besides the monopoly of the Indian fur traffic would pass from the hands of Virginia traders, if a more direct and rival route

were opened up through the province of Pennsylvania to
the headwaters of the Ohio. Selfish considerations are
just as likely to have influenced the one side as the other.
When we recollect the long contest for the Monongahela
region and a large part of Westmoreland county as originally constituted, reaching through the dark days of the
Revolution, even after the new road was made, we need
not wonder at the jealousy and opposition of Virginians to
any project or enterprise that would in the least jeopardize
their supremacy in that coveted locality.

Washington could not yield the point with a very good
grace. He predicted defeat and disaster to the expedition. September 1, he writes "All is dwindled into ease,
sloth and fatal inactivity. Nothing but a miracle can
bring the campaign to a happy issue." Bouquet convinced
Forbes that the proposed new route was preferable, and
Col. James Burd was sent forward to cut a way through
the forest and erect a stockade at Loyalhannah. Col.
Armstrong, who was a captain in this expedition, wrote
under date of Raystown, (Bedford) October 3, 1758, to
Richard Peters " The general (Forbes) came here at a
critical and seasonable juncture ; he is weak but his spirit
is good and his head clear, firmly determined to proceed
as far as force and provisions will admit, which through
divine favor will be far enough. * * * * * * *
The Virginians are much chagrined at the opening of the
road through this government, and Col. Washington has
been a good deal sanguine and obstinate upon the occasion ; but the presence of the general (Forbes) has been
of great use on this as well as other accounts. * * *
Col. Bouquet is a very sensible and useful man ; notwithstanding had not the general come up the consequences would have been dangerous. * * * * * *
I leave this place to-day as does Col. Bouquet and some
pieces of artillery."

Bouquet gave very careful instructions to Col. Burd not
to beat a drum or fire an unnecessary shot while cutting
the road through the forest. In silence but with energetic
dispatch the work was pushed forward. Nor did Bouquet neglect to drill his troops and keep them well in hand

for the kind of fighting needed to cope with the denizens of the woods. " Every afternoon he exercises his men in the woods and bushes in a particular manner of his own invention which will be of great service in an engagement with the Indians," is what Joseph Shippen wrote to his father from Bedford.

In a letter to Chief Justice Allen, written on the day of arrival at Fort Duquesne, November 25, 1758, Bouquet attributes the success of the expedition in great part to the adoption of his route. Besides being much nearer Philadelphia, the base of supplies, the route secured the favor and co-operation of the Pennsylvania German farmers on whom he had to depend for transportation and who would have been unwilling to leave their own province to follow the longer Braddock road. This contest was the beginning of the struggle for commercial supremacy which, with varying fortunes, has gone forward ever since and which now finds its leading champions in the Pennsylvania Central and Baltimore and Ohio railroads. While we would not detract one iota from the fame and merits of Washington, and feel that under the circumstances it was quite natural for him to contend for what was manifestly the interest of Virginia and the Ohio land company, we yet must say that the logic of events fully vindicated the course of Bouquet and Forbes in cutting a short and direct road to Fort Duquesne.

As Pennsylvanians, at least, we should feel thankful to the firm and sagacious man who did so much to open up the western part of our state to settlement and put matters in the best possible shape for military defence along the borders. It was hard and slow work to open a wagon track through the dense forests and over towering mountains, but with an army of over 6,000 men, including many frontiersmen and woodsmen, now was the time to have it done if the campaign was to be a complete success. Historians agree that thus twenty years were gained in the settlement of Western Pennsylvania. Forbes was a man of courage and sterling merit, and the fact that a commander such as he endorsed the Loyalhannah route, is strong proof and presumption that Bouquet had the better

cause and better argument over against his indignant col-
league, even the great and good Washington.

It is very probable, however, that this dispute may have
contributed to the neglect or disparagement of Bouquet
by biographers and historians, whose great object was to
glorify the Father of our Country and present him as a
hero and a sage under all circumstances, before as well as
during and after the War of Independence.

Forbes was a lion hearted old Scotchman. Weak and
emaciated in body but dauntless in spirit, he had himself
conveyed through the wilderness on a litter between two
horses. He reached Bedford September 15, but remained
there six weeks waiting for the opening of the road. November 1, he arrived at the Loyalhannah. A stockade
had been erected here by the road building party under
Col. Burd by direction of Col. Bouquet. This had been
assailed by the French and Indians, who made a determined sortie from Fort Duquesne to surprise and cut off
the advance guard and pioneers before the main body
could come up to their relief. But the assault was repulsed and in consequence the Indians became discour-
aged and left for their forest homes. A reconnoitering
party of 800, mostly Highlanders under Maj. Grant had
previously pushed forward from the Loyalhannah, and
had gained possession of a hill in the rear of the Fort,
but with strange infatuation they failed to improve their
advantages and opportunities. Failing to advance and
surprise the garrison and making an ostentatious display
they were soon surrounded by the French and Indians
who shot down their huddled ranks from behind trees and
ravines like so many sheep. Grant's Hill, in the centre of
Pittsburg, marks the scene of this disastrous affray. A
stand made by Col. Lewis with Provincial troops prevented the annihilation of the impracticable Scotch officer
and his Highlanders who seemed to have learned nothing
from Braddock's disaster or Bouquet's discipline. De Lig-
nery cruelly gave up five of the prisoners captured in the
route to be burned at the stake by the Indians and allowed the remainder to be tomahawked in cold blood on
the parade ground of the fort.

Washington was directed to open the last fifty miles of the road between the Loyalhannah and Fort Duquesne. On the 24th of November, 1758, Forbes and his army were encamped at Turtle Creek, near the scene of Braddock's defeat three years before.

Provisions, forage, &c., were so nearly exhausted that some advised a retreat, but the "iron-headed " old Scotchman, as Forbes was called, would listen to no such talk, but announced his intention of sleeping in the fort on the next night. That same evening a great smoke was seen ascending in the direction of the fort, and at midnight the camp was startled by the jar of a great explosion. The French had evacuated the post and had set fire to the magazine. They resolved to destroy what they despaired of defending. The last of their troops had embarked in boats and were seen hurrying down the Ohio as the British army approached.

The Highlanders were infuriated by the sight of the heads of slaughtered countrymen impaled on stakes along the race course as they neared the fort. These were victims of Grant's defeat. As one has said who was present, " foaming like mad boars, engaged in battle, they rushed madly on with hope to find an enemy on whom to accomplish retribution." But the detested foe was gone, and gone forever was French power and prestige at the forks of the Ohio. A square stockade was built and placed in charge of Colonel Hugh Mercer with 200 men. Next year a fort was at considerable cost erected on the ruins of the old fort by General Stanwix and named Fort Pitt, in honor of the English statesman, whose energetic policy had secured British supremacy in the New World. Pittsburgh was laid out at the confluence of the Allegheny and Monongahela rivers. As early as April 1761, there were 162 houses, 221 men, 73 women and 38 children in the young town of Pittsburgh, according to the returns made to Colonel Bouquet.

The capture of Fort Duquesne and the opening of the new road, proved as great a blessing to the people of Pennsylvania as Bouquet and his friends had predicted. The army speedily returned to their homes. Forbes was borne to Philadelphia, where he died a few weeks later, and was buried with great honor in Christ church.

The following extract from a letter to his lady friend at Philadelphia, written on the day of the army's arrival at the fort, shows the high estimate in which Bouquet held his hoary-headed chief :

FORT DUQUESNE, Nov. 25, 1758.

DEAR NANCY.—I have the satisfaction to announce to you the agreeable news of the conquest of this terrible fort. The French, seized with a panic at our approach, have destroyed themselves ; —that nest of Pirates which has so long harboured the murderers and destructors of our people. They have burned and destroyed to the ground their fortifications, houses and magazines, and left us no other cover than the heavens—a very cold one for an army without tents and equipages. We bear all this hardship with alacrity, by the consideration of the immense advantage of this important acquisition. The glory of our success must, after God, be allowed to our general, who, from the beginning, took those wise measures which deprived the French of their chief strength, and by a treaty at Easton kept such a number of Indians idle during the whole campaign and procured a peace with those inveterate enemies more necessary and beneficial than the driving of the French from the Ohio. His prudence in all his measures in the numberless difficulties he had to surmount deserves the highest praises.

BOUQUET IN COMMAND.

Bouquet was now in command and by judicious conferences with the Delaware Indians and energetic management, he soon restored peace and tranquility to the borders, so that the pioneer settlers met with little disturbance during the remainder of the French war. Four thousand settlers, who had left their homes in terror during the past few years, in consequence of the ravages that succeeded the defeat of Braddock and the cowardly retreat of Dunbar, now returned. Bouquet, with his Royal Americans, garrisoned the forts and posts, reaching from Philadelphia via Carlisle, Bedford, Fort Pitt, Lake Erie, Sandusky, &c. to Detroit. This regiment, largely composed of recruits from the German and Swiss settlers of Pennsylvania and

Maryland, as we have seen, held the outposts of civilization in the midst of savage beasts and savage men for
seven years. Communication was kept up largely by express riders, who, taking their lives in their hands, rode
rapidly from post to post.

BYERLY AT BUSHY RUN.

Andrew Byerly was induced to establish a relay station
for these express riders at Bushy Run, midway between
Fort Pitt and Fort Ligonier. He received a grant of several hundred acres of land from Col. Bouquet and the
proprietary government, on which he erected buildings
suitable for his purpose. Here, with his second wife and
a young and growing family, he settled down in the midst
of the wilderness, at the end of the Penn Manor, intend-
ing to carve out a home for his children.

He cultivated friendly relations with the surrounding
Indians and was soon well established, with a valuable
herd of milk cows and other comforts of civilization.
Here Bouquet spent many a pleasant hour in his trips to
and from Fort Pitt. Ecuyer was also on friendly terms
with the family. Mrs. Byerly, whose maiden name was
Beatrice Guldin, had emigrated from the Canton of Berne,
in Switzerland, the home of Bouquet. They often con-
versed about the lakes and the Alps, and friends in the
far away land of their nativity, and contrasted those peaceful scenes and associations with the rough experiences of
pioneer life in the new world. Byerly was a baker by
profession, and seems always to have been a favorite with
· military men. He had erected one of the very first inns
ever built in Lancaster, Pa., where he resided for a
long while and buried his first wife. He had baked for
Braddock's army at Fort Cumberland; and, backed by
Maj. George Washington, had beaten a Catawba warrior
in a foot race, on a wager of thirty shillings, which was
intended to test the relative prowess and fleetness of the
two races. Afterwards he removed to Fort Bedford, where
he baked for the British garrison and where his son Jacob,
a great-grand-father of the writer, was born in 1760. The

garrison being small, it was not long before he located at
Bushy Run, by the special favor and protection of Col.
Bouquet, on a very desirable grant along the Forbes road.
The letters, written during this interval of garrison duty,
from Fort Pitt, Bedford, Lancaster, &c., to his lady friend
in Philadelphia, show how irksome a life of inactivity was
to this man of action and of thought, and how Bouquet
felt isolated among the rude soldiers and uncouth frontiersmen with whom he came in daily contact. As one
who knew him well has written, "He was a man of science and sense." He delighted to associate with people
of intelligence and culture. He had no tastes for the
vulgar pastimes and pursuits that usually occupy the time
and attention of military men, when off duty, among a
rude population.

Bouquet was always a welcome guest and visitor at Byerly Station, on Bushy Run, and here he seemed to unbend
himself amid congenial social surroundings. His name
and memory has always been cherished in the Byerly family as a precious heirloom—as a sacred legacy handed down
with the benedictions of a pious and grateful ancestress.

PONTIAC'S CONSPIRACY.

The reign of peace and prosperity, which was causing
the wilderness to rejoice and blossom as the rose, came to
a sudden close in the spring of 1763. The French garrisons had been driven out of Canada and all their forts and
posts along the St. Lawrence, the Lakes, the Ohio, the
Illinois and the Mississippi had fallen into the hands of
the English as a result of the capture of Fort Duquesne
and Quebec. The Indians lamented the change and their
spirit of discontent was fanned into a flame by disappointed
French traders who led the credulous savages to believe
that the great king of France would soon drive out the
English and recover his lost dominion. Their easy social
habits and greater tendency to enter into matrimonial relations always made the French special favorites with the
red man and his daughters.

Pontiac, the great chief of the Ottawas on the shores of

Lake Michigan, became the powerful exponent and champion of the spirit of hostility against the English.

He was indeed a remarkable man. He originally belonged to the Catawba Indians. Having been captured
when a child and adopted by the Ottawas, he became not
only the war chief but also the Sachem, or civil ruler, of
his tribe by force of superior courage and ability.

He led a band of Ottawas and bore a leading part in the
defeat of Braddock in 1755, along with Charles Langlade
and other Lake Indians. The conduct of the British troops
on that occasion caused him to have great contempt for
the red coats, and he fancied that with one bold push they
might be driven east of the mountains, if not into the sea.
With great craft and secrecy he laid his plans to surprise
all the English forts and posts east of the mountains and
massacre their Royal American garrisons. Pontiac was a
born leader and had that magnetism and force of character that fitted him for the difficult and dangerous role that
he resolved to play in order to restore the supremacy of
the red men on the American continent. War belts had
been sent among the different tribes and a general willingness manifested to unite in one mighty effort to exterminate
the English. Kiashuta or Guyasutha, a head chief of the
Senecas, marshalled a part of the Five Nations to unite
with the Delawares and neighboring tribes in destroying
the garrison at Fort Pitt and the smaller posts in Western
Pennsylvania. But Pontiac was the leading spirit of the
general movement. April 27, 1763, he held a great council on the banks of the river Ecores, near Detroit. With
fierce gestures and loud, impassioned voice he denounced
the English for their injustice, rapacity and arrogance.
He compared and contrasted their conduct with that of
the French who had always treated them as brothers. He
exclaimed " the red coats have conquered the French but
they have not conquered us. We are not slaves or squaws,
and as long as the Great Spirit is ruler we will maintain our
rights. These lakes and these woods were given us by
our fathers, and we will part with them only with our
lives." He assured the council that their great father,
the King of France, would soon come to their aid to win
back Canada, and wreak vengeance on his enemies.

"The Indians and their French brethren would fight once more side by side as they had always fought; they would strike the English as they had struck them many moons ago, when their great army marched down the Mononga- hela, and they had shot them from ambush like a flock of pigeons in the woods."

The eloquence of Pontiac, backed by the harangues of other chiefs, carried everything before it. It was agreed that a deadly blow should be struck at all the forts in the following month. Eighteen nations, or leading Indian tribes, entered into the conspiracy of which Pontiac was the head centre. The adopted Catawba lad, far from his native haunts, had become the master spirit of his race. His bugle call rallied the dusky sons of the forest from the Mississippi to the Alleghanies in one fierce phalanx of savage hostility to the red-coated British. Different parts were assigned to different leaders. The general plan was to surprise and capture the garrison and destroy the forts in the neighborhood of the respective tribes and then fall like a tornado upon the defenceless settlements with fire and tomahawk.

So well kept was the secret that the storm of war came like a thunderbolt from a clear sky. Nine forts and posts were captured by strategem or assault, and their garrisons for the most part massacred. Thus fared Le Bœuff, Ve- nango, Presque Isle on Lake Erie, Le Bay on Lake Michigan, St. Joseph's, Miami, Ouachtanon, Sandusky and Machinaw. These, with the larger and stronger forts of Detroit, Niagara and Fort Pitt, were all attacked at about the same time.

SIEGE OF DETROIT.

The most difficult task of all, the capture of Detroit, Pontiac took in hand himself. And, no doubt, he would have succeeded at once had not his plans been betrayed by an Indian maiden to Major Gladwyn, who was in com- mand of that important stronghold. He was forced to the alternative of a regular siege, in which he displayed won- derful fertility of resources. Several parties sent to the

relief of the besieged garrison were surprised and cut off.
Vessels were boarded by the savages from their canoes ;
immense fire rafts were floated down the river to destroy
the ships of the English. The impetuous Dalzell, a friend
of Putnam, and an aid of Amherst, heading a sortie or
night attack upon the forces of Pontiac, was himself am-
buscaded and slain with fifty-eight of his men. A thousand warriors surrounded the fort at Detroit, but Major
Gladwyn had 300 good soldiers in the fort, and was protected by armed vessels at anchor on the river front.
Pontiac's greatest difficulty was in securing provisions for
such an immense horde of savages. A currency of birch
bark with Pontiac's stamp was employed in obtaining supplies from neutral French settlers and neighboring tribes.
To his lasting honor let it be recorded that Pontiac saw
to it that every piece of birch bark that bore his sign-
manual was fully redeemed after the war. Not a few
white individuals and communities are put to shame by the
integrity, sacrifice and fidelity of the great Ottawa chieftain. He had the vices of his race, no doubt, to some
extent, but their noblest virtues of courage, patience, fortitude, honesty and magnanimity were well illustrated in
his character. Had he succeeded in reducing Detroit and
precipitating his vast horde of besiegers upon Fort Pitt,
there is little doubt but that it would have fallen and the
English been driven to the sea.

Fortunately for the provinces, the great leader of the
conspiracy was foiled and detained in his efforts to capture Detroit until Bouquet had routed his Eastern Confederates on the bloody field at Bushy Run, after the best
contested Indian battle ever fought in the wilds of America.

SIEGE OF FORT PITT AND LIGONIER.

And now let us turn to this, the main object of our
sketch. As intimated before, the Indian uprising of 1763
was a great surprise to the military and civic authorities of
the land. It is true that there were signs of outbreak, but
nobody dreamed that it would assume such vast proportions and be fraught with such direful consequences. The

traders, who are supposed to understand Indian character and intentions better than any other class, were mostly caught in the whirlwind of disaster and overwhelmed by the suddenness of the outbreak. It was stated in the journals of that day that over one hundred traders lost their lives, and that property lost by them among the Indians or taken at the capture of the interior posts amounted to about two and a-half millions of dollars. So great a loss seems hardly possible. Fort Pitt at this time was in charge of Captain Simeon Ecuyer, a brave and skillful Swiss officer, like Bouquet himself.

On the 4th of May, 1763, he wrote Bouquet that " Maj. Gladwyn writes to me that I am surrounded by rascals. He complains a great deal of the Delawares and Shawanoes. It is this *canaille* who stir up the rest to mischief." On the 27th a party of Indians encamped near the fort and offered to trade a great quantity of valuable furs for bullets, hatchets, gunpowder, &c. They were looked upon with suspicion. On the 29th of May Ecuyer wrote an important letter to Bouquet, which seems to have been about the last that got through before communication was cut off ; for on the 17th of June Lieutenant Blane, commanding at Fort Ligonier wrote Bouquet that he had heard nothing from Fort Pitt since May 30. No further tidings were received until Bouquet cut his way through in August.

The following is Captain Ecuyer's letter in full, a copy of which, in the original French, as well as an English translation, has been kindly furnished the writer by Francis Parkman, the historian of Pontiac, &c.

FORT PITT, May 29, 1763.

SIR.—A large party of Mingoes arrived at the beginning of the month and gave up to us ten horses of poor quality. They asked me for presents, but I refused everything they had to offer except eight *merits* of Indian corn, (i. e.: 24 bushels, C. C.,) which they planted opposite Crogans' house, where they have built a town. In the evening of the day before yesterday, Mr. McKee reported to me that the Mingoes and Delawares were in motion, and had sold in a great hurry skins to the value of £300., with which they bought as much powder and lead as they pleased. Yesterday I sent him to their towns to get information, but he

found them entirely abandoned, and followed their trail and si
certain that they have gone down the river, which makes me
think that they want to interrupt our boats and close the passage
against us.   They stole three horses and a cask of rum at Bushy
Run.   They even robbed a man named Coleman of £50, (on
the Bedford road,) holding their guns against his body.   I am
assured that the famous Wolfe and Butler were the chiefs ; it is
clear that they want to break with us.   I pity the poor people on
the communication.   I am at work to put this post in the best
position possible with the few people I have.   Just as I was finish-
ing my letter, three men came from Clapham's with the melancholy news that yesterday, at three o'clock in the afternoon, the
Indians murdered Clapham and everybody in his house.   These
three men were at work outside and escaped through the woods.
I gave them arms and sent them to aid our people at Bushy Run.
The Indians have told Byerly (at Bushy Run) to leave his house
within four days, or he and all his family would be murdered.   I
tremble for the small posts.   As for this one, I will answer for it.
S. ECUYER.
If you do not often get letters from me, it will be a proof that
the communication is cut.
To Colonel Bouquet.

From this time until the tenth of August, the garrison
was cooped up in the fort, and communications cut off.

THE FLIGHT OF THE BYERLYS TO FORT LIGONIER.

Let us take another look at Bushy Run before we dwell
upon the siege of Fort Pitt.
As Ecuyer states, Byerly had received warning, but his
family was in no condition to be moved.   Mrs. Byerly
had just been confined and the departure was delayed as
long as possible, indeed until certain death was imminent
if the flight should be any longer postponed.   Byerly had
gone with a small party (perhaps Clapham's men referred
to above) to bury some persons who had been killed at
some distance from his station.   A friendly Indian who
had often received a bowl of milk and bread from Mrs.
Byerly came to the house after dark and informed the
family that they would all be killed if they did not make
their escape before daylight.   Mrs. Byerly got up from
her sick couch and wrote the tidings on the door of the

house for the information of her husband when he should return. A horse was saddled on which the mother with her tender babe three days old in her arms was placed, and a child not two years old was fastened behind her.

Michael Byerly was a good sized lad, but Jacob was only three years old and had a painful stone bruise on one of his feet. With the aid of his older brother who held him by the hand and sometimes carried him on his back, the little fellow, however, managed to make good time through the wilderness to Fort Ligonier about thirty miles distant. But although he reached his ninety-ninth year he never forgot that race for life in his childhood, nor did he feel like giving quarters to hostile Indians, one of whom he killed on an island in the Alleghany in a fight under Lieutenant Hardin in 1779, although the savage begged for quarters.

Milk cows were highly prized by frontier families in those days, and the Byerly family made a desperate effort to coax and drive their small herd along to Fort Ligonier. But the howling savages got so close that they were obliged to leave the cattle in the woods to be destroyed by the Indians. Byerly in some way eluded the Indians and joined his family in the retreat. They barely escaped with their lives. The first night they spent in the stockade, and in the morning the bullets of the pursuers struck the gates as the family pressed into the fort. Here they were compelled to remain two months, exposed to great privations and repeated assaults of Indians. Fort Pitt would have been nearer and preferable as a place of safety had it been possible to reach it. As it was they had to choose the longer road and the weaker fort as the only chance of escape from the red demons. At Fort Pitt Capt. Ecuyer put everything in the best possible shape for defence. The garrison consisted of 330 soldier, traders and backwoodsmen, who were armed and drilled for the emergency. There were also about one hundred women in the fort and a still greater number of children.

"A hospital was constructed under the drawbridge, out of range of musket shot, for patients suffering from smallpox, and the captain was very apprehensive that disease would break out in epidemic form as a result of the over-crowded condition of the fort. He seemed to have no fear of losing the fort. A letter, written at the time, says, " we are in such a good posture of defence that with God's assistance we can defend it against a thousand Indians."

Careful preparation was made for an attack. Buildings outside of the ramparts were levelled to the ground, and every morning at an hour before dawn the drum beat and the troops were ordered to their alarm posts. A heavy guard was kept on duty night and day. "I am deter-mined to hold my post, spare my men and never expose them without necessity. This is what I think you require of me," wrote the brave and judicious Ecuyer to Bouquet. It was next thing to death to expose a head on the ram-parts, or to wander outside the fortification. Lurking savages were at hand to pick off the unwary.

On the 25th of June, the Indians captured a lot of horses and cattle, belonging to the fort. A general fire was then opened on the fort from all sides. A discharge of howitzers threw them into confusion and made them act more cautiously. Next morning, Turtle Heart, a Dela-ware chief, approached the fort in the guise of friendship, and advised the commander and garrison to withdraw and take the women and children down to the English settle-ments, in order to escape destruction from the six great nations of Indians, who were coming to destroy them. He promised that they would be protected in making their escape. This was the ruse by which so many traders and smaller posts had been deceived and finally treacherously murdered after they had given up their arms. But Ecuyer was not to be caught with such chaff. He replied in a very ironical way, thanking the Delaware brothers for their great kindness, and assuring them that he and his troops could hold the fort against all the Indians that dared to attack it. "We are very well off in this place, and we mean to stay," said he. He then told them in confidence that two great armies were coming, one from the East and the other from the Lakes, to destroy the bad Indians, while the Cherokees and Catawbas, their old enemies,

B

were joining a third army in Virginia to destroy them.
This speech seemed to have a demoralizing effect upon
the savages, who withdrew for a season to meet a large
body of warriors approaching from the west.   During this
interval Ensign Price, from Fort Le Boeuf, entered Fort
Pitt with his command of a dozen men, who had gallantly
defended their little post until it was in flames from burning arrows and had then cut their way out of the rear and
escaped after great peril and suffering.   The names of
this detachment of Royal Americans, as far as given, indicate their German descent, viz. : Fisher, Nash, Dogood,
Nigley, Dortinger and Trunk.   Captain Ecuyer strength-
ened his defences with a line of palisades, and constructed
a rude fire engine to extinguish flames caused by the
burning arrows of the Indians shot against the sides and
roofs of wooden buildings.   July 26, a small party of Indians came to parley, under the lead of Shingas and
Turtle Heart.   They professed great affection for the
whites, and great concern for their safety.   The Ottawas
were coming in great force from Detroit to destroy the
garrison, and they begged their white brothers to depart
while it could be done in safety.   Ecuyer replied that he
could defend the fort for three years against all the Indians
in the woods, and that he would never abandon it as long
as a white man lived in America.   He despised the Ottawas, and warned his Delaware brothers to keep out of
reach of his bombshells and cannon loaded with a whole
bag full of bullets.   Thwarted in their crafty and treacherous schemes by which they had succeeded in destroying
Lieutenant Gordon and his entire command at Venango,
the Indians began a general attack in earnest.   Many of
them dug holes in the river banks, from which to fire on
the fort, and from all sides bullets and arrows flew thick
and fast.   The Royal Americans and border riflemen from
their loopholes drew a bead on every Indian that exposed
his person in the least.   Ecuyer was wounded in the leg
by an arrow, but kept up the hopes and spirits of his men,
while at the same time he refused to let them sally forth
to engage in a hand to hand conflict with the savages, as
many of them proposed to do.   The attack lasted five

days and five nights. Ecuyer speaks with great admiration of the conduct of his men—" regulars and the rest."
" I am fortunate to have the honor of commanding such
brave men. I only wish the Indians had ventured an
assault. They would have remembered it to the thou-
sandth generation." Bouquet wrote General Amherst,
August 11, in terms of high praise of Ecuyer for the
defence of the fort and the important additions made to
the fortifications during the investment.

In various letters, written from the fort immediately after
the siege was raised, it is stated that " to a man they were
resolved to defend the position (if the troops had not
arrived) as long as any amunition and provisions to support them was left ; and that then they would have fought
their way through or died in the attempt, rather than have
been made prisoners by such perfidious, cruel and blood-
thirsty hell-hounds. Some of the women in the fort, it is
said, helped to defend the place. Many express-riders
going to and from the garrison have been killed."

DEFENCE OF FORT LIGONIER.

At Fort Ligonier matters were even more critical than at
Fort Pitt. The stockade was bad and the garrison extremely weak but Byerly and a few other frontier settlers had
made their way into it with their families and helped to repulse the assaults of the savages. Lieutenant Archibald
Blane with a detatchment of Royal Americans was in command, and conducted the defense with great courage and
practical tact.

On the 4th of June Blane writes : " Thursday last my
garrison was attacked by a body of Indians, about five in
the morning ; but as they only fired upon us from the skirts
of the woods, I contented myself with giving them three
cheers, without spending a single shot upon them. But as
they still continued their popping upon the. side next to the
town, I sent the sergeant of the Royal Americans with a
proper detachment to fire the houses, which effectually disappointed them in their plan."

On the 17th, he writes to Bouquet, " I hope soon to see

yourself and live in daily hopes of a reinforcement. * *
Sunday last a man straggling out was killed by the Indians.
* * I believe the communication between Fort Pitt and
this place is entirely cut off, not having heard from them
since the thirtieth of May, though two expresses have
gone from Bedford to that post." On the 21st the Indians
made a serious attack for two hours. A small party of
fifteen men were so exceedingly anxious to have a closer
tilt with the savages that the lieutenant finally yielded to
their entreaties to let them out to attack some Indians that
showed themselves at a little distance. As it turned out
this was only a decoy to entrap them. About a hundred
savages lay in ambush by the side of the creek about four
hundred yards from the fort ; and just as the party was
returning near where they lay, the savages rushed out to cut
them off and would have succeeded in doing so had it not
been for a deep morass which intervened. Foiled in this
movement, more by natural obstacles then by the judgment or sagacity of the whites, the Indians immediately
began an attack upon the fort and fired upwards of a thousand shots without doing any special damage.

Bouquet was deeply concerned for the safety of Fort
Ligonier, for on its preservation depended the safety of
Fort Pitt and his own army of deliverance. A large quantity of military stores were in the magazines at Ligonier,
with which the Indians might have blown up Fort Pitt or
reduced Bouquet's troops to the greatest extremities. A
picked party of thirty Highlanders was sent by a circu-
itous route through the woods traveling by night at their
utmost speed under the escort of experienced guides.
They got close to the fort without being discovered and
then by a sudden rush and a running fight they managed
to get in without losing a man. This was a timely relief
and ensured the safety of the post until the main body could
arrive.

Next to Ligonier in the line of communication came
Fort Bedford, at a distance of fifty miles across the mountains and through the wilderness. Captain Lewis Ourry
was in command here with a mere handful of Royal Americans. On the third of June he wrote Bouquet that owing

to the arrival of express riders, (who were generally soldiers sent from one post to another at the peril of their lives,) his regulars were increased to "three corporals and nine privates." But he had a large body of settlers who, frightened by depredations of the Indians in the neighborhood, rushed pell-mell to the fort. These he organized into two military companies, aggregating 150 men. Over one hundred families had sought refuge at the fort. When the scare was over for the time being the silly people would venture out in small squads, and many were thus cut off and slain by scalping parties of skulking savages. June seventh he writes, "I long to see my Indian scouts come in with intelligence ; but I long more to hear the Grenadiers march and see more red-coats." Ten days later the country people in fancied security had returned to their plantation so that Ourry was left alone with a garrison of only twelve Royal Americans, who had not only to guard the fort but likewise take care of seven Indian prisoners. He writes to Bouquet : "I should be very glad to see some troops come to my assistance. A fort with five bastions cannot be guarded much less defended by a dozen men, but I hope God will protect us." The killing and scalping of some families on Denning's creek threw the settlers into a panic again, and in a few days the militia were back from their farms and with difficulty could be prevented from murdering the Indian prisoners. Ourry feared that the Indians, despairing of taking Fort Pitt, would fall upon and destroy the smaller posts and ravage the settlements, which they doubtless would have done had Bouquet's advance been much longer delayed. July 2d, about twenty Indians attacked a party of mowers and killed several of them. Eighteen persons in all were killed near Fort Bedford. July 3, Ourry received word from Blane of the loss of Presque Isle on Lake Erie, Leboeuf, Venargo, &c., which he sends to Bouquet with the intimation that Blane had entertained some idea of evacuating or capitulating Fort Ligonier. Bouquet replied : " I shivered when you hinted to me Lieut. Bl—'s intentions. Death and infamy would have been the reward he would expect instead of the honor he has obtained by his prudence, courage and resolution.   *   *   This is a most trying time.   *   *   You may be sure that all the expedition possible will be used for the relief of the few remaining posts."

Parkman remarks on the above letter :   " Bouquet had the strongest reason for wishing that Fort Ligonier should hold out.   As the event showed its capture would probably have entailed the defeat and destruction of his entire command."

THE SITUATION AT CARLISLE.

Bouquet had his headquarters in Philadelphia as Colonel of the first battallion of Royal Americans at the time of the outbreak of Pontiac and his confederates.   His Royal Americans, broken into detachments, had held the line of forts and posts between that place and Detroit for over six years.   As military hermits they held the outposts of civilization in the Western wilderness.   Bouquet, as we have seen, was held in high esteem in Philadelphia.

He was in the prime of life, had a fine personal presence, splendid physique and extraordinary qualities of mind and heart.   " Firmness, integrity, calmness, presence of mind in the greatest of dangers—virtues so essential to a commander; were natural to him.   His presence inspired confidence and impressed respect, encouraged his friends and confounded his foes."   Such is the estimate given of Bouquet by some of the best men of the provinces who knew him well.   He promptly reported the situation to General Amherst as Ecuyer had informed him in letters written at the end of May.   The haughty and arrogant Briton could not believe that the despicable savages would be so audacious as to besiege his forts or attack regular troops of equal numbers with their own. It is amusing to read his brag and bluster and to mark the change which in some respects seems to come over the spirit of his dream as the campaign progresses.

Bouquet evidently knew his weak and strong points and knew how to secure his hearty co-operation in measures necessary to the success of the beleaguered garrisons.

June 23, Amherst ordered Major Campbell to proceed at once from New York to Philadelphia with the remains of the 42d Regiment of Royal Highlanders, and of the 77th Montgomery's Highlanders ; the first consisting of two hundred and fourteen men, including officers, and the latter of one hundred and thirty-three. These troops had just landed from the West Indies and were in a very emaciated condition, most of them really unfit for service. The remains of five more such regiments arrived from Havana July 29, numbering in all nine hundred and eighty-two men and officers fit for duty; but by this time Bouquet was beyond Fort Bedford. Amherst seemed incapable of comprehending the magnitude of the danger.

" If you think it necessary " he writes to Bouquet " you will youself proceed to Fort Pitt that you may be better enabled to put in execution the requisite orders for securing the communication and reducing the Indians to reason." Bouquet was not the man to shirk duty or danger in such a crisis. With all the enegy of his ardent and indomitable nature he threw himself into the work of preparing an expedition for the relief of the invested forts and the exposed frontiers. He sent forward orders for the collection of stores and transportation at Carlisle as soon as the outlook became serious.

After making the necessary arrangements at Philadelphia, he hastened toward Carlisle. At Lancaster he writes to Amherst expressing confidence in his ability to open up communication with the troops sent to his assistance.

Amherst replies " I wish to hear of no prisoners, should any of the villains be met with in arms." On the 3d of July Bouquet received what he calls the " fatal account of the loss of our posts at Presque Isle, Lebœuf and Venango." The express rider who brought the message from Bedford came through in one day. He told the disastrous news to the country people who flocked about him and remarked, as he rode towards Bouquet's tent, " the Indians will be here soon."

All was consternation and alarm. Word was sent out to the settlements and soon every road was filled with panic-stricken fugitives crowding into Carlisle. The In-

dians were raiding through the Juniata regions and along
the borders of the Cumberland valley. A scouting party
found Shearman's valley laid waste, the dwellings and
stacked grain on fire, and swine devouring the bodies of
slaughtered settlers. Twelve young men went to warn
the people of the Tuscarora valley. They found the work
of ruin in full blast already and fell into an ambush in
which they were nearly all killed.

The country between the mountains and the Susquehanna was abandoned. Two thousand families left their
homes and fled to the forts and larger towns for protection.

A letter written from Carlisle, July 5, 1763, gives us an
idea of the terrible panic which existed. " Nothing could
exceed the terror which prevailed from house to house
and from town to town. The road was near covered with
women and children flying to Lancaster and Philadelphia.
The Rev.———, pastor of the Episcopal church, went at
the head of his congregation to protect and encourage them
on the way. A few retired to the breastworks for safety.
The alarm once given could not be appeased. We have
done all that men can do to prevent disorder. All our
hopes are turned upon Bouquet." Instead of finding supplies at hand for his troops and for the relief of the forts,
Bouquet found a vast crowd of despairing and starving
people, while crops were being burnt and mills destroyed
on all sides. July 13th, Bouquet wrote Amherst from
Carlisle as follows :

" The list of the people, known to be killed, increases
very fast every hour. The desolation of so many families
reduced to the last extremity of want and misery ; the despair of those who have lost their parents, relations and
friends, with cries of distracted women and children who
fill the streets—form a scene painful to humanity and impossible to describe." To procure provisions, horses and
wagons under the circumstances was indeed a herculean
task.

A few friendy Indians at the fort he with difficulty saved
from the fury of the mob of rustics. Instead of helping
him forward the settlers were rather a drawback and incumbrance, and had to be fed from the public crib.

THE MARCH TO BEDFORD.

However, in 18 days after his arrival at Carlisle, by
judicious and energetic measures, a convoy was procured
and the army set out on its perilous march.

His entire force did not exceed 500 men, of whom the
most effective were the 42d Highlanders. Sixty of the
77th regiment were so weak that they had to be conveyed
in wagons. They were intended for garrison duty at Bedford &c., while effective men at those forts were to join
the army of deliverance. The bare-legged Highlanders with
their kilts and plaids, and their infirm appearance, gave
little assurance to the anxious people who watched their
departure.

The fate of Braddock a few years previous had not been
forgotten, nor the desolation and despair that ensued.
Nearly twice as many English troops had been slain on
that fatal day as Bouquet had in his entire command,
while the Indians that now infested the woods were far
more numerous than those who routed the proudest of the
Britons eight years previous.

At Shippensburg, as at Carlisle, a great crowd of starving
people were found, who had fled from the tomahawk and
scalping knife. " On July 25, 1763 there were in Shippensburg 1384 of our poor distressed back inhabitants, viz :
301 men, 345 women and 738 children, many of whom
were obliged to lie in barns, stables, cellars and under old leaky sheds, the dwelling houses being all crowded," says the chronicles of those days. In such a state of
affairs it would seem that the provincial authorites and
frontiers-men themselves would have united in one grand
effort to drive out the savage destroyers of life and property. But Bouquet could get little or no aid from that
quarter. A suicidal Quaker policy pervaded the civil
authorities, while the settlers seemed benumbed with fear
and despondancy.

He writes to Amherst, " I find myself utterly abandoned by the very people I am ordered to protect   *   *   *
I have borne very patiently the ill usage of this province,
having still hopes that they will do something for us ; and
B*

therefore have avoided a quarrel with them." His efforts
to engage a body of frontiersmen for the campaign were
fruitless. They preferred to remain for the defence of
their families, forgetting that their homes and families
could never be secure until the savages had been driven
back to their haunts beyond the Ohio and chastised into
submission. Such a force of men, used to the woods and
enured to pioneer life, would have been of vast service in
the march.

The Highlanders were sure to get lost in the woods
when sent out as flankers. As Bouquet wrote to Amherst
July 26, "I cannot send a Highlander out of my sight without running the risk of losing the man, which exposes me
to surprises from the skulking villians I have to deal with."

Doubtless, however, the tactics resorted to in 1758 to
make his men effective against Indian attack and surprise
during the Forbes campaign, were called into vigorous
play during this march, as the outcome at Bushy Run
clearly indicates. At Bedford, where he arrived July 25,
Bouquet was more fortunate in enlisting frontiersmen and
succeeded in getting about thirty to march with the army
for flanking and scouting purposes.

Murders had continued in the settlements, three men
having been killed near Shippensburg by prowling savages after the army passed. · But thus far the troops had
met with little molestation.

THE MARCH TO LIGONIER.

Now, however, began the real perils of the march, and
greater caution was needed. Forests, rocks, ravines and
thickets abounded on every side, inviting their wily foe to
ambush the troops as they threaded their way through the
valleys and across the mountains.

But Bouquet knew exactly what the exigencies of the
situation required. July 28, the army started from Fort
Bedford. A band of backwoodsmen led the way, followed
closely by the pioneers ; the wagons and cattle were in
the centre guarded by the regulars and a rear guard of
backwoodsmen closed up the line. Frontier riflemen, or

provincial rangers, scoured the woods on all sides, making surprise impossible. Bouquet himself, with musket in hand, oftentimes led the advance. Thus they toiled along the tedious way, which Burd, under Bouquet's orders, had opened through the wilderness five years before.

The mountain air, the pure water and delightful scenery had an inspiriting effect upon the Highlanders, who grew stronger as they marched along.

August 2, the little garrison and small body of pioneer settlers, who had held Fort Ligonier for two long months, were transported with the sight of the red coats of the Royal Americans and the kilts and plaids of the Highlanders marching to their rescue.

" The Campbells were coming " indeed, as the record of the bloody fight a few days later fully demonstrates. The clan Campbell, whose members have marched so oft in many lands to glory and the grave, was well represented in the rank and file of Bouquet's army of deliverance.

The Indians disappeared as the troops approached, but no tidings had been received from Fort Pitt for weeks. Bouquet wisely resolved to leave his wagons and oxen behind, which were the most cumbrous part of his convoy, in order to advance more rapidly and be in better shape to resist attack. Three hundred and forty pack horses were loaded with supplies for the needy garrison at Fort Pitt, and on the 4th day of August the army marched about a dozen miles and encamped for the night.

Andrew Byerly and his son Michael accompanied the troops, in hopes of recovering some of their property, which had been left to the mercy of the Indians when the family had fled from Bushy Run over two months ago. After proceeding a few miles, the boy was sent back for some reason, to remain at Fort Ligonier. On his return he saw numerous Indian trails crossing the dusty road, over which the army had passed. The savages were on the alert to ascertain the number and character of the troops, and watching their opportunity to surprise and ambush them.

Bouquet had his plans well arranged for the speedy

relief of Fort Pitt in a way that would be most likely to
thwart the designs of the savages. His intention was to
push on to Bushy Run, which would be an excellent place
for man and beast to rest and recuperate for a few hours,
and then set out and make a forced march by night
through the defiles at Turtle Creek, where he expected
the savages would try to ambuscade his troops.

BUSHY RUN BATTLE.

Accordingly, on the morning of August 5, 1763, the
troops set out at an early hour over the hills, and through
the hollows of what now forms the heart of Westmoreland
county, Pa. Along the Forbes road, shrouded on all sides
by dense forests, they moved at a lively rate. By one
o'clock the jaded column had advanced seventeen miles,
and Andrew Byerly, along with a detachment of eighteen
soldiers in the advance, cheered the weary troops with the
welcome tidings that Bushy Run, their resting place, was
only half a mile distant. All were pushing forward with
renewed vigor, when suddenly the whole line was startled
by the report of rifles in the front. A fierce assault had
been made on the vanguard and the firing was quick and
sharp. Twelve out of eighteen fell in the unequal conflict that ensued before the two advance companies could
press forward to the relief of their comrades. The firing
became furious, indicating that the Indians were in large
force and were fighting with unusual courage.

The convoy of packhorses was halted, the troops were
formed into line and a general bayonet charge was made
through the forest. The yelping savages gave way before
the cold steel of the Highlanders. But just as the route
seemed' cleared in front, terrible war whoops resounded
through the woods on either flank, and an uproar among
the packhorse drivers indicated that the convoy was attacked in the rear. The troops in advance were instantly
recalled to defend the convoy. Driving away the savages
by repeated bayonet charges they formed a circle around
the crowded and frantic horses. It was a new kind of work
for the Highlanders, but they bore themselves with great

steadiness and remarkable fortitude in spite of the terrific and confusing yells of their ferocious assailants and the deadly shots that came pouring in upon them from every thicket, tree or covert, large enough to conceal a foe. Nothing but implicit confidence in their commander and in the pluck and fidelity of each other could account for their undaunted gallantry under such trying circumstances. It seemed like pandemonium broke loose. Walter Scott has described such a scene :

> "At once there rose so wild a yell
> Within that dark and narrow dell,
> As all the fiends from heaven that fell,
> Had pealed the banner-cry of hell."

Rushing up with terrific whoops, the painted demons would pour in a heavy fire, and when the Highlanders would charge bayonet they would dodge and vanish behind trees and thickets only to renew the assault the moment the troops returned toward the circle of defence.

Many brave men fell on that hot afternoon. Captain Lieut. Graham and Lieut. McIntosh of the 42d Highlanders were killed and Lieut. Graham wounded. Lieut. Donald Campbell of the 77th was wounded and Lieut. Dow, of the Royal Americans, was shot through the body, after killing three Indians.

Upwards of sixty men were killed or wounded in the action which lasted until dark. It was impossible to change position and the troops were obliged to lay upon their arms where they had stood during the fight. Numerous sentinels were posted to guard against a night attack. A space was made in the centre of the camp for the wounded, around whom a wall of flour bags was erected to protect them from the bullets which flew among them thick and fast from all side during the fight. It was indeed a sad and dreary night for the wounded.

The agony of thirst was almost intolerable, springs ran out of the hill sides near by, but the savages guarded them well with their skirmish line, and it was almost certain death to approach them. At imminent risk Byerly managed to convey a few hatfuls of water to the wounded Highlanders. A grateful shower of rain also afforded

some relief. After Bouquet had made his dispositions for
the night he proceeded to write a report of the battle to
General Amherst, evidently supposing that he was not
likely to survive the conflict the coming day. The report was written amid all the bustle of the camp when
danger and death in their most horrid forms stared him
in the face, and yet how carefully, calmly and correctly
everything of note is stated ! Here it is.

REPORT OF THE FIRST DAY'S FIGHT NEAR BUSHY RUN.

CAMP AT EDGE HILL,
26 MILES FROM FORT PITT, 5th Aug. 1763.
SIR: The second instant the troops and convoy arrived at
Ligonier, where I could obtain no intelligence of the enemy. The
expresses sent since the beginning of July, having been either
killed or obliged to return, all the passes being occupied by the
enemy. In this uncertainty, I determined to leave all the wagons,
with the powder, and a quantity of stores and provisions, at Ligonier, and on the 4th proceeded with the troops and about 340
horses loaded with flour.
    I intended to have halted to-day at Bushy Run, (a mile beyond
this camp), and after having refreshed the men and horses, to
have marched in the night over Turtle Creek, a very dangerous
defile of several miles, commanded by high and rugged hills ; but
at one o'clock this afternoon, after a march of 17 miles, the savages suddenly attacked our advance guard, which was immediately supported by the two Light Infantry companies of the 42d
regiment, who drove the enemy from their ambuscade and pursued them a good way. The savages returned to the attack,
and the fire being obstinate on our front and extending along our
flanks, we made a general charge with the whole line to dislodge
the savages from the heights, in which attempt we succeded,
without by it obtaining any decisive advantage, for as soon as
they were driven from one post, they appeared on another, till,
by continued reinforcements, they were at last able to surround
us and attacked the convoy left in our rear ; this obliged us to
march back to protect it. The action then became general, and
though we were attacked on every side, and the savages exerted
themselves with uncommon resolution, they were constantly repulsed with loss ; we also suffered considerably. Capt. Lieut.
Graham and Lieut. James McIntosh, of the 42d, are killed, and
Capt. Graham wounded. Of the Royal American Regt., Lieut.
Dow, who acted as A. D. Q. M. G., is shot through the body.

Of the 77th, Lieut. Donald Campbell and Mr. Peebles, a volunteer, are wounded. Our loss in men, including rangers and drivers, exceeds sixty killed or wounded.

The action has lasted from one o'clock till night, and we expect to begin at daybreak.

Whatever our fate may be, I thought it necessary to give your Excellency this early information, that you may at all events take such measures as you think proper with the Provinces, for their own safety, and the effectual relief of Fort Pitt, as in case of another engagement, I fear insurmountable difficulties in protecting and transporting our provisions, being already so much weakened by the losses of this day in men and horses, besides the additional necessity of carrying the wounded, whose situation is truly deplorable.

I cannot sufficiently acknowledge the constant assistance I have received from Major Campbell during this long action, nor express my admiration of the cool and steady behavior of the troops, who did not fire a shot without orders, and drove the enemy from their posts with fixed bayonets. The conduct of the officers is much above my praises.

I have the honor to be with great respect,

Sir, &c.   HENRY BOUQUET,

To His Excellency, Sir Jeffrey Amherst.

With gloomy forebodings the troops, and especially the wounded, awaited the dawn of the coming day. Wild whoops and occasional shots from the deep thickets and surrounding hillsides, indicated how eager the painted demons were to glut their vengeance. The hordes besieging Fort Pitt had all precipitated themselves upon Bouquet, knowing that if he and his supplies could be cut off and captured, the reduction of the fort would soon follow. It was a very disturbed and broken sleep that even the most securely sheltered of the troops could get at such a time.

SECOND DAY'S FIGHT, AUGUST 6.

With the first gray streaks of dawn came those incessant savage yells preluding a fierce assault on every side. Soon from every tree and bush that could conceal an enemy, a galling fire was poured upon the devoted forces of Bouquet. The Colonel himself, with his bright uniform, was a conspicuous mark, and the balls whizzed about him so thick that he concluded to change his dress. While doing so, behind a large tree, no less than fourteen bullets struck it. As on the previous day, the savages made frequent impetuous onsets in order to break through the line of defence. But they were firmly met and gallantly repulsed at every point. The gleam of the bayonets would cause them to retire swiftly to the bushes, but the moment the charge ceased they were back again with their demoniac yells, popping away at every exposed soldier. The long march and hard fight of the previous day, added to their burning thirst, " more intolerable than the enemy's fire," as Bouquet puts it, left the troops in rather sorry plight to contend with such alert and daring assailants. The Indians had every advantage on their side in the way of shelter from the fire of the troops and being without any encumbrance they could attack and retreat with the greatest ease and rapidity. The savages marked the increasing fatigue and distress of the troops and, confident of speedy triumph, derided them in bad English and vulgar ribaldry. Keekyuskung, a Delaware chief, who had taken part in the murder of Colonel Clapham and his family, and who was a ringleader in getting up the conspiracy in general, was conspicuous in this kind of work throughout the morning, as he had been also on the previous night. His taunts were all the more provoking, as he bellowed them forth from behind a large tree, because he had, in times past, received many favors from Colonel Bouquet and the Royal Americans, when on his visits to Fort Pitt.

The interior of the camp was in great confusion owing to the fright of horses on account of the terriffic war whoops resounding on all sides and the hurts received from Indian bullets. The cowardly behaviour of the pack horse men added to the danger and tumult. They forsook the poor brutes and hid themselves in terror among the bushes, from which no command or entreaty could draw them to a discharge of duty. Breaking away from the convoy many of the horses dashed madly through the woods, and through the lines of the contending forces. The crisis was fearful and only a cool head, fertile in resources and a brave heart unappalled by any danger, could meet the emergency. The heat, the toil, the thirst, the increasing and more audacious assaults of the savages began to tell seriously upon the strength and spirits of the soldiers. They were growing weaker and falling rapidly while their relentless foes were every moment growing stronger and bolder.

It was a crisis requiring the highest kind of military genius combined with indomitable resolution. Bouquet was equal to the ordeal and from the very jaws of defeat, disaster and death he snatched the most brilliant victory ever won over the Indians.

A Captain or Lieutenant Barret, commanding it is said a small Maryland detachment of provincial rangers, pointed out to Bouquet a place where a large body of the boldest of the Indians might be taken on the flank and rear by a well directed bayonet charge around the hill and up a hollow or ravine. Andrew Byerly was with Bouquet at the time, and heard Barret make the suggestion, which the Colonel quickly put into execution on a large scale by a masterly piece of strategy. Immediately Major Campbell was directed to make a rapid circuit through the woods on the right flank of the savages around the hill aforesaid, taking them in flank and rear. Captain Basset of the Royal Engineers was directed to arrange the other companies, so as to co-operate promptly with the strategic movement at the right moment. The thin line of troops that took the place of the two companies withdrawn from the front, gave away before the impetuous onset of the exultant savages and fell back upon the convoy, where they presented a line of bristling steel. The Indians fell completely into the snare and rushed with demoniac fury into the camp, certain that the fight was won.

But just as they supposed themselves masters of the field the Highlanders charged in with a wild battle cry upon their right flank. A volley was fired upon the amazed and huddled savages, but they stood their ground with wonderful intrepidity, not willing to loose a decisive victory and the great booty of stores and scalps which a moment before they felt was within their grasp. It is

agreed on all hands that on this occasion, not only in the
attack and the assault, but in meeting the unexpected
charge on their flank and rear, the Indians displayed unusual courage and firmness.

But a well directed bayonet charge no body of Indians
ever did or will stand.   Here Bouquet had them at last
where he wanted them, at close quarters where there could
be no dodging or popping from behind the trees.   The
Highlanders were at home with the bayonet and only too
glad to get a good chance at the painted villains who had
skulked behind trees while they shot their brave comrades
during the past two days.   Still the savages struggled
in hope of gaining the day, but the shock was irresistible and, perceiving that they had been caught in a trap,
they fled in tumultuous disorder.   In doing so they were
obliged to pass in front of the companies brought up on the
opposite side by Capt. Basset, from whom they received
another volley.   The four companies now vied with each
other in driving the savages through the woods beyond
Bushy Run without giving them time to reload their
empty rifles.   Many of their chief warriors were killed and
the rest utterly routed.   Among others, Kukyuskung, the
ungrateful and blatant blackguard, and the famous war
Chief called " The Wolf," were slain.

Amherst had expressed the hope that no prisoners with
arms in their hands should be taken, and his wish was
gratified.   Historians say that in the fight only one Indian was taken prisoner, and after a little examination
he was shot down like a captured wolf.   Hereby hangs
a tale, which I was told by my great great grandfather,
Jacob Byerly, and his son Joseph, on Christmas day 1855,
two and a-half years before the old Revolutionary veteran
passed away, at the age of 99 years.   He had heard it
often from his father, who was in the fight.   When the
flight of the savages had fairly begun, a Scotch Highlander dropped his musket and darted after the fugitives, as
only a fleet-footed Highlander could.   Soon he overtook
and mastered, single-handed, one of the largest of the savages, whom he was leading toward the camp, when he was
met by an officer of Barret's detachment.   " What are you

going to do with that fellow ? " said the fussy official. " I
am taking him to Colonel Bouquet. If *you* want one,
there are plenty of them running yonder in the woods,
and you may catch one for yourself," replied the Highlander. The officer drew his pistol and shot the prisoner
through the head, which cowardly deed greatly incensed
the brave Highlander and called forth the indignant re-
buke of Bouquet, when informed of the affair.

Sixty dead Indians were found on the field, and many
wounded had been conveyed away by their friends. Bouquet had won a decisive but dearly bought victory. Eight
officers were killed or severely wounded, and in all one
hundred and fifteen men, or nearly one-fourth of the
entire force had been killed, wounded or were missing, as
a result of the two day's conflict.

The pack horse drivers emerged from the bushes, and,
in company with some of the Rangers, proceeded to scalp
the dead Indians, whom the regular troops disdained to
touch.

So many of the horses had escaped through their neglect and cowardice during the conflict that a large quantity of valuable stores had to be destroyed for lack of
transportation to prevent them from falling into the hands
of the Indians after the army passed on. Litters were
made and the wounded were borne to Bushy Run, where
the army encamped to rest and refresh themselves after
the exhausting struggle of the past two days. After the
severe handling they had lately received it was supposed
the Indians would not molest them soon again. But
scarcely had they gone into camp before a volley was
fired into their midst. The angered Highlanders soon dispersed the prowling miscreants without awaiting orders to
do so. Ten of the wounded died at Bushy Run and were
buried next day where Harrison city now stands. The
Indians returned to the battle-field after night and scalped
all the dead they could find. These gory trophies they
shook at the garrison and raised the scalp haloo, as they
marched past Fort Pitt in a body, a short time before the
army appeared on the morning of Aug. 10.

As on the night before, Bouquet rested not until he had

written his report of the day's conflict, which was done in
such a complete manner that he never had occasion to
change or supplement it.

Through the courtesy of her Majesty's government I
have been furnished with an authentic copy of Bouquet's
reports of these conflicts. The official reports are in all
respects the same as given by Parkman, except the indicated omission by the copyist of the scalping operations
of the Rangers and packhorse drivers, which I have sup-
plied from Parkman's full text. But the detailed tabular
statement of killed, wounded and missing in the Bushy
Run battles I have never seen published elswhere, not
even by Parkman. It is very important and interesting,
showing the relative losses of the Highlanders, Royal
Americans and Rangers. The first named formed nearly
two-thirds of Bouquet's force, and besides having to do
the heavy work, making repeated bayonet charges, they
were not used to the Indian's mode of fighting as were
the small detachments of Rangers and Royal Americans.
Hence the loss of the gallant Scotch far exceeds that of
all other parties combined. The 42d Regiment of Royal
Highlanders bore the brunt of the fierce assaults in front
in the first days' battle and has a proud record on the roll
of honor.

BOUQUETS' REPORT OF SECOND DAY'S FIGHT.

CAMP AT BUSHY RUN, 6th Aug. 1763.
SIR : I had the honor to inform your Excellency in my letter
of yesterday of our first engagement with the savages.

We took the post last night on the hill where our convoy halted,
when the front was attacked, (a commodious piece of ground and
just spacious enough for our purpose). There we encircled the
whole and covered our wounded with flour bags.

In the morning the savages surrounded our camp, at the distance of 500 yards, and by shouting and yelping, quite round
that extensive circumference, thought to have terrified us with
their numbers. They attacked us early, and under favor of an
incessant fire, made several bold efforts to penetrate our camp,
and though they failed in the attempt, our situation was not the
less perplexing, having experienced that brisk attacks had little
effect upon an enemy who always gave way when pressed, and

appeared again immediately. Our troops were, besides, extremely fatigued with the long march and as long action of the preceding day, and distressed to the last degree, by a total want of water, much more intolerable than the enemy's fire.

Tied to our convoy, we could not lose sight of it without exposing it and our wounded to fall a prey to the savages, who pressed upon us, on every side, and to move it was impracticable, having lost many horses, and most of the drivers, stupified by fear, hid themselves in the bushes, or were incapable of hearing or obeying orders. The savages growing every moment more audacious, it was thought proper to still increase their confidence by that means, if possible, to entice them to come close upon us, or to stand their ground when attacked. With this view two companies of Light Infantry where ordered within the circle, and the troops on their right and left opened their files and filled up the space, that it might seem they were intended to cover the retreat. The Third Light Infantry company and the Grenadiers of the 42d were ordered to support the two first companies. This manœuvre succeeded to our wish, for the few troops who took possession of the ground lately occupied by the two Light Infantry companies being brought in nearer to the centre of the circle, the barbarians mistaking these motions for a retreat, hurried headlong on, and advancing upon us, with the most daring intrepidity, galled us excessively with their heavy fire; but at the very moment that they felt certain of success, and thought themselves masters of the camp, Major Campbell, at the head of the first companies, sallied out from a part of the hill they could not observe, and fell upon their right flank. They resolutely returned the fire, but could not stand the irresistible shock of our men, who, rushing in among them, killed many of them and put the rest to flight. The orders sent to the other two companies were delivered so timely by Captain Basset, and executed with such celerity and spirit, that the routed savages who happened that moment to run before their front, received their full fire, when uncovered by the trees. The four companies did not give them time to load a second time, nor even to look behind them, but pursued them till they were totally dispersed. The left of the savages, which had not been attacked, were kept in awe by the remains of our troops, posted on the brow of the hill for that purpose ; nor durst they attempt to support or assist their right, but being witness to their defeat, followed their example and fled. Our brave men disdained so much as to touch the dead body of a vanquished enemy that scarce a scalp was taken except by the Rangers and pack-horse drivers.

The woods being now cleared and the pursuit over, the four

companies took possession of a hill in our front, and as soon as litters could be made for the wounded, and the flour and everything destroyed, which, for want of horses, could not be carried, we marched without molestation to this camp.   After the severe correction we had given the savages a few hours before, it was natural to suppose we should enjoy some rest, but we had hardly fixed our camp, when they fired upon us again.   This was very provoking; however, the Light Infantry dispersed them before they could receive orders for that purpose.   I hope we shall be no more disturbed, for, if we have another action, we shall hardly be able to carry our wounded.

The behavior of the troops on this occasion, speaks for itself so strongly, that for me to attempt their eulogium would but detract from their merit.

I have the honor to be, most respectfully, Sir, &c.

HENRY BOUQUET,

To His Excellency, Sir Jefferey Amherst.

P. S.—I have the honor to enclose the return of the killed, wounded and missing in the two engagements.   H. B.

RETURN OF KILLED AND WOUNDED IN THE TWO ACTIONS AT EDGE HILL, NEAR BUSHY RUN, THE FIFTH AND SIXTH AUGUST, 1763.

CORPS.	Captains.		Lieuts.		Volunt'rs.		Serge'nts.		Corporals.		Drum'rs.		Privates.		Missing.
	Killed	Wounded	Killed	Wounded	Killed	Wounded	Killed	Wounded	Killed	Wounded	Killed	Wounded	Killed	Wounded	
42d Regt. Royal Highlanders,	1	1	1	1	..	..	1	2	..	..	..	1	25	27	..
60th Regt. Royal Americans,	..	..	..	1	..	..	..	3	1	3	..	..	6	4	..
77th Regt. Montgomery's Highlanders,	..	..	..	1	..	1	..	..	1	..	1	..	5	7	..
Volunteers, Rangers and Pack horse men,	..	..	1	..	..	..	..	..	..	..	..	..	7	8	5
Total,	1	1	2	3	..	1	1	5	2	3	1	1	43	46	5

KILLED—Captain Lieut. John Graham, of the 42d Regiment; Lieut. James McIntosh, of the 42d Regiment; Lieut. Joseph Randall, of the Rangers.

WOUNDED—Captain John Graham, of the 42d Regiment; Lieut. Duncan Campbell, of the 42d Regiment; Lieut. Donald Campbell, of the 77th Regiment; Volunteer, Mr. Peebles, of the 77th Regiment.

Total Killed, ... 50

" Wounded, ... 60

" Missing, ... 5
_____

Total of the whole, ... 115

(*Colonial Correspondence—American and West Indies—Sir Jeff. Amherst*, 1763, *Vol.* 97.)

NEW YORK, 3d Sept., 1763.

MY LORD :—On the 10th of last month Col. Bouquet got his convoy into Fort Pitt, after having been attacked on the 5th and 6th by a very numerous body of savages, which he repulsed and defeated, though not without some loss on our side. Captain Lieut. Graham and Lieut. James McIntosh, of the 42d, being killed, with an officer of Rangers, and four officers wounded—in the whole, 49 were killed and 60 wounded. As I have the honor to transmit to your Lordship Colonel Bouquet's letter with my answers, and the account I made public here of that affair, I need not repeat the praises due to the troops for their behavior, clogged as they were by a large but necessary convoy, and on a very untoward communication.

*   *   *   *   *   *   *   *   *   *   *   *

I have honor to be with the utmost respect, my Lord, your Lordship's most humble and obedient servant,

JEFFERY AMHERST.

Right Honorable Earl of Egremont.

The copies of Col. Henry Bouquet's official reports of the battles with the Indians, near Bushy Run, I have received direct from the British government, in response to a letter written last January, which was endorsed by Hon. Wm. S. Stenger, Secretary of Commonwealth ; Hon. H. P. Laird, Gen. R. C. Drum, Secretary of War Lincoln, and transmitted officially by Secretary of State Frelinghuysen.

The reports of Bouquet, written in the midst of such exciting and confusing scenes are models of exactness and reflect high honor upon him as a soldier and a scholar. Although a Swiss and well acquainted with German, French and other European languages, he wrote English better than the great majority of English officers.

With the aid of these reports and Hutchins' map, drawn up a few years after the battle, it is easy to locate the field of conflict. The first day's fight, where the 42d Highland regiment suffered so severely, took place on the Gonaware Hills, near Harrison City, located on Bushy Run. The fight around the convoy, where the savages were finally ambushed and routed, took place on the Wanamaker farm, a short distance south-east of Mr. W.'s present residence. The old Forbes road ran through the Wanamaker and Gongaware farms, along a different line from the present road, but that line is well known by Mr. W., and others, who cleared away the native woods on both sides of the Forbes road. By comparing the march and resources of Bouquet with those of other Indian fighters, we are filled with increasing admiration at his success, August 5 and 6, 1763, on the bloody fields near Bushy Run.

With a force of less than 500 men, mostly composed of raw Highlanders, unused to Indian warfare, Bouquet defended his convoy of 340 pack-horses and finally routed the horde of savages who had fought with unusual courage and sagacity. True, he lost about one-fourth of his men in killed and wounded, but an equal or greater loss was inflicted on his wily and savage foes. Compare this with the results of similar conflicts. Braddock, in 1755, with 1,400 men, lost nearly 900, and out of 85 officers, 64 were killed or wounded. And yet he was opposed by only a few hundred Indians and French, who lost only 30, all told, of their number. As a consequence, the borders were desolated for hundreds of miles and thousands of pioneers were driven from their homes or massacred.

Col. Crawford, with 500 men, in 1782, was routed, and himself, his son and son-in-law captured and burned at the stake.

Col. Loughrey, with 140 picked frontiersmen from Westmoreland, was surprised and all his force captured by an Indian detachment in 1781.

Gen. Harmer, 1790, with 300 regulars and over 1,000 volunteers was routed with a loss of several hundred of his best troops.

Gen. St. Clair, a brave and able officer, 1791, with 1,200 men, in line of battle, expecting attack and provided with artillery, and with large reinforcements near at hand, met with overwhelming defeat, and a loss of 68 officers killed 28 wounded, together with over half of his men. And these were for the most part veterans, used to fighting and commanded by gallant and experienced officers.

In the light of these and many similar conflicts in the
c

olden times or in recent years, the valor and ability of
Bouquet shine forth in replendent colors. Or take a successful Indian fighter like Gen. Anthony Wayne and we
find that Bouquet stands the peer of the greatest. Gen.
Wayne had over 1,500 veteran and mounted Kentuckians
and 2,000 regulars, including artillery in 1794. After
sharp fighting, he routed about half his number of In-,
dians, with a loss of 33 killed and a hundred of his own
men wounded. The loss of the Indians was about the same
as that of the whites. Under Braddock's mangement the
Indians killed fifty white to every one of their own number
slain, while under Bouquet's management they lost more of
their own warriors than they were able to destroy of the
whites. It is to honor the memory and perpetuate the heroism of this superb man and his gallant army of deliverance
that Westmorelanders and all patriotic citizens of West
Pennsylvania, Virginia and Ohio are invited to assemble on
the historic field of his grandest triumph, Aug. 6, 1883.

"The battle of Bushy Run," says Parkman the great
historian of Colonial times, "was one of the best contested actions ever fought between white men and Indians.
* * * The Indians displayed throughout a fierceness
and intrepidity matched only by the steady valor with
which they were met. In the provinces the victory
excited equal joy and admiration, especially among those
who knew the incalculable difficulties of an Indian campaign. The Assembly of Pennsylvania passed a vote expressing their sense of the merits of Bouquet and of the
services he had rendered to the province. He soon after
received the additional honor of the formal thanks of the
King."

The army in a few days reached Fort Pitt, to the great
joy and relief of the garrison, whose stock of provisions
were about exhausted. Bouquet wrote, as follows :

To Sir Jeffery Amhurst :

FORT PITT, Aug. 11. 1763.
SIR :—We arrived here yesterday without further opposition
than scattered shots along the road.

The Delawares, Shawanese, Wiandots and Mingoes, had closely
beset and attacked this fort from the 27th July to the 1st inst.,
when they quitted it to march against us.

The boldness of those savages is hardly credible; they had taken post under the banks of both rivers close to the fort, where digging holes, they kept an incessant fire, and threw fire arrows. They are good marksmen, and though our people were under cover, they killed one and wounded seven. Captain Ecuyer is wounded in the leg by an arrow. I should not do justice to that officer should I omit mentioning, that without engineer or any other artificers than a few shipwrights, he has raised a parapet of logs round the fort above the old one (which, having not been finished was too low and enfiladed) palisaded the inside of the area, constructed a fire engine, and, in short, has taken all precautions, which art and judgment could suggest, for the preservation of this post, open before on three sides, which had suffered by the floods. The inhabitants have acted with spirit against the enemy, and in the repairs of the fort. Captain Ecuyer expresses an entire satisfaction in their conduct.

The artillery and the small number of regulars have done their duty with distinction.

Sir Jeffery Amherst's letters add to the above accounts, that by his last intelligence the number of savages in the two actions of the 5th and 6th of August slain, was about sixty, and a great many wounded in the pursuit. That the three principle ringleaders of those people, who had the greatest share in fomenting the present troubles and were concerned in the murder of Col. Clapham, &c., viz: Kikyuscuting, and the Wolf and Butler, were, according to the information sent him, killed; the two former in the field, and the last at Fort Pitt.

THE OWNERSHIP OF THE BUSHY RUN TRACT.

It has been asserted by some writers, in recent as well as colonial days, that Col. Ephraim Blaine was in command of Fort Ligonier, which he bravely defended with provincial troops until Bouquet came along, after which he accompanied the army as commander of the pack-horse brigade, and took an active part in the battle of Bushy Run, where he came near losing his life, &c. He then resolved that some day he would become the owner of that historic field.

All this is pure fiction, evidently gotten up for a special purpose, in order to invalidate the claims of the Byerlys to the grant on Bushy Run, originally given by Col. Bouquet and secured by settlement and valuable improvements.

The name and record of Lieut. Archibald Blane, (not Blaine), who defended Fort Ligonier with a detachment of Royal Americans in 1763, have been confounded with those of Col. Ephraim Blaine, who first appears as a commissary sergeant in Bouquet's campaign of 1764. Neither Lieutenant A. Blane nor Colonel E. Blaine was in the Bushy Run battle. The former wrote Bouquet a letter from Fort Ligonier, immediately after the battle, congratulating him on his recent victory at Bushy Run. See Parkman's Pontiac, Vol. II., p. 160. See also page 407, of Washington — Irvine correspondence — where Ephraim Blaine's record is correctly sketched.

The truth is Ephraim Blaine jumped the older and original Byerly claim by a patent, confirmed by the Pennsylvania Executive Council in the distracted days of 1786, long after the death of the elder Byerly, and when his widow and children were in no shape to dispute his unjust usurpation. For forty-one pounds of provincial currency, when that currency was comparatively worthless, he managed to get a technical title to the old Byerly tract of over 300 acres along the Forbes road, on the historic field of Bushy Run ! This was bad enough surely, but to make him one of the chief heroes in the fight, to boost up the · unjust claim, is to violate not only the rights of a family but the rights of humanity. It pollutes the fountains and muddies the sacred stream of history itself.

It was no great credit to be in command of the pack-horse brigade at the Bushy Run battle, as Col. Bouquet's report indicates. And we do Col. Blaine's memory a service by relieving him from the equivocal position in which certain prominent individuals placed him in the suit for ownership of the battle-field, when they testified that Col. Blaine took part in the battle of 1763 as commander of the pack-horse brigade, &c.

Hon. Jos. H. Kuhns, who was counsel for the Blaines in the later stages of the suit, (when Blaine's friends claimed that he had bought Byerly's right and title) told the writer a few weeks ago that the general feeling at the time of the trial was that the Byerlys had right and justice on their side. The presiding judge, being a resident

of Carlisle and a special friend of the Blaines, was blamed
with partiality. Until recently Mr. Kuhns believed the
fiction about the presence and narrow escape of Col.
Ephraim Blaine in the battle, &c.,which had been palmed
off in the courts, &c., at the trial.

But after learning the real facts in the case, and seeing
how the names and records of Lieut. Archibald Blane and
Col. Ephraim Blaine had been confounded, he wrote me
the following candid note on the subject :

GREENSBURG, Pa., May 2, 1883.

Rev. Cyrus Cort :

REV. AND DEAR SIR.—Your esteemed favor received. I am
satisfied that the story of Blaine's claim to the battle ground is
apocryphal. He was an intruder upon Byerly, who was, in
point of fact, the first actual owner of the ground by occupancy
and legal authority of the proprietary government of Penn'a.

Respectfully,   JOS. H. KUHNS.

So much for the question of original and rightful ownership of Bushy Run battlefield. Byerly removed his family
to Fort Bedford, by advice of Bouquet, until peace was
firmly established at the end of next year. He then returned and occupied the grant on Bushy Run. About
the time of the breaking out of the Revolutionary war, he
took his son Andrew to Lancaster, Pa., to give him a
chance to get an education at the home of his step-sisters.
While on this visit the old gentleman died, and was buried
at Strasburg, in that county. I am indebted to Ad. J.
Eberly, esq., and Rev. J. A. Peters for the following facts,
which should have been stated at page 17 :

Record book B, page 349, contains a deed from James
Hamilton, esq., to Andreas Byerly, for a lot of ground on
east side of North Queen street, a frontage of 64 feet and
4½ inches and a depth of 245 feet, in the town of Lancaster, Pa., dated October 25, 1745.

The baptismal records of the First Reformed church of
Lancaster, Pa., mention Andreas Byerly as standing spon-
sor for a child, Feb. 3, 1745. So also on May 3, 1750, he
and his wife served in same capacity for a child by name
of Houck, from Strasburg Twp., and again for a Backen-

stopp, Feb. 4, 1753, under the pastorates of Revs. Schnorr-bock and Otterbein, respectively.

The Byerly family resided for greater safety at Fort Walthour during the Revolution. Jacob served in several campaigns against the Indians, and killed a chief in a fight near Brady's Bend, when quite a young man. ⸱

Mrs. Byerly was a very intelligent, humane and pious woman. She had been well trained in the doctrines of the Reformed Church of Switzerland. She did good service as a nurse and a kind of doctoress during those dark and dangerous days. But her care was extended to the soul as well as body. She established a Sunday school for the intellectual and religious training of the neglected children at the fort, and in various ways was a public benefactress. Some years after Mr. Byerly's death she was married to a Mr. Lord, an Englishman. She lies buried among her children at the old Brush Creek grave-yard. Andrew Byerly had four sons, viz. : Michael, Jacob, Francis and Andrew. Their descendants are scat-tered over a great part of the United States. Jacob en-tered the Revolutionary army at sixteen, and saw hard service for several years in helping to guard the frontiers against Indians and Tories. His son Andrew was major in the War of 1812, and guarded the ships of Commodoie Perry's fleet, while being built on Lake Erie. Benjamin was a lieutenant and Joseph a private, as also his son-in-law, Skelly, in the same war. Benjamin was likewise sheriff and assemblyman.

Captain George A. Cribbs, who fell at the head of his men at the second battle of Manassas, was married to a grand daughter of Jacob Byerly, and Sergeant Cyrus Rankin, who fell on the Peninsula, was a great grandson.

Mrs. James Gregg, of Greensburg, is a granddaughter of Michael, and Daniel C. Byerly, deceased, was a grand-son.

Prof. Andrew Byerly, of Millersville Normal School, is a grandson of Andrew II.

The descendants of Francis Byerly are numerous in Iowa. Michael, Jacob and Francis married three sisters named Harmon, whose mother was Christina Lenhart, from Holland. Jacob was married in old Fort Walthour, by 'Squire Trouby, during the Revolution. He and his son Joseph are buried with fine military monuments at Brush Creek graveyard.

EVIL RESULTS OF PROVINCIAL APATHY.

After their discomfiture at Bushy Run, the Indians moved from their towns along the Alleghany and Ohio rivers into the Muskingum country, where they fancied themselves entirely safe from molestation, while at the same time they could carry on their depredations by sudden incursions into the white settlements. It would have been wise policy and an immense saving of life and treasure had they been followed at once to their forest fastnesses and brought to terms by a display of military prowess in their own haunts.

This was exactly what Bouquet proposed to do. As soon as he had brought his heavy convoy through from Fort Ligonier to Port Pitt, he made strenuous efforts to secure reinforcements for such an expedition into the heart of the Indian country.

August 27, 1763, he wrote General Amherst from Fort Pitt that with a re-inforcement of three hundred Provincal Rangers he could destroy all the Delaware towns " and clear the country of that vermin between this fort and Lake Erie." He bitterly complained that the provinces would not even furnish escorts to convoys, so that his hands were completely tied, He candidly admitted the importance and value of provincials for service against the savages in the woods, something which Amherst, like Braddock before him, was loth to do.

October 24, 1763, he writes the haughty and obstinate Amherst as follows : " Without a certain number of woodsmen I cannot think it advisable to employ regulars in the woods against savages, as they cannot procure any intelligence and are open to continual surprises, nor can they pursue to any distance their enemy when they have routed them ; and should they have the misfortune to be defeated, the whole would be destroyed, if above one day's march from a fort. That is my opinion, in which I hope to be deceived."

The Quaker Provincial authorities, backed by the Dun-
kard and Mennonite elements among the Germans, seemed
to be utterly insensible to the dangers and sufferings of
the exposed settlements near the borders.   In their more
secure abodes in the older settlements they would prate
about the wickedness of war, and try to justify their impracticable theories by extensive scriptural quotations.

St. Paul teaches that civil government is a divine institution, and its representatives must not bear the sword in
vain, but be a terror to evil-doers and a praise to them
that do well.   See Rom., 13.

All this was ignored, and in place of it was substituted
a perverted theory of non-resistance.   The exhortations
to individual Christians to forego the gratification of private or personal revenge, on the ground of the old law of
retaliation, was applied to civil rulers and governments in
a way that was contrary to reason and Scripture.

The Great Cove, in Blair county, was settled by Dunk-
ards as early as 1755.   These were exposed to Indian
raids.   " Gottes wille sei gethan," they would say, while the
brutal savages were tomahawking their wives and children,
in whose defence they would not lift a finger.   They
seemed to think that it was the Lord's will that the devil
and his agents should have full swing without opposition.

The strong and vigorous Scotch Presbyterian and the
German Reformed and Lutheran elements of the population had no patience or sympathy with such sentimental
views.   When their families or friends were being ruthlessly slaughtered by the savages, they were filled with
indignation against all who either directly or indirectly
abetted the cruel destroyers of life and property.

Large numbers of Reformed and Lutheran families had
settled along the Codorus, the Conewago, the Monocacy
and Connocheague streams of Pennsylvania and Maryland,
where regularly organized congregations existed already
in 1748, as we learn from the " Life and Travels of Rev.
Michael Schlatter."   So also at Winchester and other
points through the Shenandoah Valley.

The Royal American Regiment, as we have seen, was
largely composed of this element and commanded by ex-

perienced German and Swiss officers, who had seen service in the armies of the Dutch Republic.

The horrors of savage warfare fell upon these settlements and soldiers, together with their Scotch-Irish neighbors, in the Conococheague settlements.

The friendly Conestoga Indians in Lancaster county and the Moravian Indian converts along the Lehigh were blamed for harboring and abetting some of the marauding Indians, and the full force of popular fury was arrayed against them. When homes were being daily desolated, parents tomahawked and scalped, and children carried into heathen captivity, it was natural for the people to hate the name of Indian and to be filled with wrath at any one who would protect or countenance any member of the race. The supineness of the Provincial Assembly, and their failure to second the efforts of such a man as Bouquet was discouraging and demoralizing and provoking in the extreme to the regular troops, who had suffered so much on the outposts, and to the hardy pioneers in the advanced settlements. The Paxton Boys, in their riotous conduct at the Lancaster jail and in their march to Philadelphia, helped to awaken the Quakers from their dream of lethargic indifference. The Royal Americans had been kept in the woods for over six years, and now Amherst sought to compel regulars to remain in service after the long term of enlistment had expired. These causes combined to produce great discontent, both among officers and men. They were expected to hold many important posts and keep up long lines of communication in the midst of the wilderness, surrounded by prowling and hostile savages. Lieut. Archibald Blane and the gallant Capt. Ecuyer asked Bouquet to be relieved from labors and responsiblilities too heavy for their strength and resources. And Bouquet himself chagrined, at some action of the British government which seemed to shut the door of promotion against foreign born officers, and worried out of patience by the ingratitude and neglect of the provinces, felt himself constrained to do the same thing.

c*

Amherst had left for England, disgusted with the situation and angry at the provinces for want of co-operation. General Gage had taken his place as commander-in-chief. Bouquet wrote Gage, June 20, 1764, asking to be relieved of the command, the burden and fatigues of which were too great for his strength to endure much longer.

He thus refers to the condition of the troops at the same time: " The three companies of Royal Americans were reduced, when I met them at Lancaster, to 55 men, having lost 38 by desertion, in my short absence. I look upon Sir Jeffery Amherst's orders forbidding me to continue to discharge, as usual, the men whose term of service was expired, and keeping us seven years in the woods, as the occasion of this unprecedented desertion. The encouragement given everywhere in this country to deserters, screened almost by every person, must in time ruin the army unless the laws against harbourers are better enforced by the American (provincial) government."

But Gage would not consent to relieve so useful a man in such an emergency. It was agreed that two strong bodies of troops should proceed into the Indian country to do what Bouquet was anxious to do the previous summer, i. e. chastise the savages into submission in their own native strongholds. Bradstreet was to take a large force by way of the Lakes and co-operate with Bouquet, who was to march with his Bushy Run veterans (what was left of them) and a large force of provincial rangers to be raised in Pennsyslvania, Virginia and Maryland.

The Pennsylvania Assembly voted to raise three hundred men to guard the frontiers and one thousand to join Bouquet's expedition into Ohio. Virginia and Maryland at first refused to do anything for the common defence.

MASSACRE OF A SCHOOL-MASTER AND TEN SCHOLARS.

The summer of 1764 was rapidly passing away, and nothing effective had yet been done. The Indians continued their ravages and penetrated deeper and deeper into the settlements, killing and slaying the defenceless people.

"In 1764, July 26, three miles northwest of Greencastle, Franklin county, Pa., was perpetrated what Parkman, the great historian of Colonial times, pronounces 'an outrage unmatched in fiend-like atrocity through all the annals of the war.' This was the massacre of Enoch Brown, a kind-hearted exemplary Christian schoolmaster, and ten scholars, eight boys and two girls. Ruth Hart and Ruth Hale were the names of the girls. Among the boys were Eben Taylor, George Dustan and Archie McCullough. All were knocked down like so many beeves and scalped by the merciless savages. Mourning and desolation came to many homes in the valley, for each of the slaughtered innocents belonged to a different family. The last named boy, indeed, survived the effects of the scalping knife, but in a somewhat demented condition.

The teacher offered his life and scalp in a spirit of self-sacrificing devotion if the savages would only spare the lives of the little ones under his charge and care. But no ! the tender mercies of the heathen are cruel, and so a perfect holocaust was made to the Moloch of war by the relentless fiends in human form. The school house was located on the farm now occupied by Mr. Henry Diehl, and formerly owned by Mr. Christian Koser. It stood in a cleared field, at the head of a deep ravine, surrounded by dense forests. Down this ravine the savages fled a mile or two until they struck Conococheague creek, along the bed of which, to conceal their tracks, they traveled to the mouth of Path Valley, up which and across the mountains they made good their escape to their village, near the Ohio.

It is some relief to know that this diabolical deed, whose recital makes us shudder even at this late date, was disapproved by the old warriors when the marauding party of young Indians came back with their horrid trophies. Neephaughwhese, or Night Walker, an old chief or half-king, denounced them as a pack of cowards for killing and scalping so many children.

But who can describe the agony of those parents in the Conococheague, settlement weeping like Rachel for her children and refusing to be comforted ? Or who can describe the horror of the scene in that lonely log school house, when one of the settlers chanced to look in at the door to ascertain the cause of the unusual quietness.

In the centre lay the faithful Brown, scalped and lifeless, with a Bible clasped in his hand. Around the room were strewn the dead and mangled bodies of seven boys and two girls, while little Archie, stunned, scalped and bleeding, was creeping around among his dead companions, rubbing his hands over their faces and trying to gain some token of recognition.

A few days later the innocent victims of savage atrocity received a common sepulture. All were buried in one large, rough box at the border of the ravine, a few rods from the school house where they had been so ruthlessly slaughtered. Side by side, with head and feet alternately, the little ones were laid with their master, just as they were clad at the time of the massacre. Strange to say, no memorial tablet has ever been erected over their remains. Tradition has preserved the exact location of the common grave of master and scholars, and it is not too late yet for grateful, patriotic and philanthropic Christian people, enjoying the blessings of civilization, peace and prosperity, to render this duty of the living to the martyred dead.

August 4, 1843, or seventy-nine years after the slaughter, a number of the principal citizens of Greencastle made excavations to verify the traditional account of the place and manner of burial. Some remains of the rough coffin were found at quite a depth from the surface, and then the skull and other remains of a grown person, alongside of which were remains of several children. Metal buttons, part of a tobacco-box, teeth, &c., were picked up as relics by those present, among whom were some of our citizens still living with us in a green old age, viz: Dr. Wm. Grubb, Dr. J. K. Davison, Geo. W. Zeigler, Esq., and Gen. David Detrich.

There was a good deal of talk at the time about the propriety of buying the adjacent grounds, laying out a road and erecting a monument; but nothing definite was ever done. Mr. Koser, the owner of the farm, took a lively interest in the matter, and in lieu of a better memorial planted four locust trees to mark the corners of the grave. Two of these only survived and are mentioned by S. H. Eby, Esq., Sup't of Common Schools, in his interesting report, published 1877. But, alas! even these imperfect historic landmarks were cut down a few years ago for the sake of making a few posts, and Mr. Koser's well-meant efforts to preserve the identity of the grave have thus in a measure been thwarted. The stumps remain as frail indices by which the exact location of the grave may still be accurately determined.

Such is the present state of the case as ascertained last Wednesday (April 11, 1883), on a visit to the spot by Gen. David Detrich, Col. B. F. Winger and Rev. Cyrus Cort."

The foregoing is an extract from an article that appeared in the Greencastle *Press*.

I am glad to be able to report that as a result of the visit just mentioned, steps having been taken by public spirited citizens of Greencastle to have the grave of Brown and his martyred scholars duly marked by a permanent monument at an early day.

Atrocities like these helped to arouse the slumbering provinces to the necessity of bold and energetic measures.

CAMPAIGN OF 1764.

On the 5th of August the two Pennsylvania battallions under Lieut. Colonels Francis and Clayton were assembled at Carlisle. Gov. Penn had come up from Philadelphia with Col. Bouquet and addressed the troops. He spoke of the necessity of chastising the Indians " for their repeated and unprovoked barbarities on the inhabitants of the Province, a just resentment of which added to a remembrance of the loyalty and courage of our provincial troops on former occasions he did not doubt, would animate them to do honour to their country, and that they could not but hope to be crowned with success as they were to be united with the same regular troops and under the same able commander who had by themselves on that very day, the memorable 5th of August, in the preceeding year, sustained the repeated attacks of the savages and obtained a complete victory over them."

Gov. Penn also reminded them of the exemplary punishments that would be inflicted on the grevious crime of desertion, if any of them were capable of so far forgetting their solemn oath and duty to their king and country as to be involved in it. Col. Bouquet then took command of the troops, regular and provincial. After four days of necessary preparation for the long march, the army set out.

Col. Bouquet gave very strict " orders to officers and men to observe strict discipline and not to commit the least violation of the civil rights or peace of the inhabitants."

His care and conduct in this respect stand forth in happy contrast with that of many militia or emergency men who came up the valley to defend the borders from invasion a hundred years later, but who in the end were more harmful and more dreaded by the loyal people of the borders than the disciplined host of Southern invaders under Lee.

DESERTIONS OF PROVINCIAL TROOPS.

In spite of all precautions, no less than 200 desertions took place by August 13, when the army reached Fort Londoun.

Bouquet asked permission to fill up the contingent, which was granted by resolution of the governor and commissioners August 16. He then applied to Colonel Lewis for 200 Virginia volunteers, to take the place of the deserters. With the co-operation of Governor Fauquier the men were soon raised and joined Bouquet at Fort Pitt in the latter part of September.

These Virginia volunteer riflemen were among his best troops, but in the end, Virginia ungratefully left Col. Bouquet in the lurch as regards their payment.

At Fort Loudoun, Bouquet received a very presumptuous and characteristic letter from Col. Bradstreet, telling him that he need not proceed any farther, inasmuch as peace had been concluded with the Delawares and Shawanese. At that very time these same tribes were scalping settlers in all directions. Bradstreet was ambitious to gain all the glory of the campaign. Instead of minding his own business and compelling the Lake Indians to bring in their captives and give proper guarantees of submission, he turned aside in his course to attend to the business assigned to Bouquet, who was his superior officer. As the whole scheme was a ruse on the part of the Ohio Indians to gain time and prevent Bouquet's advance, he and General Gage were both indignant at Bradstreet and repudiated his officious intermeddling.

Without delaying an hour, Bouquet pushed forward. September 5, he had reached Fort Bedford, where more Pennsylvanians deserted, taking along their arms and horses. A large reinforcement of friendly Indians,.promised to be sent from the Six Nations by Sir. Wm. Johnson, never arrived. At Ligonier he received from Gen. Gage the hearty endorsement of his own conduct, and the repudiation of Bradstreet's unwarranted and premature negotiations with irresponsible representatives of the Ohio Indians.

ARRIVAL AT FORT PITT.

He passed safely over the historic field of Bushy Run to Fort Pitt, where he was rejoiced to receive the Virginia reinforcement. Ten Indians came to the opposite bank of the river, proposing a conference. Finding that they were evidently spies, endeavoring to gain important information, he detained two of them as hostages, and sent another one with two messengers to Bradstreet and a statement to the Ohio Indians that if any harm was done to these two men, the Indian hostages in his hands should be put to death at once and dire vengeance executed against their entire nation. Several Iroquois Indians came into the fort, pretending great friendship, and assuring him that the Ohio Indians would speedily return all the white captives. They spoke of the difficulty of penetrating the hilly forests and the great numbers of the Indians who would oppose the army, but who would soon fulfil all his stipulations if he only remained quietly at Fort Pitt. The whole object of these crafty envoys was evidently to delay the campaign until bad weather and lateness of the season made it impossible.

Bouquet saw through their designs and sent them to tell the Delawares and Shawanese, &c., that he was on his way to punish their cruel and perfidious conduct unless they made prompt and complete submission to his terms.

THE MARCH INTO OHIO.

Early in October the army left Fort Pitt to cut a road directly through the unexplored wilderness of Ohio. The Colonel assured the troops of his confidence in their bravery and told them that "he did not doubt but that this war would soon be ended, under God, to their own honor and the future safety of their country, provided the men were strictly obedient to orders and guarded against the surprises and sudden attacks of a treacherous enemy, who never dared to face British troops in an open field."

Large droves of sheep and cattle were taken along for subsistence, besides great droves of packhorses loaded with flour and other provisions. The Virginia woodsmen acted as scouts and flankers in front and on the sides, whilst the pioneers cleared the road through the dense forest. The army, with flocks and herds and camp equipage, followed the pioneers at the rate of seven or eight miles a day, moving constantly in a series of concentric hollow squares, with flocks, herds, baggage, packhorses, &c., in the centre. Thus in line of battle and guarding carefully against ambush and surprise, they moved steadily forward. Skulking Indians were watching every movement, but no direct attempt was made to interfere with the progress of the troops. The strictest discipline was enforced. Before leaving Fort Pitt two soldiers had been shot for desertion, and all superfluous women ordered back to the settlements. One woman was allowed to each corps, and two nurses for the general hospital. These were needed to look after the children and female captives, whose recovery was one chief object of the expedition. In ten days the army reached the Muskingum, and was now in the heart of the Indian country. Near the fording of that river, they saw the wigwams of 100 families of Tuscarora Indians who had fled in terror at their approach. The two soldiers sent to Bradstreet, now appeared, having been detained by the Delawares on trifling pretexts until they saw the invasion was an overwhelming success. They brought word that the chiefs would come in a few days to hold a conference.

COUNCIL ON THE MUSKINGUM—CAPTIVES RESTORED.

Bouquet marched along the Muskingum until he found ample forage in the broad meadows for his cattle, sheep and packhorses ; he erected a palisaded depot for provisions and baggage. Soon a number of chiefs appeared, stating that great numbers of warriors were eight miles distant, and that a place and time should be appointed for council. He designated a spot near the river bank where he would meet them next day. A party of woodsmen soon prepared a rustic arbor, where English officers and Indian chiefs might meet under shelter. Every precaution was used to prevent a surprise or attack. Guards were doubled and no straggling allowed. The soldiers were drawn up so as to make the most stunning impression upon the minds of the savages. And truly it was a wonderful sight to see such a vast body of troops fully equipped in the midst of the wilderness, with flocks and herds, and other resources needed for a protracted campaign. The scene was as picturesque as it was astounding in its display of miltary prowess.

The Highland grenadiers were there with their plaids, kilts and tartans, whom the Indians styled, " petticoat warriors" on account of their queer dress. The Royal Americans were on hand with their bright red British uniforms, the duller garb and duller trappings of Pennsylvania troops and the fringed hunting frocks of the Virginia backwoods riflemen made such a combination of military pomp and power as has been rarely seen in any land.

The chiefs came at the appointed hour—Kiashuta, or Guyashuta, the chief of a band of Senecas, Custaloga chief of the Delawares, Keisnauchtha, chief of the Shawanese, each with a band of warriors, were the leaders along with Turtle Heart, Beaver, &c., they tried to frame excuses for their teacherous conduct, blaming it on the rashness of their young men and the western tribes led in person by Pontiac, they begged for peace and promised to return to him all white prisoners in their hands.

Bouquet thoroughly understood the Indian character, and knew what demeanor and tactics suited the occasion. He told them to return next day to receive his answer. Inclement weather prevented their proposed meeting until the twentieth. Instead of calling them brothers he began : "Sachems, War chiefs and Warriors." He then addressed them with great spirit, and in severe and impassioned language. He pointed out the absurdity of their trifling excuses, and reminded them of their unparalleled treachery and cruelty in plundering traders and settlers, capturing children and in assulting the king's troops in the woods at Bushy Run, last summer. He denounced their continued murderous forays upon the border settlements, and condemned their repeated failures to bring back the white prisoners in their hands. He will not be deceived longer by their false promises. "If," said he, "it were possible that you could convince us that you sincerely repent of your past perfidy, and that we could depend on your good behavior for the future, you might yet hope for mercy and peace. If I find that you faithfully execute the following preliminary conditions, I will not treat you with the severity you deserve. I give you twelve days from this date to deliver into my hands at Waukatamake, all prisoners in your possession without any exception, Englishmen, Frenchmen, women, children, whether adopted in your tribes, married or living amongst you under any denomination and pretence whatsoever, together with all negroes. And you are to furnish the said prisoners with clothing, provisions and horses to carry them to Fort Pitt. When you have fully complied with these conditions, you shall then know on what terms you may obtain the peace you sue for."

Bouquet was as wise and sagacious as he was brave and generous. The manner as well as the sentiments of his address made a deep and lasting impression upon the supplicating savages. Their haughty spirit was completely humbled.

They abjectly promised to comply fully with all the conditions. The Delawares had already delivered up eighteen prisoners. They handed over eighty-three small sticks indicating the remaining number of prisoners in their hands, whom they promised to bring in as soon as possible. The Shawanese failed to respond properly to the Colonel's wishes, either by appearing at the council with their kings or by bringing in the captives in their hands. A sharp message was sent to them not to trifle with the patience of the commander. The army marched some thirty odd miles further to the Forks of the Muskingum, where it was agreed to await the prisoners instead of at Waukatamake. The principal chiefs of each tribe he kept in his possession as hostages to secure the fulfillment of pledges. Great care had to be taken to prevent a general stampede of the tribes and the murder of all the prisoners in their hands as well as to secure a full compliance with the conditions of restoration. Bouquet's management inspired them with confidence and respect, while at the same time it filled them with terror and brought them into complete submission 'to his commands. Runners were sent out in all directions, and soon several hundred captives were brought into camp. Among these were ninety Virginians, of whom thirty-two were adult males and the rest were women and children ; one hundred and sixteen Pennsylvanians, forty-nine men and sixty-seven women and children were also returned. Many of the volunteers had wives, children and relatives among the captives, and the scenes that took place at the recovery and recognition of the long lost loved ones were touching in the extreme. With great sorrow and reluctance the Indians parted with these adopted members of their households. For, be it remembered, that when once an Indian had adopted a captive, the captive was henceforth treated as a member of the family and not as a slave. The captive women were, as a rule, absolutely free from insult and were not even obliged to marry against their will. · The reverse of this is the case among many of the Western and South-western tribes of Indians at the present day, who treat their captives as slaves and always outrage the women. Many of the Shawanese warriors were absent on hunting expeditions, so that nearly a hundred captives could not be reached. Hostages were given for the safe delivery of these at Fort Pitt. Bouquet maintained a stern and indignant demeanor until all conditions were fulfilled as far as possible, knowing that any other deportment under circumstances would be mistaken for timidity and indecision. Kindness can only be appreciated by a savage when he knows you have ability to overwhelm him if refractory. Having fully convinced them of his prowess and displeasure at everything like duplicity, Bouquet convened the chiefs in the rustic council house again and intimated his satisfaction with their conduct and his desire to arrange for a lasting peace.

Guyasutha, the celebrated Seneca chief, who had been the leading spirit of the eastern wing of Pontiac's conspiracy, and had led the forces around Fort Pitt and at Bushy Run, made the opening speech in the metaphorical

and eloquent language so characteristic of Indian orators.
"Brother," said he, addressing Col. Bouquet, "with this
string of wampum I dispel the thick cloud that has hung
so long over our heads, that the sunshine of peace may
once more descend to warm and gladden. I wipe the tears
from your eyes and condole with you on the loss of your
brethren who have perished in this war. I gather their
bones together and cover them deep in the earth, that the
sight of them may no longer bring sorrow to your hearts,
and I scatter dry leaves over the spot, that it may depart
forever from memory. The path of peace, which once
ran between your dwellings and mine, has of late been
choked with thorns and briars, so that no one could pass
that way, and we have both forgotten that such a path
had ever been. I now clear away all such obstructions
and make a broad, smooth road, so that you and I may
freely visit each other as our fathers used to do. I kindle
a great council fire whose smoke shall rise to heaven in
view of all the nations while you and I sit together and
smoke the peace pipe at its blaze."

The orators of each tribe spoke in similar strain promising to lay down their arms and live hereafter in peace with
the English. Bouquet replied to each and all as follows :
" By your full compliance with the conditions which I imposed you have satisfied me of your sincerity and I now
receive you as brethren. The King, my master, has com-
misioned me, not to make treaties but to fight his battles ;
and though I now offer you peace it is not in my power
to settle its precise terms and conditions. For this I refer
you to Sir William Johnson, his Majesty's agent and
superintendent for Indian affairs, who will settle with you
the articles of peace and determine everything in relation to trade. Two things, however, I shall insist on.
And first you are to give hostages as security that you
will preserve good faith and send without delay a deputa-
tion of your chiefs to Sir William Johnson. In the next
place these chiefs are to be fully empowered to treat in
behalf of your nation ; and you will bind yourselves to
adhere strictly to everything they shall agree upon in your
behalf."

These conditions were readily complied with, and chiefs duly designated for the mission to Sir William.

And now having gained all his points, Bouquet to the great joy and relief of the Indians extended for the first time the hand of friendship, which hitherto he had resolutely refused to do.

Nettowhatways, the chief of the Turtle tribe, having failed to co-operate properly in the peace measures, Col. Bouquet deposed him and directed his tribe to elect another chief and present him as their proper representative, which was done a few days later.

Nov. 12, Red Hawk, Nimwha, Lavissimo, Bennevissico, and other leading Shawnese chiefs made their submission. Red Hawk instead of proposing in usual Indian style to bury the hatchet (which might in that case be dug up again) said that they as younger brothers would take it out of the hands of their older white brothers and " throw it up to God " that they might never see it again.

He then produced copies of treaties made in 1701 as, an evidence of the friendly relations of their ancestors. He promised that the remainder of the prisoners would be brought into Fort Pitt in the spring which pledge was kept. Many of the captives had become so fond of Indian life that it was with difficulty that they could be induced to return to Christian homes. McCullough, one of the captives in his narrative says that Rhoda Boyd and Elizabeth Studibaker escaped from the whites and went back to the Indians. Mary Jemison, who had married among them, fled with her half-breed children and hid until the troops left the country.

This would indicate that after their adoption captives was as a rule treated kindly and as members of their own families by their Indian captors.

One of the Virginia volunteers had lost his wife and a child two years old in an Indian foray into the settlement six months before. What transports filled their hearts when he met her with a babe three months old at her breast ! Quickly he took her to his tent, and furnished suitable clothing for her and her babe. But what had become of the two-year-old darling captured with its

mother ? She could not tell, except that it had been separated from her and taken elsewhere after their captivity.
A few days later a child was brought, in which was supposed to be the one in question. The mother was sent
for, and at first was not certain that it was her child, but
after carefully scrutinizing it she recognized its features,
and was so overcome with joy that she dropped her young
babe and, catching up the newly found child, she clasped
it to her heart, and with a flood of tears carried it off.
The father, picking up the child that she had let fall, followed his overjoyed wife and thus again the family circle
was unbroken. The rough soldiers, and even the stolid
savages were moved to feelings of sympathetic tenderness
by such touches of human nature, which make the whole
world of mankind akin.

November 18, the army set out for Fort Pitt, followed
by many affectionate Indians, who sought to help the captives along in their homeward journey. In ten days the
fort was reached just in time to escape severe winter
weather. The regular troops (Highlanders and Royal
Americans), were placed at the different forts and posts
on the line of communication, while the volunteers returned with the captives to the provinces. Those captives,
whose friends had not been able to go with the army,were
taken to Carlisle, where many persons who had lost children by the Indians, flocked to discover, if possible, their
captured kindred. One German woman, from East Pennsylvania, came in search of a daughter, who had been
carried off nine years before. She identified one of the
young female captives as her long lost child, but could
gain no token of recognition in response to her loving entreaties. The old lady lamented that the child that she
had often sung to sleep on her knee had forgotten her in
her old age. Bouquet, like a man of sense and humane
instincts, told the woman to sing one of the songs or
hymns that she used to sing to her when a child. Mrs.
Hartman, the mother, obeyed as best she could, singing
part of a very appropriate German hymn, of which I will
give several verses, together with a translation by Rev.
Samuel R. Fisher, D. D., deceased.

Allein und doch nicht gantz alleine
  Bin ich in meiner einsamkeit,
Dann wann ich gantz verlassen scheine,
  Vertreibt mir Jesus selbst die zeit.
Ich bin bey Ihm, und Er bey mir,
So kommt nun gar nich einsam für.

Alone and yet not all alone
  Am I, in solitude though drear,
For when no one seems me to own
  My Jesus will himself be near.
I am with Him and He with me,
I, therefore, cannot lonely be.

Komm ich zur welt; man redt von sachen,
  So nur auf eitlekeit gericht;
Da muss sich lassen das verlachen,
  Der etwas von den Himmel spricht.
Drum wunsh ich lieber gantz allein,
Als bey der welt ohn Gott zu seyn.

Seek I the world? Of things they speak,
  Which are on vanity intent;
Here he is scorned and spurned as weak
  Whose mind on heavenly things is bent.
I rather would my lone way plod,
Than share the world without my God.

Verkehrte konnen leicht verkehren,
  Wer greifet pech ohn kleben an?
Wie solt ich dann dahin begehren,
  Wo man Gott bald vergessen kann?
Gesellschaft, die verdachtig sheint,
Wird ofters nach dein fall beweint.

With ease do perverts perverts make;
  Who handles pitch his hands will soil;
Why then should I with those partake,
  Who of His honor God despoil?
Society which we suspect,
We often afterwards reject.

*   *   *   *   *   *   *   *

Wer wolte dann nun recht erkennen,
  Das ich stets in gesellschaft bin?
Und will die welt mich einsam nennen,
  So thun sie es nur immerhin.
G'nug, dass bey mir, wann ich allein,
Gott und viel tausend engel seyn.

Who will not then with candor own,
I have companions all I crave?
And will the world still deem me lone?
. Then let it thus forever rave.
Enough ! I've God and angels' host,
Whose number can its thousands boast.

The sweet accents of her German childhood, fell upon
her enraptured ears like the song of angels, and with a
gaze of fond recognition, and a passionate flood of tears,
the long lost daughter rushed into the outstretched arms
of her devoted mother.

Scenes like this threw a halo of religious romance
around the expedition of Bouquet. Rev. Ruben Weiser
has drawn out the story of Regina Hartman, the German
captive, with confessedly large drafts upon the imagination. He draws Conrad Weiser into the drama, although
the great Indian interpreter had already been dead four
years ! This is not more absurd than to foist in a German
hostler to interpret between Mrs. Hartman and Col Bouquet, who was well acquainted with German, French, &c.,
or his efforts to make Regina pass through a certain religious process.

Peace and tranquility were restored to the borders
without bloodshed, and hundreds of captives were brought
back from heathen bondage to blessings of Christian
homes and civilization. Bouquet was the hero of the
hour. Early in January, 1765, he arrived in Philadelphia.
The people and authorities everywhere vied with each
other in expressing their highest esteem for his character,
and grateful recognition of his services. The friends and
relatives especially of recovered captives were filled with
affectionate and reverent admiration.

PUBLIC THANKS TO BOUQUET.

January 15, 1765, the Assembly of Pennsylvania at its
first setting, adopted a congratulatory and complimentary
address, heartily thanking him for his great service to that
province, by his victory at Bushy Run, Aug, 6, 1763, his recent campaign against the Ohio Indians, during which he

had laid the foundation of lasting peace and rescued hundreds of Christian brethern from savage captivity ; and, finally, they thanked him for his "constant attention to the civil rights of his Majesty's subjects in this province."

In like manner the House of Burgesses for the Colony and Dominion of Virginia, thanked Bouquet for his invaluable services in subduing the Indians, and recovering so many of their people from captivity.

They further requested the Governor to recommend Bouquet to the ministers of King George, as an officer of distinguished merit, in this and every former service in which he had been engaged. The gallant and chivalric Colonel replied in grateful acknowledgment and generously awarded much of the credit of the success of his recent campaign to the efficiency of the provincial troops, and especially commended Col. Lewis for his zeal and good conduct during the campaign. Col. Reid, who was second in command, also received honorable mention from him as well as all officers, regular and provincial, who served in the expedition.

INJUSTICE AND INGRATITUDE OF VIRGINIA.

But every sweet has its bitter, and the oft-told tale of ingratitude and injustice to benefactors must, alas, be repeated. Virginia was lavish in her praises, as well she might be, for she had profited greatly by the campaign ; but when it came to foot the bill of expenses for her small body of splendid troops during the campaign, she repudiated the obligation ! "Tell it not in Gath, publish it not in the streets of Askelon !" Pontiac, the heathen savage, put such conduct to shame by scrupulously redeeming every piece of birch bark currency issued in his name for supplies during the siege of Detroit.

At length, after great personal annoyance and embarrassment, Bouquet induced the Pennsylvania Assembly to pay the Virginia troops for services and expenses incurred during the campaign of 1764.

By so doing Pennsylvania in some degree atoned for a multitude of past sins of neglect and indifference. But

D

Bouquet was stung to the quick by the conduct of the Virginians, and begs Gen. Gage to relieve him from his present command in order that he might make a trip to Europe. His request was granted. He wrote to Gage March 4, 1765, "the disgust I have conceived from the ill-nature and ingratitude of those individuals (the Virginia officials) makes me accept with great satisfaction your offer to discharge me of this department, in which I never desire to serve again, nor, indeed, to be commanding officer in any other, since the new regulations you were pleased to communicate to me ; being sensible of my inability to carry on the service upon the terms prescribed."

This had reference to some rigid prescriptions which he supposed fully closed the door against the promotion of foreign born officers.

He seems to have intended to return and settle in the provinces, or remove obstacles in the line of promotion, for the day before writing the above letter to Gage, i. e., March 3, 1765, he was naturalized by the Supreme Court of Pennsylvania, in accordance with a late act of Parliament.

BOUQUET'S PROMOTION.

And now to his great surprise and the gratification of all good men, Bouquet receives tidings that the King had promoted him to the rank of brigadier general.

April 15, 1765, he wrote his grateful acknowledgment of the unexpected honor, which also gave assurance of preferment to other deserving foreign-born officers, who were among the most devoted subjects of the King. Letters of congratulation came pouring in, especially from officers who had served under him.

Capt. George Etherigton, of the first battallion of Royal Americans, who so narrowly escaped massacre at Michillmackinac in May, 1763, wrote Bouquet as follows from Lancaster, Pa., April 19, 1765 : "Sir, though I almost despair of this reaching you before you sail to Europe, yet I cannot deny myself the pleasure of giving you joy on your promotion, and can, with truth, tell you that it gives great joy to all the gentlemen of the battallion, for two reasons : first, on your account ; and secondly, on our own, as by that means we may hope for the pleasure of continuing under your command. You can hardly imagine how this place rings with the news of your promotion, for the townspeople and German farmers stop us in the street to ask if it is true that the king has made Col. Bouquet a general ; and when they are told it is true, they march off with great joy ; so you see the old proverb wrong for once, which says he that prospers is envied ; for sure I am that all the people are more pleased with the news of your promotion than they would be if the government would take off the stamp duty."

Dr. Wm. Smith, Provost of the University and historian of his campaigns, spoke the common sentiment when he said Bouquet had become "as dear by his private virtues to those who have the honor of his more intimate acquaintance as he is by his military service to the public." For this reason "it is hoped he may long continue among us, where his experienced abilities will enable him, and his love of the English constitution entitle him, to fill any future trust to which his Majesty may be pleased to call him."

It had been Bouquet's hope and desire to visit England and to return again to the scenes of his earlier career among the Lowlands of Holland and the mountains of Switzerland, but the king assigned him to the command of the Southern military department, and as the Indians had recently become troublesome in that locality, he repaired to his new field of action without unnecessary delay.

LEAVES FOR PENSACOLA. WILL AND DEATH.

Before leaving Philadelphia he made his last will and testament, which I copied a few weeks ago at the office of the Register of Wills, in Philadelphia. It is in his own handwriting, and reads thus: " In the name of God, Amen. I, Henry Bouquet, Brigadier General of his Majesty's forces, serving in North America, have thought fit to dispose of my estate, real and personal, after my death, in the following manner : I give and bequeath for the use of the Hospital of Pennsylvania, forty pounds of that currency. I give and bequeath to my friend, Thos. Willing, Esq., five tracts of land of two hundred acres each, surveyed or to be surveyed for me in Trough Creek Valley, by virtue of the warrants granted me at the land office, and now to the amount of thirteen, including one to be given by Geo. Croghan, Esq., in the hands of Mr. Robert Callendar, living near Carlisle, in Cumberland county ; amounting in the whole to two thousand eight hundered acres, for which I paid only the warrant money. I give and bequeath to John Schneider, the boy who is bound to me, the sum of fifty pounds currency to be paid him when he is of age by Col. Haldimand, to whom I recommend my other servants. All my just debts are to be paid, consisting at present in one thousand pounds sterling, besides interests to Mr. G. Heneman, solicitor of the Swiss troops at the Hague in Holland—in my note in hand to account current with Mr. Adam Hoops, the note being for two hundred and fifty pounds being without interest—in a bond upon mortgage to Mr. Roberts for the sum of one thousand pounds currency with interest. I give and bequeath to my father, if then living, or after him, to Col. Lewis Bouquet, and to his heirs all the effects of any nature, whatsoever, which I may be possessed of in the continent of Europe, without exception. I constitute and appoint my friend, Col. Frederick Haldimand, my heir and executor, and to him I give and bequeath all and everything which 1 may die possessed of in North America, without any exception whatever, upon the condition of paying my just debts and above legacies. My estate, consisting for the present in the farm called *Long Meadows enlarged*, situate in Frederick county, in the Province of Maryland. [Bouquet received the grant for this estate Sept. 16, 1763. It contained, as owned by him, 4,163 acres of very valuable land. Frederick county, Maryland, at that time included Washington county, within whose present limits the estate was located near the Pennsylvania line.] The deeds whereof are now in the possession of the above named, ——— Roberts. The said farm to be sold with the saw-mill, tan yard, houses, tenement and appurtenances on the same for the payment of my debts and legacies—in the eighteen hundred acres of land above mentioned, to be surveyed for me in this Province and remaining after deducting the five tracts given to Mr. Willing—in my share of the She- pody lands if then in my possession—in my apparel, bag- gage, furniture, stores, &c., in my pay and arrears which may be due me at my death—in my share of the Carolina Plantation after the accounts are fully settled between Messrs. Guinand and the others concerned, all of which I bequeath to Col. Haldimand, and I hereby annul and de- clare void, and of no effect, any other will which I may at any time have made previous to this day, as this present will and testament contains my last and real intentions and disposition, and is to take place accordingly. In witness whereof, I have wrote, (written) signed with my own hand and affixed my seal to this last will and testament, in the City of Philadelphia, in Pennsylvania, this twenty-fifth day of June, in the year of our Lord one thousand seven hun- dred and sixty five.   HENRY BOUQUET.

Signed, sealed, published and declared by the testator as his last will and testament in our presence who sub- scribed the same as witnesses in his presence and at his request.   BENJAMIN CHEW,
                                          JO. TURNER,
                                          THOS. TURNER.

The will was probated Nov. 1, 1765, on oath of the Turners, the other witness, Mr. Chew, being the register general. Soon after this and evidently with a good deal of reluctance, Gen. Bouquet set out for his new station at Pensacola, where he arrived Aug. 23, 1765, in the deadliest season of the year, and at once fell a victim to the fever so fatal to unacclimated persons. The following extract from the *Pennsylvania Magazine* for Thursday October 24, 1765, tells the sad story : "On Tuesday last arrived the sloop William, Capt. Rivers, in thirty-six days from Pensacola, by whom we learn ten sail of transports with troops (to relieve those on that station that are going home) arrived there, and that there has been a great mor- tality among them, ten or twelve dying of a day, amongst which was the gallant and worthy officer, Brigadier Gen.

Bouquet. This gentleman had served his Majesty all the last war with great distinction. He was promoted from conscious merit not only unenvied, but even with the approbation and good wishes of all who knew him. His superior judgment and knowledge of military matters, his experienced abilities, known humanity, remarkable politeness and constant attention to the civil rights of his Majesty's subjects, rendered him an honor to his country and a loss to mankind. He arrived the 23d of August, and died September 2." Thus in the midst of his growing fame and in the full vigor of manhood this superb man, who had faced death unscathed a thousand times in the forests and thickets of Pennsylvania, met his untimely end from insidious disease, just as he was about to begin his career on a new theatre of action in the far distant south.

He died universally regretted, and his character and example were commended by contemporary writers as worthy of imitation by young officers who desired to win a lasting fame in the public service. He sleeps in a soldier's grave, far from home and kindered, far from those who knew him but to love him. But warm and grateful hearts in the North land cherished his memory and fame with fond affection 118 years ago. And although for a time oblivion's waves seemed to have almost engulfed him, yet we see the dawn of a brighter day and feel assured that the fame of Bouquet will shine forth bright and beautiful as in days of yore. In the forum of all grateful hearts, among the descendants of Colonial ancestors or pioneer settlers, a monument deserves to be erected to the memory of Henry Bouquet more enduring than Parian marble or Corinthian brass. Reverently and gratefully I pay him this tribute, and would that it were indeed an amaranthine chaplet to adorn and perpetuate his memory, yea to call forth the homage of the good, the brave and the true, as the centuries go marching down the corridors of time.

BOUQUET'S GRAVE UNKNOWN.

Bouquet's grave at Pensacola is unmarked and unknown. During the past ten months very thorough researches have

Leen made by the military authorities on the Gulf, but all in vain, as the subjoined letters indicate.

WAR DEPARTMENT, ADJUTANT GENERAL'S OFFICE, }
WASHINGTON, February 13, 1883. }

MY DEAR SIR : Your letter of the 9th inst. enclosing one addressed to our Ministe1 at Great Britain, has been received. It affords me great pleasure to aid you all I can in this matter, and I have accordingly submitted your letter to Mr. Lowell, to the Hon. the Secretary of War, for transmission to the Secretary of State for such action as may be consistent with public interests.

Referring to your inquiry of the 9tb ult., respecting the remains of Bouquet, I regret to inform you, that the commanding officer at Fort Barrancas, Fla., to whom your request was referred, reports under the date of the 7th instant, that he has made search and inquiry in Pensacola regarding the whereabouts of Gen. Bouquet's remains, but has not been able to learn anything about them. He further states that the oldest cemetery at Pensacola was commenced in 1780, and that those best posted in the matter have informed him that all the cemeteries at that place were destroyed prior to 1780, and that there is no trace of them left.

The old cemeteries at Pensacola were probably destroyed in 1781, when that town was besieged and taken by the Spanish General Galvez.

I will make further inquiries regarding Bouquet's remains and apprise you of the result.   Yours very truly,

R. C. DRUM,
REV. CYRUS CORT, ·   *Adjutant General.*
Greencastle, Franklin County, Pa.

WAR DEPARTMENT, ADJUTANT GENERAL'S OFFICE, }
WASHINGTON, March 21, 1883. }

DEAR SIR : I have received General Hancock's answer to my inquiries regarding Bouquet's remains.   ·

He informs me that upon the receipt of my letter he referred it to several officers who have been stationed at Fort Barrancas, Fla., for any information or suggestions they might have in this matter ; that they named certain persons who, they thought, could probably furnish the desired information, but that all efforts in that direction have thus far proved to be unsuccessful.

The commanding officer of Fort Barrancas again visited Pensacola, with a view of obtaining some information of the remains of Bouquet, supposed to have be buried there. He interviewed a number of gentlemen, old residents of that town, and states that none of them have ever heard of Bouquet.

He also searched the old cemetery, which was deeded by the Spanish to the Catholic church in 1781, but without success, and finally states that—unfortunately—the records of the cemetery as well as those of the Catholic church, were destroyed by fire last summer, and regrets to state that it is impossible to gain any information at Pensacola regarding the whereabouts of Bouquet's remains.   I am, yours very truly,
                                            R. C. DRUM,
The REV. CYRUS CORT,   *Adjutant General.*
Greencastle, Franklin County, Pa.

General Drum has shown great zeal and persistency in this research.   He has always manifested deep interest in the character and career of Col. Bouquet, and as a Westmorelander of old and honored lineage, he is anxious to have justice done to the hero of Bushy Run.   It remains for the present generation to mark aright the field of Bouquet's greatest triumph by a monument as lasting as the hills which were consecrated by the blood and valor of his heroic soldiers.   Appropos to this part of my subject I will append a poem, which was written in a freight car on the Iowa prairies, whilst the writer was transporting his horse and household goods from one field of pastoral labor to another, Nov. 19, 1880, the thermometer being several degrees below zero.

BOUQUET'S GRAVE.

He sleeps in an unknown grave,
    In a far away land,
    By the South Sea strand,
Bouquet sleeps the sleep of the brave.

Sleep on, Oh son of the free !
    Where the blood of the Scot,
    From the field where you fought,
Ran down to the boundless sea.

Ah ! was it not grandly meet,
    That the gallant Bouquet,
    In that land far away,
Should lie where the surges beat.

Oh Sea ! be an urn for the men,
And a requiem bell
For the hero who fell,
Till the muse shall be grateful again.

Alas ! 'Tis a burning shame,
That the Keystone state
Should be tardy or late
To cherish the Switzer's fame.

Redeemed were your woody hills
By the Swiss and the Scot,
Let them ne'er be forgot
While valor the bosom thrills.

Awake ! Ye sons of the North !
And the deeds of these men
Clasp to your hearts again,
And fondly cherish their worth.

Oh, land of the brave and free !
Bright as the noonday sun,
Long as your streams shall run
Let the fame of the Switzer be.

A MONUMENT DUE BOUQUET.

In an article written for Frank Cowan's paper, on the
Bushy Run battle, nearly eleven years ago, I asked the
question " does not Westmoreland county, yea all Western
Pennsylvania owe a monument to Henry Bouquet ?" In my
centennial speech at Hannastown, a year ago, I enlarged
upon the same thought and, I trust, that in the Providence
of God, I may see the day when the dear old county of
my nativity will thus honor herself, as well as the grand
hero who has made her soil historic ground. All public
spirited people should aid in such a work. It will stimulate the young to emulate one who, amid perils and privations, by sterling merit and conscientious fidelity to duty,
rose from obscurity to become the peer of the greatest and
best.

It will help to demonstrate that no flight of years or
changes of human governments and institutions, can oblit-
erate the memory of genuine worth and true manhood, as
illustrated in the history of Henry Bouquet.

D*

With Pericles, as amplified by Edward Everett at Gettysburg, we may say of illustrious men "The whole
earth is their sepulchre and all time the millenium of their
glory." Wherever heroic deeds have been done, wherever the battles of human civilization have been fought and
won, that is hallowed ground, full of deepest interest to
every thoughtful, true-hearted man.

"These are the shrines to code nor creed confined
The Delphian vales, the Palestine, the Meccas of the mind."

Bushy Run battlefield ought to be, and I feel assured
will be looked upon, in years to come, as such a shrine.
Here savage barbarism, as represented by Pontiac and
Guyasutha, two of its noblest representatives, met the
vanguard of civilization, culture and progress, under the
matchless leadership of Bouquet. Here, too, was fought
and won the battle which virtually established the supremacy of the Anglo Saxon race, in the great valley of the
Mississippi.

"The land is holy where they fought
And holy where they fell."

Not by British blood and valor *per se*, but by Swiss and
Scot, Royal Americans, Provincials and Highlanders from
Caledonia hills, by these other branches of the great Teutonic host, the Aryan or Indo-Germanic family of nations,
was this typical battle fought and won 120 years ago.

It is meet that the German-Swiss and Scotch-Irish elements should possess this goodly land, as they do this day,
forming the bone and sinew of Westmoreland's sterling
population.

And it is meet that they should not forget the pit out of
which they have been dug, nor the rock from which they
have been hewn.

The toils and privations of our colonial ancestors should
be held in grateful and everlasting remembrance. They
braved the perils of old ocean and of life in the Western
wilderness, amid savage beasts and more savage men, for
the sake of religious principle, and that their children
might be freeholders and freemen in the best sense of the
term. Let us prize the precious birthright as something

more precious than silver or gold. "Man shall not live by bread alone, but by every word that proceedeth out of the mouth of God." Ideas, principles, sentiments cultivating a pure and progressive Christian manhood, are of vastly more account than the filthy lucre, on which so many set their hearts. The scenery and associations of childhood and youth are educational. They stamp their impress upon the soul for weal or for woe. Inspiring historical treasures are beyond all price. Many are the lines of thought and currents of history that centre in and around the honorable and eventful career of Henry Bouquet. As good men did in days of old, so now would I commend his as a character and example worthy of study and imitation by the young and all entrusted with official positions.

CONCLUDING REMARKS.

Bouquet willed a large tract of land in Trough Valley, (Huntingdon or Mifflin Co., Pa.,) to Mr. Thos. Willing. This was a brother of Miss Annie Willing, his fair correspondent. His extensive Long Meadows estate in Maryland lay a few miles north or north-east of Hagerstown, Md., and is now owned by the Lehmans, Willems, Cresslers, and others.

Col. Haldimand, his legatee, and executor, was his special Swiss compatriot and military comrade. He figured somewhat in the Revolutionary War, and became governor-general of Canada, from which post he retired in 1785, to die in his native Switzerland. Many of Bouquet's most valuable papers are included among those of Haldimand, at present, in the British Museum. The time to write a complete biography of the man has not yet arrived.

Mr. G. D. Scull, of Philadelphia, residing at Oxford, England, expects to publish a very limited edition of some of these papers during the ensuing year. He claims that on one occasion Bouquet saved Philadelphia from sack and pillage, the proof of which will doubtless appear in his book. I had hoped to be able to refer to this proposed publication in the preparation of this sketch, but have been disappointed.

PONTIAC'S SUBMISSION.

Pontiac, for a season remained defiant, even after his confederates had submitted to the terms of Bouquet. When Capt. Morris went to him with proposals of peace, he met him on the outskirts of his camp, and refused to take his hand. With flashing eye, he exclaimed, "The English are liars." And yet he spared the captain's life, as he afterwards did that of Lieut. Fraser, Mr. Croghan, and other peace envoys, although his warriors were anxious to slay them. He sought the country of the Illinois, with 400 warriors, where the flag of France still floated, as it had done since the days of La Salle, Tonti, &c., in 1680.

He urged the different tribes to rise again and fight for the preservation of their race, and threatened to destroy those who shirked. French traders had all along led him to expect aid from their great King. At length, he was fully convinced, by replies of French officers, in response to his embassies sent to Fort Chartres and New Orleans, that all hope of help from that quarter was vain. He then gave up the contest, and agreed to meet with other confederates at the great council, held by Sir Wm. Johnson, to arrange definitely the terms of peace, secured by the campaigns of Bouquet.

Croghan, who met him repeatedly and experienced his magnanimity in restraining warriors who were anxious to kill the British peace-agent, speaks thus of the great Ottawa chieftain : "Pontiac is a shrewd, sensible Indian, of few words, and commands more respect among his own nation than any Indian I ever saw could do among his own tribe."

Late in the fall of 1765 Capt. Sterling descended the Ohio in boats, and passed up the Mississippi with one hundred Highlanders of the 42d regiment to Fort Chartres, of which he took formal possession in the name of Great Britain.

It was fitting that "those veterans whose battle cry," as Parkman says, "had echoed over the bloodiest fields of America," should consummate on the banks of the Father of Waters the work begun at Bushy Run, and es-

tablish forever Anglo-Saxon supremacy in the new world.
In due time Pontiac appeared at the great council held
by Sir Wm. Johnson during the latter part of July, 1766.
The following are the opening sentences of his speech:
" Father, we thank the Great Spirit for giving us so fine a
day to meet upon such great affairs. I speak in the name
of all the nations to the westward, of whom I am the
master. It is the will of the Great Spirit that we should
meet here to-day ; and before him I now take you by the
hand. I call him to witness that I speak from the heart ;
for since I took Col. Croghan by the hand last year, I
have never let go my hold, for I see that the Great Spirit
will have us friends."

PONTIAC'S ASSASSINATION AND ITS EXPIATION.

Everything was amicably adjusted at the council, and
Pontiac, with many presents, returned to the Maumee,
where he spent one season. He afterwards seems to have
located in the region of the Illinois Indians, who were
jealous of his presence, and who approved of his assassination. Accounts differ in regard to this affair, Mr.
Parkman adopts the Cahokia theory i. e., that Pontiac
was killed at that place by an Illinois Indian who had
been bribed to do the foul deed by Williamson, an English trader, who feared that Pontiac, while on a drunken
spree, was about to stir up trouble against the English,
and thus interfere with his traffic. Mr. Matson contends
that Pontiac was fatally stabbed by Kineboo, the chief of
the Illinois Indians at a council, held near Joliet, in that
state.

One thing is certain, the Illinois Indians were held responsible for his assassination. All the tribes that in
former days had felt the magic spell of his eloquence and
had responded to his bugle call, now leagued together to
avenge the death of Pontiac by a war of extermination
against the Illinois Indians.

The following extract I take from an article which I
prepared for the *Guardian* for August, 1882, on the basis
of Matson's theory :

" Runners were sent to the Winnebagos, of the North, and the Kickapoos, of the South-west, who agreed to help avenge the death of the great Pontiac. Over the remains a council was held by the allies, who swore by the great Manito of war not to lay down the tomahawk until the fallen chieftain's death should be avenged by the destruction of the Illinois Indians, who abetted the cowardly deed of Kineboo. The Miamis united with the tribes already mentioned, and Bernet, the white outlaw, also with a band of warriors, joined in the bloody strife. The com-bined forces made the most formidable Indian army ever collected in the West. Death and annihilation to the Illinois was the sav-age oath of the ferocious avengers. The smaller towns along the Illinois river were first destroyed, and finally La Vantum, their great capital, which was defended by their bravest warriors, was suddenly assaulted. The skull and cross bones of Pontiac were borne on a red pole by the avengers. Their first attack met with a bloody repulse. A council of war was called by the invaders, at which the leading war chiefs, with fiery eloquence, advocated that nothing short of extermination of the Illinoisans would meet the demands of the case or be acceptable to the great Manito of war. The Illinois warriors had spent much of the night in dancing and premature rejoicing over the repulse of the assailants, and were taken by surprise in the morning. After terrific carnage, the allies were again repulsed with great slaugh-ter. But again and again they returned with reinforcements to the conflict. Thus for twelve long hours the carnival of death went on in and around La Vantum, the great Indian city of the West. Night came on, and still the battle raged, until a heavy rain storm put an end to hostilities. During the darkness and storm the Illinois Indians crossed the Illinois river in their canoes and ascended Starved Rock, the old site of Fort St. Louis, where Tonti had so signally repulsed the Iroquois. Here the remnant of 1200 Illinois Indians, including 300 warriors, rallied and thought themselves secure. But the allied forces, not content with the destruction of the town and other property of the Illi-nois, quickly surrounded the Rock, determined to avenge the death of Pontiac by the complete annihilation of all who in any way approved of his assassination. With ferocious yells they rushed up the rugged pathway on the only accessible side of the rocky summit. But brave and desperate Illinois warriors, with war clubs and tomahawks, sent them bleeding and mangled down the steep declivity. Again and again did the fierce avengers attempt to storm the almost impregnable heights. Many were slain as soon as they reached the summit, and hurled over the precipice into the river below. After losing many of their brav-

est warriors, the allies gave up the assault and began the slow
and tedious work of starving out the besieged Illinoisans. At
the time of the attack upon the town a French and Indian half-
breed warrior, named Belix, who had greatly distinguished himself in previous battles, was being married to the beautiful daughter of Chief Kineboo. When the assault was made upon the
Rock, Belix stood foremost and most valliant among the defenders, and with his war-club dealt death-blows upon many of the
assailants. His bride stood near by to encourage her gallant
lord, but when she saw him fall with skull cloven by a tomahawk,
she uttered a wild scream and sprang over the Rock, falling from
crag to crag until her lifeless body dropped into the river below.
Fifty-one years had elapsed since the rock had been abandoned
by the French, and the palisades and earth-works afforded but
little protection against sharp-shooters who took possession of
neighboring cliffs and joined in a galling fire upon the Illinois.
Kineboo, whose rash and dastardly act had precipitated the war,
was killed in this way. But soon a rampart, sufficient to ward off
bullets was erected by the besieged along the exposed edges of
the precipices. But the worst enemy now began to assail them.
Hunger began to gnaw at their vitals with remorseless tooth. The
small supply of provisions, brought along in their flight from La
Vantum, were soon exhausted. The Rock of refuge became an
altar of sacrifice, of whole burnt offering, to the Illinois in the
end ; for their relentless foes never relaxed in the siege until the
last Illinois but one had perished. A warrior, the solitary exception, let himself down by a buckskin cord into the river on a
dark and stormy night and escaped, but all the rest,—warriors,
squaws and pappooses perished. Some of the squaws, in the de-
lirium of hunger and thirst, would spring with their infants into
the river. Warriors would make a sortie only to be slain or
driven back by the merciless avengers. Some feasted on the
dead. The death-song was chanted, and at last, when a final
assault was made, only a few feeble survivors remained to be
tomahawked. Thus perished the once powerful and arrogant
Illinois, and thus terribly was the assassination of the great Pontiac avenged. Great must have been the magnetism of the man
in life and death who marshalled the conspiracy which nearly
drove the English east of the Alleghenies, and which combined
the savage hosts of the lakes and the prairies to expiate " the
deep damnation of his taking off " by a holocaust that is unparalleled even in the history of savage warfare and retaliation.
Well may the old site of Fort St. Louis, on the Illinois river,
near Ottawa, Illinois, the scene of the first white settlement in
the Mississippi valley, two hundred years ago, be called Starved

Rock, in commemoration of that closing tragedy and catastrophe in the history of the great tribe whose name is perpetuated not only by the river along which they roved, fished and hunted, and fought their numerous foes, but also by the title of one of the greatest and most prosperous states in the American Union."

Thus was expiated the death .of Pontiac, over whose grave, as Parkman says, "more blood was poured out in atonement than flowed from the veins of the slaughtered heroes on the corpse of Patroclus."

Let justice be done to the memory of the man who broke the eastern wing of the great conspiracy at Bushy Run, Aug. 6, 1763, and rolled back the advancing tide of savage barbarism. All honor to Colonel Henry Bouquet and his heroic army of deliverance, who consecrated by their blood and valor, the green hills of old Westmoreland and made them historic forever.

WESTMORELAND COUNTY BEFORE AND DURING THE REVOLUTION.

Westmoreland county was created by Pennsylvania provincial authorities in 1773, and originally included all that part of the State west of Laurel Hill. A dozen other counties have since been created out of the same territory, so that for Western Pennsylvania it may be said that "Old Westmoreland" was the mother of counties.

Hannastown, a hamlet a few miles north-east of Greensburg, was the first county seat. Here justice was first dispensed, west of the Alleghenies, according to the civil code. William Crawford, afterwards burnt by the Indians, was the first presiding justice, and Arthur St. Clair was the first prothonotary. The first court fixed the price of a gill of whiskey at four pence ; toddy, one shilling ; West India rum, six pence ; cider, per quart, one shilling six pence ; strong beer, per quart, sixpence.

The jail was made of rough, unhewn logs. Punishments were fines, whipping, standing in pillory or stocks, cropping off ears and branding.

Rape, sodomy, robbery, mahem, arson, burglary, witchcraft and concealing of a bastard child were punishable with death, as well as murder. Virginia set up rival claims to a large part of the territory included in Westmoreland county, and created West Augusta county to cover it. Lord Dunmore, her Tory Governor, organized a court at Pittsburgh Feb. 21, 1775, to offset the claims of Pennsylvania. Dr. John Connolly, a resident of Pittsburgh, was the Virginia agent, and representative of Dunmore. He published a manifesto Jan. 1, 1774, inviting settlers to meet at Pittsburgh on the 25th proximo for conference, assuring them of the protection of Virginia.

Arthur St. Clair, a justice of the peace of Westmoreland, issued a warrant and had Connolly arrested for a short time and confined in the log jail at Hannastown. Connolly, after his release, issued warrants and arrested the Westmoreland justices of the peace. The conflict continued for about a year. Virginia's claims were recognized at Fort Pitt and in the Monongahela region. Yohogania county was created Nov. 30, 1776, out of part of Augusta and included the greater part of Alleghany and Washington counties. Virginia courts were held for five years under these auspices. Virginia's price for lands being cheaper than those of Pennsylvania, the settlers in those regions generally sided with her in the dispute. At Bushy Run, Hannastown and Ligonier, with adjacent settlements, Pennsylvania interests and claims were upheld. This conflict of jurisdiction caused great trouble and uneasiness, which was not allayed fully until the completion of the western end of Mason and Dixon's line, after the Revolution.

From the date of Bouquet's peace, dictated to the Indians on the Muskingum, until the outbreak of the Revolution, there was comparative peace and tranquility, so far as the Indians were concerned. The fur traders plied their lucrative traffic without molestation. The country began to fill up rapidly. When the War of Independence began, the sectional disputes were forgotten and a common purpose was manifested to resist the encroachments of Great Britain. Hannastown has the honor of not only being the first seat of civil justice, west of the Alleghanies, but of leading the van in sounding the note of defiance in a formal public declaration of the sentiments that stirred the heart of the persecuted colonies. On the sixteenth of May, 1775, a convention was held at Hannastown, which denounced the acts of British usurpation and tyrrany, and took measures to provide for the common defence.

Westmoreland was prompt in electing delegates, July 8, 1776, to attend the convention, which met in Philadelphia, July 15, 1776, to lay the foundations of a government, "based on the authority of the people only."

That convention included many of the best men of the state—wise in counsel, brave and energetic in action. Men like Franklin, Clymer, Hiester, and Rittenhouse. Westmoreland sent as her delegates — James Barr, Edward Cook, James Smith, John Moore, John Carmichael, James Perry, John McClellan and Christian Lavingair.

Before taking their seats or casting their votes, they were required to subscribe to the following : " I, — —, do profess faith in God, the Father, and in Jesus Christ, His Eternal Son, the true God, and in the Holy Spirit, one God blessed forevermore ; and do acknowledge the Holy Scripture of the Old and New Testament to be given by divine inspiration." A very correct and orthodox profession of the fundamental doctrines of Christianity. The convention adjourned September 28, 1776, after framing an excellent form of government, by the people and for the people. In fact, their work has formed the basis for all the state constitutions since adopted.

And now came the horrors of war. To the everlasting disgrace and infamy of Great Britain, it must be said that she offered large bounties to cruel savages for the scalps of the frontier settlers, men, women and children.

The British Governor, Hamilton, who had control at Detroit and along the northern frontiers, gave standing rewards for scalps, but offered none for prisoners. In consequence the Indians compelled the poor captives to carry their plunder to the immediate vicinity of Detroit, where, after having endured indescribable sufferings during the journey through the wilderness, the poor creatures were put to death and scalped in cold blood to get the bounty. DePeyster, under orders from Haldimand, acted more humanely as commandant at Detroit. He encouraged the Indians to bring in live meat, as the prisoners from the borders were called, rather than scalps, which he did not like to see. In this way he saved 300 frontier prisoners from a barbarous death. Prowling bands of savages continually ravaged the borders, and Westmoreland was a favorite resort for the scalping parties. The old war path of the Catawbas and Cherokees from the south and southwest, with a tributary trail or path from Tennessee and Kentucky, went right through the heart of Westmoreland to the headwaters of the Susquehanna, in western New York, where lived the Iroquois, or Six Nations, their inveterate enemies. After the conquest of the southern tribes by their powerful northern foes, they made periodical trips to pay tribute or show proper obeisance to the conquerors.

The Mohawk Pluggy, located on the eastern branch of the Scioto, with a lawless and miscellaneous gang of marauders, made frequent forays into the settlements along the Ohio and its branches.

Generals Hand and McIntosh, Col. Brodhead and Gen. Irvine commaded Fort Pitt during the Revolution, and although many expeditions were projected and a few abortive ones undertaken to carry the war into the Indian country, nothing serious was ever accomplished in that line to check the repeated incursions of the savages. Such a campaign and commander as carried terror to their hearts in their own native haunts in 1764, would have secured safety and tranquility to a large extent. But the desultory and fragmentary efforts put forth from time to time for aggressive movements against the savages and tories, as a rule only resulted in greater hardships for the frontier settlers.

McKee, the Girty's and other tories who had grudge against the frontier settlers, led on the savage demons with great craft and daring against the exposed frontiers.

In April, 1778, a Westmorelander wrote, "God only knows what may be the fate of this county ; but at present it wears a dismal aspect." May 1, 1779, another wrote, " The savages are continually making depredations among us ; not less than forty people have been killed, wounded or captured this spring." A year later and the prospect was still more gloomy. Over forty settlers had been slain in the Monongahela region, and the raids were frequent from the northern Allegheny regions. " It really began to look," wrote Butterfield, " as though Westmoreland would again become a wilderness. The people, in a half starving condition, huddled in and about the forts and block-houses. The troops at Fort Pitt were ragged, unpaid, poorly fed, and of course discontented and inefficient. In August the Maryland corps deserted their posts on the frontier of Westmoreland, and in a body marched across the mountains. Lochry and his 150 picked men were surprised and destroyed in 1781. Crawford, another county official, met with terrible disaster and death in 1782 ; and thus the chapter of horrors and frontier suffering goes on. Brodhead and some of his subordinate officers got at loggerheads, and in the midst of quarrels among officers at Fort Pitt the work of desolation prospered.

Gen. Irvine was appointed, but although many campaigns were talked about, none but such as Crawford's, Williamson's, &c., badly managed affairs, were actualized. The main army was engaged in the last death grapples with the British Lion along the Atlantic coast, and the western settlers were largely left to the mercy of the savages. The British were emboldened even to fit out an expedition to capture Fort Pitt. Three hundred British and Tories, and five hundred Indians, assembled with twelve pieces of artillery, on Lake Jadagua (Chatauqua), in 1782, with this intention. Having learned, through a spy, that the fort was much stronger than had been supposed, the main object of the expedition was given up. The usual method of border warfare was then adopted, and marauding bands went into the different settlements. A feeling of unrest and apprehension pervaded the frontier. Many had been shot down and scalped, and prisoners carried off from the immediate vicinity of Forts Walthour, Klingensmith, &c. This sense of alarm found very timely and forcible representation in the petition of German settlers on Brush Creek, addressed to General Irvine, commander at Fort Pitt, June 22, 1782. It sets forth the despondency and distress of the people on account of continued calamities (Crawford's fate had just been learned). They speak of the great peril attending the gathering of the harvest, nearly ripe, and beg for some troops to protect them as they seek to gather in the crops, which are needed to save them from famine—as much to be dreaded as the scalping knife. This petition was signed by ancestors of many living Westmorelanders, viz.: George, Christopher, Joseph and Michael Waldhauer (Walthour,) Abraham and Joseph Studabedker, Michael and Jacob Byerly, John and Jacob Ruthdorf, Frederick Williard, —— Wiesskoph (Whitehead), Abram Schneider, Peter and Jacob Loutzenheiser, Hanover Davis, Conrad Zulten, Garret Pendegrast and John Kammerer. This petition is given by Butterfield, without the names of signers, on pages 300-301, of his valuable book, "Washington Irvine Correspondence."

ATTACK ON HANNASTOWN.

Three weeks later, July 13, 1782, a large detachment of the aforesaid Chatauqua expedition burst upon Hannastown, the county seat of Westmoreland. They burned the town, and came very near capturing the fort, into which a few of the frightened settlers, with Michael Huffnagle, the prothonotary, at their head, had fled for safety. Captain Matthew Jack, by his courage and presence of mind, saved many lives on that disastrous day, as he rode gallantly from point to point, even through the encompassing lines of whooping savages. Miller's station, near by, was raided by the Indians, and the greater part of a wedding party was captured, including the wife and daughters of Robert Hanna. Captain Brownlee, and several others, were tomahawked, after being led captives a few miles. Dwellings were destroyed, together with many horses and cattle. The settlers were so terror-stricken that the ripened harvest was not gathered in many places, and great want ensued. Connolly, the renegade Tory, whom Gen. St. Clair had confined in the log jail at Hannastown, is supposed to have led this party, together with Guyasutha, the famous Seneca chief.

About 20 persons were killed or captured in this foray. On the 13th of July, 1882, the centennial of this attack and repulse of the Indians and Tories at Hannastown, was celebrated by a large assemblage of Westmorelanders, in the woods near the old site of Hannastown. Hon. Jacob Turney presided, and made the opening address. Addresses were also made by Hon. Daniel Kane, Judge Bigham, Ex-Senator Cowan, and Rev. Cyrus Cort.

RELIGIOUS CHARACTERISTICS OF EARLY SETTLERS.

It is gratifying to know that amid their dangers and hardships, those Teutonic pioneers in old Westmoreland forgot not the God of their fathers.

On May 1, 1782, when the Reformed Cœtus (Synod) met at Reading, Pa., a petition was received from " A congregation in Westmoreland county, near Pittsburg, in the back part of Pennsylvania, a new settlement, where no ministers have yet been." They " very earnestly entreated for a good minister, to whom they promise to pay annually 80 pounds sterling, besides other necessaries of life."

Rev. John William Weber, having expressed a willingness to go west and take charge of this mission enterprise, the Reverend Cœtus recommended him and advised the Westmoreland people to give him a regular call. He arrived in Sept., 1782, and preached through what now constitutes Westmoreland, Washington and Fayette counties, and at Fort Pitt, where the traveler Schopf met him in October, 1782. The congregations at Harolds and Brush Creek were organized a few months after Rev. Weber's arrival in Westmoreland. Here worshipped the Turneys, Drums, Barnharts, Marchands, Trubys, Mechlings, Kemmerers, Kifers, Klines, Byerlys, Whiteheads, Saams, Klingensmiths, Kunkles, Walthours, Baughmans, Thomases, Detars, Harrolds, Grosses, Henrys, Corts, Keppels, Kiehls, Shrums, Painters, and many other ancestors of Reformed and Lutheran families.

Previous to the coming of Rev. Weber many of these German pioneers used to meet at the house of Loutzenheiser and Davis to read the scriptures, sing the sweet hymns of the German fatherland, hear a sermon read by some competent person, and engage in other religious services as best they could.

They frequently carried their rifles with them, when they went to worship in the early days of Rev. Weber's ministry. Prowling savages lurked in the thickets for many years. Amid such perils and privations, those pioneer settlers carved out homes for their children and turned the western wilderness of Penn's woods into a fruitful field. Surely a grateful posterity should honor their memory and rise up and call them blessed, while enjoying the goodly fruits of their pioneer toil.

At a still earlier date the Scotch-Irish, led by pastors Finley, Power, McMillan, Dodd, Smith, &c., occupied the Sewickly and other settlements, and already in 1781 the old Redstone Presbytery was organized. " The incursions of savages " prevented the first meeting being held at Laurel Hill, the appointed place, and so it met at Pigeon Creek.

It is meet, as already said, that the descendants of the hardy Scotch-Irish and German-Swiss should occupy the green hills and fertile valleys of old Westmoreland. By the blood and the sweat and the toil of their pioneer ancestors, this goodly land has been rescued from savage barbarism. Hallowed be the memory of the brave men and women who nobly stood in the breach in the hour of trial and danger.   •

Pennsylvania has been compared to a sleeping giant, not yet fully conscious of her vast power and resources. With unappreciated modesty, she has failed to assert her rights, and especially has she neglected to cherish aright the rich legacies of the past, bequeathed by an honest and patriotic ancestry. It behooves us to gather up the historic treasures that rightfully belong to our grand old Keystone commonwealth.

Our own self-respect and independent manhood demands this. It is no less a duty to posterity than a debt of gratitude to our heroic ancestry. The educational effect will be stimulating and ennobling in all respects.

For the sake of religious principle, our forefathers crossed old ocean's wave and braved the dangers of pioneer life in the new world. In the midst of untold perils, they were true to the principles of civil and religious liberty, as we have already seen, and here on our native hills was fought the decisive battle of Christian civilization against heathen barbarism.

ADDENDA.

Referring back to page 11, it is proper to remark that Bouquet and Washington were personally on good terms, and did not impugn each others motives.

Many persons will doubtless feel prompted to contribute toward the erection of a monument to Henry Bouquet, after reading the record of his gallant achievements. All such will please send funds or written pledges to James Gregg, Chairman of Finance Committee, Greensburg, Pa., subject to the disposal of the Executive Committee— Coulter, Kline and Gregg—for that purpose.

P. S.—After this pamphlet was nearly all in type, I learned that at a meeting ·held subsequent to June 19, 1883, it was decided to invite the following gentlemen to address the meeting at Bushy Run battlefield, Aug. 6, 1883, viz:

Hon. James G. Blaine, of Washington, D. C.; Dr. Sam'l Wilson, of Allegheny City, Pa.; Gen. James A. Beaver, of Bellefonte, Pa.; Hon. William S. Stenger, of Harrisburg, Pa.; Rev. Cyrus Cort, of Creencastle, Pa.; Wm. M. Darlington, of Pittsburgh, Pa.; Hon. W. U. Hensel, of Lancaster, Pa.; Hon. Silas M. Clark, of Indiana, Pa.; Hon. Wm. Koontz, of Somerset, Pa.

POEM.—Frank Cowan, Esq., of Greensburg, Pa.

ERROR.—On page 54, instead of " Schnorrbock " read " Schnorr, Vock."

THE

BOUQUET CELEBRATION

ON

BUSHY RUN BATTLEFIELD,

IN

WESTMORELAND COUNTY, PA.,

AUGUST 6, 1883.

Edited by REV. CYRUS CORT, of Greencastle, Pa.,
in Behalf of the Bouquet Memorial Committee.

LANCASTER, PA.
STEINMAN & HENSEL, PRINTERS.
1886.

DEDICATION.

TO the Memory of Henry Bouquet and the 1763 Army
of Deliverance, composed of Scotch Highlanders, Royal
Americans (mainly of German-Swiss extraction), and Provincial Rangers — nearly one-fourth of whom by their
blood, and all of whom by their valor, consecrated the field
of Bushy Run, August 5th and 6th, 1763.

May the descendants of the hardy Scotch-Irish and
German-Swiss Pioneer Settlers, whose goodly heritage they
rescued from the savage destroyer, always show themselves
worthy such heroic defenders.

TABLE OF CONTENTS.

THE BOUQUET CELEBRATION.

THE celebration of the one hundred and twentieth anniversary of the victory won by Colonel Henry Bouquet over the Eastern Confederates of Pontiac, at Bushy Run, Aug. 6, 1763, brought together the largest and finest concourse of people ever assembled in Old Westmoreland county.

The magnificence of the demonstration in honor of the gallant Bouquet and his Army of Deliverance, compensated in some degree for the long delay in commemorating their heroic achievements.

The battle of Bushy Run, or Edge Hill, was not only memorable as an exhibition of dauntless courage and consummate military skill under the most desperate circumstances. It was so decisive and important in its immediate and remote results, that it well deserves perennial remembrance.

To perpetuate the memory of the great event itself, and its splendid commemoration, Aug. 6, 1883, a memorial committee was appointed with the unanimous approval of the vast assemblage convened in Gongaware's woods on celebration day. After some delay, they herewith present the result of their labors.

Every movement of this kind has its history, in the light of which it can only be properly understood and appreciated.

Accordingly it has been deemed advisable to give a brief sketch of the various steps that led the way to the celebration of Aug. 6, 1883, as a proper introduction to the full account of the celebration itself.

I

The Renaissance, or renewal of interest in Bouquet and his campaigns on the part of those more immediately identi-,fied with the recent celebration, dates back to the autumn of 1872.

On the 25th of September, of that year, Dr. Frank Cowan published an article in his newspaper, giving an account of a visit to the battle-field of Edge Hill, or Bushy Run, and a sketch of the battle itself, as given in the old, provincial work of Dr. William Smith. The young editor lamented the dearth or total absence of local traditions respecting the battle as compared with the Burning of Hannastown. He accounted for this on the ground that the battle was fought by foreigners, none of whose decendants had ever located near the scene of the conflict, &c. At the end of nearly two months, a mutilated copy of Mr. Cowan's paper, with the aforsaid article, fell into the hands of Rev. Cyrus Cort, then residing at Vinton, Iowa. Mr. Cort immediately wrote a lengthy article, giving an account of the battle of Bouquet and a number of incidents and traditions connected with it, which he had received from his great grandfather, Jacob Byerly, and his son Joseph on Christmas day, 1855, several years before the Revolutionary veteran ended his days in his ninety-ninth year. Jacob Byerly was a son of Andrew Byerly, the founder of Byerly Station at Bushy Run, and along with the rest of the Byerly family, barely escaped with his life to Fort Ligonier, in the latter part of May, 1763. After being closely besieged for two months, Col. Bouquet came to their relief with his Scotch Highlanders, Royal Americans, and a few Provincial Rangers. Andrew Byerly went along with the army, and was in the advance when the battle of Aug. 6, 1763, began on Gongaware's hill. He took an active part in the two days' conflict, and through him some very interesting incidents have been handed down to posterity which were never published until recent years. The article of Rev. Cort, besides supplementing the editorial of Mr. Cowan as regards incidents of the battle, urged upon the people of Westmoreland the duty of erecting a durable monument to the memory of Bouquet and his Army of Deliverance.

The editor heartily commended the article to the attention of his readers, and called upon all who were interested in the history of Old Westmoreland, the mother county, to record without delay all traditional incidents and adventures with which they might be acquainted.   Thus the matter rested until December, 1880, when Rev. C. Cort published an article on Bouquet and his campaigns in the *Guardian*, a monthly magazine printed at Philadelphia. A revised edition of this article, with a poem on "Bouquet's Grave," was issued a few weeks later in pamphlet form. The *Guardian* article was republished in a short time by many of the papers in Southern and Southwestern Pennsylvania, and created a good deal of interest in the hero of Bushy Run.   A short time previous, George Harrison Fisher, Esq., of Philadelphia, had published in the *Pennsylvania Historical Magazine* some interesting correspondence between Col. Bouquet and a Miss Willing, together with a sketch of the gallant Swiss officer.   This was embellished with a fine steel engraving of Col. Bouquet, taken from an original painting in possession of the Fisher family.

Rev. Cort was not aware of the article of Mr. Fisher until after the publication of his own.

Again there was a pause until the centennial observances of the burning of Hannastown, July 13, 1882.   As one of the speakers on that occasion, Rev. Cort in the course of his address made the following reference to Bouquet and Bushy Run : "This is an age of centennials, and I am glad that the centennial boom has struck Old Westmoreland.   It should have struck you nineteen years sooner.   It has always appeared passing strange to me that Westmoreland county, and Western Pennsylvania failed to celebrate with centennial memorial services the victory of Bouquet in the heart of our noble old county on Aug. 6, 1763.   It is true that many of us were off to the wars in 1863, and had more important work in fighting battles for the preservation of the Union than to commemorate the deeds of colonial days.   But there were enough men and women at home to have made the welkin ring with the grateful notes of centennial commemoration.   An event so critical, so decisive and far reaching in its results, should be commemorated by annual as well as centennial observances.   The heroic deeds of Col. Bouquet, the gallant German-Swiss commander, the Scotch Highlanders and Colonial Volunteers, that formed the little army of deliverance, deserve to be held in grateful and everlasting remembrance by all the descendants of the thousands of pioneer settlers in Western Pennsylvania and Virginia, who were then delivered from the horrors of savage warfare. Had such deeds of valor, and such inspiring associations been connected with any spot in New England, the Yankees would have made it pay long ago in more ways than one. ˉ Bouquet's battle-field, near Bushy Run, a few miles west of here, should be hallowed as historic ground, and honored by the erection of a monument that would vividly call to remembrance the deeds of the dauntless heroes who consecrated it with their blood and valor one hundred and nineteen years ago.''

In the latter part of October, the battle of Bushy Run was brought prominently before the public in the bi-centennial celebration at Philadelphia. Rev. Cyrus Cort, who was in the city at the time, wrote an article on his return home, which was published in all the Greensburg papers. We give the following extracts as bearing directly on the subject in hand, and because the article helped greatly in preparing the way for the celebration which came off, as suggested, on the succeeding anniversary of the victory of Bouquet :

The battle of Col. Bouquet with the Indians at Bushy Run in 1763, formed a prominent feature in the gorgeous tableau that paraded the streets of Philadelphia on Wednesday night, October 25th, during the great Bi-Centennial celebration. Comparatively few of the spectators were well enough posted in the colonial history of the Keystone Commonwealth to understand or appreciate the representation which held so conspicuous a position in the grand pageant Even so well informed and cautious a paper as the *Ledger*, spoke of it next day as a fight between the British soldiers and the early settlers ! It seems that Major Beane received the suggestion from Mr. Stone, the Librarian of the Pennsylvania Historical society, who considers the victory of Bouquet over the Indians at Bushy Run, the decisive or turning point in the conquest of the vast region west of the Alleghenies by the Anglo-Saxon race. The representation was rather too much of an anacronism. British soldiers and Indians were armed with the latest improved modern rifles. The very essential Scotch Highlander and Colonial Volunteer, features of the conflict, were ignored in the tableau for lack of proper costume for the characters, as the writer was informed by Major Beane. But certainly the Scotch societies, or the Caledonian club, that took part in Tuesday's parade, could easily have furnished this, and thus have made the representation much more correct as well as picturesque.

The point, however, to which I wish to call the attention of Westmoreland this time, does not concern the success of the tableau representation of the battle of Bouquet so much as the importance of the event itself, and the rich historical treasures that necessarily cluster around the locality where that desperate and decisive conflict took place. Allow me in this connection to repeat a few sentences of my Hannastown Centennial address, delivered on the 13th day of last July :

[Here follow extracts already quoted from the Hannastown address which need not be repeated.]

The sentiments then expressed have been strikingly confirmed by the estimate of the learned Librarian of the Pennsylvania Historical Society, and by the unusual prominence given to the battle of Bouquet in the recent Bi-Centennial tableaux in Philadelphia.

In my monograph on Col. Bouquet, several years ago, I set forth the same views. It seems to me that it is high time that Westmorelanders, and the descendants of the Colonial settlers, should make an earnest practical effort to mark the battle-field of Rouquet, a short distance east of Harrison City, on the old Gongaware and Wannamaker farms. With the map of Hutchins, the royal geographer, executed soon after the battle, and published with Dr. William Smith's account of Bouquet's expedition, and with the aid of local traditions, this could be done without much difficulty. The little spring from which my great-great-grandfather Byerly carried a scant supply of water in his hat to the wounded Highlanders and volunteers, who were almost perishing with thirst during the two days conflict, would help to locate an important part of the field.

*   *   *   *   *   *   *

Old residents can easily designate the fields where the old forest trees contained so many bullets, when their land was cleared a generation or so ago. The exact route of the old road between Fort Ligonier and Fort Pitt could no doubt be definitely fixed at this point, so as to help determine the exact locality of the battle. The committee having charge of the Soldiers' Monument enterprise, of which, I believe, Gen. R. Coulter, Hon. Jas. C. Clarke, Gen. Thos. Gallagher and John Armstrong, Esq., are members, could not only locate the outlines of Bouquet's battle-field, but would be a very good committe to receive funds and devise a suitable monument in honor of Col. Henry Bouquet and his gallant army of deliverance.

*   *   *   *   *   *   *

The proposed soldiers' monument to Westmoreland military heroes might be so designed as to commemorate Colonial heroes like Bouquet,

Revolutionary heroes like St. Clair, War of 1812 heroes like Markle, or Major Andrew Byerly, (whose command defended Commodore Perry's fleet while it was being built on Lake Erie), Mexican war heroes, &c., as well as the heroes of the latest and greatest of our American wars.

*   *   *   *   *   *   *

At all events, I trust that suitable efforts will be made at an early day, to define the main features or outlines of Bouquet's battle-field. Vice President Jourdan, of the Historical Society at Philadelphia, called my attention to the fact that Bancroft or some other standard author, stated that the scene of Bouquet's battle was unknown. I remarked that the statement was not correct, and that the battle was fought in the heart of Westmoreland county, a short distance east of Harrison City. Bullets, bones, &c., had in former days, been found there in great numbers, and the local tradition, together with the map of Hutchins, would enable any intelligent person to locate the battlefield. I am confident that the Pennsylvania Historical Society would cheerfully give room in their valuable magazine for any communication on the subject which such a committee as I have designated might choose to make. In this way justice might, in a measure, be done to the memory of the departed heroes, while at the same time a pilgrim shrine would be erected in the grand old county of our nativity, that would increase in interest and importance as age after age rolled by. Might not the next 4th of July, or the 5th or 6th days of August be made memorable by a celebration, sham battles, speeches, &c., that would give the movement a successful impulse? Judging from the interest he manifested in the monograph on Col. Henry Bouquet, several years ago, and more recently in one on "Baron Steuben and his relations to the Reformed Church," I believe Adjutant General R. C. Drum would honor and grace such an occasion with his presence if invited by such a committee.

So also, public spirited Westmorelanders from all parts of the county, and from all parts of the Union, many of whom have become distinguished in civil and military life, would esteem it a privilege and pleasure to take part in such a demonstration. Let us begin at the beginning in this matter of commemorating the deeds of departed heroes and benefactors whose names are linked inseparably with the history of old Westmoreland. Thus can we best secure proper remembrance and honor in the end for the scarred veterans and heroic dead of our late war, and at the same time stimulate intelligent interest and generous emulation in the minds and hearts of the rising generation. The fame of their illustrious men is one of the noblest heritages of a people. Those who will not gratefully cherish the names and deeds of heroic ancestors and benefactors, will scarcely do aught that posterity will delight to honor. For the sake of the living champions of constitutional liberty and union, and for the sake of unborn generations, no less than for the sake of the illustrious dead of Colonial days, I trust that Westmorelanders will do speedy and ample justice to the memory of Colonel Henry Bouquet, and the 1763 army of deliverance.

GREENCASTLE, Franklin Co., Pa., Oct. 30.   CYRUS CORT.

The county papers generally favored the proposed celebration and articles furnished by Rev. C. Cort and Hon. Jos. H.
Kuhns in furtherance of the movement were, from time to
time, published in the Greensburg *Daily Press*, and in several of the weeklies.

April 25, 1883, a committee consisting of Rev. C. Cort,
S. A. Kline, Esq., Maj. J. M. Laird, A. B. Kline, Esq. and
Curtis Gregg, visited and located the Bushy Run, or Edge
Hill battle-field in its main features, and selected a grove
covering the same for the proposed celebration.

MEETING IN THE GREENSBURG COURT HOUSE.

On the following evening a public meeting was held in
the Court House at Greensburg, to arrange for the celebration. Ex-Governor Latta presided, and General Coulter
and Hon Jacob Turney acted as vice presidents, with Maj.
Laird, Frank Vogle and Curtis Gregg as secretaries.

In an address of over half an hour, Rev. C. Cort reviewed
the career of Col. Bouquet, and described the battle of
Bushy Run and its far reaching results. He urged the propriety of getting up a celebration at the next anniversary of
Bouquet's victory on that bloody field. Bouquet as the
champion and chief builder of the Forbes road, from Bedford to Fort Pitt, in 1758, had rendered signal service to the
province of Pennsylvania.

A committee consisting of Revs. Love, Moorhead and
Lucien Cort, and Philip Kuhns, Dr. Kline and A. M.
Sloan, Esq., presented a series of resolutions providing for
the celebration by religious services of a commemorative
nature, in all the churches of the county, Aug. 5, and by
addresses, poem, military display and pic-nic dinner in the
grove on Bushy Run battle-field, Aug. 6, 1883.

Committees were appointed as follows:

Committee of Arrangements to secure and prepare grounds for the
celebration: Amos B. Kline, J. B. Laux, Lewis Wannamaker, E. F.
Houseman, Lewis Gongaware, William Moore, Mr. Shadwick, Jos.
Clark, Robert Byerly, Wm. G. Shuster, Abner Cort.

Committee on Finance : Jas. Gregg, Esq., Geo. F. Huff, Capt. J. J.
Wirsing, Dr. Sowash, Wm. B. Skelly, Paul Lauffer, David Snyder,
Jno. Rankin, Sebastian Baer, Esq., Hon. N. M. Marker, H. F. Ludwig, Esq., Hon. John Hugus, and George Plumer Smith, of Philadelphia.

Committee on Invitation : General R. Coulter, Hon. Jos. H. Kuhns, Hon. Jacob Turney, Hon. John Latta, Maj. James M. Laird, G. D. Albert, Esq., John A. Marchand, Esq., Dr. Frank Cowan.

Committee of Reception at Bushy Run on Monday—viz : Hon. John Latta, Hon. James R. McAfee, Col. Geo. F. Huff, John Kuhns and A. D. McConnell, Esqs.

The chairmen, R. Coulter, Jas. Gregg and Amos B. Kline, were appointed an executive committee to fill all vacancies and have a general oversight of the celebration.

A few weeks previous to the celebration, Rev. C. Cort published, by request of the executive committee, a pamphlet of one hundred pages on "Col. Henry Bouquet and His Campaigns." This document was received with words of hearty commendation by the religious, as well as secular press, German and English, in Pennslvania, Ohio and New York. Lengthy extracts from it were inserted in the Pittsburg dailies a few days before the celebration took ·place. In this way the name of Bouquet and Bushy Run became familiar to thousands who had never heard of them before, and a deep interest was created in the approaching celebration. Thus, too, the questions of some of the Pittsburg dailies two months previous, "Who is Bouquet, What Did He Do," &c., were measurably answered in a way that raised the subject far above the plane of ridicule.

Amos B. Kline, with his colleagues on the committee of arrangements, did their work well. With the assistance of County Surveyor Wm. Miller, John Kuhns, Esq., Ed. Potts, Louis Wannamaker and Rev. C. Cort, the battle-field was definitely located and the exact positions of Bouquet's troops and their savage assailants, clearly indicated. The first and second positions of the troops ; the lines held re- · spectively by the Highlanders, the Royal Americans and Provincial Rangers ; the location of the pack horses, the cattle and the Flour Bag Fort, occupied by the wounded, in the two days' fight were definitely marked with flags and handboards, and pointed out as they had not hitherto been for a hundred years.

THE GATHERING OF THE CLANS—AUGUST 6, 1883.

All the necessary preliminary arrangements having been completed, the friends and promoters of the celebration awaited the dawning of the memorable 6th of August, 1883, with anxious hearts. It came bright and beautiful, as balmy and propitious a day as could have been desired for such an occasion. And never did the sons and daughters of Old Westmoreland turn out in such a vast and magnificent array as they did on that memorable day. Old and public-spirited citizens like Gen. Thos. F. Gallagher, who had attended all important convocations of our people for a generation past, declared that the concourse assembled on Bouquet's battle-field, Aug. 6, was by far the largest and grandest of them all. It was the largest assemblage of any kind ever convened in Old Westmoreland, and by far the largest of the kind ever convened in Western Pennsylvania. Estimates of the numbers present vary greatly, ranging from 8,000 to 25,-000. Dr. Samuel Stewart, who had considerable army experience, named the latter number. It was estimated that between 2,500 and 3,000 vehicles were on the grounds or in the groves, fields, fence corners, &c., within a circuit of two miles. A large number of hacks ran during most of the day from Manor and Penn Stations, and thousands footed it from the railroad and neighboring towns. At Irwin, business was largely suspended, and L. Kunkle, with four Percheron horses, hauled on a large wagon, seventy-two persons to the battle-field. All other vehicles had been engaged weeks ahead.

"What would Colonel Bouquet have thought of this," exclaimed Ex-United States Senator Cowan to General Beaver, as they met at the outskirts of the crowd, on the General's arrival. It was indeed a mighty host to honor the memory of Bouquet and his Army of Deliverance, on the very scene of their heroic achievements, after the lapse of 120 years. If the ovation was long in coming, it made up in a measure for the delay by its splendid character and magnificent proportions. It was worthy the man and the occasion, and did high honor to Old Westmoreland, the mother of counties, and the mother of the great majority of

1*

those assembled on the historic field, in social and patriotic communion.

THE ORGANIZATION OF THE MEETING.

A large stand had been erected in Gongaware's woods by the committee of arrangements, on part of the old Bushy Run battle-field. The stand was tastefully decorated with American flags and with several flags of the Swiss Republic, loaned for the occasion by the Swiss consul at Phil-·adelphia. The coat-of-arms of the Cantons of Berne and of Vand, the home of Bouquet, painted on large metallic shields, with their brown bears and motto, "Liberte et Patrie," held a conspicuous place. Relics in large numbers from Provincial and Revolutionary times, covered the tables. Prominent among them was a bayonet, found in a clearing on the battle-field, in good state of preservation, two years ago. Amos B. Kline, Esq., chairman of the committee of arrangements, called the meeting to order at half past ten o'clock, and nominated General Richard Coulter as presiding officer. The General made a short speech as follows:

GENERAL COULTER'S REMARKS.

Gentlemen and Ladies: You all know the object of this meeting. We are here to commemorate the memory of a brave and skillful commander, and a military achievement that had far greater influence in determining the character of the Western end of the State, than any event of later years. In the stirring times of later wars, the battle of Bushy Run had been forgotten. Its importance had not been appreciated, and it received but a small share of the attention which it deserves. But I am not going to make any speech. It is my duty to see the programme carried out.

Prayer was then offered by Rev. B. F. Boyle, of Irwin.

On motion of Dr. Frank Cowan, a committee consisting of Geo. D. Albert, Esq., Rev. Cyrus Cort and E. B. Kenly, was appointed to prepare a memorial of the celebration.

The following is the list of vice presidents and secretaries:

Vice Presidents : Hon. Jos. H. Kuhns, Hon. Jas. C. Clarke, Greensburg; Robert M. Cavett, Irwin; Samuel Rock, Esq., Adamsburg;

Daniel Kuhns, Jno. C. Rankin, Jacob Gongaware, Jesse Brinker, Penn township; Jacob Rugh, J. J. Hazlett, Esq., Hempfield township; Dr. Jas. Fulton, Salem borough; H. M. Jones, Salem township; Dr. Rugh, Finton Torrence, Franklin township; Obediah McKeown, Washington township; John Townsend, Allegheny township; Isaac Irwin, Burrell township; Jonathan Whitesell, Bell township; Robert Fostor, Loyalhanna township; General Thos. Gallagher, John M. Stewart, New Alexandria; David Brown, Samuel Gorgas, Derry township; Col. John Oursler Col. Geo. Anderson, Latrobe borough; Col. John Johnston, James Rogers, Unity township; John Fausold, Mt. Pleasant township; Capt. Wm. Jordan, O. P. Shupe, Mt. Pleasant borough; Jacob Stoner, Huntingdon, East, township; Samuel Bell, Dr. Sutton, Huntingdon, South, township; Dr. Patton, Hon. E. C. Leightty, West Newton; Maj. M. M. Dick, Geo. Waltz, Sewickley township; Geo. Campbell, Cook township; John Hubbs, Samuel McLain, Donegal township; Howard Covode, Hon. John Hargnett, Ligonier borough; Col. David Hoover, Frank Ford, St. Clair township; Hon Daniel Kaine, Fayette county; Dr. J. M, Service, Dr. Kerr, Philadelphia; Robert Paul, Rev. T. R. Ewing, Indiana county; I. W. Hughes, Bedford county; Hon. Thos. J. Bigham, Francis Torrence, J. P. Fleming, Hon. J. E. Parke, Allegheny county; Robt. L. Johnson, Esq., Hon. D. J. Morrell, Cambria county; Hon. Ed. S. Golden, John W. Tohner, Armstrong county; Simon Hughes, Esq., Edward Scull, Somerset county; John T. Shryock Zanesville, Ohio.   ,

Secretaries : Frank Vogle, Greensburg *Democrat ;* Jas. B. Laux, Greensburg *Press ;* E. V. B. Laird, Greensburg *Argus ;* D. S. Atkinson, Esq., Greensburg *Tribune and Herald ;* Thos. J. Keenan, Chas. Shryock, Pittsburg *Times ;* Geo. H. Welshonse, E. C. McCurdy, Pittsburg *Dispatch ;* J. G. Blair, Daniel Robinson, Pittsburg *Chronicle;* Robt. W. Herbert, Pittsburg *Post ;* L. M. Ackley, Pittsburg *Commercial-Gazette ;* I. M. Newcomer, Scottdale *Tribune ;* Chas. Fink, Latrobe *Advance ;* E. C. Hough, West Newton *Press ;* Jas. B. Sanson, Indiana *Democrat.*

At this time the scene was a very animated one.   An immense assemblage stood in front of the grand-stand, eight brass bands, from Greenburg, Latrobe, Ligonier, and other localities made the welkin ring with their martial and patriotic strains,   It was with difficulty that General Coulter succeeded in silencing some of them, so as to enable him to proceed with the programme.

He then introduced Rev. C. Cort, of Greencastle, Pa., who made the opening address, as follows :

ADDRESS OF REV. CYRUS CORT.

Ladies and Gentlemen, Friends and Countrymen : We have longed to see this day, and we now see it and are glad. We have met in the leafy grove, under heaven's blue arch, in this temple not made with hands, to honor the memory of Colonel Henry Bouquet and the 1763 Army of Deliverance. The skies are bright and the heavens smile upon us. It is right and proper that we should leave our shops and our stores, our mines and our farms, to mingle thus in social and patriotic communion. It is high time, indeed, that this should be done. Greensburg should have been called after Bouquet. Many of your sons should have been namesakes of the gallant Swiss hero, to whom we all owe so much. Instead of this many living in sight of this historic field of his triumph, were ignorant of the first A B C of his history. Even the little village called after him, a couple of miles up the Manor, some of you used to spell with one "u," and two t's, and two e's, (Boquette) instead of *Bouquet,* as the grand warrior wrote it.

But all this dense ignorance has passed away, and even some of the Pittsburg newspaper men, who inquired a few months ago, "Who is Bouquet ?" are beginning to get some light into their darkened understandings. Let the good work go on. Every gallant young man ought to have a button-hole forget-me-not bouquet on his coat to-day, and every young lady ought to have the beau without the quet— only let them take care that they have not too many strings to their bow, or too many beaux to their string. One is enough, if he is good, and too many if bad.

But all jokes aside.

I am heartily glad to see you here to-day. This is indeed a grand assemblage of the beauty and chivalry. Fair women and brave men of Old Westmoreland, and honored citizens of the Republic from abroad, distinguished in the forum and the field, are here to grace and honor the occasion with their presence—men who have poured out their blood like water on the battle-fields of the Republic.

As a grateful and progressive people, we dare never forget the toils, the dangers and hardships of our pioneer an-

cestors. The wilderness has been turned into a fruitful field
and the desert made to blossom like the rose, but it was by
the sweat and blood of brave and hardy men ; the fruits ot
whose labor we now enjoy.

This is hallowed ground, and sacred are the memories
that cluster around this spot. One hundred and twenty
years ago, this very forenoon, the representative champions
of Christian civilization and human progress made the
gallant charge around and through this grove that rolled
back the exulting hosts of barbarism. Here was executed
that masterly stratagem that shattered the right flank and
front of the encompassing host of savages. Here was broken
the eastern wing of Pontiac's great conspiracy. Here it was
that Bouquet plucked the flower of safety and success from
the nettle of danger. Here, from the very jaws of defeat,
disaster and death, he snatched a glorious victory. Here
the die was cast and the stakes were lost, and lost forever,
by the impetuous confederates of Pontiac. Here was fought
and won the battle that decided Anglo-Saxon supremacy in
the Valley of the Mississippi. Here the kilted and
plaited Highlander, from Caledonia's hills, the red-coated
Royal Americans (mostly of German and Swiss extraction),
and their comrades, the Provincial Ranger, from East Pennsylvania and .Maryland, all fought side by side, and
triumphed under the masterful leadership of that superb officer who hailed from the Alpine Mountains of Republican
Switzerland. This is indeed hallowed ground on which we
stand to-day.

> "A shrine to code nor creed confined,
> A Delphian vale, a Palestine ;
> A Mecca of the mind."

All true-hearted men and women will delight to honor the
memory of the gallant heroes who fought and fell on this
bloody field. But we, who are the beneficiaries of their
self-sacrificing toil and valor, we, in whose veins flows the
blood of Scotch-Irish and German-Swiss ancestors ; above
all, we, whose pioneer ancestors were rescued from the
tomahawk and scalping-knife of the blood-thirsty savages,
we, my countrymen, one and all, may well unite in paying
homage to the memory of the brave men who consecrated

these hills and these vales with their blood and their dauntless courage 120 years ago.

> " The land is holy where they fought,
> And holy where they fell."

The lofty example of heroism, the steadfast devotion to
duty even unto death, the magnanimous response to the cries
of panic-stricken settlers and of beleaguered frontier garrisons in deadly peril, the virtues that exalt and adorn human
nature, which were illustrated on this gory field in trying
days of yore, dare not be forgotten—all this is full of instruction and inspiration.

"There is a spirit in man, and the inspiration of the
Almighty giveth him understanding."

"Man shall not live by bread alone, but by every word
that proceedeth out of the mouth of God."

The Almighty gives us words of direct revelation as we
have them recorded in the Sacred Scriptures, and words of
Providential manifestation in the unfoldings of history;
words of solemn import and energizing power for all who
have ears to hear and eyes to see. Ideas and sentiments,
such as come from ennobling historical associations and
surroundings, are more to be prized than silver or gold.
They enter into the warp and woof and become part of the
texture of communities and nations.

And here to-day, my countrymen, we gather for ourselves
and our children some of the rich, historic treasures of the
past, and we catch an inspiration in contemplating the
worthy deeds of departed heroes and benefactors of the
human race. Life is flat and stale and monotonous, indeed,
when it lacks sentiment and enthusiasm—I mean enthusiasm
in the true sense—the stirrings of Deity within us, prompt-
ing us to realize high ideas of manhood and womanhood in
whatever sphere Providence may call us to occupy.

"Without enthusiasm nothing truly great was ever
achieved," says Senecca, the greatest of heathen moralists.
It gives rapture to the poet, heroism to the warrior, devotion to the martyr, ardor to the patriot, lifting them above
their narrow selfishness into the plane of superhuman effort
and consecration.

The will, the intellect, yea our entire being in body and

soul must be enthused with grand ideas of truth and duty if we shall ever effectually help forward the race in its ceaseless efforts to reach the final goal of history and humanity.

A stagnant and treadmill existence, indeed, is that of the Mongolian and other Orientals who are largely destitute of sentiment and enthusiasm.

But we, who represent a cosmopolitan population ; we who belong to the great Republic of the New World, which embraces in one vast national existence all the historic tribes of humanity, the kindred streams of the great Teutonic or Indo-Germanic family of nations, we must gather and cherish the achievements of by-gone ages and especially those that so deeply concern our own life and history.

Only by learning aright the lessons of the past can we go forward with safety and courage in the future. Rooted and grounded in principles and sentiments that have stood the test of the ages we may take hostages of futurity and march in the vanguard of human progress. Then, as Tennyson has expressed it :

" Not in vain the distance beacons forward, forward, let us range ;
Let the great world spin forever, down the ringing grooves of change ;
Through the shadows of the globe we sweep into the younger day ;
Better fifty years of Europe Than a cycle of Cathay   *   *   *
Oh, I see the crescent promise of my spirit hath not set ;
Ancient founts of inspiration well through all my fancy yet."

Yes, one year of American life full of vigorous thought and progress is better than a thousand years of monotonous treadmill Oriental existence.

Civilization, and especially Christian civilization, makes history possible. The red men roamed through these forests for countless ages, but their lives and their labors were like water spilt upon the ground which can never be gathered up for the benefit of others. No reliable records have they to show the pit from which they were dug and the rock from which they were hewn—hence fundamental elements of progress and improvement are lacking.

Great men lived before Agamemnon but they had no Homer to sing their praises and immortalize their deeds, and so far as instruction and inspiration to others are concerned they lived and toiled and struggled in vain.

In order to be true to ourselves and those who shall come
after us, we must cherish and record the deeds of those who
have gone before us as the master spirits of our race.
Among these the pioneers who took their lives in their
hands to carve out homes for themselves and their children,
dare not be forgotten.

The muse of poetry and the muse of history must be invoked, as we have invoked them here to-day, in behalf of
one of

> ‑ " The few, the immortal names
> That were not born to die."

The contemplation of noble characters and great achievements is in itself ennobling.   It lifts us out· of the narrow
rut of our own selfishness into a higher and purer atmos-
phere.

Anniversary commemorations, orations, poems, historical
records, monuments such as I hope to see crown these hills
in honor of Bouquet, these enshrine, crystalize, and local-
ize, great and decisive events.

They are educational and stimulating to the young in the
highest degree.   As the soul of Thucyides was enthused
with the lofty resolve to emulate the works of Herodotus when
he heard them read for the first time at the Olympic games,
so amid such scenes as these the young and gifted sons of
genius feel within them the kindlings of high and honorable effort.

" Immortal fame is a grand thought,
It is worthy the toil of the noble hearted."
" Fame is a spur to brave and honest deeds
And who despises fame will soon renounce the virtues that deserve it."

But fame must have an enduring basis of genuine worth
and merit ; fraud and falsehood vitiate everything that they
touch.   Not only the makers, but the lovers of lies, shall
be excluded from the company of the blessed in the New
Jerusalem above.   We must love and seek truth as the ·jewel
of the soul, as the pearl beyond all price, as that which
allies us to the great and omnipotent Jehovah.   Justice and
judgment are the habitation of His throne, the place where
His Honor dwelleth.

The poorest widow, with a just cause, is stronger before

the final tribunal of history and of God than the mightiest monarch that ever sat upon an earthly throne. " The hypocrite's hope shall perish." " The refuge of lies shall be swept away." There is a Nemesis of History which sooner or later avenges the wrongs of the past and vindicates with just judgment the inexorable claims of truth and righteousness.

The locomotive may take the place of the pack horse, the four horse reaper and steam separator may take the place of the sickle and the flail of our forefathers, the telegraph may take the place of the express rider, and ten thousand other improvements be made in art and science and material industries, but the old-fashioned principles of morality and religion are unchangeable, and eternal " Jesus Christ is the same, yesterday, to-day and forever." " The holiest among the mighty, and the mightiest among the holy, who with His pierced hands has lifted empires off their hinges, turned the streams of centuries, and still governs the ages."

As Julia Ward Howe has expressed it in the Grand Battle Hymn of the Republic :

Let the Hero born of woman, crush the serpent with his heel,
He has sounded forth the trumpet that shall never call retreat,
He is sifting out the hearts of men before His judgment seat ;
O, be swift, my soul, to answer Him; be jubilant my feet.
In the beauty of the lilies, Christ was born across the sea,
With a glory in his bosom that transfigures you and me,
As he died to make men holy,
Let us die to make men free,
While God is marching on.

Yes, make men free! free in the highest and noblest sense of that word.

" He alone is free whom the truth makes free, and all are slaves beside."

For the sake of religious principle, our forefathers came to this new world, and we are degenerate sons of noble sires if we barter away the precious birthright. Let us be true to the God of our fathers, and He will never forsake us.

Men and women of Westmoreland, and all good people here assembled, this is a great day, a "red letter day" in the history of our grand old county.

Here, on this ground, hallowed by the blood and struggles of the Swiss and the Scot, on this historic field of Edge
Hill and Bushy Run, let us dedicate our lives anew to the
sacred cause of Christian civilization and constitutional liberty.

Bouquet was a free-born Switzer. In the land of Tell and
Winkleried he breathed the air of freedom. In the armies
of the Dutch Republic, the pioneer of our own great Republic, he gained his first laurels and won distinction. His
sword was always drawn in behalf of the land that best represented the cause of civil and religious liberty.

He sincerely loved the British Constitution, the principles of Magna Charta, dear to every Anglo-Saxon heart.
He indignantly resigned his high position in the King's service, when he thought it involved some degree of humilia-
tion, which he, as a high-souled man, could never brook.

For what he was in himself, for what the poor Swiss boy
from the shadow of the Alps made of himself as the peer of
the greatest and best among the foremost nations on the face
of the earth ; for what he did for us and our pioneer ancestors, we commend his example, we honor his memory
and invoke for him an undying fame.

"Cold in the dust the cherished form may lie,"

As it has lain for lo ! these 118 years, in an unknown
grave in the sunny South.

" But that which made this man and men like him, can never die."

With Pericles and Edward Everett, we may say of illustrious men, "the whole earth is their sepulchre, and all
time the millennium of their glory."

Oh, land of the brave and free !
Bright as the noonday sun,
Long as your streams shall run,
Let the fame of the Switzer be.

————

The papers state that Rev. C. Cort spoke in a loud, clear
voice, and was frequently applauded.

General Coulter then introduced the poet of the day, who
delivered his production in good style, as follows :

THE POEM OF DR. FRANK COWAN.

THE BATTLE OF BUSHY RUN.

What! Poet, wouldst thou sing of war?—of human strife and slaughter?
Of severed limbs and shattered bones?—of heart's-blood shed like
water?—
Of Murder in its maddest mood, agasp with fiery breath,
Leaving the world without a sun, a blackened waste in death?

Aye, wouldst thou, in this Christian land, extol the God of War?—
Or Scythian Sword, the Roman Mars, the Scandinavian Thor,
Or Mexic monster, Hindoo ghoul—whatever it may prove,
Forefend against it, Jesus Christ, thou God of Peace and Love!

Yea, Man of Peace, I sing of war!—of butchery and blood!—
Heads hot with rage, hearts hard with hate, and hands with gore im-
brued!—
Destruction crushing into dust the noblest forms of earth
Th' Eternal and the Infinite unite in giving birth!

Yea, war! red-handed, raging war! in its most direful form;
The struggle for existence in a fierce organic storm!
The lightning's flash, the dart of death, the sword, the barb, the ball!
The thunder's crash, the vanquisht's groan, the victor's shout o'er all!

Sublime, thou call'st the storm at sea, the wind and wave contending,—
Sublime, the earthquake suddenly the very mountains rending,—
And the volcano belching fire and smoke for miles afar,—
But what are these but bubbles when compared with human war!

Consider, for a moment, MAN, the all-involving world
Turned outside-in in flesh and blood, and into action whirled—
Sphere crushing sphere, sun burning sun, an universal jar!—
And thou canst measure if thou wilt the majesty of war!

But why this eulogy of war, this bright and happy day,
Within this peace-appareled wood, in holiday array,
Where men and women, boys and girls, commingle without strife,
As if with darkness Death had left the world to light and Life!

Here, where we stand, the battle raged : the hosts contending, those
Whom time and place and circumstance had made relentless foes—
The Civilized and Savage man—the White and Red of hue—
The East and West of place of birth—the Old World and the New!

A symbol battle of the world! A race opposing race,
Expanding in significance throughout all time and space ;
The victory declaring for the good above the evil,—
Life over Death,—Heaven over Hell,—a God above a Devil!

In proof whereof, The Continent, from one sea to the other,
To fifty millions of mankind a mighty nation-mother!—

Her breasts outnumbering countlessly the dugs of the Diana
The old Ephesians painted black—Earth bearing Man and Manna!

A mother to increase until exhausted with old age,
Five hundred million sons or more in civil strife engage—
Depopulating cities, states—leaving the land a prey
To those by might and worth decreed, a better race than they!

So Rome and Greece, and Egypt fell—the glories of an age,
In the unfinished book of time a multilated page ;
Like ox and ass with broken backs, their usefulness outlived,
The world the better for their death, their ultimate achieved !

So Turkey, China fall to-day—their masses much more fit
To mingle with the mundane mud than to emerge from it;
Like the Great Auk and Dodo, or the Saurians of the Past,
The world the better for their bones in solid stone encased !

Then let the cheer go round and round, for war, relentless war !
That purifies the planet till it glows a heavenly star !
Sweeping away the weak and vile—as in this very wood—
Leaving the globe a heritance to him of worthiest blood !

Aye, let the cheer go round and round, in honor of the few
Who on this field of battle won a New World for their due—
This glorious Land of Liberty! the worth-reward of Man !
AMERICA, the Mighty, where HE IS THE KING THAT CAN !

This closed the literary exercises of the forenoon. It
was now after twelve o'clock and the meeting took a recess
for dinner.

DINNER.

In families and groups of families the vast assemblage
partook of a pic-nic dinner in the grove and adjacent fields.
Everybody seemed to be in excellent spirits and a grand
good time they had of it. The trip to the battle-field, the
bracing and balmy air and the pleasurable excitement of the
occasion added a relish to the repast by increasing the
keenness of the appetite. The lemonade and restaurant
stands did a thriving business. Not a few persons lost their
friends in the crowd and had to depend upon some good
Samaritan for rations. Rev. Cort, in a vain attempt to find
his commissary stores, ran across Gen. Beaver and his three
boys who had just come upon the grounds. The General's
horses were provided for in Wannamaker's barn and the

party then set out in search of friends with whom they expected to get dinner. But it was a useless seach amid that
seething mass of humanity. Messrs. Hazlet and Stark, with
their families, had just finished a sumptuous repast but had
plenty and to spare. The overplus they kindly placed at
the disposal of the General, the preacher and the boys, all
of whom heartily enjoyed their improvised meal at the edge
of the grove. The General then made a rapid survey of
the field of battle, springing along so nimbly and rapidly
on his crutches that his clerical guide had hard work to
keep up as he sought to explain the respective positions of
Bouquet's Highlanders, Royal Americans and Rangers on the
one hand and that of their savage assailants on the other.
All this while Col. Geo. F. Huff, ex-Gov. Latta and other
members of the Reception Committee were on the lookout
for Gen. Beaver in order to furnish him escort and enter-
tainment. The afternoon proceedings, however, brought
all speakers and committees into right relation with each
other at the grand stand.

A little Indian (Guyatau or Guito) of the Seneca tribe,
from the Cattaraugus Reservation, under the care of Mr.
Gibson, of Dunbar, Fayette county, Pa., was on the stand,
dressed up in full Indian costume and attracted great attention. Guyasutha, the chief of the Senecas located in Ohio,
was the leading spirit among the Indians in this battle and
in the siege of Fort Pitt and subsequently in the attack on
Hannastown. (See appendix). Hence this little copper-
colored, dark-eyed Indian, with tomahawk and other war-
like equipments, was looked upon as a representative of the
vanishing race of red men who made these woods hideous
with their war-whoops 120 years ago to-day. Guyatau or
Guito is seven years old and a smart looking Indian boy.
In striking contrast with him in appearance and historical
association there sat with his mother on the same platform,
a few feet distance from Guyatau, Ralph Bouquet, a fair-
skinned, light-haired, rosy-cheeked, blue-eyed white boy,
the four-year-old son of Rev. Cyrus Cort, and the great-
great-great-grandson of Andrew Byerly, the founder of
Byerly's Station at Bushy Run about 1760, and an important actor in the bloody drama enacted on these hills in

those trying days of yore. Andrew Byerly was one of the
advance guard of eighteen who received the first fire of the
savages, Aug. 5, 1763, on Gongaware's hill—twelve of the
eighteen fell—two companies of the Highlanders rushed forward to the rescue when the conflict soon raged, not only in
the front, but on both flanks and the rear, for the savges had
completely surrounded Bouquet and his little army. Byerly
rendered valuable service during the fight, and at the imminent risk of his life, carried water in his hat to the
wounded Highlanders famishing from thirst during the terrible night of suffering and suspense between the two days of
conflict. (For fuller notice of Andrew Byerly, &c., see
pages 23, &c., 51, &c., of pamphlet on "Col. Henry Bouquet and His Campaigns.")

AFTERNOON PROCEEDINGS AND SPEECHES.

The appearance of General Beaver on the platform, cre⁻
ated great enthusiasm among the assembled multitude which
had now crowded together again in front of the speaker's
stand.

The sea of smiling faces, the thousands of handsome and
well dressed ladies and their gallant escorts, parents with
their children, beaux with their sweethearts, sitting and
standing among the forest trees and anxious to see and hear
the one-legged hero, whose blood had been poured out so
freely on so many battle-fields of the Republic, presented a
scene never to be forgotten by those who were privileged to
behold it. Visitors from a distance spoke with admiration of the fine appearance and excellent behavior of the
people. Everybody seemed happy and anxious to promote
the comfort and happiness of their fellows. There was one
drawback, however. Eight brass bands were scattered
through the grove, and each of these bands seemed to think
that they ought to be heard whenever they felt like blowing
their horns. Rev. W. W. Moorehead, of Greensburg, Pa.,
had offered an appropriate and fervent prayer, and General
Coulter had introduced General Beaver amid the applause
of 10,000 enthusiastic people. But still the bands kept
tooting away. By extra effort on the part of his aids, com-

parative quiet was' secured, and General B., in a pleasant manner and loud, clear voice, proceeded to speak as follows:

ADDRESS OF GENERAL JAMES A. BEAVER, OF BELLEFONTE, PA.

Ladies and Gentlemen :—I confess to you that my coming here to-day has been more for my own gratification and instruction than with the hope or for the purpose of saying anything either to gratify or to instruct the good people of Westmoreland county. My boys and I have driven more than 160 miles from our home rather for the purpose of learning what Westmoreland county is, and what has been done by your ancestors both for you and for us, than for the purpose of adding to your knowledge of history or of the men who made history, or of increasing the pride and intensifying the interest which you must have in the historical associations which crowd around this locality and this occasion. (At this point the music of a brass band almost drowned the speaker's voice, and he laughingly exclaimed: "There is too much of this thing; I never could blow against a brass band." The crowd joined in a hearty laugh and General Coulter leaning far over the railing toward the unruly musicians shouted: "Are there not enough good people out there to stop that band?" But the band played on. The crowd still seemed to enjoy it. Gen. Beaver after waiting a minute turned to those in the immediate neighborhood and said : "Coulter forgets that he is not commanding a brigade; there was a time when he could say to a brass band, stop, and it stopped; play, and it played; but that time has gone by, my old friend, the brass band is on top." Renewed laughter.) Order being finally restored the speaker continued :

Coming from our home in Bellefonte south of Bedford, and then turning westward, we endeavored to follow the old military road that was laid out for General Forbes by Colonel Bouquet (or rather by Col. Burd under Bouquet's supervision), to Ligonier which was afterwards extended by Washington to Fort Pitt. We were unable to follow its immediate route altogether, inasmuch as it has been replaced by roads with better grades which cross it ; but following

the same general direction we gathered enough to see, and
in some measure to understand how the men who established
our civilization were compelled to toil and to march, and
to suffer in order that we might enjoy the civilization and
the advantages which we have to-day. It is a wonderful
inspiration for a Pennsylvanian who has some knowledge of
the history of this general locality to come over these mountains, and recall as he crosses them how much our fathers
labored and suffered and wrought out in toil and blood in
order that they might hand over to us the great heritage of
civilization and of freedom which we enjoy, and which we
are bound to preserve and hand over to our children and
children's children. I have lately re-read some of the history
which relates to the expedition under the command of Col.
Bouquet, which left Bedford with the design and for the
purpose of relieving the beleaguered garrison at Fort Pitt.
It is a wonderful story, full of romance and daring, but I do
not propose to go into its historical details. All who are
here have doubtless heard of the gallant commander of the
expedition, Col. Henry Bouquet. He was a man of the
most wonderful versatility and varied acquirements and of
undaunted bravery, and yet, of such wisdom and gentleness
that he was enabled to secure the co-operation of the people
of the eastern part of the State, who, it must be confessed,
were at that time a little "twisty" and unwilling to give
that cordial help and co-operation in military campaigns
that were absolutely necessary to secure the full fruits of victory. Bouquet, by his wisdom and gentleness quite won
the admiration of our Quaker population in the eastern
part of the State, and succeeded in procuring with their apparent sanction the necessary votes of supplies and men
which enabled him to make his subsequent 1764 campaign,
which brought permanent peace to the frontier settlers until
the war of Revolution began. This is not the time nor the
place, nor does it fall to my province to recount the details
of the campaigns of which the battle of Bushy Run was a
part, nor yet to sketch the life and character of the gallant
commander who displayed such heroic bravery and wise intelligence in making the dispositions of his forces, which
enabled him to win immediate victory upon the field which

is in our sight. There are certain practical questions which
grow out of this event which, it seems to me, press upon
our attention, and should receive our careful consideration.
Go to yonder hill-top and picture if you can how this wise,
brave Swiss Colonel protected his 340 pack-horses and their
drivers (for those of you who had experience in the army
will readily understand that the drivers were harder to
manage than the horses), and surrounded on all sides by
hordes of savages, who were confident of the scalps and
supplies of the little army which they had surrounded, not
only saved his transportation and supplies, but by skillfull
manœuvring and brave fighting after a two days' battle
drove the savages from their well chosen position, and finally gained the object of his expedition. No stretch of our
imagination can picture to us the kind of warfare which
was carried on to protect our fathers against the savage
hordes who were trying their utmost to blot out the little
spark of civilization which was lighted in this Western
region, and which the early settlers were than trying to fan
into a flame. Those of us who have some knowledge of
modern warfare and some experience in the late war so
happily ended, can scarcely conceive of the situation in
which this little army of Bouquet was placed.

You remember, my comrades, that if we did not have
about three days' rations in our haversacks, and fully five
days more in the wagon train, and if we did not have
further, a railroad or a river by which to bring up our supplies, and a telegraph line to keep us in communication
with the outside world, we were supposed to be in danger
of being cut off and "gobbled up." But here is a man
with less than a thousand men ; aye, with less than half of
that number, who struck out from Bedford across the mountains by a road which had been constructed some five years
before, who left his wagon train at Fort Ligonier and started
thence with all his supplies upon pack-horses with his rangers,
his Royal Americans, his Highlanders and his Light Infantry
through the wilderness to relieve the beleaguered fort at
the junction of the Allegheny and Monongahela rivers.
The mode of warfare is so thoroughly foreign to our present
conceptions of military operations that no stretch of the

2

imagination, I say, can enable us to comprehend what was involved in the campaign to which we have referred, and which was carried to such a successful issue by Col. Bouquet. My admiration for the man, however, has led me to wander, and I come back to the practical thought which I wish especially to present, which is this: that as the men whom we have in mind to-day lived and labored, and some of them laid down their lives for us and for what we hold most dear to us, so we are to see to it not only that what was left us should be preserved and handed down to our children, but that their memories should be perpetuated in an endur-ing way, so that our children and our children's children may learn what was done on these hills, before the remem-brance of it has faded out of the minds of men and locali-ties can no longer be clearly designated. We, in Pennsylva-nia have less of local pride and of interest in our local history than have the people either of New England or New York; as a consequence, many localities full of historical and romantic interest are unmarked and comparatively unknown. We have in this State a society known as the Historical Society of Pennsylvania, whose headquarters are in Phila-delphia. It is doing a vast amount of good in preserving the early records of our settlers, and publishing them through the medium of the *Pennsylvania Magazine.* This society, however, is unfortunately largely local in its agencies and ends, and therefore local in its results. Its aim is to reach out through the entire State and to enlist the interest and co-operation of men in every section. Unfortunately, however, it has been unable so far to do this as fully as we could wish. Although I live east of the Allegheny moun-tains, we, of that locality are classed and have come to consider ourselves as belonging to Western Pennsylvania. It would be much better if we could co-operate with the society of which I have spoken, but if this cannot be done, we should undoubtedly seek to co-operate with a similar society which has been organized in Pittsburg for the bene-fit of that locality and, I take it, for that of all Western Pennsylvania. Through one or the other of these agencies not only should what has been written with reference to this battle be preserved, but the relics which remain of it and everything which relates to it should be gathered and deposited under their auspices.

Here is a bayonet; it formed a part of the equipment of one of the Highlanders, doubtless, before whose terrific bayonet charge the Indian gave way. It should be placed where it would become an object lesson to all beholders of the fight at Bushy Run and should stimulate inquiry in regard to that battle and those who took part in it. Local historical societies in connection with either one ·or the other of the greater societies already named, should be organized in our several localities so as to co-operate with them and secure for them just such relics as I have mentioned. The place where the battle was fought should be so marked that coming generations would have no difficulty in telling where it is and learn through its monuments of the heroism of those who won its great victory. Monuments which would serve tell not only where the battle was fought and the victory won, but who fell in the fight, and who they were and what they did in winning it. We are brought face to face to-day with this bit of colonial history. We learn more than we have ever known perhaps of Col. Bouquet and his little army—of their bravery and of his wisdom and courage ; and yet he has largely dropped out of American history as it is learned by the masses of this generation. Over these hill-tops his ·name ought to be perpetuated. Through the influence of this day the memory of his achievements should be revived ; and their influence in shaping the welfare of this region gratefully recalled. One of the boasts of my lineage is that I am mainly of Pennsylvania German stock. There is good reason perhaps,ı why the memory of Col. Bouquet and his followers is so little regarded. Following his campaigns, came the exciting events which culminated in the war of the Revolution. That, of course, to us Americans was the great event in our history. Our interest centres in that; and our American historians are more interested in preserving the names of the men who participated in it, than those brave spirits who served the mother country in the Indian wars which preceded it. This perhaps, is the reason why the memory of Washington, St. Clair and Mad Anthony Wayne overshadows, and their achievements overtop, and to a great extent blot out the memory and achievements of this brave German-Swiss. We have a history of which we need not be ashamed. Let us be interested in preserving it and making it known to the world and to our descendants. We owe it to those who made the history; we owe it to ourselves; we owe it to those who are to come after us. Let us therefore co-operate with Judge Parke and Mr. Bigham and the other gentlemen who have come here from Pittsburg and are interested in preserving the historical records of this region of Western Pennsylvania.

It is a great pleasure, I assure you, to join with you in the commemoration of this great event. I see not only Westmoreland, but Armstrong, Allegheny, Fayette and other counties represented on these grounds. Such gatherings are good, not only because they remind us of what others have done and suffered, but because of the social features which surround them, and other opportunities thus afforded for renewing old friendships and making new ones. Gratefully mindful of the men and the achievements of the past, true to obligations of the present and trustful as to the future, let us gather up the lessons of to-day, and carry them with us as an inspiration and an incentive in the life which we are to live for the benefit not of ourselves alone, but of those who are about us and are to come after us.

At the close and also frequently during the progress of his speech, the sentiments of General Beaver were greeted with hearty applause.

Hon. John E. Parke, of Pittsburg, president of the Western Pennsylvania Historical Society, delivered the following address on the French and Indian war and the causes that led to the same, &c.

ADDRESS OF JUDGE JOHN E. PARKE.*

PONTIAC'S PLOT.

We have been called together this day to celebrate one of the most important and interesting events connected with the history of our country. On this spot, sacred to the memory of the past, one hundred and twenty years ago, the gallant and accomplished Col. Henry Bouquet, with his heroic little band of Highlanders and Anglo-Americans, having passed the rugged and dangerous defiles of the Allegheny, arrived at Bushy Run, August 5, 1763.

The prominent events connected with Bouquet's expedition, and their subsequent development into permanent settlements, the ingredients of which are of the highest importance in perpetuating the fame of these gallant men, who left the confines of civilization to brave the dangers of an unknown country, the simple outline of which, when drawn with fidelity, possess marvelous interest to the student of nature. The elaboration of these events I will leave to others more competent to do justice to the subject.

The imagination fails to conceive incidents more romantic, than those which sober truth reveals in the career of those who penetrated the Western wilds in order to create new homes for themselves and families, impelled by those powerful motives of human action—ambition and a love of liberty.

In the career of many of the early adventurers, we see these passions overruling all others. They stand out in bold relief as grand heroes worthy of a representation in the annals of the country. In the delineation of their deeds, and of those who follow after them, who occupied what they had won, by faith, courage and indomitable perseverance, are prominent features in the picture. These were the necessary elements of success in the wide and dangerous fields of adventure, and were ever present in great abundance when required in laying the foundation of their future homes.

*Judge Parke had engaged to secure the attendance of W. D. Moore, Esq., of Pittsburg, but that gentleman was unable to fulfill the engagement, and upon a few hours' notice, the Judge was obliged to prepare himself to fill his place.

Many of the events which have rendered Western Pennsylvania conspicuous in the history of the past, leave their impress on the mind of every American citizen. They pass before us as a mighty vision, making us feel the poverty of language and weakness of eloquence when startling realities are to be described.

Old Westmoreland, whose vast territory at an early day extended so as to embace nearly all the territory lying westward from the foot hills of the Alleghenies to the Virginia borders, may be justly styled the Mother of the Western Counties, and her soil was among the first points selected by the hardy pioneer and venturesome scout to commence the work of civilization.

Here all the embarrassments of a new settlement were encountered. The terrible conflicts with the cruel and treacherous red men, isolation from society, cut off from aid and intercourse with the Atlantic seaboard, were evils of no ordinary magnitude.

The rugged passes of the Alleghenies then presented a formidable barrier, and the traveler who passed them, found himself, as it were, in a new world, where he was compelled to defend himself or perish. A continual conflict was waged between the sturdy pioneer and his implacable Indian foeman. These conflicts were for life and all that made life dear, and were, however, only marked individual acts of heroism, which produced none of those events affecting national greatness, which it is the province of the historian to record. They will, therefore, find no place in the annals of our country, yet it is to be hoped, nevertheless, that the indomitable reporter will start out in quest of traditionary lore, who will patiently listen to the reminiscences of hoary-headed men, and laboriously glean the frail and fragmentary memorials of other days.

Then will the hardy pioneer and gallant conqueror of the country, of which we are so proud, find a place, if not with heroes of history, at least with heroes of romance.

The early exploration of Westmoreland county by these avant couriers of civilization, of which there is no authentic record, are well calculated to excite an interest in the breast of every American citizen, especially those to the "manor born."

We can scarcely realize the wondrous changes that have occurred in our midst, even within the compass of our own recollection. Before the introduction of steamboats, or street railways were invented, ere the lightning telegraph and telephone had annihilated space, or the steam horse rendered distance a myth, a long time ago, to the Indian war-whoop and the midnight howl of the wolf, to the light of burning cabins, now succeed the sound of the steam whistle, the light of glowing furnaces, the sound of the ponderous engine, clang of machinery, and the whirr and clatter of the shuttle and cotton spindle.

Over this territory, hallowed by the memory of the past, the merciless red man roamed, and who claimed the country from the foothills of the Alleghenies to the great lakes of the North, over which he ruled, bidding defiance to his indomitable Anglo-Saxon foe.

The startling war-whoop, and the no less appalling cry of the panther, struck terror into the hearts of all who had the temerity to venture within the depths of the gloomy forests.

Westward through the wilderness led 'the great Indian trail to the mouth of the Beaver ; thence in a northwesterly direction to Sandusky and Detroit ; following the ridges, it passed through Trumbull and Portage counties, Ohio, clearly defined by stone-piles and marked trees. Near the confluence of the Mahoning and Shenango, forming the Beaver, another trail crossed, following a more westerly direction to the Tuscarawas branch of the Muskingum. Over these trails these wild denizens made their periodical raids, unchecked, towards the settlements, except when opposed by the avant couriers of civilization, the venturesome pioneer and brave and hardy scout. Notwithstanding the important treaties that had been made with them from time to time, they still continued their atrocities upon the defenseless pioneer, who had the hardihood to brave the danger consequent upon the settlement of an unknown country.

The memorable struggles between the legions of France

and the battalions of England for the supremacy in the
great Northwest, during which time the gorgeous Fleur de
Lis and the royal banner of St. George waved successively
over the battlements of old Fort Duquesne, was happily determined by the peace of 1763. Negotiations with this view
were entered into during the year 1762, and were finally
consummated early in the following year. By the condition
of the treaty, France agreed to surrender absolutely all her
possessions in North America to England.   Anticipating an
early peace, the former made a secret covenant with Spain,
ceding to that nation the territory of Louisiana,(in the year
1800 it was re-ceded to France, and in 1803 was purchased
by the United States for $15,000,000), which at the time
embraced a large portion of the Southwest.   The object of
this secret covenant was evidently to keep from under the
control of their hereditary enemy, the free navigation of
waters flowing through the Mississippi and Ohio Valleys
within the ceded territory.   This deception was not apparent during the negotiation; it was only made so at the time
of the execution of the treaty.   This covert disposition of
the territory, which they failed to maintain by the prestige
of arms, was a diplomatic trick, seriously involving their
national honor, and which came near defeating the object.
In view of the prostration of the country by the recent war,
England resolved to accept the situation, trusting in their
ability to acquire in the future the peaceful possession of the
disputed territory.

     With the restoration of peace, it was confidently hoped
that it would forever end the troubles and difficulties with
the Indians, who were, with a few exceptions, the allies of
France.   This, however, was a fatal mistake, as it proved
the prelude to a most cruel and devastating war, destructive
alike to life and property throughout the entire Western
frontier.   The contemplated and simultaneous uprising of
the several hostile tribes was so unexpected that the outposts were in a great measure unprepared to repel successfully, their murderous onslaughts, except in the instance of
the attack on Fort Pitt, Detroit and Ligonier.

     Hitherto the Indians who had been held in subjection by
the French had been won over by a doubtful diplomacy

and apparent kindness, so that the relations existing between them were of the most friendly character.

When, however, they discovered that they were to be
handed over under the treaty to their foe, they indignantly
refused to consent thereto. The onward and steady progress of civilization carried forward by the indomitable
Anglo-Saxon race, assured them that submission on their
part would end in extermination; to prevent such a calamity,
then was the time to act, while the forts were feeble and
wide apart, and the settlements scattered and thinly popu-
lated.

The war familarily known as the Pontiac war, so called
because this great war chief was the genius who devised and
inaugurated it, and who carried it on with that relentness,
cruelty so characteristic of the North American Indian.
Pontiac's personal efforts, however, were confined chiefly to
the neighborhood around Detroit and the lakes, while the
operations on the borders of the Ohio were entrusted to
warriors equally fierce and unrelenting.

As far as the English and Colonists were concerned, the
contests were principally confined to Forts Pitt, Detroit and
Ligonier. All the frontier forts, except those three and
Niagara, fell without an effort at defense, the latter was considered too well fortified to be molested, so that the three
former were the only ones that successfully resisted the advancing tide of savage vengeance; whilst there was nothing
left of the unfortunate garrisons and the settlements around
them but a mass of smouldering ruins. Immured within
the gloomy depths of a mighty wilderness, isolated from all
intercourse with civilization, these gallant defenders not
only maintainted their posts, but actually carried the war
into the heart of the enemy's country, and, at the point of
the bayonet, wrung from them an unwilling peace.

The movements, therefore, on these three forts, and the expedition that subsequently went out from them against the
savages, comprises the entire history of the wars as far as it
relates to our own military movements. The sparse and
scattered locations of our frontier defenses through the vast
wilderness lying between the great Northern lakes and the
Ohio and Misissippi Valleys, were but rude log enclosures,

2*

principally located on the lines of water communications, but frequently met with in the heart of the forests, garrisoned by a mere handful of soldiers, and the emblem of sovereignty floating above them, seemed more of burlesque than the distinguishing mark of a mighty and powerful nation. These forts, situated so distant from each other, were but mere dots in the interminable wilderness.

The presence and maintenance of these isolated outposts inflamed the spirits of the haughty chiefs, who had the sagacity to believe that if the struggle for the supremacy was maintained and accomplished by their foes, it would be the foreshadowing of the red man's coming fate.

To resist this encroachment on their rights, the head chiefs of the various tribes who inhabited the country, then only known and travelled by their own hunting and war parties, determined to crush out at once the power of their foes.

The Shawnees, Delawares, Senecas, Wyandots and Miamis, who considered themselves the exclusive masters of the territory, being moved by their hatred and fear of their Anglo-Saxon foemen, joined together in a common cause, in order to wipe out at once, by a simultaneous movement, the further progress of civilization.

Although rumors of this confederation occasionally reached the military authorities, they did not wholly ignore them, but rather treated them with a cool indifference, highly discreditable to their military education, for if prompt measures had been carried out on the first intimation of alarm, the sacrifice of life and the destruction of the outposts might have been prevented.

It was in consequence of this fatal indifference that when the storm burst upon the forts and defenseless settlements, it came like the mighty tornado, carrying terror and destruction as it sweeps its irresistible course.

The period of time selected by the tribe to carry into effect their purposes, evinced their profound knowledge and sagacity. Operations were delayed until the harvests were safely garnered, so that their foes with the provisions provided for their sustenance, might be destroyed at the same time—thus clearing the wilderness of their foes, at least, for the time being.

Fort LaBœuf, on French creek, Venango on the Allegheny, Presque Isle, on Lake Erie, La Bay, on Lake Michigan, St. Joseph, Miami, Sandusky and Michilmackinas, went down in gloom one after another, with scarcely any resistance. Many of them fell by stratagem, and their garrisons were cruelly massacred ; others capitulated and shared the same fate ; out of all, only one, LaBœuf escaped. The defense of the latter proved futile, the Indians having succeeded in firing the adjacent buildings. The garrison took refuge in the woods, and ultimately escaped.

The royal banner of St. George, wherever it floated over mountain, prairie and stream within these vast domains, was stricken down. Forts Pitt, Niagara, Ligonier and Detroit still remained intact, and the hardy settlers who had escaped the murderous tomahawk and scalping-knife, fled for safety within their protecting walls. The intrepid trapper and venturesome trader were followed up with untiring zeal, and when taken, were horribly tortured and ruthlessly butchered in cold blood, in a manner only known and practiced by these human sleuth-hounds.

The stout pioneer in the clearng, and the loved ones in the log cabin, fell alike before the rifle and tomahawk.

The sound of the woodman's axe and the boom of the morning and evening gun of the lonely forts went down in silence together, and the fires of civilization and the smoke thereof, as it gracefully ascended above the tree tops,were ex tinguished in blood. Those who escaped the murderous raid left their rude homes to the torch of the foe, and sought safety in flight, carrying with them a tale of blood and cruelty, the bare recital of which filled the border settlements with terror and dismay. In the midst of these scenes of gloom and desolation, the indomitable defenders of Forts Pitt, Detroit and Ligonier watched with vigilance the movements of their treacherous assailants, thus assuring the safety of the forts, their flags gallantly spread to the breeze, the only emblems of Anglo-Saxon power and of civilization in a land now covered with teeming cities, girdled by the wires of the electric telegraph, and traversed by a mighty network of railroads.

Judge Parke was followed by Hon. T. J. Bigham, of Pittsburg, who spoke as follows:

ADDRESS OF HON. T. J. BIGHAM.

I have attended, I believe, all the historical celebrations in Westmoreland county of late years. Some years ago I attended the celebration at Greensburg, and I was at Hannastown one year ago. I am not in good health. My wife let me come here on condition that I would not make a . speech. I am a native of this county, having been born at the other end of the manor. I was born and lived there until I went to college. My ancestors settled there about two years after this battle at Bushy Run. We did not celebrate the one hundreth anniversary of this battle, as the battle of Gettysburg occurred just about that time.

At the time of the Bushy Run battle this county was in Cumberland—the capital was Carlisle. At one time it included nearly the whole of Western Pennsylvania. This was all called Mother Cumberland, just after the battle of Bushy Run. I am in favor of preserving the records of the early history of Westmoreland. I am seventy-four years old and have been, next to Judge Parke, the most busily engaged in the old historical celebrations. There was one or two battles in Fayette county, by Washington, and one in Armstrong. Col. Armstrong led all Pennsylvanians to Kittanning, and destroyed that nest of Indians. I always like to attend these meetings if I am able to get out at all.

The old Residenter's Society of Pittsburg is designed to imitate the Historical Society of Pennsylvania. Judge Parke wishes to enlarge this society. Most people have lost a knowledge of the French and Indian war. A reporter came up to me and asked me about this war. I said " Is it possible that the young generation don't know anything about this war?" France claimed to have discovered the mouth of the Mississippi river, also the St. Lawrence. It was then a kind of rule that the nation that discovered the mouth of the river had the right to the territory which it drained. France claimed every foot of ground that she thought was hers, and named it New France.

Louis XIV., in the estimation of the French, was a grand

monarch, and he claimed all the country west of the Mississippi and Ohio. Louis XXV entertained the same idea. The English had settled east of the Allegheny mountains. The English charter included all the country from ocean to ocean. We passed through the country where Braddock was defeated in July, 1755, this morning. In 1758 William Pitt, after whom Pittsburg is named, was called to the helm of the British Empire. He was the greatest statesman of the last century; no European statesman excelled him. Before this time the armies in America had bad leaders. Pitt sent good men to take command. Wolfe and Forbes were sent over to fight the French and Indians. The war continued some seven or eight months and was ended just before the battle of Bushy Run. Great Britain never was so powerful as she was at that time. The whole of this country east of the Mississippi was owned by her. In India war was carried on, and the whole of that country, with a population greater than the United States to-day, was ceded to England. She was never so great a nation as at that time, not even after the battle of Waterloo, where the whole of Europe was repulsed. Our interests were with Great Britain, and I think if England had not succeeded in the French and Indian war we would not be as far on in industry and civilization as we are at the present time.

Pontiac is said to have led part of the force which defeated Braddock. He summoned his men and made a great speech, in which he told them that the Great Spirit had come to them and they resolved that they would destroy our ancestors. The tempest broke out in June. Guyasootha was the commander of the party which attacked this place. He was the principal man that led the warriors under Pontiac. Pontiac himself was besieging Detroit. It is not known definitely that Guyasootha was the commander in the battle, but it is highly probable he was here. I rejoice that Bouquet was successful. They attempted to play the same trick on Bouquet as they did on Braddock, but he turned the tables on them. They fought the whole afternoon of the fifth, night parted them and they fought the battle again the next day.

This place was a sort of half-way station between Ligonier and Fort Pitt. He intended to rest his men at Bushy Run

and march through the wilderness near Turtle Creek at
night, where he expected to meet the Indians. At this
battle he managed his men in two files. He then sent forward two companies to make the attack, but this was a
failure.

The Indians supposed this to be a real retreat, and got
out from the woods and then had to fight Bouquet's men on
both sides. That was just the reverse of the position in
which Braddock was. The Indians in the woods were
formidable, but out of them the white man could get the
best of them. Bouquet just re-acted Braddock's Field, but
got the Indians into the trap. After they were driven back
they fled away to the Muskingum country. Some time ago
some young lawyers came in my office, and I asked them if
they knew who Bouquet was? My son spoke up and said
that he was a Frenchman.

I request that the people of Harrison City petition the
Court to change the name of Harrison City to that of Bouquet. It would mean something to have Bouquet City instead of Harrison City.

From infancy I heard talk of the burning of Hannastown.
Braddock forbid his men to get behind trees but made them
keep in regular order, and in this way the Indians had the
advantage.

Bouquet made another tour in 1764 into the Muskingum
country to effect a treaty with the Indians in which he was
successful. In 1765 he was sent to Florida. He contracted
a fever there and died.

In 1762 all the country east of the Mississippi was ceded
to the English. Pontiac did not hate the French as much
as he did the English, for he knew they would not harm
so much in the way of making settlements and in cultivating land. The Anglo-Saxons were industrious. My ancestors were Irish. If the French were industrious they
could have found plenty to do in the Mississippi valley.

THE CONCLUSION.

When Judge Bigham's speech was ended the benediction
was pronounced by Rev. D. B. Lady, of Manor, and the

literary exercises of the day were brought to a close between three and four o'clock in the afternoon.

Letters were received from distinguished gentlemen of our own and other lands, some of which are hereto appended.

REVIEW OF THE GRAND ARMY POSTS.

While Gen. R. Coulter was presiding at the speaker's · stand during the delivery of the last two addresses, Gen. James A. Beaver, Gen. Thomas F. Gallagher, Col. John Johnston and other military men reviewed the Grand Army Posts on the top of Gongaware's Hill, the scene of the first day's fight between the Indians and the two companies of Highlanders and where a large number of Bouquet's men were buried at the close of the battle.

G. A. R. Post, No. 4, of Latrobe, arrived in the grove on Sunday evening and encamped there during the night. On Monday they were joined by two brass bands from that place and others of their comrades until their number reached about 50. Irwin Post, (190) mustering 75 men and headed by the Paintertown cornet band, and Turtle Creek Post, (199) with 25 men and a martial band, arrived early in the day. Later the Greensburg Post, with 40 members and a martial band, and Fort Ligonier Post, with 40 members and a brass band, reached the grove. Still later the Sewickley Cavalry, commanded by Capt. Samuel Bell and Lieuts. Millken, Martin and McCune, 70 strong, and headed by a martial band, rode up to the rendezvous of rejoicing. There were other members of Posts in neighboring towns and counties in attendance, but not as organizations. The excellent Salem cornet band and Citizens' band of Greensburg were likewise present and added their harmonious strains to the almost ceaseless flow of music during the day.

Headed by the Citizens' band, of Greensburg, the battle-scarred veterans to the number of about 300 with their respective bands, made a few evolutions around the hill-top and then marched past the Generals in fine style. They were followed by the Cavalry in picturesque costumes.

The distinguished reviewers expressed themselves highly gratified with the military display.

Shortly before the review began Rev. C. Cort introduced Revs. A. E. Truxal, John W. Love, Geo. H. Johnston, Thos. J. Barkley and A. B. Kline to Generals Beaver and Gallagher. As soon as the introduction was ended Gen. Beaver remarked: "Gentlemen, I am very glad to see you here and I appoint you all to act as members of my staff." Several of the clergy received orders immediately to clear the space in front of the General and his party so that the veterans could' pass muster without being crowded. This was no easy task under the circumstances.

Col. Oursler, of Latrobe, and others deserve great credit for securing the presence of so many G. A. R. men.

Herewith we append some of the letters received by those in charge of the celebration.

LETTERS FROM PUBLIC OFFICIALS, &C.

PHILADELPHIA, Aug. 2, 1883.

To the Honorable Committee on Invitation for the Bouquet Celebration :

Gentlemen : Your kind invitation to participate in the celebration of the battle of Bushy Run, in honor of my distinguished countryman, Gen. Henry Bouquet, on the 6th instant, has come to hand in time. Please accept my sincere thanks for the same and believe me, it would afford me great pleasure, to meet you on such an occasion of intense gratification to my patriotic feelings. To see the history of another of my compatriots, who devoted his life and gallant services to the existence and security of this land of freedom in its early stages,—a republican by birth and spirit, instrumental in the early struggles of this great Republic,—drawn from oblivion and placed in its well deserved position before the people, cannot but fill my heart with pride for the hero of your celebration and with warmest thanks for the gentlemen who have taken in hand this noble task. While I, therefore, deeply regret to be prevented, by my arduous duties from accepting your kind and honoring invitation, I thank you gentlemen, all of you, who have the noblest interest, started and brought to a happy issue this timely and creditable celebration, from all my heart. I also convey to you my warmest thanks from the countrymen in my consular district and especially from the members of the Swiss National Festival Society, in this city, whom I have made acquainted with your object, and who, in their last meeting, by resolution, unanimously passed, have authorized and requested me to do so. With sincere hope and conviction, that your festival may be a great and complete success, I remain, gentlemen, very respectfully yours,   R. KORADI, *Consul of Switzerland.*

In a personal letter to Rev. Cyrus Cort, Herr Koradi

states that he has forwarded copies of the former's historical pamphlet to the Prefect at Rolle, the Chief of Department of Public Instruction at Lausanna, to the Federal Chancery at Berne and to the Swiss Legation at Washington.

EXECUTIVE MANSION, WASHINGTON, July 12, 1883.

My Dear Sir: The President desires me to acknowledge the receipt of your kind note of the 7th inst., inviting him to be present at the celebration of Bushy Run, on the 6th of August next, and to express his regret that engagements covering that date will prevent its acceptance. Thanking you in his behalf for the courtesy of the invitation, I am, very truly yours, O. L. PRUDEN, Sec'y.

R. COULTER, ESQ., Ch'm, etc., Greensburg, Penn'a.

WASHINGTON, July 17, 1883.

Sir: I much regret that it will not be in my power to accept your courteous invitation to be present at the celebration of the 120th anniversary of the battle of Bushy Run on the 6th of Aug. next. Very faithfully yours, J. S. SACKVILLE WEST.

R. COULTER, ESQ., Greensburg.

EXECUTIVE DEPARTMENT, COMMONWEALTH OF PENNA.,
OFFICE OF THE GOVERNOR,
HARRISBURG, July 11th, 1883.

GENERAL R. COULTER, Greensburg, Pa.

Dear Sir: I am in receipt of your very kind invitation to attend the celebration of the 120th anniversary of the battle of Bushy Run, August 6th, and regret my inability to be present. Accept my thanks and believe me your obedient servant, R. E. PATTISON.

STATE OF OHIO, EXECUTIVE DEPARTMENT,
OFFICE OF THE GOVERNOR,
COLUMBUS, July 11, 1883.

R. COULTER, ESQ., Greensburg, Pa.

My Dear Sir: By direction of the Governor, I have the honor to acknowledge the receipt of an invitation to him to be present and participate in the celebration of the battle of Bushy Run, to be held on the battle-field on Monday, August 6th. The Governor is greatly obliged for your kind remembrance of him and regrets that engagements already made cover the dates named and will prevent his acceptance. Very truly yours, F. D. MUSSEY, Private Secretary.

WAR DEPARTMENT, ADJUTANT GENERAL'S OFFICE,
WASHINGTON, July 18, 1883.

R. COULTER, ESQ., Chairman :

Dear Sir: In reply to your invitation to General Drum to be present at the celebration of the battle of Bushy Run on August 6th, I beg to inform you that the General is at present absent on a "tour of inspec-

tion," and will not return to this city before the date named, otherwise
I have no doubt he would take pleasure in joining the celebration.
Very Respectfully,

HENRY TURNBULL.

Letters of regret were also read from ex-Governor Hart-
ranft; Mayor King, of Philadelphia; Hon. W. U. Hensel,
of Lancaster, and Prof. Samuel Wilson, of Allegheny City.

APPENDIX.

In response to enquiries sent by Counsul Koradi, through the Prefect of Rolle, to the custodians of the archives of the Canton Vand, at Lausanne, in Switzerland, Rev. C. Cort received some valuable data from Mr. J. Berney, the Chief of Public Instruction for the Canton Vand.

This came too late for the Bouquet pamphlet, for which it was desired, but we will insert the main points here.

In the Parochial Register of the Reformed Church of Rolle, the entry is made March 25, 1735, that Henry Bouquet had been examined, along with others, with a view to participate in the Holy Communion. His age is stated to be 16 years. This agrees with other data which state that Henry Bouquet was born in the year 1719.

It is further stated in this document of Mr. Berney, that Henry Louis Bouquet was the oldest of seven brothers; that he entered the service of Holland, in 1736, and afterwards passed into the service of Piedmont, where his brilliant career and intelligence attracted the Prince of Orange, who invited him to command a company of his guard. During the leisure hours of garrison duty, he cultivated the sciences and became intimately acquainted with distinguished professors in Holland, at the University of Leeyden, &c. From this, it appears that our hero had a middle name, which he seldom or never used. Louis Bouquet, evidently the uncle referred to in the will of Henry Bouquet (see page 76, of Bouquet pamphlet), became General Quartermaster and Lieutenant-Colonel in the Regiment Stuerler, in the service of the Netherlands, and renounced his citizenship of Rolle, April 14, 1750, and was discharged from his duties as a citizen, October 8, 1750, evidently with a view of be-

coming a citizen of Holland, where he had risen to distinction. Several members of the Bouquet family served with
distinction in foreign countries, we are told ; particularly in
Holland, where, among others, one of his uncles was an
engineer officer. This may have been Colonel Louis, already described.

The Bouquet family were citizens of Rolle, and one of its
members belonged to the council of that town or city.

In the letter, forwarding the document, Consul Koradi
writes :

" Just as I thought, when reading your very interesting pamphlet,
in which you give such a clear and minute report of my countryman,
that I wondered where you got all these details from ; the report I got
does not bring anything new. The only point of importance is the
proof by it, that Henry Bouquet really was a native of Rolle, a Swiss from
the Canton of Vand, and that Bouquet was his correct oirginal name ; that,
therefore, the suggestions of the Pioneer of Cincinnati, that he was a
German, and his name Frenchified, from Strauss, into Bouquet, was
wrong."

This was the conclusion arrived at, on other grounds, by
Rev. Cort (see pamphlet, page 5).

The archives of Vand also state that :

" In 1754, the British government confided to him and fellow-coun-
tryman, Haldimand, of Yoerden (also in the Canton of Vand), the organization of a brigade, named the Royal American, into which he
drew several other fellow-citizens of the Canton of Vand, among whom
was DuFes, of Monden, and Vullgamott, of Lausanne."

Subsequent to the publication of the Bouquet pamphlet
and the Bushy Run Celebration of August 6, 1883, Wm.
M. Darlington, Esq., of Pittsburg, Pa., informed Rev. C.
Cort that he had spent a good deal of time in an effort to
ascertain the exact location of Bouquet's grave, at Pensacola, many years ago. He had an old drawing of the fort
and barracks at Pensacola, made in 1772, which would seem
to locate the grave and monument of Bouquet, if the exact
position of the old barracks can be determined.

Mr. Darlington says that one of the principal clerks of
the British Museum told him that the Canadian government
paid a thousand pounds sterling, or five thousand dollars,
for a manuscript copy of the Bouquet-Haldimand papers,
which were presented to the British Museum by a grandson
of Haldimand.

On page 83, of the Bouquet pamphlet, reference is made to G. D. Scull, an American resident of Oxford, England, who had collated some of the more important Bouquet papers for publication, a limited number of which, at ten dollars a copy, was to be printed at an early date. The following letter from Mr. Scull to Rev. Cort, will be of interest in several respects. He had previously written that Bouquet was deserving of perennial remembrance, and he was delighted to learn of the proposed celebration at Bushy Run.

RUGBY LODGE, NORHAM ROAD, ⎱
OXFORD, Aug. 17, 1883. ⎰

DEAR SIR:—I am extremely obliged to you for the copy of " Bouquet and his Campaigns," received some days ago. I assure you, I have read it with great interest and pleasure. Of a certainty you are General Bouquet's qualified and well-appointed biographer. What a pity that your well directed search for his grave, at Pensacola, ended in total failure.

Lieut. Francis Hutcheson, in 1763, was with Bouquet in his expedition against the Ohio Indians, and acted, at times, as his secretary. Bouquet invited Hutcheson to go with him to Pensacola, where they arrived, and Bouquet was buried eight days after. He was appointed a Major of Brigades afterwards. Hutcheson acted as administrator to Bouquet's estate, at Pensacola, had a vendue, and brought up North the net balance in bills on London and New York—$3,566.03½—which was handed over to Colonel Haldimand. Among the items of expense are amounts paid six soldiers for carrying the corpse to the grave, $3. Left with Captain Valoe to finish railing around the General's grave, $30, and $11.05 for scantling round ditto.

Among the things put in an inventory, and which were probably handed over to Colonel Haldimand, are :. A gold watch, with a seal, coat of arms and compass, a sum of coin, Johannes and ½ do., doubloons, guineas and ½ do., 2 negro men and 1 girl, 24 pieces of silver plate, 1 pipe of Madeira, 3 quarter-casks do., 2 casks Rhenish, 2 demijohns claret, cask of bottled beer, scarlet coat, with broad gold lace, scarlet, gold-laced frock and breeches, 18 pairs of silk stockings, 9 pairs thread do., 33 shirts, 10 white waist coats, 15 ruffled caps, 11 cotton do., 17 stocks, 4 pairs white spadderdashes, 1 plaid night gown, 1 silk night gown, 1 Huzzar cloak, 1 silver-mounted sword, 1 cutlass, 1 case pistols and furniture, 2 boxes containing 5 wigs, etc.

Major Hutcheson afterwards became Colonel Haldimand's private and military secretary. I am quite in the dark if anything has yet been done to bring out my Bouquet correspondence in Philadelphia. I am grievously disappointed at the result.

Very truly yours,   G. D. SCULL.

Looking at matters from our modern standpoint, we may smile at the mention of some of the articles in the foregoing list. But Bouquet, like all other men, must be judged by his own times, and the customs of the age and country in which he lived. ·An inventory of the personal eff ects of George Washington and other Revolutionary patriots would not differ materially from the one given above.

The inventory confirms what we know from other data, that Bouquet was a generous-hearted host, a good liver and a man of elegant tastes.

CELEBRATION ITEMS.

Gen. James A. Beaver and his three sons arrived in Greensburg on Saturday evening, and stopped at the Fisher House until Monday morning, when they drove to the Bouquet battle·ground, where the General took part in the celebration. He was on his way to Conneaut Lake, where his brigade will go into encampment at the close of the week.

Andrew Byerly, of Sharpsville, Mercer county, a great grandson of Andrew Byerly, of Bushy Run fame, arrived in Greensburg on Saturday, on his way to Bushy Run, and was the guest of Ex-County Treasurer James Gregg.—Prof. Andrew Byerly, of Millersville Normal School, an establishment of seven or eight hundred students, is also a great grandson.

Mrs. Rev. Cyrus Cort, two sons—Paul and Ambrose—and cousin, reached this place at noon on Saturday, from Greencastle, in a carriage drawn by one horse. They came by way of Forts Bedford and Ligonier—the same road taken by Col. Bouquet and his army when on his way to relieve Fort Pitt. They were three days en route, the distance traveled being one hundred and twenty-five miles. They spent one night at Ligonier, the site of the fort by that name, where Andrew Byerly, the great-great-great-grandfather of Mrs. Cort's sons, was cooped up by Pontiac's confederates, after making a narrow escape from Bushy Run, where Byerly kept a relay station for express riders midway between Forts Pitts and Ligonier. Mrs. Cort joined her husband at this place, who arrived here by rail on Thursday morning last, accompanied by his four-year-old son, Ralph Bouquet, to help perfect arrangements for the celebration.

A bayonet used by the Royal Infantry, and found on the Bushy Run battle-field by C. Gongaware in 1881, and presented to Rev. Cyrus Cort, of Greencastle, was on exhibition. It is in a good state of preservation. The blade part is sixteen inches long and bears the appearance of having been a very formidable instrument of war.

OLD BOB, THE WAR HORSE.

The celebrated war horse upon which Col. George Covode was shot and killed, is here. He is owned by W. H. Covode, Esq., of Ligonier. He is now 32 years old, and was through the following engagements : Gaines Mill, Charles City Cross Roads, Hedgeville, Antietam, Markham Station, Kelly's Ford, Middleburg, Gettysburg, Upperville, Shepherdstown, Trevillian Station, Todd's Tavern, Sulphur Springs, Deep Bottom, St. Mary's Church, Ream's Station, Stony Creek, &c. Col. Covode rode Bob around Richmond twice, during which he was shot in the neck, the only wound the horse received.

That intrepid son of Mars, Colonel Rogers, divided the Indian honors with Guito, the Seneca youth. The valiant Colonel was gotten up as a great brave in a fearful and wonderful costume, with rings, feathers and a great battle-axe as ornaments. To attempt a description of his outfit would be to essay to "paint the lily." It is enough to say that his make-up was purely and typically Rogerian and that he was the observed of all observers.

Captain Samuel Bell, of South Huntingdon township, with a company of 100 uniformed men on horseback.

A delegation of five arrived from Irwin on bicycles.

J. V. Stephenson, Adison Barnhart, Harry Huffman, Eli Beck, Joseph Guffey and B. J. Johnston arrived at 9 o'clock on bicycles.

Several amusing incidents occurred while the surveying party were engaged in marking the battle-field.

John Layton (colored) assisted at the work, and his mind was evidently quite wrought up by hearing details of the fight. He gave vent to his feelings by such exclamations as these : "I tell you what, didn't William Penn and his soldiers have a hard time of it here ? What terrible sufferings our ancestors had to go through," &c.

After hearing the story of Kuykyuskung, (pages 40–42 of Bouquet pamphlet), some of the boys concluded to have a little fun and do some marking on their own account. Accordidgly they marked a board as follows, and nailed it to a large oak tree by the roadside, and near the scene of Bouquet's final strategic movement so disastrous to the savages : "Here one bloody injun, Kookyoosti, was kilt." A great crowd surrounded that tree on Celebration Day, and many pieces of its bark were taken away as relics.

The large Swiss national flag with its red field and white cross in the centre, presented a fine appearance, as did also the smaller one with its gilt fringing.

MONUMENT COLLECTIONS.

A number of gentlemen were furnished with subscription lists to get contributions for the monument proposed to be erected to Col. Bouquet and his army on the battle-field. But it seems very little was done for this laudable object, except by some of the citizens of Irwin and Stewartsville and vicinity, who, besides raising $56 to help defray expenses of the celebration, also gave forty dollars ($40) toward the monument fund. This $40 with a goodly part of the $56, were given by descendants of Andrew Byerly, of Bushy Run. If

Greensburg, Penn., Harrison City, Manor, and other places would do as well in proportion, a granite memorial column would soon crown the summit of the battle-field, which would permanently identify the place and perpetuate the memory of the decisive conflict and the gallant heroes through all coming time.

Several hundred dollars more are needed for this monument fund, which we trust the public-spirited citizens of Western Pennsylvania will contribute at an early date. A grand work has already been accomplished by the celebration of August 6, 1883, and the various publications relating to Bouquet which it called forth. But without the monument the projectors and advocates and actors in that commemoration feel that the main object of their endeavors remains to be realized. This fund is in charge of General Coulter, Amos B. Kline and James Gregg, (Treasurer), of Greensburg, to whom contributions may be safely entrusted. Furnish them $300 more, and the monument will be put up, and a grand dedication service will bring to a fitting conclusion the praiseworthy efforts to honor the memory of Henry Bouquet and the 1763 Army of Deliverance. One way of helping the cause is to circulate the pamphlet relating to Bouquet, his campaigns and the celebration of the Bushy Run victory. As the *Freiheit's Freund*, of Pittsburg, stated in one of its issues, these pamphlets "ought to be put into the hands of every school boy and girl in Pennsylvania." As a limited number of copies have been printed and the work not stereotyped, the time will probably soon come when they will be as rare and expensive as Bouquet's original narrative, a copy of which recently brought upwards of fifty dollars. And yet without them no Pennsylvania library can be considered complete. Their preparation has been a labor of love on the part of him who has borne the chief burden of toil and expense from a sense of gratitude to the noble Swiss hero who rescued his ancestors from the tomahawk and scalping-knife of the merciless savages. But thousands of others in our Keystone Commonwealth, yea, all over this great Republic, are also greatly indebted to Henry Bouquet, and should esteem it a duty and privilege to help perpetuate the memory of his noble character and his heroic deeds.

GUYASUTHA.

The reputed leader of the savages at Bushy Run battle and the siege of Fort Pitt, was Guyasutha, the chief of a band of Seneca Indians located in Ohio, who, along with the Mingoes, belonged to the Ioquois or famous Six Nations, from Central and Western New York. His name is spelled in half a dozen different ways. As a young brave he went with Washington from Logstown to LaBœuf in 1754. He was a leading character in the conference with Gen. Bradstreet when that conceited officer was hoodwinked by the wily savages near Lake Erie in 1764. A few weeks later he had to deal with a different style of man in his conference with Col. Bouquet on the Muskingum. His eloquent and politic speech on that occasion is given in the Bouquet pamphlet, page 68. In April and May, 1768, he was leading actor at a conference at Fort Pitt. When Washington descended the Ohio in 1770 Guyasutha visited him and was recognized as one of his companions in 1754.

In 1775, two days after the Westmoreland patriots had promulgated their Declaration of Indpendence, on May 16, at Hannastown and Fort Pitt, Guyasutha, who had just returned from Niagara, held a conference at Fort Pitt with Majors Trent and Ward and Captain Neville. Capt. Pipe, a Delaware chief, and Shade, a Shawnese chief, and several other Shawnese, took part. Guyasutha announced that the Six Nations and their allies in Ohio would remain neutral during the impending war between the British and the American Colonists. He said: " Brothers, we will not suffer either English or Americans to pass through our country. Should either attempt it we will forewarn them three times, and should they persist they must abide the consequences. I am appointed by the Six Nations to take care of this country, that is, of the Indians on the other side of the Ohio, and I desire that you will not think of an expedition against Detroit, for, to repeat, we will not suffer an army to pass through our country.''

In 1782, July 13, Guyasutha led the attack on Hannastown. He seems to have been the greatest leader of Pontiac's Eastern confederates, but had his forces shattered at Bushy Run by Bouquet, after the best contested battle ever fought by the red savages on American soil. In view of his prominence, the war is sometimes called "Guyasutha's War," as well as "Pontiac's War." Finally, he died near Pittsburg, at an advanced age, leaving his name to the beautiful plain on the Allegheny river, where his remains now rest.

Neville B. Craig gives most of the foregoing facts in his History of Pittsburg (pages 136–9), and was personally acquainted with Guyasutha, when he tarried superfluous on the stage a striking emblem of the decayed condition of the Six Nations, as in the prime of life he had been a fit representative of their power and glory. Once the Iroquois carried dismay to all the savage tribes between the Atlantic and the Father of Waters, and between the Gulf of Mexico and the great Lakes of the North. Yea, to French and English alike, in Canada and the United States. They were the recognized lords of the savage wilderness, and exacted tribute from the powerful Catawbas and Cherokees in the distant South, who traveled along the war-path through the wilds of Westmoreland, from year to year, with tokens of obeisance and servitude to the great Council House at Onondaga. And thus, like the old Romans, their power and glory, founded on rapine, has departed, in spite of all their superior courage, energy and governmental genius.

CONCLUDING REMARKS.

A shade of sadness comes over us as we bring this memorial volume to a close. A number of public-spirited citizens, who took part in the celebration, and who were most highly gratified and warmest in their congratulations over its success, have passed away since that memorable sixth of August, 1883. Hon. Joseph H. Kuhns, who seemed to renew his youth in his efforts to promote the commemoration ; General Thomas F. Gallagher, the stalwart hero of Gaines' Mills and South Mountain ; Dr. Samuel Wilson, who was stricken down with fatal disease on the eve of the celebration, in which he fondly hoped to take part ; ex-Senator Cowan and others, distinguished in forum and field, have passed across the river. This is a solemn reminder that we, who remain, "should be up and doing," to finish the work so grandly begun.

MEMORIAL

OF

ENOCH BROWN

AND

ELEVEN SCHOLARS,

Who Were Massacred in Antrim Township, Franklin
County, Pa., by the Indians, During the
Pontiac War, July 26, 1764,

CONTAINING

ADDRESSES OF GEORGE W. ZIEGLER, ESQ., REV. CYRUS CORT, HON.
PETER A. WITMER, REV. F. A. WOODS AND DR. WM. H. EGLE,
AND POEM OF JOHN M. COOPER, ESQ., AT THE DEDICA-
TION OF THE ENOCH BROWN PARK AND MONU-
MENTS, THREE MILES NORTH OF GREEN-
CASTLE, PA., AUGUST 4, 1885,
WITH CENTENNIAL SERMONS, APPENDIX, &C.

———————

*Edited by REV. CYRUS CORT, in behalf of the
Enoch Brown Monument Committee.*

———————

LANCASTER, PA.
STEINMAN & HENSEL, PRINTERS,
1886.

DEDICATION.

*TO the Teachers and Scholars of all the Schools, secular
and religious, in Franklin County, Pa., who aided by
their contributions and their labors in securing the Enoch
Brown Park and Monuments; also, to the Christian people and public-spirited citizens of the county, and of other
counties, who helped along the good cause with their generous gifts, this volume is affectionately dedicated. " The
righteous shall be in everlasting remembrance."*

TABLE OF CONTENTS.

MONUMENT ON THE SITE OF ENOCH BROWN SCHOOL HOUSE.

Enoch Brown Memorial.

INTRODUCTORY SKETCH.

A FEW years after the French and Indian Wars came the
Pontiac War of 1763–4, when the great chieftain of
the Ottawas marshaled the tribes between the great lakes
and the Alleghenies into hostile camps against the English
and their colonial subjects. His avowed purpose was to
drive the red coats and pale faces into the sea. No less
than ten forts between Detroit and Fort Pitt were captured,
and most of their garrisons massacred. Detroit, Fort Pitt
and Ligonier were closely besieged for months by the savages.
Col. Henry Bouquet with a force of about five hundred
men, mostly Scotch highlanders, broke the eastern wing of
Pontiac's conspiracy by defeating his confederates under
Guyasutha, &c., after a desperate two days battle at Edge
Hill or Bushy Run, Aug. 5 and 6, 1763. The gallant commander begged for a few hundred more troops with which
to penetrate to the haunts of the Indians in central Ohio
and thus bring the war to a decisive close. But the Quaker
provincial authorities disregarded his appeals for the much
needed reinforcements. As a consequence, prowling bands
of savages made frequent raids into the settlements, killing
and scalping the pioneer settlers in Pennsylvania, Maryland
and Virginia regardless of age, sex or condition. In one
of these forays into the Cumberland Valley on the twenty-
sixth day of July, 1764, there was perpetrated, what Parkman, the historian of Colonial times, pronounces " an out-

A

rage unmatched in fiendish atrocity through all the annals of the war.''

This was the cold-blooded massacre of Enoch Brown, a worthy Christian school-master, and eleven scholars, at a little log school-house in Antrim township, three miles north of where Greencastle now stands.

Eight years before to the very day (July 26, 1756,) John McCullough, eight years old, and his little brother had been carried away captive by five Delaware Indians and a Frenchman, from their home, a few miles southwest of the school house, and at this time John was living as an adopted son, among the Delaware Indians on the banks of the Muskingum. In his narrative, as published in Border Life, &c., it is stated that the massacre of the school-master and scholars was perpetrated by three young warriors from that locality, who brought the scalps of master and scholars back as bloody trophies of their trip into the settlements. Neeppaugh-weese, Night Walker, an old chief or half king, and other old Indians denounced them for killing so many children and called them cowards, the greatest affront that could be offered them.

The original MSS. of the McCullough narrative, now in the possession of John McCullough, a grandson of the captive lad, contains no reference to the massacre, but the family are confident that their ancestor furnished the account as given in Border Life, &c.

Others have claimed that the massacre was perpetrated by a squad of Seneca Indians from western New York. Richard Bard in his narrative states that his father was at work near the place of massacre on the 26th of July, 1764, and owing to the strange movements of his dog he concluded that Indians were skulking in the thicket near by. He retreated to the house and in about an hour saw a party commanded by Capt. Potter (afterwards Gen. Potter of the Revolution) who were in pursuit of a party of Indians, who had on that morning murdered a school-master named Brown with ten small children, and had scalped and left for dead one by the name of Archibald McCullough, who recovered. * * According to the story of the boy, two old Indians and a young Indian rushed up to the door soon after the opening of the morning session. The master, surmising their object, prayed them only to take his life and spare the children, but all were brutally knocked in the head with an Indian maul and scalped. Some of the traditions represent the Indians as shooting the master down when they approached the door, and that on his knees he begged them to spare the lives of the little ones.

Parkman, in his "Conspiracy of Pontiac," Vol. 2, says : "In the centre lay the master, scalped and lifeless, with a Bible clasped in his hand ; while around the room were strewn the bodies of his pupils, miserably mangled, though one of them still retained a spark of life. The deed was committed by three or four warriors from an Indian village near the Ohio."

The savage fiends made good their escape, and the horror-stricken settlers buried the master and ten scholars in a large box, placed alternately head and feet in opposite directions in a common grave a few rods from the scene of slaughter. Seventy-nine years afterwards (Aug. 4. 1843) the traditional account of the burial was verified by excavations made by about twenty citizens of Antrim township, including Geo. W. Ziegler, Esq., Dr. Jas. K. Davison and Gen. David Detrich who still remain with us in a hale old age. Christian Koser, the owner of the land, planted four locust trees at the corners of the grave ; two of these grew for thirty odd years, when, strange to tell, they were cut down for posts. There was danger that the sacred spot would pass into oblivion. Col. B. F. Winger, Gen. David Detrich and Rev. Cyrus Cort visited the location in the spring of 1883, (April 11), and a month later, May 14, laid the matter before a meeting of the citizens of Greencastle, at which Geo. W. Ziegler, Esq., presided. Steps were taken looking to the purchase of the land and the erection of a monument, but nothing definite was done until the attention of the Franklin County Centennial Convention of April 22, 1884, was called to the subject.

This convention, composed of representative men from all parts of the county, appointed a committee, consisting of Rev. Cyrus Cort, Wm. G. Davison, Col. G. B. Wiestling,

Dr. A. H. Strickler and Benj. Chambers, to devise plans for raising funds to erect a monument, &c.

At the afternoon session of the Convention the committee reported as follows:

Your committee appointed to prepare a proper plan for securing permanent results from the Centennial Celebration in the shape of a Monument to the memory of Schoolmaster Enoch Brown and the ten school children massacred by merciless savages, July 26th 1764, respectfully report the following for the consideration of this Convention :

Resolved, That the sum of at least two thousand dollars be raised for the purpose of securing a suitable amount of land on the farm of Capt. Jacob Diehl, in Antrim township, including the spot where Schoolmaster Brown and his ten children were massacred by the Indians, July 26th, 1764, and where they are now buried; and of enclosing the same with a suitable fence and likewise of erecting an appropriate monument to their memory and keeping the same in permanent repair.

Resolved, That the aforesaid fund shall be raised in the name of the teachers and scholars of all the schools in the county, including common schools, select schools and Sunday schools.

Resolved, That all the teachers and scholars of the schools aforesaid be earnestly requested to contribute at least one dime each toward the fund on or before Sept. 9, 1884, and the names of all teachers and scholars so contributing or collecting at least one dime shall be recorded in a suitable book to be preserved in the archives of the Historical Society of Franklin County.

Resolved, That the committee of the respective townships be directed to take immediate steps to have the foregoing school collections taken up, either by the teachers at present or lately in charge of the schools, or by some suitable person in each school district.

Resolved, That in aid of this fund we recommend that a collection be taken at all the memorial religious services held on the Sunday preceding the Centennial Anniversary, viz: September 7th, 1884.

Resolved, That in further aid of this fund we recommend that the Executive Centennial Committee be directed to request the various railroads in the county to contribute a generous rebate on all excursion tickets issued on account of the Centennial Celebration.

Resolved, That a committee of five be appointed to receive the funds and carry into effect the action proposed in the foregoing resolution in regard to the purchase of land, erection of monument, &c.

Resolved, That the above committee be directed to request the Court of Franklin County, or other competent authority, to appoint three trustees to invest not less than five hundred dollars of the funds in securities approved by the court, the annual proceeds to be devoted to keeping the grounds, monument and fences in good condition and repair.

Resolved, That the newspapers of the county be earnestly requested to urge the importance of this memorial feature of the Centennial upon the attention of the people of Franklin county.

The report was unanimously adopted by the Convention, and on the motion of Col. Wiestling, the committee called for in the seventh resolution was appointed as follows: Rev. Cyrus Cort, (chairman); Dr. A. H. Strickler (treasurer); Hon. D. W. Rowe, Capt. R. J. Boyd and Col. W. D. Dixon.

On the following day, April 23d, the committee contracted with Capt. Diehl, through Col. B. F. Winger, for the enclosed tract or field which contains the site of the school house, the grave of Enoch Brown, and scholars, together with the spring adjacent.

April 29th, the land was surveyed under the supervision of Col. Winger, along with Rev. Cort, Dr. Strickler and Col. Dixon of the committee. Capt. Diehl obligated himself in writing to give a deed for the land as soon as the surveyor had completed his plot and estimates. The committee pay at the rate of twenty-five dollars per acre.

The committee bought more land than was at first contemplated, for the reason that it was cheaper to purchase the entire field of a fraction less than twenty acres at $25 per acre, than to buy four or five acres in the heart of the field for $30 per acre, fence it in with a strong and durable fence and give bonds to keep the same in good repair for all time to come, which was the alternative presented by the owner of the tract.

The surplus land can be sold and the cost of outside fencing saved, together with the expense and liability of a bond binding through all time and necessitating an investment as large as the cost of the entire field. A public road has been laid out along the north side of the Enoch Brown Park as the tract is now called. It required a great deal of work to reclaim the historic spring and clear off the ground between it and the grave. For several weeks during the hottest weather the chairman of the committee, assisted by other public spirited citizens, "worked with head, heart, hand and horse" to accomplish this praiseworthy undertak-

ing, as the poet John M. Cooper, Esq., expressed it in his
report of the dedication services in the Carlisle *Volunteer.*
The contract for erecting the monuments was awarded to
Mr. W. N. Meredith, of Mercersburg, for the sum of $500,
the committee furnishing the limestone foundations. Hundreds have visited the Park since dedication day, and have
uniformly expressed their gratification with the monuments,
iron fences and improvements made by the committee with
the funds at their command. Other items of historic interest are omitted here because they appear in the addresses.

MONUMENT OVER THE COMMON GRAVE OF ENOCH BROWN AND TEN SCHOLARS.

THE DEDICATION CEREMONIES.

THE following account of the dedication ceremonies, organization, speeches, &c., we cull in the main from the Greencastle *Press* of August 6, 1885:

UNVEILING AND DEDICATION.

August 4, 1885, was indeed the red letter day for Mother Antrim. Never before in her history was there such an outpouring of her beauty and chivalry to honor and grace a public occasion as that which congregated at Enoch Brown Park on Dedication Day. The two previous days had been · stormy and foreboding. The long wished for rain had deluged the earth in torrents and many feared that the weather would be unfavorable for the ceremonies. But there never dawned a lovelier day for the occasion than last Tuesday. At an early hour a stream of visitors began to pour out over the hills to the Park until about 5,000 people had assembled on the historic field. The large monument on the site of the school house, which can be seen from afar, first attracted attention, and around it a large concourse of people were soon assembled. Then the beatiful monument of smaller proportions over the common grave of Schoolmaster Enoch Brown and ten scholars was next visited, and around it many lingered with deep and melancholy interest. Then the historic spring at the foot of the hill, a few yards off, drew the multitude, not only to gratify curiosity, but to slake their thirst, and thousands there partook of nature's cooling beverage, as did the scholars of Enoch Brown one hundred and twenty-one years ago. It was equal to the large demands, although one hundred and fifty gallons had been dipped out the previous evening after dusk.

Shortly after 11 o'clock Rev. Cyrus Cort arrived with Poet Cooper and Historian Egle and daughter in his carriage, the morning train on which they came from Harrisburg having been delayed about half an hour.

The meeting was called to order by Col. B. F. Winger, Chief Marshal. Mounting the base of the monument the Rev. Cort made a few preliminary remarks and then four little girls and nine boys, viz., Rose Winger, Libbie Seacrest, Sally Whitmore and Carrie Hawbecker, Paul Cort, Paul Sunners, Ambrose Cort, Ambrose Walck, Harry Fuss, Elmer Pentz, George Pentz, George Gorden and Willie Meredith, pulled the cords, the mantle of red, white and blue fell and the monument stood forth a thing of beauty and strength, the delight of all beholders. It is indeed a massive affair. On the top of four feet of solid masonry underneath the ground are nearly four feet of dressed limestone of immense proportions from Hawbecker's Williamson quarry. On the top of this limestone foundation, which is five feet square, is placed the granite base of the monument, four feet square and seventeen inches high, and weighing 4,600 pounds. Next comes the polished die or sub-base, three feet square and two feet high, on the four sides of which are engraved the inscriptions. On the top of this stands the shaft of the monument, two feet square at the base, ten feet high and tapering gracefully to a pyramidal apex. The shaft weighs 4,100 pounds. Enclosing the monument is a very substantial iron fence, fifteen feet square. The following are the inscriptions:

On the East side:

SACRED TO THE MEMORY OF SCHOOL-MASTER ENOCH BROWN AND ELEVEN SCHOLARS, VIZ: RUTH HART, RUTH HALE, EBEN TAYLOR, GEORGE DUNSTAN, ARCHIE McCULLOUGH, AND SIX OTHERS, (NAMES UNKNOWN) WHO WERE MASSACRED AND SCALPED BY INDIANS ON THIS SPOT, JULY 26, 1764, DURING THE PONTIAC WAR.

On the North side :

ERECTED BY DIRECTION OF THE FRANKLIN COUN-
TY CENTENNIAL CONVENTION OF APRIL 22, 1884, IN
THE NAME OF THE TEACHERS AND SCHOLARS OF ALL
THE SCHOOLS IN THE COUNTY, INCLUDING COMMON
SCHOOLS, SELECT SCHOOLS AND SUNDAY SCHOOLS.
FOR A FULL LIST OF CONTRIBUTORS SEE ARCHIVES
OF FRANKLIN COUNTY HISTORICAL SOCIETY OR RE-
CORDER'S OFFICE.

West side inscription, next to grave :

THE REMAINS OF ENOCH BROWN AND TEN SCHOL-
ARS (ARCHIE MCCULLOUGH SURVIVED THE SCALP-
ING) LIE BURIED IN A COMMON GRAVE, SOUTH 62¼
DEGREES, WEST 14½ RODS FROM THIS MONUMENT.
THEY FELL AS PIONEER MARTYRS IN THE CAUSE OF
EDUCATION AND CHRISTIAN CIVILIZATION.

On the South side :

The ground is holy where they fell,
  And where their mingled ashes lie,
Ye Christian people mark it well
  With granite column strong and high ;
And cherish well forevermore
  The storied wealth of early years,
  The sacred legacies of yore,
  The toils and trials of pioneers.

The latter are the concluding stanzas of a poem published
last Spring in the town papers and in the Guardian, a
monthly magazine issued in Philadelphia.

The small monument was unveiled at the grave by Rev.
Cort after a few preliminary remarks.   It is a very chaste
A*

and pretty structure, composed, like the larger monument, of Concord granite. It is about seven feet high and two feet square at the base. On the side facing the grave is this inscription, "The grave of Schoolmaster Enoch Brown and Ten Scholars, massacred by the Indians July 26, 1764." Around it is also a solid iron fence ten feet square. A heavy stone wall has been erected near the south end of the grave and considerable filling has been done. The Mercersburg band played a dirge at the large monument and the Greencastle and Shady Grove bands at the smaller when the unveiling took place. The assemblage then repaired to the stand erected in the grove belonging to the Park, where the remaining ceremonies were conducted according to the published programme.

George W. Ziegler, Esq., was chosen President for the day and made a short address heartily approving the cause which had brought the people together and commending the Monument Committee for its faithful and energetic labors. Rev. J. D. Hunter then offered a very appropriate prayer. The Reformed church choir, under the lead of Prof. Collins assisted by a few amateurs, sang "America," "My Country, 'tis of Thee," and afterwards the "The Infant Martyrs," a hymn composed by Dr. Henry Harbaugh on the martyred babes of Bethlehem who were slain by King Herod. The organization was completed by the election of the vice-presidents and secretaries, viz.:

Vice Presidents, Rev. J. Spangler Kiefer, Hagerstown, Md.; General David Detrich, Dr. James K. Davidson, Captain Jacob Deihl, Antrim; Jacob Hoke, Judge Kimmel, Rev. Herbert, Chambersburg; Jacob B. Brumbaugh, Peters; Simon Lecron, D. C. Shank, George J. Balsley, D. O. Nicodemus, Washington; Joseph Winger, Montgomery; Dr. Frick, Quincy; Rev. Kappenberger, John Hoch, Mercersburg; Rev. Bahner, Waynesboro; Rev. Riddle, Fairfax, Va.; Andrew K. Kissecker, Tiffin, Ohio. Secretaries, W. G. Davison, W. C. Kreps, Greencastle; Bruce Laudebaugh, G. W. Atherton, Mercersburg; William A. Ried, Antrim; A. N. Pomeroy, Chambersburg.

Rev. Cyrus Cort, chairman of the Monument Committee, then made the presentation speech, which was well received and warmly applauded by the audience. The speaker was heartily congratulated from all sides at the close.

PIC-NIC DINNER.

At this point a recess of an hour was taken to partake of a pic-nic dinner in the woods. It was an interesting and picturesque sight to see families and groups of families enjoying the sumptuous meals which they spread upon the leaves and grass or upon improvised tables throughout the beautiful grove. The speakers, Witmer, Woods (and lady), Egle (and daughter), and poet Cooper, together with some of the clergy, were entertained at one table near the stand by President Ziegler, Marshal Winger and Chairman Cort and their families, and seemed to greatly enjoy their dinner and the surroundings. A balmy breeze floated among the trees, and nature and Providence combined to make the scene one long to be remembered, adding a peculiar zest to the spirit of hospitality and good will that pervaded the occasion.

AFTERNOON SESSION.

After dinner the exercises at the stand were resumed. Rev. J. W. Knappenberger, of Mercersburg, made a short and very appropriate prayer. Peter A. Witmer, Esq., of Hagerstown, Superintendent of Public Schools of Washington county, Md., made an eloquent and able address, conveying the cordial greetings of a sister State and a neighboring county, endorsing heartily the movement. He said: "Enoch Brown was a nobler hero than the blood-stained warriors or thousands of others who were so often honored in this way. The school house was the symbol of our civilization and that brave and self-sacrificing man, who was ready to yield his life as a sacrifice for his scholars, was a pioneer and a martyr in a blessed cause. He was worthy the high honors shown him to-day." Rev. F. M. Woods, of Martinsburg, W. Va., then delivered an excellent speech in fine style. He paid a glowing tribute to the sterling Scotch-Irish pioneer settlers, who came to this new world that they might have freedom to worship God. They were ready to leave kindred and country and sunder the dearest earthly ties for conscience sake. They asked not "Will it pay?" "Will it be popular?" but "Is it right?" and, fearing God, they had no fear of man. What added peculiar interest to Rev. Mr. Wood's remarks is the fact that he is married to a daughter of Rev. D. X. Junkin, who is a descendant of Eleanor Cochrane. His wife sat immediately behind him on the platform, and seemed to enjoy the occasion beyond all others present, which is saying a great deal.

Next came the poem, by John M. Cooper, Esq., the gifted bard of Antrim. Like all other productions from Mr. Cooper's pen, it was beautiful and classic. It threw a halo of poetic fancy around the memory of the martyred schoolmaster and scholars.

Finally Dr. Wm. H. Egle, of Harrisburg, Pa., delivered in an effective manner the historial address of the occasion on "Pontiac and Bouquet," with especial reference to the part taken by Provincial troops in the campaign of 1763–4. He contrasted these distinguished leaders of the red and white races as the representatives of savagery and civilization, and sketched graphically the leading events in the campaigns of 1763–4. He paid a glowing tribute to the memory of Enoch Brown (he called him Enoch all the time), the brave, true-hearted schoolmaster, who fell with his scholars before the brutality of incarnate fiends. The Doctor evidently has no special love for the Indian character and believes that the uncivilized red man illustrates fully the doctrine of total depravity. He paid a very handsome compliment to Rev. C. Cort, not only for his persevering and successful efforts in behalf of the Enoch Brown Monument, but as the author of an "elegant work" on Bouquet and his campaign of 1763–4.

At the close Col. Winger moved a vote of thanks to the speakers and poet, and that they be requested to furnish copies of their speeches and poem to the Enoch Brown Monument Committee for publication. A vote of thanks was also returned to the five bands present for their gratuitous services, viz: The bands of Mercersburg, Clay Hill, Shady Grove, New Franklin and Greencastle.

The benediction was finally pronounced by Rev. John R. Agnew, a grandson of Mary Ramsey, one of the scholars of the Enoch Brown school, who Providentially escaped the massacre.

Col. Wiestling was to have made the reception speech, but was unable to be present. His substitute failing to appear, the following letter was read: '

MONT ALTO, July 29, 1885.

Rev. Cyrus Cort, Chairman Enoch Brown Monument Committee :

MY DEAR SIR: For several weeks I have had but little respite from severe suffering from acute rheumatism following in the wake of a sprained knee. This has so disabled me that business matters have accumulated on my hands to such an extent as to render it exceedingly improbable that I can ever attend the unveiling ceremonies on August 4.

Although (as I advised you) I feared this contingency, yet I feel sadly disappointed, and deeply regret my inability to celebrate with you what I consider an important event. I know it will be interesting; I know you will be happy, because the consciousness of having faithfully fulfilled the trust committed to you by the people of Franklin County through their representatives in convention, cannot but make you congratulate each other as I heartily do you all. Yes, I congratulate the citizens of our county on the successful consummation of the crowning feature in the programme of the Centennial celebration, so happily woven into history by the untiring and effective labors of your committee. The convention made no mistake in determining upon the crowning memorial, it did not eir in providing the way to secure means for its accomplishment, and it was equally fortunate in selecting a committee of ability, industry and unswerving integrity to its commission, a committee, the chairmanship of which you have a right to be proud. As compensation for my absence I enclose my check for twenty dollars additional contribution to the Monument fund; but how I am to be compensated for the loss of my anticipated pleasure in being with you, I know not.　　　　　　　Very truly yours,

GEO. B. WIESTLING.

The following letter was also read from Rev. Prof. Jos. H. Dubbs, D. D., Professor of History, &c., in Franklin and Marshall College :

Rev. C. Cort:

MR DEAR SIR: I regret that it will not be in my power to be present at the dedication of the Enoch Brown Monument. It is in my opinion an occasion of profound interest, and I hope it may command the general respect which is manifestly deserves. We have in this country but imperfectly learned the lesson that in honoring our ancestors we honor ourselves; but the day will surely come when your disinterested labors in this direction will be fully appreciated.

I remain fraternally yours,

JOS. HENRY DUBBS.

The following letter from Governor Pattison and extracts from letters of Horatio Seymour and Thos. G. Apple to Rev. Cort were read :

FROM THE GOVERNOR.

EXECUTIVE DEPARTMENT, COMMONWEALTH OF PENN'A, }
OFFICE OF THE GOVERNOR, HARRISBURG, July 28, 1885. }

B. F. Winger, Esq., Greencastle, Pa.

SIR : I am directed by the Governor to acknowledge your very kind invitation to attend the ceremonies of the unveiling and dedication of the monument erected to the memory of Enoch Brown and his ten scholars who were massacred by Indians one hundred and twenty-one years ago, three miles north of Greencastle. The Governor regrets that his official engagements which cover the 4th day of August will require his presence at Erie, Pa., as President of the commission to establish and maintain a Home of Pennsylvania Soldiers and Sailors. For this reason he cannot be present. But he directs me to express his sincere gratification that the memory of the pioneer school-master is thus to be perpetuated and that the children who with him were stricken down at their humble shrine of learning are not forgotten by those who live in the enjoyment of the Christian civilization of the present day.

I am   Very truly yours,

THOS. T. EVERETT,
Private Secretary.

The people then returned to their homes highly gratified with what they had seen and heard at the Enoch Brown Park. All were pleased with the monuments, the iron fences and other improvements made by the committee. All were delighted with the literary exercises. The poet, who is an excellent judge of large experience, remarked in the evening " I never heard four better speeches on any public occasion than those delivered to-day." He repeatedly announced his intention to bring his entire family to Antrim township at an early day to show them the beautiful and lasting monuments and all the historic scenes belonging to the Enoch Brown Park. He considered it by far the grandest day ever seen in Mother Antrim, and said that the crowd around the speaker's stand was larger than " he had ever seen listening to a speech of any kind in Franklin County."

Many and hearty were the congratulations showered upon the chairman of the monument committee at the close of the meeting. He felt amply rewarded for all the toil and trouble which the monument project has given him by the outcome of this red letter day.

Chief Marshal Col. B. F. Winger performed his duties with great tact and efficiency. The following is the list of aids as appointed and revised by himself, viz: Wm. Snyder, Charles B. Cayl, Edward S. Snively, John W. Kuhn, D. I. Binkley, John H. Baumbaugh, John McCulloch, Upton G. Hawbaker, Dr. Leslie Lecron, C. C. Pentz, Henry Lenherr, W. L. G. Unger, Seth Dickey, Dr. H. G. Critzman, Jeremiah Ashway, Claggett Seacrest, Wm. J. Zacharias, Max Ways, J. W. Wister, Capt. L. Henkell, Paul L. Cort, Geo. W. Frye and George Crunkleton.

SPEECH OF GEORGE W. ZIEGLER, ESQ.,

OF GREENCASTLE, PENN'A.

George W. Ziegler, on being chosen president of the meeting, spoke as follows:

LADIES AND GENTLEMEN:—I thank you for the honor of the position assigned me as presiding officer of this large and respectable meeting on this very interesting and important occasion; and permit me to congratulate you on the bright and glorious sun that greets us from a cloudless sky, to cheer and gladden our hearts in the enjoyment of the ceremonies and intellectual feast that awaits us.

The wooded hillside upon which we are now assembled is sacred and historic ground, consecrated and hallowed by the wanton and brutal destruction of human life and spilling of innocent blood more than a century ago.

On the 26th day of July, A. D. 1764, a small squad of hostile and treacherous Indians made their appearance upon these grounds, and with revenge and murder in their hearts they stealthily stole their way to the southeastern declivity of this hill, where then stood an humble pioneer school house, occupied by teacher Enoch Brown and eleven of his scholars (thank God the number present on that eventful day was not greater), and as soon as it was reached they suddenly and fiercely rushed in, and with glaring eyes and upraised bludgeons in their hands confronted them, and, deaf to the noble appeal of humanity on the part of Brown to spare the lives of his scholars, at the sacrifice of his own, and their piteous shrieks and cries for mercy, they at once commenced the slaughter of master and children, and in cold blood massacred the whole school, save little Archie McCullough, whom they supposed dead, but who afterward revived; and while teacher and scholars were still agonizing in the throes and convulsions of death they proceeded in the awful and horrible work of securing their scalps, that they might bear them back, in their blood-stained hands, as trophies of their victory to the bloodthirsty chieftain, who had no doubt detailed them on their revengeful mission of destruction and death.

This act on the part of the Indians is unquestionably the most cowardly, bloody and atrocious tragedy that stains the annals of our border warfare in the Cumberland valley, during the dark and bloody days of its Colonial history; and, although more than a hundred years have come and gone since its enactment, yet we cannot listen to its recital without a sigh and shudder of sorrow and regret for the sad and lamentable fate of its innocent victims.

But enough of this awful and horrible story, and let us now joyfully turn to its interesting and fitting sequel, which is about to reach its culmination in the ceremonies of this day.

At a meeting of the Franklin County Centennial Convention, held in Chambersburg, on the 22d day of April, 1884, the Rev. Cyrus Cort and Col. George B. Wiestling, and other public spirited gentlemen of the convention, induced that body to take action for the adoption of certain necessary measures for the promotion and consummation of the laudable and commendable movement inaugurated at a meeting held by a number of the liberal minded citizens of the borough of Greencastle, on the 14th of May, 1883, looking to the erection of a monument, &c., to the memory of Enoch Brown and his scholars, massacred on this hill on the 26th of July, 1764.

And to these preliminary movements and the untiring labors of the Centennial, County and Monument Committees, and for the faithful, proper and speedy manner in which they prosecuted the work assigned them by the Franklin County Centennial Convention, we stand greatly indebted this day for the two beautiful and appropriate monuments which now grace and adorn this hill.

The larger of these monuments stands on the site occupied by the rustic school house at the time of the massacre of Schoolmaster Brown and his scholars; and the other, on the small mound, beneath which their sacred dust has long since mingled and now peacefully slumbers in the common grave in which they were buried.

And what could have been more fitting than the manner and place of their burial? all deposited in the same grave, and near beside the little spring, still issuing from the foot of this hill, and where master and scholars together were wont to slake their thirst during the interim of weary school hours.

These monuments were fashioned by skilful, artistic hands, and wrought out of the most enduring materials (Eastern granite and Pennsylvania limestone), and rest on deep and solid foundations, and will for many long centuries to come rescue from oblivion the sacred and hallowed spots they are intended to perpetuate. And I feel warranted in the prophecy, that should some distant antiquary, more than a thousand years hence, make a pilgrimage to this historic hill, that he will find them still intact and standing as erect as we behold them this day.

Enoch Brown needed no monument to perpetuate his name, it is indelibly engraven in the history of the State, and there it will remain forever. "His is one of the few immortal names that were not born to die."

Yet, as a proper and fitting mark of love and honor to this faithful teacher and his lamented scholars, and in fulfillment of a sacred and long neglected duty, these monuments have been erected and we have met here to-day to dedicate them to their memory.

NOTE.—I was present at the exhumation of the remains of Teacher Enoch Brown and his scholars, and according to the most authentic evidence on the subject it took place on the 4th of August, 1843. It

was my mournful privilege to gaze upon their still remaining moulder-
ing bones and other relics connected with their burial, and these not only
established beyond all doubt the identity of the place of their burial,
but also the truth of the traditional story that they were all buried in
one common grave.   GEORGE W. ZIEGLER.

PRESENTATION SPEECH OF REV. CYRUS CORT.

MY CHRISTIAN FRIENDS:—We are glad to meet you here
to-day. We have had a plentiful rain. He giveth grass for
the cattle and herb for the service of man. And now the
skies are bright and the heavens smile upon us. That gracious
Providence which has enabled us to bring all the difficult
and dangerous labors of this monumental project to a safe
and successful conclusion, without harm or accident, still
continues to favor us. To the Lord be all the praise, the
honor and the glory of the achievement.

The greatest leader and lawgiver of the human race tells
us to "remember the days of old and consider the years
of many generations." This is the parting counsel of Moses.
It is the swan song, yea, the key-note of the swan song of
that man of God at the close of his earthly pilgrimage.
The trials, the sufferings and heroic deeds of their ancestors,
the gracious dealings of the great Jehovah in former years,
were to be kept in everlasting remembrance. A reverential
historic spirit is one of the noblest attributes of true manhood. It is also one of the safeguards of society. It pro-
motes the best interests of religion and patriotism. Such a
spirit makes great account of memorial occasions. It
brings us into living communion with the heroic past. Under
the guide and inspiration of a reverential historic spirit the
Hebrews and Greeks marched in the vanguard of human
history in developing the ideas of religion and classic culture.
In the interest of that spirit we are assembled to-day. To-
day we rescue from oblivion hallowed scenes consecrated by
the martyr blood of innocent childhood and the self-sacrificing privations of pioneers. To-day we commemorate a
typical event, full of pathetic interest and engrave it as a
memorial in the rock forever. The massacre of School-

master Enoch Brown and ten scholars and the horrid mang-
ling of the eleventh on this spot by the Indian savages,
July 26, 1764, was an "outrage," says Parkman, "unmatched in its fiendlike atrocity through all the annals of
the war," that terrible Pontiac war, so full of bloodshed
and horror. It was an event indeed almost unique in human
history. Hundreds of years before the dawn of the Christian era a band of bloodthirsty Thracian soldiers wantonly
butchered the teacher and all the scholars belonging to a
boys' school at Megalissus in Greece. For thousands of
years that event stood alone as an example of human bar-
barity, as a contrast between civilization and barbarism,
until it was outdone by the massacre of Enoch Brown and
his scholars on this very spot 121 years ago. Here Ruth
Hart and Ruth Hale, George Dunstan, Eben Taylor, Archie
McCullough and six other innocent children were knocked
on the head like so many beeves and the bleeding scalps
torn from their mangled heads and that of Master Enoch
Brown. O ! bloodiest chapter in the book of time ! Here
a holocaust was offered to the red Demon of war by the red
demons of the savage wilderness.

My Christian friends, it is a sacred duty that we discharge
to-day in this tribute of the living to the martyred dead.
Long, too long have the martyrs waited for this memorial.
No class of men or women deserve more to be held in
grateful and everlasting remembrance than the hardy pioneers who rescued the wilderness of this new world from
savage beasts and savage men and changed it into a fruitful
field. As citizens of this magnificent valley we enjoy the
fruits of their toils, their sacrifices and privations, and let us
never forget the memory of their deeds and sufferings. Because Enoch Brown was an honored, useful and trusted
instrument in the higher phases of that work of pioneer
civilization and progress ; because he fell as a self-sacrificing
martyr in that cause at the post of duty and of danger ;
because his eleven scholars fell as innocent victims and true
martyrs in that cause of education and Christian civilization
we set apart these monuments and these grounds as sacred
to their memory forevermore.

We believe that Enoch Brown was a good and true man.

Had we not thought so we would never have toiled as we have done to bring this movement to a successful close. He was a genuine Christian schoolmaster of the olden time, one who taught his scholars not only how to read, write and cypher, but who taught them also the first principles of our holy religion as recorded in the oracles of the living God.   Amid perils he taught such principles as make good citizens and faithful Christians.   Indeed, one of the cherished traditions of the terrible tragedy is that Schoolmaster Brown was shot down with the Bible in his hand before he could make any resistance and on his knees begged only that the innocent children might be spared. Parkman, in describing the ghastly sight that met those who first entered the school house after the massacre says: '' In the centre lay the master, scalped and lifeless, with a Bible clasped in his hands; while around the room were strewn the bodies of his mangled pupils.''   Another tradition says that Mr. Linn, while working in a meadow in the vicinity, heard the shot that killed Schoolmaster Brown, and when he and others came to see what was the matter they found little Archie McCullough, who survived the scalping, sitting by the spring near by washing the blood from his face and mangled head.   He told them that when the four Indians opened the door Master Brown, knowing well their object, begged them to take him as their victim and let the innocent children return to their homes.   The same instant he was shot down, and then he and the children were quickly toma-hawked and scalped by two of the savages while the other two stood with murderous weapons in the doorway.   Other traditions, handed down directly by Betty Hopkins to Gen. Detrich and others, go to show that Enoch Brown did his duty as a true-hearted man, who felt the awful responsibility of the sacred trust committed to him.   Betty Hopkins was a worthy Christian woman, forty years old at the time of the massacre, living within a mile of this very spot.   She saw the mangled bodies of master and ten scholars committed to a common grave by the grief-stricken and horror-stricken community 121 years ago, and her story of the burial was corroborated by the exhumation 79 years after the burial. No word derogatory to the courage or character of Enoch

Brown ever came from her lips in the sixty odd years that
she lived in this locality after the tragedy, which was the
one great absorbing theme of her conversation.   Often did
the General, when a boy, and other young friends read at
her request her favorite chapter in the Bible (the 17th of
the Gospel according to St. John), and then listen in return
to the story of the massacre of Enoch Brown and his ten
scholars.   At length this remarkable woman, this traditional
and Providential bond between the living and the dead,
passed away at the good old age of 104 years, when she was
consigned to her last resting place by the General himself.
Apart from all traditionary accounts, one way and another,
there is enough in the very nature of things to vindicate the
memory of Enoch Brown from all aspersions of cowardice
or incompetency.   Cowards are not apt to teach school on
exposed frontiers in perilous times.   The Scotch-Irish pioneer settlers were heroic, God-fearing people.   No matter
what some of their descendants may do they would have
died in their tracks rather than disappoint a trust, and they
would never have entrusted the lives and education of their
precious children to an incompetent poltroon.   They were
brave and true themselves and expected courage, honor and
fidelity from all in official position.   And when the savages
came in all their fiendish fury and desolated ten Christian
homes at one fell swoop, by butchering those innocent children on this very spot, when there was bitter lamentation
and weeping throughout the Conococheague settlement and
Antrim's hills resounded with the wails of mothers refusing
to be comforted over the destruction of their darling household treasures, think you that those true-hearted, high-souled
men and women would have buried their precious children
in a common grave with Enoch Brown had they not esteemed the schoolmaster as a good, true man, who did all
he could to protect and save the little ones entrusted to his
care?   Never, never, would they have given him such an
honorable sepulture along with their slaughtered innocents
had he not been a worthy and deserving man.   We know
little of the particular families represented in this massacre.
The McCulloughs still remain among our most worthy citizens.   The Harts and Hales, the Dunstans and Taylors,

who patronized this school and who furnished a victim each, have removed or become extinct so far as we know. We know of others, however, who attended this pioneer school, who were Providentially absent on that fatal day, and by their high character we may judge in a measure the teacher and scholars in general. Here came Eleanor Cochrane, who became the wife of Captain Joseph Junkin, a hero of the Revolutionary War, whose right arm was shattered by a musket ball at the battle of Brandywine. She bore him 14 children, 10 sons and 4 daughters. Two of the sons, George and D. X. Junkin, became ministers of the Gospel, and two of the daughters married ministers. In all about thirty of the sons, sons-in-law and grandchildren are in the ministry, and a still larger number are ruling elders. Three of the sons were officers in the war of 1812–14. One of the granddaughters is the wife of Col. Preston, at Lexington, Va., and a gifted poetess. Another granddaughter was the wife of the renowned chieftain of the Southern Confederacy, Stonewall Jackson. A granddaughter is the wife of the reverend gentleman (Rev. Woods,) who will speak to you from this stand to-day and we are glad to have her with us on the platform enjoying these memorial services in honor of the martyred companions of her ancestors. What possibilities are enshrined in the life of one little girl! Here also came Mary Ramsey, the grandmother of our venerable and beloved friend, Rev. John R. Agnew, also present with us, and the grandmother also of his excellent wife and other notable members of the Agnew family and its kindred branches. Two of Mary Ramsey's nieces, the Misses Irwin, married sons of President Wm. H. Harrison. Here also came the Poes, renowned in civil as well as military affairs. You have all heard of the Poe boy who played truant on that particular day and watched mowers in a meadow and caught a thrashing from his strict old father for telling a lie in the evening, claiming that he was at school not having heard of the massacre. Bad boys no doubt have often thought of this as a justification for playing truant. The moral of the fable being that the boy who plays truant saves his scalp. It reminds one of the dialogue between a father and a son who was hard to get out of bed in the morning: "Tom, get up;

the early bird gets the worm." "Served him right. If he had not been up so early he would not have been caught." Now, my friends, I have a new revelation to make, which mars the proportions of the old story somewhat. Last Saturday I received a letter from Mrs. Fannie B. Campbell, well-known to many present, under date of July 29, at Clifton Springs, N. Y. Mrs. Campbell writes : " Dear Mr. Cort : Yours received to-day. The only tradition I have from the Poe family of the massacre of Enoch Brown and children, is that grandfather James Poe was a scholar attending the school at the time, but was detained that day by his mother objecting to his going on account of the cold. He was a very small boy, and had to be sent on horseback in charge of a servant. On that day the horse was at the door waiting for him when his mother interfered. So his life was spared and like the small boy in the Sunday school book, he lived to grow up and go to the Legislature twenty years." That is the latest tradition of the Poe story, and it would be a very acceptable substitute for the truant story if they had only left out that cold wave right on the 26th day of July, 1764. Benj. M. Nead, Esq., tells us in Dr. Egle's " Historical Notes," that at the time James Poe was a lad 16 years old, and went with the party of settlers under Lieut. Potter in pursuit of the Indians who had massacred the schoolmaster and scholars at Guitner's school house. This spoils the truant boy story again. These conflicting traditions show how even good, reliable people get things mixed. They remind us of the man who said he once saw wheat standing so thick that wild turkeys could run over the tops of the heads without sinking to the ground. When asked about the size of the turkeys he said they were whoppers. One day he shot one and it was so heavy that he threw it over his shoulder and it was so large that the head dragged in the snow behind him. When some one remarked that that must have been a queer country where they had snow in harvest time, he replied, " I believe I did get my story a little mixed." So is it with many of these floating traditions. They are a good deal mixed. But be that as it may, the Poes and Potters did really stand in close relationship to this school. The Lieut. Potter who led in pur-

suit of the bloodthirsty Indians afterwards became a General in the Revolutionary army and James Poe was Captain
under him and was married to his daughter. *James Poe
was for many years an honored Representative and Senator
in the State Legislature. His son Thomas was Adjutant and
a very gallant soldier in the war of 1812-14, and fell mor-
tally wounded in the battle of Chippewa. This gives us an
idea of the class of people who patronized the school of
Enoch Brown on these grounds 121 years ago. They belonged to the best class of pioneer settlers, people who came
to America for conscience sake, that they and their children
might have freedom to worship God. An eminent historian
(Dr. Wm. H. Egle) from the capital of our own Keystone
State is here to-day to tell us about Pontiac "the lord of
the savage wilderness," who marshalled the savage hordes
as no Indian chief ever marshalled them before or since, in
that great war of which this massacre of the master and
scholars was one of the characteristic incidents. He will
tell us also about the superb man who hailed from the Alpine
mountains of Republican Switzerland, the heroic Bouquet,
who with his Scotch Highlanders, his German-Swiss Royal
Americans and Provincial Rangers, signally defeated the
confederates of Pontiac at Bushy Run the year before this
massacre occurred, and vainly begged the Quaker provincial
authorities to furnish needed reinforements of a few hundred men, that he might penetrate the forest fastness and
conquer peace on the banks of the Muskingum ; how after
a year of cruel delay and fourteen days after this massacre
he at length was able to set out from Carlisle on that memorable campaign of 1764, which brought peace and tranquility
to the borders and restored several hundred white captives
to the blessings of Christian homes and civilization.
Strange, passing strange it is, that the plowshare should so
long have been allowed to pass over the site of the school
house and the harvests fertilized by the blood of master and
scholars should so long have been reaped on this sacred spot.
Strange that the common grave of master and ten scholars,

---

*Both of these officers lie buried at the Brown's Mill graveyard, a few
miles east of the Enoch Brown Park.

that this the most sacred historic spot of our noble old county, should remain so long without monumental column or memorial tablet, to be profanely trodden under foot of man and beast. Thank God that reproach no longer rests upon the people of Franklin county and Antrim township. In this hour of rejoicing, when the capstone is to be brought forth, as it were, with shoutings, let us not forget the veterans who forty-two years ago exhumed the remains of Enoch Brown and scholars, who identified the grave and verified the tradition of their common sepulture. Without their pioneer work the waves of oblivion would doubtless long since have obliterated all traces of that hallowed spot, fuller of pathetic interest than any other in all the broad domain of the Cumberland Valley. We are glad to welcome these veterans to-day. They bind us with golden chains to the hoary past. We are glad to have one of them, Geo. W. Ziegler, Esq., preside over these memorial services, who has been a great help and inspiration in this movement. Also to have two others, Dr. J. K. Davison and Gen. Detrich, as vice presidents, all enjoying a good old age. In the language, slightly modified, of the immortal Webster to the veterans of Bunker Hill, sixty years ago, allow me to say " Venerable men ! you have come down to us from a former generation. Heaven has bounteously lengthened out your lives that you might behold this joyous day. You are now where you stood forty-two years ago this very hour with your brothers and neighbors in philanthropic efforts. Behold how altered. The same heavens are indeed over your heads, the same fountain flows at your feet. But all else how changed ! Alas! you are not all here—Koser, Michaels, Rankin, Sites, Grubb, Rowe, Mitchell, Osbaugh, Short, Shirey, Atherton, our eyes seek in vain for you amidst this broken band. You are gathered to you fathers but live in our grateful remembrances. * * All is peace and God has granted you this sight of your country's happiness ere you slumber in the grave forever. He has allowed you to partake of the reward of your patriotic toils ; and he has allowed us, your sons and countrymen, to meet you here and in the name of the present generation, in the name of your country, in the name of liberty and civilization, to thank you. * * May the

B

Father of all mercies smile upon your declining years and bless them."

We are glad to hail to-day as our gifted Poet and a true son of Antrim, one who years ago labored to bring about this very memorial work which has at last been accomplished under the auspices of the county at large. All honor to the pioneer settlers and all honor to the pioneer workers in the movement to honor the memory of Enoch Brown and his slaughtered scholars.

On the 22d day of April, 1884, a convention of representative delegates from all parts of Franklin county, met in the Court House at Chambersburg, to devise measures to promote the proper celebration of the one hundredth anniversary of the organization of the county, on the coming 9th of September. In the progress of their deliberations, it was resolved at the instance of Col. Geo. B. Wiestling, that a permanent memorial of the Centennial should be erected in the form of a monument, to perpetuate the memory of Schoolmaster Brown, and the ten scholars ruthlessly massacred by the Indians on this spot, 120 years previous. An appeal was made by the convention to the patriotic and Christian liberality of all the churches and schools, both secular and religious, week day and Sunday schools throughout the county, in aid of this enterprise, also to public spirited citizens in their individual capacity. The Centennial Executive Committee at Chambersburg was directed by the Convention to secure a generous rebate in aid of this monument fund, from all the railroads, on all excursion tickets issued on account of the Centennial Celebration. This was the unanimous action of the Convention, and the sum of at least $2,000 was pledged to the Monument Committee, which I have the honor to represent, wherewith to buy the land, erect the monument and make all other needed improvements. The Monument Committee have honestly and earnestly striven to carry out in good faith the wishes of the County Centennial Convention as best they could with the means placed at their disposal. They had a right to expect the generous assistance and hearty co-operation of every preacher, teacher, scholar and public spirited citizen of the county. The faith of the entire county was pledged to make the monumental project a grand success. But, alas! your committee was doomed to bitter disappointment. A generous rebate amounting to $758 was contributed by the railroads, as the Convention had requested, but $334 of that rebate never came into the hands of our Monument Committee. The bad example of this breach of faith in official circles was contagious and had a demoralizing effect. The majority of churches and schools of all kinds have utterly failed to do their duty in the premises. In all, up to date, your Committee has received less than $1,400, instead of at least $2,000, solemnly pledged by the sovereign convention, April 22, 1884. Of this amount, $91.77 has been contributed by the churches; about $260 by the week day schools, and the same amount ($260) by the Sunday schools of the county. Had it not been for the liberal subscriptions of individuals, headed by Geo. W. Ziegler, Esq., amounting in all to $335, your committee would have been seriously hindered in the prosecution of their work. Although the public schools of Greencastle with their six teachers and hundreds of scholars, only gave $5.75, yet Antrim township and Greencastle raised the handsome sum of $332. Well done for Mother Antrim! She has raised nearly one-fourth of the entire cost.

We point to this noble and enduring granite monument erected on the very spot where Enoch Brown and his ten scholars shed their precious blood, 121 years ago; we point to the smaller, but equally enduring and appropriate monument, which, beautiful in its simplicity, a few rods from here, marks the spot where repose in a common grave the mortal remains of the massacred master and scholars; we point likewise to this picturesque park of field and forest, containing a fraction less than twenty acres, all paid for and held in fee simple by your committee in trust for the people of the county, this tract which encloses the historic spring at the bottom of the hill, where little Archie McCullough washed the streaming blood from his face and scalpless head; we point to these memorials and possessions as the best answer to the question as to how we have discharged our duties as custodians of the Enoch Brown Monument Fund. In the face of all manner of obstacles; in spite of all manner of misrepresentation and abuse, we have persistently labored to carry out in good faith the patriotic and benevolent intentions of the Centennial Convention.   As the walls of Jerusalem were built in the days of Nehemiah, with sword in one hand and trowel in the other, so this monument project has been carried forward.   The memory of Enoch Brown, the noble-hearted, self-sacrificing Christian schoolmaster, has been vindicated against unjust aspersions, and after the lapse of 121 years, a granite monument, as enduring as the grand old mountains that loom up in majesty on the sides of the North, now covers the spot where he and his youthful scholars fell as pioneer martyrs in the cause of education and Christian civilization.

The question has been asked time and again, ''What good will the monument do?   Why go to all this trouble and expense about people killed 121 years ago?''   We can not expect to satisfy some people with any argument that we may offer.   Like the terrapins or land turtles that lately crawled around the grave of Enoch Brown and scholars, they have no reverential historic spirit and mope about most sacred scenes concerned entirely with the question, what shall we eat or what shall we drink?   But for thinking men and the rising generations the monuments will teach an important lesson and have an enobling educational influence. It will open up to many a most important chapter of history and fill their hearts with gratitude to the brave men and women who bore the brunts in the fierce struggle between civilization and barbarism.   In the language of Horatio Seymour, in his letter to the chairman of your committee, these monuments '' will tell us of the past and instruct with regard to the duties of life and the virtues of patriotism. We feel as we look upon them that the dead speak to us. They will do much to instruct and improve our citizens.'' It will show that this generation had some higher thoughts and aspirations than the mere scramble after filthy lucre, the degrading worship of Mammon.   As Webster argued at Bunker Hill, it will evoke and appeal not only to lofty thoughts, but to that other important part of our being which has so much to do with the interests of religion and patriotism, '' to sentiment and imagination.''   And where in all the realms of romance and fancy do we find a more pathetic story than the massacre and common burial of Enoch Brown and scholars? The simple recital of this terrible tragedy stirs emotions at times too deep for tears. And, my friends, rest assured that when all the beauty and chivalry of Franklin county, here assembled to-day, shall sleep beneath the green clods of the valley, this place will be a pilgrim shrine, increasing in interest as age after age rolls by. These are

> "Shrines to code nor creed confined,
> The Delphian vales, the Palestines,
> The Meccas of the mind."

I pity the person who has so little patriotic and religious sentiment as to ask, as some are doing: "What good will the monument do? Might not this money have been applied to more useful purposes? Why not give it to the poor or the Children's Aid Society of Chambersburg?" This is but the doleful echo of that harsh old mercenary and selfish spirit which found its proper exponent in Judas Iscariot, who was filled with indignation because the grateful Mary anointed the blessed Master with three hundred penny-worth of precious ointment. "Might not this have been sold and given to the poor," exclaimed the arch traitor and thief. Over against this sanctimonious and Pharisaic spirit we place the gracious words of the blessed Master: "Let her alone. Why trouble ye her? She hath done what she could. She hath wrought a good work on me. Against the day of my burying she hath kept this. For ye have the poor with you always, and whensoever ye will ye may do them good, but me ye have not always. Verily I say unto you, wheresoever this gospel shall be preached throughout the whole world, this also that she hath done shall be spoken of for a memorial of her." Like the odor of a sweet smell the fragrance of that self-sacrificing deed of love comes floating down the ages full of instruction and heavenly benediction. Away with that low, groveling, utilitarian spirit which dares to rob the world of its beauty, its sunshine and song, which measures by dollars and cents the immeasurable debt of gratitude due our heroic pioneer ancestors!

Thank God, the debt so long unpaid, and the work so

long delayed, has not been entirely forgotten. All honor to
the Centennial County Convention, of April 22, '84, and to
all the good people who have helped with their dimes and
dollars to build the monument. We wish the monument
was worthier the wealthy county on whose bosom it stands.
But such as it is, we take pleasure in handing it over to the
teachers, scholars and citizens of Franklin county. Here is
·embodied the spirit of generous-hearted patriotism. Here are
concentrated the offsprings of the poor and the rich, the dime
of the bare-footed school boy and school girl, and the liberal
benefactions of the wealthy. Here, too, the rich and poor
will meet together for ages, and dwell upon the toils and
trials of pioneer settlers, as illustrated in the massacre and
burial of master and scholars in a common grave.

And now, in behalf of the Enoch Brown Monument Committee, appointed April 22, 1884, by the Franklin County
Centennial Convention, I hand over these monuments, these
hallowed grounds, all these rare historic treasures, to the
teachers, scholars and people of Franklin county, to be cherished throughout all coming generations. Without debt or
incumbrance, we give them. Here in my hand I hold the
deed for these lands in fee simple given in trust for the use
of the schools and the people. Take them, and may they
be an inspiration and a benediction through all coming time,
helping posterity to "remember the days of old and consider
the years of many generations." God bless the teachers,
scholars and people of Franklin county.

ADDRESS OF PETER A. WITMER, ESQ.

OF HAGERSTOWN, MD.,

And Superintendent of Public Schools in Washington County, Md.

Upon the invitation of the committee having charge of
these memorial ceremonies, I am here, as a representative of
your sister State of Maryland, to join in the tribute which
we are met to pay to the manly sacrifices, and heroic endur-
ance of the pioneers who here conquered the untamed wildness of nature, that we, their children and successors, might

enjoy, in peace and prosperity, the fertile soil, the health-giving climate, the beautiful scenery, and the happy homes which have made the Cumberland Valley the synonym of the " Paradise of America."

We are met, as I understand it, to recall the days when this beautiful valley was covered with primeval forests, and a robust, but some crude, civilization was pressing forward to conquer the wildness of nature and the still more stubborn wildness of the savage inhabitants who roamed at will over these hills and through these valleys. We stand, to-day, on what, one hundred and twenty years ago, was the utmost verge of American civilization. Beyond, toward the setting sun, was a howling wilderness; yonder, toward the rising sun, thirteen feeble colonies, apparently depending for existence upon the mother country across the seas, inhabited by less than 3,000,000 people, constituted the Anglo-Saxon contingent which was to win to civilization and to freedom the grandest empire the world has ever seen. To-day that conquest has been made. Look around you and behold it. An almost limitless expanse of territory, reaching from ocean to ocean and from the lakes to the gulf; embracing every variety of surface, soil and climate, studded with cities and villas, with commercial marts and thriving inland towns, through which courses, in ceaseless pulsations, the full tide of an ever restless commerce ; traversed by 125,000 miles of railways, which carry your products on the wings of the winds, chequered by 500,000 miles of electric wires, which transmit intelligence with the velocity of thought, watered by a thousand rivers, which make your valleys bloom and bourgeon like an Eden; filled with an active, busy, bustling population, the whole ruled by what we believe to be the best government ever organized by man. See, all over your land, the studios of art, where the skill of the painter makes, instinct with beauty, the living canvas, and the sculptor's genius moulds the breathing marble into forms of life, and soul and passion ; your courts, where Justice sits enthroned, crowned with a people's majesty, your halls of Legislature, where eloquence " rules her wilderness of free minds," your schools, and colleges, and universities, where the youth of the land are trained to meet like men the responsibilities of life, your eleemosynary institutions, where charity comes like a benediction to so many weary hearts, your Sunday-schools, the great auxiliaries of the church in the work of human redemption; and, finally, your churches, the beautiful architectural creations of Christian ingenuity, and opulent devotion, whose spires are pointing the hopes of immortal flocks to the great Unseen Shepherd, while their choirs and organs pour forth, over hill and valley, a full tide of choral harmony, which, swelling in one grand diapason to the heavens, dies away at last in soft melodious cadence, at the foot of the throne of Him whose praise it celebrates.

This and more than this is your country. Such is the structure which has been reared upon foundations laid strong, and deep, and broad, by the men whose virtues and heroism we are here to-day to recount and commemorate.

In this connection I have been asked to refer to the part which Maryland took in the stirring events which have been so eloquently portrayed by the gentlemen who have already addressed you, and whilst I shall not enter upon historical details, I may say, generally, that Maryland in the colonial days stood fast by the fortunes of her sister colonies. Her fame is full of honor, in peace and in war. Sprung directly from the loins of the mother country, her sons inherited the spirit of freedom which wrung from King John the Magna Charta, and, subsequently, from England's royal line, still greater concessions. Imbued with that spirit, the founders of Maryland, when they landed on St. Mary's shore, planted there the emblem of Christ's suffering and man's salvation, and forever dedicated her soil to civil and religious liberty. She contributed freely of her blood and treasure to defend herself and her sister colonies from the rude assaults of the savage, and the more insidious but more dangerous advances of English tyranny, and if she failed to send a proper contingent to the Pontiac war it was because she was even then resisting the first attempts of England to tax the resources of the colonies to fill her depleted coffers. She became, as you all know, with your own great State, a child of the Revolution, and received upon her head its baptism of fire and blood.

The Maryland Line met the scarlet uniform and the glittering steel of England from the first dark hours of Bunker Hill to the final and triumphant glory at Yorktown, and she points with pride to her brilliant record through all that long and bloody career.

It is enough to know, my friends, that through the sufferings, the sacrifices and the many achievements of our fathers, to whose memory we have this day met to do honor, we are permitted to enjoy the priceless blessings of American liberty, and I shrink from claiming for the State which I have the honor to represent, and which I love so well, credit or fame, in any degree above that which belongs to each of the whole glorious thirteen.

But this occasion suggests another train of thought. We are here to dedicate a monument to the humble man, Enoch Brown, the teacher, who with his pupils, and on this very spot, fell a victim to the savage ferocity of the Indian and to duty. The world is full of monuments, but their inscriptions usually blazon the deeds of warriors, statesmen, poets. Rarely does the world rear the monumental pile to the humble school teacher. Fidelity, honor, faith, truth may all be his, and a moral heroism which, in the path of duty, scorns to turn aside from death; but these evoke no admiration. The glamour of war, the triumphs of eloquence, the rapt genius of poetry and art—these only are deemed worthy the homage of men. But here, one hundred and twenty-one years ago, a nobler man than warrior, politician, or poet, fell a martyr to duty and to civilization; therefore, it is fit that we raise this monument. It is right that the moral heroism, the undaunted courage, the sublime and splendid disregard of self and life which Enoch Brown exhibited should be perpetuated in stone, which, I trust, will be as enduring as the eternal hills that now look down upon it. True, he who lived so well, and died so nobly, and sleeps so calmly here, may not know what we now do.

> No storied urn, or animated bust,
> Back to its mansion calls the fleeting breath;
> Nor Honor's voice provokes the silent dust,
> Nor Flattery soothes the dull, cold ear of death;

but I believe that at the last Grand Assize, when the Judge

B*

of all the earth shall pronounce humanity's final doom, ft shall be said of Enoch Brown, as Christ said of Mary, he hath done what he could.

With the spirit of our Great Exemplar, he begged his brutal murderers to spare his pupils and take his life as a vicarious offering for them, And here is one great lesson that teachers may well learn—the lesson of love for those placed under their care. Love your pupils and they will reciprocate the feeling with all the fervor that glows in young hearts. Let them feel that you are their friend, not their master, and the spirit of insubordination will give way to confidence and trust.

This brings me, my friends, to a brief presentation of another subject which the mandate of your committee imposes—the educational idea suggested by these ceremonies.

Time will not permit me to enter into any general history of education, nor indeed, of this country. A rapid review of educational movements in your own great commonwealth is all that can be attempted.

It is well known that education in our early colonial time, and for many years after, was under the supervision and control of the various religious organizations of the country, and it is altogether probable that the school conducted here by Enoch Brown was, in some sort, a parochial school.

It is true that almost every colony had on its statute books provisions for the establishment of schools for the general education of the people, in other words, public schools; still these laws were, for different reasons, generally ineffective and inoperative.

As early as 1787, the General Government, in the famous ordinance for the government of the North-West Territory, set apart the sixteenth section of land in every township for the maintenance of public schools, basing their action upon the memorable declaration, that "Religion, morality and knowledge, being necessary to good government and the happiness of mankind, schools and the means of education shall be forever encouraged." Under this, and subsequent similar grants, an aggregate of not less than 140,000,-000 acres of land have been set apart by the Government for educational purposes. Thus, early in the history of our country, the General Government placed itself upon record as committed to the principles upon which our free or common schools of to-day are founded. Coming to the history of public instruction in your own great State, we find that so early as 1682, William Penn inserted in the form of government for his new province the provision, that "The Governor and the Provincial Council should erect and order all public schools," but the authority so vested was not exercised until many years after.

Your constitutions of 1776 and 1790 both contained provisions for the establishment of schools throughout the State, in which the poor were to be taught gratis, but the benevolent intentions of those who enacted these provisions were thwarted from the fact that they imposed the badge of poverty upon a certain element in the community, who resented with spirit the reproach which they believed such legislation was intended to fix upon them. The Act of your Assembly, passed in 1809, contained the same objectionable features and it was not until 1818 that legislation was secured, through the efforts of a number of the most prominent citizens of your State, which was supposed to abolish all class distinctions. This legislation was, however, local in its character, and applied only to the city of Philadelphia, and, even there, failed to remove the impression that it fixed the stigma of pauperism upon the poorer classes, as all previous laws were supposed to have done. The experiments which had been tried, and the efforts which had been made to establish a common school system, culminated in the passage of an Act in 1834, amended and improved in 1836, which is really the first common school law of this commonwealth. It established schools for the instruction of youth without regard to social or pecuniary condition. It established them upon the broad principles that public education is a public necessity, and must be maintained at public expense—that access to your schools must be free to all, just as access is free to any other public institution established for public comfort, convenience and use. There has been legislation affecting your public schools since 1835, but this legislation incorporated only such improvements as experience and an advancing civilization suggested, and now your school system stands boldly out as one of the most important factors of those splendid commercial, social and educational results which Pennsylvania to-day presents to the world. A State which appropriates annually ten millions in money for the support of 2,300 teachers, and the education of 1,000,000 of her children, may well be proud of her educational record.

And now, my friends, is it necessary to inquire what this school system is worth, or to ask whether the results justify the expenditures? As one who has been identified with the work of public instruction, in my own State, for the last eighteen years, I say, with entire confidence in the truth of my statement, that your public school system is worth all that you pay for it.

We assume as postulates the trite propositions first, that our form of government is founded in and rests upon the virtue and intelligence of the people; secondly, that the public or common school is the best vehicle for the dissemination of this public virtue and popular intelligence. I shall not stop to discuss these propositions, since, whilst they do not probably challenge universal assent, we apprehend no gentleman would risk his reputation for knowledge of the essential characteristics of our national life by disputing the first, and no ambitious politician, aspiring to the spoils of office, would venture to do violence to the settled convictions of his constituents by publicly demurring to the second. The school house is everywhere, all over this land, regarded as an exponent of our civilization, I may say, indeed, as one of its pioneers, for whenever on broad prairie, or in fertile Western valley, or on auriferous mountain side, the sturdy emigrant presses his way to subjugate the forest, turn the virgin soil, or open the mine, there, too, we find the school house, at once the emblem of our civilization and the perpetual promise of intellectual progress to our country. I know that there are men in every State, and in every community, men who, while professing to criticise only defects in the system, strike at its very life. These gentlemen say that your public school system is simply a great charity for the benefit of the poor, and should therefore be limited to the most elementary instruction, while the money intended for its support should be doled out with something of the liberality which a miser exhibits in dispensing alms. Your schools, my friends, are no more a charity than your courts or your roads maintained at public expense for the benefit and convenience of all. Again these critics say the training received at public schools unfit some people for their proper sphere in life, in other words, it makes the poor young man dissatisfied with his lot. In answer to this, I thank God that it does. Who shall fix any boy's future position in this life, in this age, and especially in this free America, where we recognize no royalty of blood but that which shows itself in an honest, earnest, manly life; no aristocracy but the aristocracy of the intellect; no nobility but that which derives its letters-patent from the King of Kings. I thank God for the aspirations which glow in the young hearts of the poor boys all over this land toward a better, a nobler and a higher life, and I pity the folly and the imbecility of the man who would seek to repress these aspirations or fix in a mould the future destiny of the youth of this country. As well attempt to bridle the winds or chain the cyclone, or to crush out the hope that lives in every Christian heart, of a happy life beyond the dark-flowing river. I appeal to every father and mother in this presence not to repress or hamper the development of mind in their children. We know not what possibilities of action and achievement are wrapped up in their young souls, and we should prove recreant to every parental duty and relation should we attempt to fix limits to the development of these possibilities.

That we are a much better educated people than we were a half century ago will not be disputed, and this is due, in our opinion, in a great degree, to the prevailing belief that education enables a man to lift himself in the social scale and generally to improve his condition in life. The public school is the most potential agency in this general diffusion of intelligence, and it, therefore, becomes a people, who would occupy a front rank among the States of the Union, to foster their public school system.

It may have defects, it has defects, but its work is none the less important, and its triumphs have been none the less decisive, and my admonition to you, my friends, citizens of this great commonwealth, is to protect it, cherish it, and with a spirit rising into chivalry, and a love deepening into reverence, defend it through sunshine and storm.

To the teachers of Franklin county, who have contributed of their means and their labors to raise this monument, and who are here to commemorate the work and the service of one of their honorable profession, I may be permitted a word by way of suggestion and encouragement. I would have them remember that this is an age of remarkable mental activity. In every department of thought we note the earnest inquiries and anxious investigations of the fore-most minds of the age. It would be strange if in investiga-tions so far reaching, and all embracing the educational field, should be neglected. It has not been neglected, and in no department of inquiry shall we find greater activity than in that which concerns so vitally the welfare of the youth of this country. It is, therefore, your duty as intelli-gent teachers to keep fully abreast of the advanced thought of the day upon all questions relating to the proper educa-tion of children. You must not forget that you are the vanguard of that grand procession of the nations which is pressing along the world's highways to the world's ideal standard of perfection. It is your mission to teach the youth of the country that there are nobler things in life than military glory, or hoarded wealth, than the arts of the poli-tician, or the tricks of modern statesmanship—that a pro-gressive civilization is leading us onward and upward to higher and grander purposes of existence, to be wrought out not on the battle field, nor in heated political contests, nor even in the busy marts of trade, but in the quiet, peaceful homes, all over this broad land, where every unbought grace of life shall find its full development, and every manly in-stinct some object worthy of its loftiest aim.

Your work embraces all humanity, and in its elevation of that humanity to a higher plane, in inculcating just concep-tion of moral, social and political duty, and in illustrating a broader brotherhood, a more generous civilization, and a more spiritual Christianity, there are fields of bloodless tri-umph grander far than ever hero conquered, and there are guerdons to be won, such as we award to-day to Enoch Brown, richer far than the laurel crown of olden Greece. May you, as teachers, by the honest, intelligent and conscientious discharge of every duty deserve to win that grander triumph and to wear that richer guerdon ; and may we all, my friends, as parents and guardians, be faithful to every obligation which our relations to the children impose, and so rest in the hope that they will revel, for ages and ages 'to come, in the full fruition of the splendid realities which we so fondly anticipate for them and for our country.

ADDRESS OF REV. F. M. WOODS,

OF MARTINSBURG, W. VA.

THE SCOTCH-IRISH PIONEERS OF OUR COUNTRY.

It is difficult for us to realize that only one short century and a quarter have passed since the hands of ruthless savages were steeped in the blood of helpless victims, upon the very spot where here to-day we stand. When you tell me that once this fair field was stained with the carnage of murdered school children ; that this lovely valley once rang and re-echoed with the wild shout of the redman, I feel disposed to ask, in view of what now meets the eye, how many hundreds of years must have elapsed since these things were seen and heard?

God's purposes of grace and of providence unfold very fast. The Indian was an unprofitable tenant of this great land, and it was needful for him to give way to another and better. Selfish greed drew multitudes, who thought to pluck the Indian's title from his hand by violence and fraud. The Spaniard must stand condemned as the bloody and unjust aggressor, in that day when justice shall poise her infallible scales, to determine the relative guilt of the Christian and the pagan. The Castilians and the many adventurers who followed in their wake, proved themselves as little worthy to hold the continent as their predecessors had been. These were not the men whom God had in preparation for the inheritance of this vast estate. They were but as the dust, and the chaff and the dried leaves, which the coming storm gathers up upon the weapons of its vanguard and tosses in wild sport before it. The rain which enriches the earth and makes it fruitful, and supplies its fountains, comes in the storm, carrying the lightning for its torch, and the thunder for the diapason of its martial music. Another race of people, trained in a different school; animated by different ambitions; impelled by different motives, were destined to cross over into this fair land and claim it in the name of the great King, and to establish His throne as the basis and security of their own rights and the glory of their wide dominion. The stones of this great temple of freedom were being hewn in the vast quarries of Europe. Rabid fanaticism was made to be the pedagogue to train and discipline a body of men and women for the task of rescuing this country from the grasp of its heathen occupants, and of redeeming it to liberty.

The history of this valley and of the entire country, is very largely influenced by the character of the Scotch-Irish Presbyterianism of those early days. The Scotchman persecuted in his own country, migrated to the west of the channel dividing him from Ireland, and there sought liberty of worship. Mingling his blood with that of his new neighbors, there resulted a compound of force and tenacity, which has made the Scotch-Irishman almost a distinct race of being. Finding no rest for the sole of his foot in this home of his adoption, he again took his life in hand and gathered up his meagre substance, launched forth upon the ocean to find his abode where religious liberty could be enjoyed. This brought him to America, where he could worship God according to the dictates of a conscience enlightened and instructed by the word of God. These are the men whom we are proud to call our forefathers; and theirs was a faith to which their descendants for a thousand generations may well be glad to do reverence. May we and our children, and theirs in turn, have the wisdom and the grace, and the courage to emulate it!

It is proper for us, to-day and here in the presence of this beautiful monument, to recall some of the more salient

points in the character of those old worthies, to whose noble
principles and true bravery we owe so much. For with their
sword and their bow they achieved for us the glorious
record of independence.

1. It is to be noted that they were not worthless adventurers or mere explorers, or the apostles of a godless civilization. They were not the seekers of worldly treasure sim⸗
ply. It was not mercenary greed which influenced their zeal.
They were in search of a religious home, and of liberty of
conscience. It was the honor of God and the blessings of
the gospel of peace which they were resolved to secure.
These privileges were denied them in their fatherland.
They could easily have purchased a peace and remained in
the countries from which they came, had they been willing
to abjure their principles and their faith, and to sub-
mit with plastic grace to the imperious will of a religious
despotism. The three Hebrews of Martyr Spirit, could
have obtained a like disgraceful immunity, could they have
smothered the protests of their faithful consciences and
bowed in tame submission to the Chaldean monarch's tyrannical will, and worshipped the great image which he set up in
the plain of Dura. But fired by the mighty impulse of indomitable principles, they chose the flames rather than
cowardly obedience. Of like character was the spirit of
these dauntless men, who with wives and mothers, and
daughters, forsook all and followed Christ into these wild
wastes. They brought the precious Bible with them, and
they loved its truths, and fed upon them as upon manna.
The word of God was the Man of their counsel. They
sought unto it in all their troubles and shaped their lives by
it. Their children were taught "to fear God and to keep
His commandments," understanding that herein is "the
whole of man." Their religion was to them a constant
living reality. They did not keep it as a fashionable pre-
tense, a flimsy robe of bright fastastic texture, which never
saw the light, except on public and stated occasions. It
was their "vade mecum." In the field, or in the forest ;
at home or on the march, or in the face of the foe, their God
was their first consideration. Right was the law of life and
the principle of action to them.

It will be readily conceded that men of this character
could not be easily diverted from their purpose. Neither
fear nor favor could disarm them. It is Christian principle
which makes the best citizen, the best friend, the best
neighbor, the best ruler. Christian principle makes the
best pioneers. When men go out to do better for their
rights with the Bible in their hands, and the fear of God in
their hearts, they are a dangerous foe to meet. It is extremely difficult to persuade them of defeat. They strike
with an arm of iron, and the fire of their wrath is unquench-
able till justice is satisfied and truth has been vindicated.
The men who sought these shores for gold and silver, or in
the spirit of discovery, were not the men who gave nerve
and stability to the institutions whose foundations were laid
amid the troubled waves and the rushing waters of those
early days. The spirit of John Knox and of Patrick Hamilton, and of Geo. Wishart, is alone able to meet and overcome the obstacles which the men of that day had to en-
counter.

2. The sufferings and trials to which these early settlers
were subjected in the Old World, were a further step in the
preparations through which Divine Providence was fitting
them for their high and honorable destiny. Inured to hardship
and to honest toil, the valorous sons and daughters of England, Scotland, France, Holland, Switzerland, Germany
and Ireland, fearlessly came to these shores to conquer the
unsubdued forests and win a righteous peace, and enjoy a
godly independence. Holding to the essential principles of
our common Presbyterianism, and deeply imbibing the
rugged truths of a sturdy Calvinism, they were well calculated to "endure hardness as good soldiers of Jesus Christ,"
and to bring into subjection the rude natives and their howling desert home. They were accustomed to be driven from
their homes and from one country to another. They were
hunted like wild beasts. They had seen their comrades
butchered in cold blood. Wives and husbands were torn
cruelly from each other, and their children were slaughtered
heartlessly before their eyes. They were exposed to hunger
and thirst, and nakedness, they learned by the bitterness of
experience, the full value of every privation. Their Chris-

tian (!) persecuters on that side of the ocean were more
merciless and savage than the bloody Indian with his scalping-knife and tomahawk on this. Raised in comfort, many
of them in luxury, they gave up home and became wan-
derers and strangers, dwelling in dens and caves. But these
things only served to give an iron tone to the nerves of their
spiritual being. Hardship had no terrors for men of this
stamp. They were trained by dark adversity for the gigantic
struggles of the arena on this western continent. Their arms
were made strong to fell the great trees, and to subdue the
ground, and to drive back the cruel foes who met them in
these forests. The task was far removed from the conditions of the child's play. Theirs was the death-grasp with
an enemy who was in furious earnest. He who would meet
these Greeks, must himself be a Greek of the Greeks. "Behold they that wear soft clothing are in Kings' houses"—
not on the borders, fighting the Indians, and daring their
lives for truth and freedom to worship God.

3. It was furthermore of the first importance that these
pilgrims and exiles, from beyond the seas, brought with
them a very true conception of the nature and worth of
right education. Their scientific curriculum may not have
been so extensive and pretentious as that in which we glory
to-day, "Darwinism," "survival of the fittest," "evolu-
tion," "molecules," and "protoplasm" and "the physical
basis of life," had not then loomed up into such clearly
defined proportions as they have since done. And the venerable anthropoid monkey had not yet been introduced into
good society as the noble progenitor of a degenerated offspring. But notwithstanding these melancholy defects in their
early education, our fathers knew something of their Bibles,
and they valued it sufficiently to teach it to their children
as an essential element in a thorough course of mental training. Their sons and daughters were taught the importance
of worshiping God and of "keeping His commandments."
The silly affectation by which the parents of this modern
day seek to screen themselves from the keen thrusts of a
guilty, reproaching conscience for neglecting the religious
education of their children, saying that the child must be
left to exercise its own judgment and choice, unbiased by

parental influence, is a cunning trick of the old adversary,
the wily serpent, who loves nothing so well as to fold his
slimy coils upon the family hearthstone, and to pollute with
his presence the family altar. By this device he reaps yearly
a bountiful harvest of priggish free-thinkers, and no-thinkers,
and upstart fledglings, who think nothing so smart as a
foppish pretension to a driveling skepticism which can giggle
and nothing more, when the solemn realities of God, of
death and of eternity are mentioned; and he reaps it from
the harvest-field of the church. Far be the day removed
from us and from our land when the Bible shall be excluded
from our schools. Cursed be the genius of an education
which leaves the heart ungarnished and the moral nature,
the "inward part," the "hidden part," to become a garden
of weeds. It becomes a Christian people to pay a worthy
tribute to the old parochial school system, wherein the Word
of God was a recognized text-book, and the rule and
standard of conduct. The early settlers of this country
were very anxious to bring the blessings of their school
within easy reach of their children. In every little community the school-house and the fort were established near
together, and were the two points of chief concern next to
the church itself.

A mournful interest gathers around the memory of that
good man, Enoch Brown, whose sad death the men of this
generation has wisely and justly determined to enshrine in
the hearts of their children forever. "Honor to whom honor
is due." Washington is held in the affections of a grateful
nation. Our great heroes of war, our statesmen, our scholars
and scientists are horored by the nation, by the nations.
Shall we allow this noble man, who fell bravely at the humble
post of his duty, to sink under the waves of oblivion! Let
his name be made known, and his worth be written upon
the shaft of the imperishable granite! And let the principles which he inculcated be magnified in the sight of our
children, that they may learn to value truth and to exalt it
in their lives.

Of the few scholars who providentially survived the terrible massacre of the school of Enoch Brown, on the 26th
of July, 1764, two especially were appointed to attain to the

parentage of a great number of sons and daughters, who shall rise up "to call them blessed."

One of the little girls became in the course of years the mother of the large and distinguished family of the Chambers', * of the adjacent city which bears their name. Another of those little girls was Eleanor Chochrane, aged seven or eight years, who was kept at home from the school on that fatal day by her parents. On the 24th of May, 1779, she was united in marriage to Captain Joseph Junkin, a brave and distinguished soldier and officer of the Revolutionary war. In virtue of this union she became the mother of fourteen children, ten sons and four daughters. These in turn became the parents of numerous offspring, which shows no alarming signs of becoming extinct at the present time.

Their children of the second and third generations exhibit much of the same true Calvinistic courage and strength of character which marked the older type.

We find in this family comforting evidence that our God is a covenant keeping God. Of the large family born to the pious Joseph Junkin and Eleanor Cochrane, two of the sons, George and David, became distinguished ministers of the Gospel, distinguished for learning and talent; but also for their holy zeal and consecration to the Master's work. Two of the daughters married ministers. Of the descendants in the next generation many became office-holders in the church. In all twenty or more of the children and grandchildren of Joseph and Eleanor Junkin have become ministers of the Gospel; and probably thirty have been chosen to the office of Ruling Elder. And there are very few if any of the children who are not Christians. God signalizes Himself in remembering His mercy.

A son of David X. Junkin, George, who lives in Virginia, is married to a great great granddaughter of Gen. Andrew Lewis, whom I suppose to be the officer who commanded the Virginia troops which joined Col. Henry Bouquet, when he marched into Ohio to punish the Indians for this atrocious massacre.

Thus in the fifth generation on the one side, and in the third on the other, the blood of the Virginia Lewises and

*See page 71.

of the Pennsylvania Cochranes unites in a family of eleven children, ten of whom are now living.

Of the family of Dr. George Junkin, two sons are able ministers of the New Testament. One is a distinguished and successful lawyer in Philadelphia. One of his daughters, Eleanor, was the first wife of the great Confederate General, T. J. Jackson, better known by his sobriquet of "Stonewall" Jackson. Another of his daughters, Mrs. Margaret J. Preston, wife of Col. J. S. L. Preston, of Lexington, Va., is widely known by her sweet and thrilling touch of the poet's lyre, which has awakened an echo of rapture in so many hearts, bringing light to those that walk in darkness and gladness to those bowed down with grief and sorrow.

But among so many why select only a few, when all are worthy? Let us all together give thanks to God for "His wonderful works to the children of men." After one hundred and twenty-one years, as our tardy memorial to the merits of well-nigh forgotten worth, we reverently unveil and dedicate this beautiful shaft, which shall ever serve to quicken our thoughts of the stirring times witnessed upon this classic spot.

POEM OF JOHN M. COOPER.

ENOCH BROWN.

Looking down the long vista that brings to our view
The face of this vale when her homesteads were new,
We see through the haze of the far-reaching years
A scene so pathetic it moves us to tears.
On the slope of a hill, near the edge of a wood,
With settlements scattered around it, there stood
A little log school house, with plain battened door,
And roof of lap shingles, and rough oaken floor.
'Twas the height of the summer and Sol's golden tide
Flowed in through a long row of glass in the side,
While the air, as if weary from journeying far,
Seemed scarcely to stir through the door wide ajar.
Within sat the master, with hair white as snow,
And eleven small children all ranged in a row,
And their lessons they droned as their primers they thumbed,
Till the little log house like a big bee-hive hummed.

Both master and children were happy that morn,
And had danger been hinted, would laughed it to scorn;

For the farmers were down in the mead making hay,
And the lambs skipped each other like children at play ;
And the kine, of their burden relieved by the maid,
Chewed their cud with content in the orchard's green shade ;
And the partridge piped clear in the stubble of grain,
And the robin was blithe down the red cherry lane ;
And the low voice of doves came with soft, soothing sound,
From the forest that bounded the school-house around ;
And the watch-dog lay dreaming, nor broke on his ear
E'en a faint sound of warning that danger was near.
The fair face of nature was bright with a smile,
Yet devils, red devils, stole here all the while.

The master had risen with bible in hand,
God's message to read to his tender young band,
When, sudden as wolves on the fold fast asleep,
Three savages came through the door with a leap—
Three red painted demons, with eyes wild aglare,
Like tigers whose nostrils scent blood in the air—
Three devils incarnate, with purpose as fell
As if formed in the black rankling bosom of hell.

The lion whose jungle bold hunters invade
Can defend it with weapons that nature has made,
But alas ! the good master who fell here that day
Had no weapon defensive—he only could pray—
And prayers to the bloodhound let loose on the trail,
Though offered by angels, will nothing avail.
With a stroke of the hatchet his gray head they clove,
And deep in his bosom the dagger they drove ;
And unmoved by their terror, the children they smote,
Till life gave its last gasping throb in the throat.
Then red-handed devils shot down yonder dell,
Like hot hissing flames through the wide flues of hell.

When the afternoon sun shone that sad, fateful day,
Some one had occasion to wander this way,
And struck by the silence, looked in at the door,
And his heart froze with horror, for there on the floor
Lay master and children, all covered with gore,
As if through the roof there had fallen a rain
Of mingled and horrible flesh, blood and brain.
And there Archie McCullough, with face all red
With the blood of his own poor bleeding head—
He alone living—his playmates all dead—
Was crawling around and calling the slain,
And patting their faces—alas ! how vain—
In his childlike effort to wake them again.

The alarm being sounded, a youth on a steed
Went spreading the news with the uttermost speed—
No bit in the mouth nor a saddle on back,
No curb but the halter quick loosed from the rack.
The mettlesome steed seemed to understand
The terrible errand they had in hand,
And the swelling veins in his silken side,
And the luminous glow of his nostrils wide,
And the nervous spring of his arm and thigh,
And the curve of his neck and the flash of his eye,
As he haughtily tossed his foretop high,
Seemed plainly to say he would do it or die.

Then he swallowed the hill at a single bound,
And startled the settlements far around
With the rapid, resounding and furious pound
Of his shodden hoof on the hard dry ground,
As up winding road and through narrow lane,
And out on the winding road again,
And into the woods, where he shook the oak
And frightened the deer with his thunder stroke,
And over the clearing and down the ravine,
Wherever the smoke of a cabin was seen,
(Leaping the fences and leaping the bars
As a comet would leap over moon and stars,)
He carried his rider, who, gasping for breath,
Kept shouting his terrible message of death—
Of master and children stark dead and still,
In the little log school house on Guitner's hill.
The cheek of the mother grew pallid with fear,
And swooning she murmured " red devils are here."

Then the rake was let drop on the freshly cut hay,
And the scythe left to rust in the swath where it lay,
And the rifle was snatched from its place on the wall,
And the shot-pouch was filled up with powder and ball,
And the settlers went forth in hot search for the foe
Who had brought on their households this burden of woe.
But pursuit was in vain, and in sadness they turned
To their desolate homes, where dim vigil lamps burned,
And the mother sat mourning the child of her womb,
As it slept the deep sleep that leads down to the tomb.

Though long seem the hours whose seconds are grief,
The space between death and interment is brief,
And not long did the stricken mourn over their dead,
Ere the loved ones were laid in their last earthly bed :
First the master, with honor well due to his years ;
Then the children around him, and over all tears ;

And the hearts of a multitude throbbed in their breast
As the turf on their cold, silent bosoms was pressed.
In sorrow, with weeping, they laid them away,
And the bones of the martyrs are there to this day ;
And so long as a star shall look down from the sky,
May this stone stand to point out the place where they lie.

Together they suffered, together they died,
And together they buried them side by side ;
And together they rose on angels' wings
Where the music of harps with golden strings
Greets the sinless souls that cross over the river
To dwell in the Land of the Blessed forever.
And the face of the Lord shone bright, and he smiled
As he said in low, loving accents mild,
"Suffer the children to come unto me,
For of such must the kingdom of heaven be."
And he ordered the angels to fashion a crown,
Lined with velvet soft and with eider-down,
To bedeck the bruised head of old ENOCH BROWN.
Red devils can never break in and slay
Where that good old master is resting to-day.

ADDRESS OF DR. WM. H. EGLE,*

OF HARRISBURG, PA.

"MEN OF ANTRIM: Let us go backward one hundred
and twenty-two years, to Anno Domini, One Thousand
Seven Hundred and Sixty Three. The lilies of France had
already given place to the cross of England, and thus ended,
forever, the fond dream of the former—the establishment of
a French empire in America. Founded in religious enthusiasm, culminating in persecutions shocking to civilization,
they attempted to cement and continue their power by en-

---

* Owing to the lateness of the hour, Dr. Egle only delivered part of the able
address which he had prepared for the occasion, on "Pontiac and Bouquet."
He had promised to revise the entire document for this publication, but a mul-
tiplicity of other pressing duties prevented him from doing so. He has, however,
revised, and somewhat enlarged the synopsis, published in the *Valley Spirit*,
Aug. 5, 1885, which we furnish below. The Doctor felt that this was all that
was really necessary, inasmuch as a large part of the ground traversed in his
speech had already been covered by the pamphlet on "Col. Bouquet and His
Campaigns," and by the proceedings of the Bouquet Celebration at Bushy Run,
Aug. 6, 1883, which are now published in full, along with the ceremonies of the
Enoch Brown Dedication.

C

listing the brutality of the Aborigine, working cruelty and
bloodshed, but as ever the case, resulting in the downfall of
those inaugurating such horrors.   The last of the French
soldiers had returned to their homes, yet the resentments and
bitter hatred they had ruthlessly kindled in the minds and
hearts of the savages remained.   The Indian of to-day is
only a prototype of those of a century ago.   They are just
as perfidious and treacherous now as they were then—and
it is only possible that by education and the power and
grace of Christianity, that they may become loyal inhabitants of a great country.   We are no admirers of the Indian
character, and in all our researches into the history of
America, find the same traits and the same brutal instincts,
which to-day fire the savage breast of the perfidious
Apache."   The speaker continued on a further description
of their character.

   Then taking up the theme of his address, "Pontiac and
Bouquet," he outlined the history of Col. Bouquet in his
warfare against the savages, who so ruthlessly desolated the
homes of the frontiersmen of that early period, and recounted
the engagements had with them.   After a vivid description of the condition of the country and people in
1763–64, and the atrocities of the Indians, the orator said :
"We now come to a dark transaction in the bloody annals
of Border life, which we have especially assembled on this
day and hour to recall.   Located near this spot, in the summer of July, 1764, was a small log building, in which a
pious school-master, Enoch Brown, taught a group of happy
little children.   It was in harvest-time, on the 26th of July.
While those in their teens were assisting in gathering the
crops, the smaller ones only engaged in study.   The lessons
of the early forenoon had nearly all been recited, and the
scholars and their faithful teacher and friend were anticipating a recess from study.   None can imagine the consternation and horror pictured on the faces of the late joyful group
when rushing through the opened door came a band of
brutal Indians.   How and whence they came, unperceived
by the settlers, and by chance, upon this gronp of children
no one relates.   It was a moment of awful suspense, as the
'Ugh' of the savages awoke the quiet of that summer's day.

Immediately the brave-hearted school-master, fully realizing the situation and the peril of the hour, bade the monsters take his life, but spare the innocent children, who were crouching in fear before the angry and infuriated red demons of the forest. There was no pity or mercy in that ruthless horde. At once the work of butchering began, and in less time than it can be related, the bloody deed was consummated. Hurriedly securing the scalps of teacher and scholars, as trophies of a victory, the inhuman monsters with hellish satisfaction, retraced their steps and were lost in the wilderness beyond."

"Why tarry the children? was the inquiry of the anxious frontier mother, as she looked out from her rude home towards the path to the school-house. Presently, anxiety gave way to alarm, and the male members of the family were sent out to learn the cause of their absence. How sad the discovery! It was indeed 'Holy Innocents' Day' in this new land of ours, and one which you, my friends, have seen fit to remember. And yet, I think I hear some say, what of this dark and bloody deed so disgraceful to humanity, so horrifying to all the finer feelings of our nature,—why commemorate, why not allow oblivion to cast an eternal shadow over the transaction? My friends, if it was only the atrocious butchery of that day, we might well cover over and hide it from earthly annals forever. But in that sanguinary hour there were the grand and ennobling characteristics of Christian manhood and glory shining forth ; which have come down to us through all the cathedral aisles of time, and prompted us to erect in this place this memorial. The deed perpetrated one hundred and twenty-one years ago, is a land-mark in the history of this locality, and this stone will be a constant reminder of the sufferings endured by your ancestors, who indeed made the wilderness to blossom as the rose, and founded through many trials and great sufferings, homes you now enjoy in peace and plenty. That heroic teacher, with the Bible in his hand imploring his brutal murderers to take his life and spare the innocent ones around him, eminently deserves the voiced recognition here given. The band of children, slaughtered through savage hate, most of whose names are unknown to us, have a sacred memory which you do well to record. Their lives were sacrificed not without some grand purpose. It touched, at least, the hearts of the Quaker Assembly, who at once determined to place the country in defence. It nerved the souls of the settlers to defend their homes and wipe the heathen from the land. And, citizens of Antrim and this highly favored locality, you have done a good thing in the erection of this memorial.

Dr. Egle took up the campaign of Bouquet after the massacre here and alluded with words of praise to the Findlays and Dixons, the Maclays and McDowells, the Armstrongs and Chambers's, the Jacks and Johnstons and Potters who accompanied him. Referring to a later period he said : " Among the hundreds of Scotch-Irish who served in the war of the Revolution from the Antrim, Letterkenny and Lurgan of old not one turned Tory. Born among privation and tyranny, in the sternness of integrity and heartfelt piety, with the Bible in one hand and the trusty rifle in the other, let us give the meed of praise to the early settlers of this locality, whose crowning excellence was their devotion to religion and their unflinching duty to God and man."

After tracing Bouquet's course in the west with his army, partly made up of the men just described, narrating the recapitulation of the Indians and the ultimate success of the brave commander, Dr. Egle concluded : " Thus ended the power of the Western Indians, and the war inaugurated by Pontiac and Kyasutha closed. The peace which ensued lasted for a period of ten years, and confidence and security were given to the pioneers of the west. The frontiers were removed from this locality west of the Alleghenies, and never more did the foot of the hostile savage tread this beautiful valley. It was during this period of quietude that emigration to the valley of the Ohio's headwaters was permanently commenced—when the foundations were laid of great and powerful States now holding a controlling influence in the American nation. To Col. Henry Bouquet, the gallent Swiss officer, more than to any other who served in the French and Indian war, are we indebted for much of the prosperity which followed. He was incomparably a strong man—firm and decided as an officer and intrepid as a soldier. His remains rest in an unknown grave on the Florida coast, but his name and fame are inseparably connected with the history of our State. He did signal service in his day and generation, and the influence of his heroic deeds has thrilled unumbered hearts through the years which have intervened.''

''Pontiac and Bouquet! The first the personification of a savage Napoleon, brutal, inhuman and treacherous—murder and lust glaring his eye-balls—pollution and baseness in all his acts. The latter—a man standing out grand and glorious, fulfilling life's noble destiny, magnanimous as he was brave, a soldier by education, but an upright citizen and Christian gentleman. The former not the ideal representative of his race, but the true, with all the evil of human nature; the latter with the God-like attributes of mankind.''

''Men of Antrim, I am done. With the work you have this day completed do not imagine that your duties of life are finished. In commemorating the virtues of the schoolmaster of the long ago you should not forget the glorious principles which underlie all noble actions. Instil into the minds of your children a reverence for the good, by precept as well as by example. If the pious teacher of one hundred and twenty-one years ago deserves this commemorative stone, let the remembrance of the events of that era frequently cause you to reflect upon the blessings you enjoy and thank God that you live in prosperous peace.''

ji ..i b r iu

APPENDIX.

THE CHRISTIAN NAME OF SCHOOLMASTER BROWN.

Considerable ado was made last summer by one of the Chambersburg papers over a supposed mistake in the name of the martyred schoolmaster. It was alleged, on the pretended authority of Dr. Egle, that his name was Hugh instead of Enoch. In a conversation with the writer on the evening of Dedication Day, in presence af Poet Cooper, Dr. Egle emphatically remarked that he never had authorized such statements. Said he, "I never said that the schoolmaster's name was Hugh or that it was not Enoch. In my speech to-day I repeatedly called him Enoch. We must take tradition where we have no history that positively contradicts it. I spent several days in Carlisle recently examining the old lists of Cumberland county taxables, &c., but found no mention of either Enoch or Hugh Brown among them." General David Detrich and his aged sister, Mrs. Diehl, also Mrs. Scott, besides other old citizens, affirm that Betty Hopkins always called the schoolmaster *Enoch ;* Mrs. Scott heard her call him Enoch nearly eighty years ago. Capt. C. F. Bonner is a great grandson of the massacred teacher, and says all the family traditions gave him the name "Enoch." Ancient papers which would doubtless have made this matter perfectly clear were thoughtlessly destroyed many years ago.

Andrew N. Rankin, Esq., of Jamaica, N. Y., states that his grandmother's maiden name was Brown and that her father was a cousin of the murdered schoolmaster. She had often told him the story of the massacre and had not only called the master Enoch, but had given the reason why he was originally named Enoch. He was born in Ireland, where thirteen is considered unlucky. Being the thirteenth child in his father's family his parents sought to ward off bad luck by naming the child *Enoch*, after the first man "who was translated without tasting death." See Gen. 5, 24. 'Squire

Rankin (the father of A. N.) was a leading spirit in the work of exhuming the remains of the teacher and scholars, August 4, 1843. He also furnished, along with George W. Ziegler, Esq., the detailed account of the same, which was afterwards published by I. D. Rupp in the county history and inserted from time to time in the county papers. The Irish device to ward off bad luck from Enoch Brown seems not to have been very successful, and yet, humanely speaking, we can say, in the light of present surroundings, that there was good luck in the bad luck. Providence overruled the massacre, we believe, to secure from the Provincial government for Bouquet the reinforcements for which he vainly pleaded the year before. And but for this massacre and the self-sacrificing spirit shown in that fiery ordeal, history would know nothing of Enoch Brown, the martyred schoolmaster, and no monument would perpetuate his memory.

ENOCH BROWN POETRY.

The following is the full text of the poem, the last two verses of which form the inscription on the south side of the monument :

A POEM—IN MEMORIAM.*

With anguish sore and bitter woe,
    The hearts of Konoshick† are wrung
Alas! the cruel Indian foe
    Has slain the tender and the young.

As Rachel wept in Judah's land
    O'er infants slain by tyrant king,
So Antrim wails her martyr band,
    Her homes with lamentations ring.

As heroes fall, at duty's post,
    So fell the master and his school,
A sacrifice, a holocaust,
    To border life and Quaker rule.

The place is holy where they died,
    In Christian faith and childhood pure,
And where they laid them side by side,
    In common grave and sepulture.

---

*By a friend of the monument, February 10, 1885.
†One of the old ways of spelling Conococheague.

And ye, who now in safety dwell,
  In Cumberland's enchanting vale,
Revere the spot and mark it well,
  Where long was heard the mother's wail.

For not in vain the martyrs die,
  Their death brings life to pioneers,
Who gain the burden of their cry,
  Relief denied in former years.

Bouquet has sought the tiger's lair
  With trusty lion-hearted men;
Kind Heaven grants the settlers' prayer,
  The Dove of Peace returns again—

The tomahawk and scalping knife,
  Long red with Anglo Saxon gore,
The symbols dire of savage strife,
  Are seen on Antrim's hills no more.

The ground is holy where they fell
  And where their mingled ashes lie,
Ye Christian people mark it well
  With granite column strong and high.

And cherish well, forevermore,
  The storied wealth of early years,
The sacred legacies of yore,
  The toils and trials of pioneers.

THE QUAKER POET.

While Prof. J. Fraise Richard was gathering data for the history of Franklin county, he wrote a letter to John G. Whittier, the New England poet, requesting him to write a poem on the massacre of Enoch Brown and the school children. The following letter was received by Mr. Richard in reply, viz:

OAK KNOLL, DANVERS, Mass., }
3d month 19, 1886. }

DEAR FRIEND: I am glad to know that the people of Franklin county have erected a monument to the memory of the noble, Christian

c*

schoolmaster and his slain children, and that the history of the county
is to be written by thyself.   In my state of health I do not feel equal to
the exciting effort of writing a poem on so sad a theme.   But I thank
thee for thy letter and enclosed circulars, and am truly thy friend,

                                                JOHN G. WHITTIER.

HON. HORATIO SEYMOUR ON THE MONUMENT.

In December, 1881, the Greencastle *Press* published a
letter from Hon. Horatio Seymour to Rev. Cyrus Cort,
stating that "it is time that our people are made acquainted
with our obligations to the German and Holland lineages,"
and thanking him for an article on Baron Steuben, which
Rev. Cort had furnished the *Reformed Church Messenger*
about the time of the Yorktown Centennial Celebration.
Mr. Seymour had been chiefly instrumental in having an
invitation sent to the Steubens of Germany, by the American Government, who he thought deserved it as well as the
Lafayettes of France, to participate in that centennial celebration.   Baron Steuben was the efficient drill-master and
Inspector General of the Revolutionary Army at Valley
Forge and vastly improved its discipline and effectiveness.
He managed the siege and commanded a division in the
trenches which was about to storm the camp of Cornwallis
at the very hour that the flag of surrender was hung out.
After the war he was for some years an elder in the Reformed
church in Nassau street, New York city, in which church a
memorial tablet was placed by his aide, General North, after
the Baron's death.   Mr. Seymonr recently celebrated his
75th birthday and at the same time his Golden Wedding.
In connection with this event Rev. Cort sent him copies of
several poems written a few months ago in honor of similar
events celebrated by his uncles, Simon Cort at Denver, Col.,
and Daniel Cort at Zwingli, Iowa, and their wives.   He
enclosed at the same time one of the Enoch Brown circulars.
Mr. Seymour promptly acknowledged the receipt of these
documents in an autograph letter to Rev. Cort, which we
believe will be of special interest now that the distinguished

Statesman has passed away along with his beloved wife, under very pathetic circumstances.

UTICA, N. Y., July 9, 1885.

MY DEAR SIR.—I am under obligations to you for sending me copies of your verses written on the Fiftieth anniversaries of the marriages of your kinsfolk, Mr. and Mrs. Simon Cort, and Mr. and Mrs. Daniel Cort. They are very happily conceived and expressed. I am also interested in the circular with regard to the Enoch Brown Monument. I have given some time and attention to the erection of monuments in commemoration of events. Such monuments have done much to teach about the past and to instruct with regard to duties of life and the virtues of patriotism, &c. We feel as we look upon them that the dead speak to us. A number of such monuments were put up in this section about the time of our national centennial year. They have done much to instruct and improve our citizens. I trust the effort to put up the Enoch Brown Monument was successful. Again thanking you for sending me the verses and the circular about the monument, I am

Respectfully yours,

HORATIO SEYMOUR.

To the Rev. Cyrus Cort.

REPORT OF THE TREASURER OF THE ENOCH BROWN MONUMENT FUND, JANUARY 4, 1886.

To amount received:

H. M. Gilmore, Chambersburg,.....................................$	1 00
German Street Grammar School, Chambersburg,................	1 80
Public Schools of Chambersburg,.....................................	69 30
Chambersburg Academy,..	6 00
Collection Presbyterian Churches, Chambersburg,..............	36 95
Zion's Reformed Church and Sunday School, Chambersburg,..	15 00
Methodist Sunday School, Chambersburg,........................	6 00
First Lutheran Sunday School, Chambersburg, ...	15 17
King Street U. B. Church, Chambersburg,.......................	5 11
Public Schools and Sunday Schools, Quincy Twp., per Col. Wiestling, ...	88 67
Individual contribution, Col. Wiestling, ...	20 00
Individual contributions from citizens of Greencastle and vicinity,...	140 25
Presbyterian Church and Sunday School, Greencastle,.........	25 00
Reformed Church and Sunday School, Greencastle,............	28 14
Methodist Sunday School, Greencastle,...........................	2 00
Public and Select Schools, Greencastle, ...	10 10
Carried forward,... $	470 49

Amount brought forward,................................$	470 49
Brown's Mills Public Schools,.............................	13 75
Antrim Grove　　"　　"	9 20
Clay Hill　　"　　"	2 00
New Haven　　"　　"	2 25
Pleasant Retreat　"　　"	4 50
Cedar Grove　　"　　"	12 50
Highland　　"　　"	10 00
Bushtown　　"　　"	3 75
Middleburg　　"　　"	1 30
Shady Grove Sunday School,.............................	9 50
Paradise　　"　　"	4 85
Reformed Church, Middleburg,.............................	1 73
Jacob Hershey and others.............................	3 45
Mrs. Martha J. Nevin, Stephen Keifer, Dr. Wm. H. Egle,	
Dr. L. B. Rowland and others, per Rev. C. Cort,.........	35 84
Citizens of Mercersburg, ...	28 50
Lutheran Sunday School, Mercersburg,....................	2 40
Reformed　　"　　"　　"	5 40
Mercersburg College,.............................	4 35
Reformed Sunday School, Fort Loudon,....................	2 58
Public Schools of Fort Loudon,.............................	3 46
Welsh Run Presbyterian Sunday School, ...	5 03
Union Sunday School, Lenhersville, ...	6 00
Individual contributions from citizens of Waynesboro and	
Washington townships,.............................	39 00
Washington township Public Schools,.....................	33 12
Waynesboro Public Schools,.............................	7 80
Methodist Church, Waynesboro,.............................	3 01
U. B. Mission Church,　　"	2 45
Harry C. Strickler,　　"	1 00
Cave Dale Public School, Peters township,..............	3 15
St. Stephen's Sunday School, Upton,.....................	15 65
Union Church Services, Upton,.............................	1 85
C. M. Deatrich and others, St. Thomas,.................	14 10
Methodist Sunday School,.............................	3 25
Amberson's Valley Sunday School, ...	13 50
Carrick U. B. Sunday School,.............................	80
Spring Run U. B. Sunday School,.............................	5 45
Spring Run Public School,.............................	5 40
Dry Run　　"　　"	3 40
Concord and Wolff's Sunday School, ...	2 15
Basket collection per Rev. George, Strasburg, ...	2 20
Union Sunday School, Strasburg,.............................	6 60
Union　　"　　"　Greenwood, ...	2 50
Centre　　"　　"　Path Valley,.............................	3 98
Lutheran Sunday School, Orrstown, ...	1 12
Carried forward,................................$	814 31

Amount brought forward, ...$ -814 31
Church of God, Orrstown, ... 1 33
Public School, Orrstown,.. 1 55
Blue Spring Sunday School,.. 3 50
U. B. Sunday School, Guilford township,...................... 5 30
Marion Public School,... 18 60
Cedar Grove Public School, ... 10 35
Falling Spring Public School,.. 2 30
B. F. Crawford and others,... 3 00
Sylvan Sunday School,.. 11 73
Carrick M. E. Sunday School, ... 1 80
New Franklin and Bethel Sunday School, ... 10 00
Fayetteville Lutheran Sunday School,............................ 7 82
Greenvillage Lutheran Sunday School, Smoketown U. S. S.,
    Clark's School, Salem School, Garfield, Row District
    and Scotland U. B. S. S.,.. 15 95
John A. Zullinger and others, Southampton township, ... 10 32
Williamson Union Sunday School,...................................... 5 05
Norman   "   "   " Lehmaster's station,......... 5 90
R. R. Rebate from Centennial Executive Committee,........... 423 91

    Total,..$1,352 72

    By amount paid :   CONTRA.

Captain J. Deihl, for land,..$ 484 69
W. N. Meredith, for Monument, ... 491 50
U. G. Hawbecker, for stone and cement, ... 27 50
Brewer & Winger, for stone,.. 3 60
S. Z. Hawbecker, for stone cutters, &c.,.......................... 29 96
Henry Lohr, for dressing stone,....................................... 5 25
S. P. Stouffer, for dressing stone,................................... 5 25
C. C. Pentz, for mason work, ... 10 00
D. A. Pentz, for mason work,.. 7 50
Charles Martin, for stone cutting,.................................... 12 00
S. S. Easton, for labor at monument,............................... 6 00
Wesley Lizer, for hauling stone,...................................... 2 00
Greencastle *Press*, for printing circulars, badges, &c.,........... 18 25
M. A. Foltz, for printing circulars, &c.,............................. 15 00
G. W. & D. Zeigler, for satin ribbon, ... 3 45
U. N. Speilman, for U. S. Flags,...................................... 1 45
B. F. Winger, expenses of trip to Mercersburg and for mail-
    ing dedication circulars,... 3 33
Daniel Foreman, carriage for speakers,........................... 2 00
D. B. Keefer, for iron fences,.. 142 24
W. B. Lear & Son, for placing iron fences, ... 12 24

    Carried forward,...$1,283 19

Amount brought forward,............................$ 1,283 19

Clippinger & Spielman, for terra-cotta pipe,.....................   1 80
J. S. Snively, for lumber used in dedication platform,...........   2 85
Luther Palmer, for hauling lumber,...............................   2 00
Rev. C. Cort, for printing, postage, trip to Mt. Alto and Get-
    tysburg to examine granite, cement for terra-cotta piping,
    telegraphing, ice on Dedication Day, in all, ...   9 77
Postage paid by Treasurer, ...   60
                                                               ──────────
                                                               $1,300 20
                                                               ══════════

Balance in hands of Treasurer, ...$ 52 52
                                                               ══════════

Respectfully submitted,
                                        A. H. STRICKLER, *Treas.*,
                                                Waynesboro, Pa.

NOTE BY EDITOR.—In addition to the two hundred and eighty odd
dollars credited in the above list to citizens of Greencastle and Antrim
township, they gave in labor and hauling upwards of fifty dollars, right
in the midst of harvest, making in all nearly one-fourth of the entire
cost, and making fully one-third of the cost without counting the surplus land. Well done for Mother Antrim! Leaving out the railroad
rebate only about $600 remains, or less considerably than half the cost,
as the contribution of Franklin county outside of Antrim township.

INCORPORATION.

The following articles of Incorporation were duly approved by the Court of Franklin county, Pa., Dec. 7, 1885,
and the Enoch Brown Park and Monument Association was
created a body politic, or corporate in law in accordance
therewith, by decree of the Honorable Court, on petition of
Cyrus Cort, Robt. J. Boyd, A. H. Strickler, W. D. Dixon
and B. F. Winger. The same are recorded in the Prothonotary's office and also in Charter Book, Vol. 1, page 244,
&c., in Recorder's office of said county.

ARTICLES OF INCORPORATION.

FIRST : The name of this incorporation shall be known as the " Enoch
Brown Park and Monument Association."

SECOND : The object of this association shall be to honor and perpetuate the memory of Schoolmaster Enoch Brown and eleven scholars massacred by Indians, July 26, 1764, by securing in fee simple from Capt. Jacob Diehl, and holding in perpetuity for cemetery, social, religious and patriotic uses for the schools and citizens of said county, the grounds in Antrim township, a few miles north of Greencastle, containing the site of the school-house where the massacre occurred, also the site of the common grave in which the master and ten scholars lie buried, and the adjacent spring a few rods southwest of said grave, and the avenue leading to the public road, north of the Park, together with the monuments, iron fences and other improvements erected on said grounds, under the auspices of this Association.

THIRD : The Enoch Brown Park, aforesaid, of Greencastle, Pa., shall be the regular place of business af this Association, and July 26, at 10 A. M. the time of the annual meeting, which shall always be held at the Park, unless otherwise ordered by a majority of the Association in writing.

FOURTH : This Association shall exist in perpetuity, and its members shall have no power to sell, mortgage or encumber the grounds which contain the site of the school-house and grave, now marked by granite monuments, or the adjacent spring.

FIFTH : The officers of this Association shall be a president, secretary and treasurer, with duties and powers usually appertaining to said offices.

SIXTH : The names and residences of its members are as follows: Cyrus Cort, (President), Greencastle ; Robt. J. Boyd, (Secretary), Upton ; A. H. Strickler, (Treasurer), Waynesboro ; W. D. Dixon, St. Thomas and D. Watson Rowe, Chambersburg, all of said county.

SEVENTH : Any vacancy occurring in this Association, or among its officers by death, removal or resignation, shall be filled by election at the next annual meeting, or at a special meeting called for that purpose, and none but citizens of Franklin county shall be eligible for such positions.

EIGHTH : Three members shall constitute a quorum, either in person or by written proxy.

NINTH : Special meetings may be called at any time by the president, one week's notice being given the members, to transact such business as may be specified in the call, and no other, unless all the members are present, or represented by proxies with authority in writing.

TENTH : The funds in possession of this Association, and all securities representing funds, whether received by gift, legacy, or from the sale of the fifteen acres, more or less, of the surplus land bought of Captain Jacob Diehl, shall be conveyed to A. H. Strickler, Robt. J. Boyd and B. F. Winger, as trustees, and their successors in office to be appointed by the Honorable Court of Franklin county, and shall be invested in securities, approved by the Court, the annual interest or proceeds to be paid over promptly to the treasurer of this Association, to be devoted to keeping the grounds, fences, monuments, spring, etc., in good repair in accordance with the action of the Franklin County Centennial Convention of April 22, 1884, after all the necessary expenses for grounds, monuments, etc., have been paid.

ELEVENTH : Any vacancy occurring in said Board of Trustees, shall be filled by the Court of Franklin county, on notice to that effect being given by said trustees, or by the secretary of this Association.

TWELFTH : No members of this Association, or its Board of Trustees, shall be allowed to make any charges for their time or services, while attending meetings of the Association or Board, or for the performance of any official duty in furtherance of the sacred trust committed to their care by the people of Franklin county.

THIRTEENTH : This Association shall have power to make, adopt, alter or amend such rules and by-laws as may be necessary, provided they do not conflict with the foregoing articles, the Constitution of Pennsylvania, or the Constitution of the United States.

THE ARCHIE McCULLOUGH SPRING.

One of the most interesting and important features of the Enoch Brown Park, is the Archie McCullough Spring. At this spring, Schoolmaster Brown and scholars were wont to slake their thirst on the hot summer days. Here little Archie McCullough was found by Mr. Linn, according to tradition, soon after the massacre, trying to wash the clotted blood from his face and scalpless head. The water is clear as crystal, and for a slate hill spring, is remarkably cool. -

Overrun by cattle, and never cleaned out for many years, this spring was simply a miasmatic mudhole or quagmire when the Enoch Brown Committee bought the Park. Miss Susan Koser insisted that it was an excellent spring, whose waters were highly prized by her father, Captain Christian Koser, on account of medicinal qualities. For many years he kept a constant supply of it in his cellar and had great faith in its curative properties.

This testimony alone with the older traditions, induced the committee to put down terra-cotta piping, so as to drain the spring properly. They also walled it up in a substantial manner. The results were equal to the most sanguine expectations. The different parties who drank the water most freely, while fixing up the park and monument, were convinced that it had valuable medicinal properties similar to those of the Bedford mineral springs, so famous for relieving or curing kidney and liver ailments. Adding a little salt makes it taste very much like the famous Vichy water.

Large quantities can be drank without any inconvenience, except that any malarial tendency in the system is driven to the surface in the form of hives, etc., causing temporary annoyance, but conducing to greater permanent healthfullness. Restored to its pristine beauty and utility, the spring is a treasure, not only on account of the pathetic interest that attaches to it because of ancient association, but because it promises to be a practical blessing to thousands of visitors for all time to come.

MOTHER TERRAPIN.

A great many land turtles of different sizes were found among the rubbish immediately adjoining the grave of Enoch Brown and scholars. A young doctor present concluded to score one for Hugh, and marked on the shell of one of the most venerable of these creatures, the initials and date, "H. B., 1764." This was intended to give aid and comfort to the advocates of Hugh Brown, whose ghost is supposed to lurk about the park, glaring fiercely betimes at the word *Enoch*, carved in big letters on both monuments. In this way the toilers, who worked for nothing and boarded themselves, while clearing the grounds of brush and briars, beguiled the hours occasionally when the thermometer was 98 in the shade. The turtle clan or totem is an important one among every large tribe of Indians, along with the wolf and bear, etc. And among white people many may be fitly represented by grandmother terrapin, moving sluggishly over and around the most sacred associations, living, as it were, in the past, but without a particle of reverence or enthusiasm for what is noble and enduring in the past. The remarks and actions of not a few persons in our county, in reference to the monumental project during the past year, indicate that they belong to the tortoise totem. It is to be hoped

that a more intelligent, progressive spirit will actuate them
in time to come, or that their childeren may at least catch
nobler historic aspirations.

We believe that the Enoch Brown Park and monuments
will help greatly to bring about this desirable result.

THE COUNTY SUPERINTENDENT'S ABSENCE.

Everybody was delighted with the noble and eloquent
speech of Peter A. Witmer, Esq., Superintendent of Public
Instruction in Washington county, Md. He did full justice
to the important educational features involved in the dedication ceremonies and brought out in grand array from his
treasures things new and old. The question naturally arose,
where was Franklin county's own Superintendent on that
memorable occasion? Did he try to rally the educational
forces of the county to unite with all true-hearted, public-
spirited citizens in their magnificent effort to honor the
memory of the noble master and scholars who fell as pioneer
martyrs in the cause of Christian education, and who consecrated Antrim's hills with their precious blood 121 years
ago? Not a bit of it. Mr. Dysert is not that kind of a
man. He was only conspicuous by his absence, trying to
prevent others from attending by getting up a little side
show at St. Thomas, where the papers stated he intended
having a public examination of teachers on August 4, 1885.

He seemed to be in full accord with several Chambersburg papers, which did all they could to confuse the public
with regard to the time and place of the dedication ceremonies, and made a frantic effort to get up a reunion of
colored veterans in Chambersburg on that particular day to
keep the people from attending at the park. They succeeded as far as Chambersburg was concerned. Not over
three dozen of her citizens were present at the dedication
ceremonies, although Mother Antrim led the van at the
Centennial parades, September 8 and 9, 1884, when over
two thousand of her citizens flocked to the county seat,
most of them paying regular railroad fare in full expecta-

tion that all the rebate would go to the Enoch Brown monument fund, as the convention of April 22, 1884, had decided.

Superintendent Dysert's indifference or hostility to the Enoch Brown memorial was shown on other occasions. He refused to issue a card to the teachers and schools of the county, urging them to co-operate with the Enoch Brown Committee in raising funds for the monument, according to the earnest request of the Sovereign Centennial Convention of April 22, 1884. He refused to let the Enoch Brown Committee, consisting of Colonels Wiestling and Dixon, and Capt. Boyd and Rev. Cort, to lay the memorial project before the County Teachers' Institute, when the two latter appeared for that purpose in person ; also representing Col. Wiestling by proxy, November 19, 1884. He said to the writer of this note that Enoch Brown did not represent anything, not even courage, and that the bulk of the funds contributed toward the erection of the monument had better be given to the Children's Aid Society in Chambersburg. Thus, with surprising mental and moral obliquity, he set up his contracted notions as superior to the Franklin County Centennial Convention, and in opposition to the judgment of the best historians, scholars, theologians, statesmen and poets in the land. The poor privilege of presenting the cause in a five minutes' speech before the Institute was denied the representatives of the Enoch Brown Committee by Superintendent Dysert. He finally consented to let the memorial of the Enoch Brown Committee go before the Committee of the Institute on Resolutions, which he sought to construct so as to smother the memorial. But in this he was outgeneraled. The committee reported favorable action in the shape of two resolutions prepared in advance by a friend of the cause. All the teachers in the county were urged to contribute and get their scholars to give at least one dime on or before New Year. The resolutions went through without opposition, but it was given out immediately by those nearest the Superintendent's throne that they were expected to remain a dead letter. No effort was made to give them vitality on the part of Mr. Dysert and his special friends, although adopted by the Institute.

All this helps us to understand why Superintendent Dysert

was absent and why the Enoch Brown Committee had to look to another county and another State to find a Superintendent in sympathy with the sacred duty imposed upon them by the Franklin County Centennial Convention, a man whose interest and enthusiasm in the cause of education reaches beyond the mere question of loaves and fishes.

We felt that a candid presentation of these facts belonged to the history of the monument, and was due the friends of the movement to honor the memory of the massacred master and scholars. Along with many other things, too numerous to mention, they help to show the ignoble opposition the committee had to face and overcome in the prosecution of their work. Thanks to a kind Providence their efforts have been crowned with gratifying success and the Enoch Brown park and monuments are fixed and enduring facts.

A WORD OF EXPLANATION.

It was stated in the newspapers last autumn, that arrangements had been made by representatives of the Enoch Brown Memorial Committee and the Executive Committee at Chambersburg, to publish jointly a full history of the Centennial of Franklin county. In addition to the contents of the present volume, the proposed history was to have given a full account of the Centennial Convention of April 22, 1884, the parades, speeches, poem, &c., of September 8 and 9, 1884, &c. A joint contract on very favorable terms had been entered into for such publication, revised copies of the centennial speeches and poem had been secured, and the title page had already been issued, when it was learned that the majority of the Executive Committee and of its sub-committee on publication, had repudiated the action of its representative, O. C. Bowers, Esq., in making said contract with the Enoch Brown Committee and with the publishers.

B. F. Gillmore and Jas. A. McKnight, Esq., seem to be mainly responsible for this renewed breach of faith on the part of the Executive Committee or it representatives. Their conduct is all the more remarkable when we bear in

mind, that out of the three hundred and thirty-four dollars
($334) of railroad rebate, unjustly withheld from the Enoch
Brown fund by said Executive Committee, one hnndred and
thirty or thirty-five dollars ($130 or $135) had been set aside
for the avowed purpose of publishing the centennial history,
the profits or proceeds of which the Executive Committee
had publicly pledged to the Enoch Brown monument fund.
That money is still in the hands of Mr. John McDowell,
Treasurer of the Executive Committee, and no honest effort
has yet been made to redeem the pledge by publishing the
whole or even a part of the centennial history.   They ob-
jected to giving the contract to a publishing house in Lancaster, Pa., which agreed to print 1,200 copies of the entire
history for less than half the amount asked for the same job
by the two best printing establishments in Chambersburg.
The proprietors of the Greencastle *Press* had offered to do
the work and guarantee a good job, for ten dollars more
than the Lancaster bid.   To obviate the objection against
letting the job go outside of the county, the Enoch Brown
representative then proposed to compromise by accepting
the offer of the Greencastle firm, and give it to the lowest
bidder in the county, but this proposal was also rejected.

This action of the Executive Committee needs no com-
ment.   We simply state the facts in this brief, explanatory
way, that the people of Franklin county may know the reason why the centennial history appears in fragmentary form,
and why a large part of it did not appear a year sooner, according to promise.   After waiting in vain for over six
months, in deference to the wishes of Mr. Bowers, to give
the Executive Committee full opportunity to make good its .
obligations, redeem its pledges, and meet the expectations
of all honorable, public-spirited citizens, the Enoch Brown
Committee has gone forward, as best it could, with the present volume agreeably to the request of the vast assemblage
present at the dedicatory services, August 4, 1885.   As a
salve to their conscience, and to propitiate public favor,
some of the Executive Committee now propose to hand
over the $130 or $135, to the Children's Aid Society in
Chambersburg.   It is to be hoped that they will not con-
taminate and degrade a noble charity by helping it with

tainted funds. The people of Chambersburg furnished that committee with ample funds to pay all legitimate expenses, without touching a cent of the railroad rebate, set apart by the Centennial Convention for the Enoch Brown monument fund. They ought to demand an itemized report to see what has been done with all the money so freely contributed. The item of $45 for erecting a stand, worse than useless, on the public square, and of over eight hundred dollars charged by the Executive Committee for their sorry display of fire-works, requires explanation. We have seen far better pyrotechnic displays repeatedly for less than one-fourth that cost.

A distinguished historian has said that the Enoch Brown Memorial was by far the most important and interesting feature of the entire centennial of Franklin county, and yet it encountered open or covert opposition continually from those who should have been most anxious to promote its success, which has been at length achieved in spite of their hostility and injustice. It is unpleasant to make these strictures, but the truth of history demanded that the responsibility should be placed where it belongs.

ACTION OF ENOCH BROWN MEMORIAL COMMITTEE.

In this connection we deem it right and proper to define the position of the Enoch Brown Memorial Committee by presenting its official action adopted Nov. 11, 1884, at the Enoch Brown Park. This action explains itself and is as follows:

WHEREAS, The Executive Committee of the Franklin County Centennial Convention has disregarded the action of said Convention adopted April 22, 1884, and has withheld $334 of the railroad rebate which they were directed to secure for the benefit of the Enoch Brown Monument Fund, and

WHEREAS, Said Executive Committee has set at defiance our protest of Sept. 9, 1884, and has returned an insulting and ungentlemanly answer to the very mild and respectful declarations of our committee, after holding a joint conference with said Executive Committee Sept. 30, 1884, and

WHEREAS, The Executive Committee have persistently striven to create the impression through the Chambersburg papers and otherwise that our Enoch Brown Monument Committee was satisfied with their conduct in the premises, and had consented to allow over three hundred dollars of the railroad rebate to be appropriated by said Executive Committee to defray expenses of the committee in other directions, therefore be it

Resolved, That the Enoch Brown Committee has never consented to allow a cent of the railroad rebate or any other part of the Centennial fund entrusted to its care to be devoted to any other purpose, than the legitimate expenses of the Monument project.

Resolved, That we reiterate our previous declarations of Sept. 30, that our understanding of this action of April 22, 1884, was and is that all the rebate received from the railroads, which amounts to about $758, should be paid into the Enoch Brown Fund, and we regret that the Executive Committee have disregarded alike our protest and the instructions to the Centennial Convention.

PROVIDENTIAL ESCAPES FROM THE MASSACRE.

In the addresses of Rev. Cort and Rev. Woods reference is made to the Providential escape of Eleanor Cochrane, who afterwards married Capt. Joseph Junkin and became the mother of a large and distinguished family. In the "Life of Dr. George Junkin," written by Dr. D. X. Junkin, pages 16 and 17, the story of her Providential escape from massacre is told. The older members of the family, assisted by some neighbors, were engaged in a "flax pulling," and Eleanor, along with another young girl who, it seems was boarding or staying at Cochrane's while attending the school of Enoch Brown, remained at home July 26, 1764, to take care of the smaller children. Dr. George Junkin once spoke of this narrow escape of his mother and another little girl to Hon. George Chambers, the eminent jurist and polished gentleman, formerly of Chambersburg, Pa., where he died in 1866, March 25. Judge Chambers replied to Dr. Junkin, "the other little girl, thus Providentially preserved, was my mother." Her maiden name was Sally Brown. She died July 27, 1837, aged 78 years. Thus we have the mothers of three large and distinguished families, the Junkins, Agnews and Chambers, all Providentially preserved from the scalping knife of the brutal savages who vented their fiendish fury on the innocent heads of their school-mates on that dreadful day of massacre.

In addition, Eleanor Pawling was a member of the school and was Providentially detained at home on the day of mas-sacre. She became the wife of Dr. Robert Johnston, the distinguished surgeon of the Revolutionary Army, the friend and host of Washington, who sent him on an important mission to China in the early days of the Republic. Post-master Brather has the gold-rimmed tortoise snuff box pre-sented to Dr. Johnston by high Chinese officials in recogni-tion of his great medical skill.

Mrs. Catharine Scott, who is now in her 84th year, says her uncle or grand uncle, Samuel Fisher, was one of a number of boys belonging to the Enoch Brown school who played truant on that 26th of July, 1764. This confirms the old traditions to the effect that the school was unusually small on the day of the massacre, and that owing to premo-nitions, Providential detentions and wilful truancy, a large proportion of the scholars of Enoch Brown escaped the fate of the master and their eleven companions who were ruth-lessly slaughtered.

CENTENNIAL MEMORIAL SERMONS.

A LL the pastors of the different churches in Franklin
county were requested to preach Centennial Discourses
September 7, 1884, and also deposit copies of the same in
the archives of the Historical Society.

The Society publicly requested pastors to furnish copies
of their sermons, as provided by the action of the Centennial Convention.

The Joint Committee on Publication, also informed all
pastors and congregations that these sermons would be incorporated in the memorial volume, on very liberal terms, and
all were invited to confer and co-operate with the committee
to secure their publication.

And yet, only three centennial sermons have been furnished for the Historical Society Archives and for publication. Some failed to preach any centennial sermons at all,
and others disregarded repeated requests looking to their
permanent preservation and publication.

This is to be regretted. A full collection of such discourses
would have been invaluable for the future historian. Instead of favoritism towards the few pastors represented in this
volume, the charge of persistent indifference and neglect
must rest against all congregations or pastors not represented
in this memorial department.

Although this feature more properly belongs to the Centennial history, proposed to be published by the Executive
Committee, and although said committee has ample public
funds in hand to meet all the expenses, yet, from what we
have shown in our "Word of Explanation," it is not in the
least probable that said committee would concern itself
about the publication of memorial sermons. Hence we have
added them to our Enoch Brown Memorial, agreeably to
D

the wishes of some of our best citizens. Their general contents will be found to harmonize well with the object and
spirit of dedication ceremonies, for which they furnish congenial company. They, as well as the Enoch Brown Park
and Monuments, will help us to "remember the days of
old," and do just homage to the heroic pioneers who laid
the foundations of church and State.

SERMON OF REV. CYRUS CORT.

PREACHED IN THE REFORMED CHURCHES OF GREENCASTLE AND
MIDDLEBURG, FRANKLIN COUNTY, PA., SEPT. 7, 1884.

LEVITICUS 25, X : "And ye shall hallow the fiftieth year and proclaim liberty
throughout all the land unto all the inhabitants thereof. It shall be a Jubilee
unto you ; and ye shall return every man unto his possession and ye shall
return every man unto his family."

INTRODUCTORY REMARKS.

My Christian Friends :—We have met to engage in the
public worship of Almighty God, which is always our highest
duty and privilege as patriots and Christians. At the same
time we have been requested, as a congregation and as a
community, to commemorate in these services the one hundredth anniversary of the organization of Franklin county.
This is a proper request and a grateful duty to which we can
respond with alacrity. The request involves a just recognition of the religious element which is the basis of all true
prosperity and safety for communites and individuals.

We have abundance of Scriptual warrant for such services
as these. Not only are we earnestly admonished by the
great leader and law-giver of ancient Israel to "remember
the days of old and consider the years of many generations;" not only does the sweet Psalmist exhort us to "walk
about Zion and go round about her ; tell the towers thereof,
mark well her bulwarks and consider her palaces, that we may
tell it to the generation following," but special times and
seasons were hallowed by divine appointment under the Old
Testament dispensation to commemorate the goodness and

protecting care of the great Jehovah, the Covenant keeping God of Abraham, Isaac and Jacob. Festivals of a religious, social and patriotic character frequently brought the people of Israel to Jerusalem to commemorate important events in their past history, to secure rights of person and property in the present and fill them with hope and courage to meet future obligations and responsibilities. What was the great central, controlling Passover festival but a vivid commemoration of their deliverance from the sword of the destroying angel and the thraldom of Egyptian bondage? At the same time it was so ordered as to have a prophetic reference to the future deliverance of all mankind from the sword of divine justice, from a worse than Egyptian bondage to sin and Satan and assure them of a happy admission to a better country than even that goodly land of Canaan in the time of its greatest glory.

So the Feast of Tabernacles and of Pentecost were important annual festivals, continually reminding them of the wanderings and privations of their fathers in the wilderness, the giving of the Ten Commandments, the ingathering of the first fruits of the harvest and their consequent duty to give tithes to maintain the public worship of Almighty God, whose protecting care they had experienced in so marvellous a degree.

The climax or culmination of all these patriotic and religious memorial services was reached in the year of Jubilee. Our text refers to that great epoch and benign institution in the history of God's gracious dealings with His covenant people—"And ye shall hallow the fiftieth year, &c."

THE SABBATIC IDEA PREDOMINATES.

The number seven was the governing factor in Jewish festivals. They were to "remember the Sabbath day to keep it holy," * * "the Lord blessed the Seventh day and hallowed it." Not only was there a Sabbath of days but a Sabbath of weeks, a Sabbath or Sabbatic year, and a grand Sabbatical cycle of years, rounded off with the Jubilee year.

Thus, from Passover to Pentecost was seven weeks, or seven times seven days preceding the Pentecostal Feast, which commemorated the giving of the law on Mt. Sinai and provided for the offering of the first fruits of the harvest, a grand harvest home festival. Then every seventh year was a Sabbatic or sacred year, during which the land rested and the spontaneous fruits of the soil were common and free to all classes of society. And finally, after seven times seven years, the fiftieth year was hallowed as the great Jubilee season of God's covenant people.

It was ushered in at the close of the great Day of Atonement, after the whole nation had humbled itself before the Lord in fasting and prayer. On that day alone in all the year the High Priest, after repeated typical sacrifices for his own sins and those of the people, entered the Holy of Holies, typifying the entrance of Christ Jesus into heaven, where He ever lives, to intercede for us.

THE YEAR OF JUBILEE—A JOYOUS AND BENIGN INSTITUTION.

When these peculiarly solemn services were over and this most sacred day of all the year was ended the year of Jubilee began. With a mighty blast of trumpets sounding forth from Jerusalem, and from all the cities, villages, mountains and valleys of Judea, the opening of the Jubilee year was proclaimed. It was indeed a gladsome time, not only on account of the joyous festivities peculiar to the season. It brought in great permanent blessings, especially for the poor and unfortunate classes of the community. The text tells the grand story in language that well befits the trump of Jubilee, "Proclaim liberty, &c." A universal balance sheet was struck. All debtor and creditor accounts were squared. All mortgages were cancelled. All bond servants, or slaves of Hebrew origin, were set free. Families impoverished during the previous fifty years were restored to the home and possessions of their ancestors.

The land of Canaan, as you are aware, was divided between the tribes and families of Israel by lot, at the time that Joshua took possession of it in the name of the Lord of hosts. Each family had its distinct and just proportion of the public domain. If lost by misfortune or mismanagement during the previous fifty years, this origina inheritance or patrimony was sure to come back to the descendants of the original owners whenever the year of Jubilee came round.

It was a wise and merciful provision, guarding the people against landed monopolies and moneyed aristocracies, which are a curse to any country and which sooner or later by their unjust extortions bring anarchy and pave the way for military despotism. The year of Jubilee sounded the death knell of oppression and monopoly. Liberty and equality then rejoiced over tyranny and injustice. The lowly were exalted and the purse-proud found their common level. That Jubilee year was indeed a season of genuine rejoicing for all pious and patriotic Jews.

All generous-hearted people could rejoice not only in being permitted to meet in family reunion and communion in the home of their ancestors. They could also share in the general joy of all generous hearts over the return and happy reunion of families long separated by poverty and misfortune. When one member of the body suffers all the others sympathize more or less in that suffering. So it is with the body politic and the Mystical Body or Church of our Lord Jesus Christ. When one class of society is wronged or oppressed there is a corresponding weakness in the whole system of government that permits it. Now it was the design, the merit and peculiar glory of Jubilee year that it provided a safeguard and remedy for the ills of society. It acted as a grand alterative, a balance-wheel, a clearance day, a judicious bankrupt act, based upon principles of inherent justice and rectitude.

THE JUBILEE FEATURE STILL NEEDED IN OUR OWN LAND.

Some such institution, or an arrangement of the framework of government securing similar results, would be a blessing in our own land and an effectual safeguard against dangers that now loom up portentously. No thoughtful man can look at the present condition of affairs in our beloved country without serious concern for the future peace and safety of the Republic.

With grasping corporate monopolies and selfish, avaricious millionaires controlling mining, manufacturing and commercial interests and even invading the public domain in violation of all law and justice, there is great danger of subversion to our most cherished institutions. They seek not only to absorb or control all the wealth of the country. They have frequently corrupted the ballot-box with their ill-gotten gains, defiled the halls of State and National legislation and dragged the judicial ermine in the mire. A day of reckoning and wrath must come sooner or later to all such bare-faced workers of iniquity. As Christian patriots we should seek to apply the proper constitutional remedies before the very foundations of our government are destroyed. No such unjust and demoralizing condition of affairs could exist under the Jewish commonwealth when administered according to the principles laid down by the Supreme Lawgiver of heaven and earth. The right of eminent domain stood in the Almighty Maker of heaven and earth, and was not vested in any man or set of men. In the 23rd verse of this chapter He solemnly sets forth this fundamental principle : "The land shall not be sold forever ; for the land is Mine."

The civil and ecclesiastical ordinances of Judaism set at defiance all the crafty schemes of land grabbers and monopolists. As in other respects the Mosaic code forms the fundamental basis of legislation among all civilized nations, so in this matter of land distribution and ownership we would do well to enshrine in some way the essential features of the Jubilee year provisions. The homestead laws in some of the Western States look somewhat in this direction, but they have often been made a cloak for downright dishonesty and have worked to the detriment of the debtor as well as creditor class, by creating usurious rates of interest owing to increased risks of investment.

Long before the Declaration of Independence was adopted by delegates of the American colonies, renouncing allegiance to King George the Third and the British Parliament, because of usurpations and tyrannical violations of the principles of the Magna Charta and Bill of Rights, so dear to every Anglo-Saxon heart; long before the Colonies declared themselves free and independent States, the old bell in the State House in Philadelphia bore the prophetic as well as Scriptural legend of the Jubilee year, which forms so significant a part of our text: "Proclaim liberty throughout all the land unto all the inhabitants thereof." Personal free-

dom, as well as national independence, has long since become a fact instead of a name. Not a slave can be found
in all this broad land between the Atlantic and Pacific.

But with all our boasted freedom we are largely becoming
hewers of wood and drawers of water for unprincipled
monopolies and law-defying corporations. Eternal vigilance
is the price of liberty. And here is a question that comes
right home to our hearthstones and concerns the happiness
of the people and the safety of the Republic. The land of
a country ought to be in the hands of those who occupy
and till the soil or personally superintend its cultivation, and
not in the hands of foreign capitalists or grinding railroad
corporations, as is now, alas! so largely the case in the far
West. Then there would be little occasion or justification
for labor strikes and communistic deliverances of a revolutionary character, which frequently threaten the peace and
safety of the country.

Such a disposition of the land of the nation would inaugu-
rate a genuine political and social jubilee for millions of our
most useful citizens. The same remark applies to Great
Britain and other nations also. The spirit and main features
of such a sovereign remedy for gravest dangers that threaten
our nation, are found in the provisions regulating the celebration of the year of jubilee in the days of old.

OUR OWN FRANKLIN COUNTY CENTENNIAL.

My Christian friends: I have called special attention to
these matters in the beginning of this centennial memorial
discourse, because they are necessarily involved in a proper
treatment of my text, and because the subject is one that
concerns deeply our welfare, as individuals, as families, and
as a nation.

The text, along with corresponding Mosiac deliverances
and institutions already mentioned, gives ample scriptural
warrant for memorial centennial celebrations, such as engage our attention to-day. All centennial occasions are
multiples of the jubilee unit of fifty years. This is simply
the second jubilee year of our existence as a county. Scripture encourages and teaches us to engage in more frequent

memorial observances than centennial periods can furnish. Important events in the political and religious history of a people should be commemorated once in the life time of each generation, or say once every fiftieth year.

Some, indeed, are of such supreme importance, the birth of the Saviour, for instance, or the birthday of a nation, as to demand annual commemorations which Christmas and the Fourth of July celebrations regularly furnish.

Others, like the organization of counties should move in cycles, and no cycle is so old, appropriate or inspiring as the jubilee cycle of fifty years. Whether or not the anniversary of the organization of our noble county was celebrated fifty years ago, we know not. But our duty to celebrate on this second return of the jubilee year is all the same.

This is an age of centennials, semi-centennials, bi-centennials, ter-centennials, and even the 400th anniversary of the birth of Luther, the great Saxon Reformer, and of Zwingli, the great Reformer of Republican Switzerland, have recently been fitly commemorated. Eight years hence, the four hundredth (400) anniversary of the discovery of America will attract universal attention. This is all right and proper. Anniversary occasions properly observed are good institutions. They help to cultivate a reverent historical spirit, which is one of the best safeguards of society. The words and deeds, the trials and triumphs, and even the mistakes and failures of our forefathers are full of instruction. The first commandment with promise " Honor thy father and thy mother" is violated wherever important events of the hoary past are not commemorated. The present is the child of the past, for whose lessons it must have due respect, in order to become the honored parent of the future. A nation, a church or a civilization is strong and enduring only as it is rightly grounded in its past history.

We can only briefly dwell upon those events that specially concern the immediate beginnings of our local history in both its civil and religious aspects.

THE ORIGIN OF THE COUNTY—ITS SCOTCH-IRISH AND GER-
MAN-SWISS ELEMENTS.

When Antrim township, in which we reside, was first created in 1741, it formed part of Lancaster county. When
Cumberland county was formed in 1750, Antrim became
part of the same. Franklin county was created Sept. 9,
1784, and was almost identical with Antrim township, as
originally constituted, out of whose territory all other townships in the county were formed with the exception of War-
ren, Metal, Fannet and part of Peters townships. The
Indian title to these portions of the county was not extin-
guished until 1758. Hence, Antrim may rightly be called
"The mother of townships." Long before these dates, en-
terprising settlers had located in this beautiful and fertile
valley. The Scotch-Irish were first on the ground. Benja-
man Chambers located at the junction of Falling Springs
with the Conococheaque in 1730, by consent of the Indians
who were as yet friendly to the white settlers. The orders of
the Provincial government to the proprietary agents were to
send the Germans into York county and the Lehigh region,
and to send the Scotch-Irish into the Cumberland Valley.
The two elements had not harmonized well in Lancaster
county, where they frequently got into broils with each
other on election days. While this order of settlement was
the general rule, there were some notable exceptions. Jacob
Schnebele, the founder of the Snively (as the name is now
written) family, located in Antrim township in 1734, or just
150 years ago. He was of German-Swiss stock. His descendants are numerous, and the Snively family is respected
by all. We are glad to have a goodly number of them in
our own Reformed congregation, who are present with us to-
day. Likewise representatives of the Crunkleton family,
whose ancestor also came here as one of the four original
settlers in 1734. No descendants of the other two (Rhoddy
and Johnston) remain. A number of us (your pastor for one)
have the mingled blood of Scotch-Irish and German-Swiss
ancestors coursing through our veins.

Along the adjacent Maryland line, which was then supposed to be farther north than at present, the Seiberts, Zel-
    D*

lers, Stalls, Cushwas, Kershners, Ankenys and other German-Swiss families located in those early provincial days.
In 1748, Rev. Michael Schlatter, the pioneer missionary of
the Reformed Church, visited a very devout Reformed congregation of German-Swiss people on the Conococheague,
near the present site of St. Paul's Reformed Church, between Clear Spring and Hagerstown, Md., about a dozen
miles from here.   The ancestor of the noted Schley family,
of Frederick City, Md., taught a Reformed Church Parochial School at Monocacy, as Frederick City was then called
in those pioneer days.   Capt. Jonathan Hager, the founder
of Hagerstown, (laid out in 1762,) belonged to the Reformed
Church, and accidentially lost his life while preparing material for the first Reformed Church erected there at the be-
gining of the Revolutionary war.   In fact, the printed forms
of naturalization used at that time in the province of Maryland, required the applicant for citizenship to furnish cer-
tificates from officiating ministers, that they were communicant members of the " *Reformed or Protestant Congregation,*" as the certificate of Heinrich Stall, granted and signed
at Frederick by Reverdy Johnson, in 1764, fully proves.
This document is now in possession of our venerable towns-
man, William Fleming, who is a great grandson of Heinrich
Stall.   That heroic man, Gen. Henry Bouquet, one of the
finest scholars and the best military man of colonial times,
was a German-Swiss and a member of the Reformed Church.
His Long Meadows estate of 4,163 acres, was located only
a few miles from here, and lay on both sides of the Pennsylvania and Maryland line.   His famous Royal American
Regiment was composed mainly of German-Swiss soldiers,
recruited in the provinces.   They held for seven years the
long line of forts and block-houses, reaching from Philadelphia through the wilderness to Detroit, and bore the brunt
of battle and hardships in those dark and trying days.

THE REFORMED CHURCH IN FRANKLIN COUNTY.

Rev. Weymer, the faithful pastor of the Reformed Church
in Hagerstown, Md., from 1770 until 1790, was the first Reformed minister to preach the gospel regularly within the
bounds of Franklin county, Pa.   In 1784 or 1785, as near

as we can learn, he organized congregations at Greencastle, Grindstone Hill and Chambersburg. Hence, we have double reasons to commemorate this year of our Lord, 1884. It is the centennial of the Reformed Church of our town and county, as well as the centennial of the county itself. This is a happy coincidence, a blending of civil and ecclesiastical events, which ought to make this centennial season doubly interesting and precious to our household of faith in Franklin county.

Along with the other heroic pioneers, whose memory we gratefully cherish to-day, let the name of JACOB WEYMER be mentioned with reverential honor. He was a man of genuine Apostolic character, a missionary in the full sense of that term ! Besides preaching to Reformed people all over Washington and Frederick counties, Md., he made missionary tours through the valley of Virginia, all over this part of Cumberland Valley and over the mountains into the Juniata region, going once a year to Huntingdon county, Pa. His remains lie buried in the rear of the First Reformed Church of Hagerstown, but no one knows the exact location of his grave. The absence of a monument is not an evidence of ungrateful neglect on the part of the Reformed people of Hagerstown, as Dr. Harbaugh intimates in his biographical sketch. It was his desire and dying request (a fact evidently unknown to Dr. Harbaugh) that his grave should be unmarked. He said the good Lord would know where to find his body on Resurrection Day. John Calvin, the great Reformed Theologian and Disciplinarian, made a similar request, and great as he was, and honored as he is by millions of Christians in all lands, of him it may be said, as it was said·of old, respecting the burial of Moses, the leader and law-giver of ancient Israel, ''the place of his sepulchre knoweth no man unto this day.'' Nevertheless their works do follow them, and they rest from their labors.

The Reformed and Lutherans in Greencastle, worshiped together in a log church at first. The Lutherans built a church of their own, and in 1808 the Reformed laid the corner-stone of a brick church, which they built on the old graveyard lot, under the ministry of Rev. Rahauser. Several years' time elapsed before the church was finished.

The successor of Father Weymer was Rev. Jonathan Rahauser, who settled in Hagerstown, in 1792. His pastoral charge took in Washington and Frederick counties, Md., and Franklin and Adams counties, Pa. At first he preached in Hagerstown, Funkstown, Boonsboro, Troxels, Greencastle, Mercersburg, Besores, Millerstown, Emmittsburg and Apple's church. In 1809 his brother Frederick took charge of Emmittsburg and Apple's congregation, along with Gettysburg, Taneytown, &c. After serving the Reformed Church at Harrisburg, as pastor for three years, Frederick Rahauser, located at Chambersburg, where he labored faithfully from 1819 until 1836. The Rahauser name is still known and honored amongst us. After the death of Jonathan Rahauser, Rev. F. A. Scholl, took charge of this particular field in 1818, and became the first resident pastor of the Greencastle charge. He resigned the Greencastle congregation Nov. 3, 1833. He labored faithfully for 21 years, when he retired from the active duties of the ministry. His field embraced all the Reformed congregations in Franklin and Fulton counties, excepting the Chambersburg charge. The corner-stone of the Union church at Middleburg was laid in 1834, in which our people there still worship.

Rev. Hamilton Vandyke and Rev. Jacob Mayer, pastor of Mercersburg charge, acted as supply of the Greencastle congregation for several years after the resignation of Father Scholl. Rev. W. C. Bennet served in the same capacity for a short time. The old church was somewhat remodled, and modernized during the vacancy.

Rev John Rebaugh succeeded Father Scholl, and was the earnest and esteemed Pastor of the Greencastle congregation from 1837 to 1851, when he resigned this congregation, but remained pastor at Middleburg, St. Paul's and Clear Spring, Md., until 1863. He was a warm-hearted genial man and a faithful pastor. The sick and sorrowing especially found in him one who could sympathize and console. His ministry marked the transition from the use of the German language to the English, which seems to have been passed over with tact and good judgment. It is a source of great regret that no official or private records have been left by any of these aged fathers in the ministry giving account of baptisms, marriages, confirmations, &c., during their pastorate here.

Rev. John S. Foulk, the successor of Father Rebaugh, introduced a new era in this respect. A Constitution and By-Laws were adopted by the congregation, and a congregational record of ministerial acts has been faithfully kept since the settlement of Rev. Foulk. Under his ministry the substantial and comfortable church edifice was erected in 1854, in which the Greencastle congregation still worships. The congregation prospered under the 7 years efficient ministry of Rev. Foulk. He was succeeded by Rev. Thos. G. Apple, D. D., now at the head of our college and theological seminary in Lancaster, Pa. With the character and results of his able ministry of nine years you are familiar. So, also with that of his successors, Drs. S. N. Callender and Moses Kieffer and the lamented pastors, Revs. S. K. Kremer and John H. Sykes. The average duration of their ministry was three years and the last two fell at the post of duty in the full vigor of manhood. Such briefly is a history of the Reformed Church in Greencastle and vicinity, during the past century. But oh! what toils and troubles, what hopes and fears, what joys and sorrows were crowded into those hundred years of congregational life! The pioneer fathers, mothers and pastors where are they? Gone to their everlasting rest and reward. It is a solemn thought that a hundred years hence, yea perhaps in half that time, not one of this audience will remain. May we so live that the Church of Christ shall suffer no harm from our connection with it, and we may at last be enabled to enter the pearly gates of the New Jerusalem, to meet the loved ones gone before.

COMPARATIVE STATISTICS OF RELIGIOUS BODIES.

At present Mercersburg Classis is identical with Franklin county in extent, with the addition of McConnelsburg charge in Fulton county, and part of Shippensburg charge in Cumberland county. This is offset by part of the Cavetown, Md., charge located in our county. The statistics of Classis for this year, shows a membership of 2,606, a bap-

tized but unconfirmed membership of 1,567, with 23 congregations, 10 pastors, 20 Sunday Schools, numbering 2,023
members.   The Greencastle charge contains two congregations, 312 members, 217 baptized members, 2 Sunday
Schools and 267 Sunday School Scholars and teachers.

The Lutheran Church, the twin sister of the great Reformation of the 16th century, has prospered side by side
with our Reformed communion in this valley.   It has 18
congregations, 2,825 communicant members, and Sunday
Schools containing 2,692 members.

The Presbyterian church represents to a large extent the
Scotch-Irish element, which originally had the vantage
ground in this county as we have seen.   It has at present
1,839 member and 1,633 persons connected with its Sunday
schools.   A great many of these are of German or Swiss
descent as their names indicate, viz : Detrich, Ziegler, Ruthrauff, Snider, Wilhelm, Kieffer, Snively, Winger, &c.   The
Methodists have 1,752 members and 1,397 Sunday school
scholars, and the United Brethren, who began their career
about one hundred years ago, claim 2,500 members in this
county.   The Tunkers or German Baptists of different
classes and shades of belief form a large part of our agricul-
tural population in particular.

THE GERMAN-SWISS ELEMENTS IN THE ASCENDANT.

Bearing in mind that the M. E. and U. B. people are
largely composed of descendants of German-Swiss settlers
who were Reformed or Lutherans, and adding these to
Reformed, Lutheran and German Baptistic members it will
be seen that the descendants of the German-Swiss settlers
outnumber those of Scotch-Irish origin fully four to one.
The Germanic element now largely owns and cultivates the
fertile farms of this grand old county.   As old Mr. Bossard
prophetically remarked many years ago they will dig out the
Scotch-Irish with their silver spades.   One hundered years
ago, when this county was first organized, a dozen lawyers
composed the bar at Chambersburg, not one of whom had
a German-Swiss origin.   Now the majority seems to be of
that stock.   We have Kimmel, Stenger, Bonebrake, Brewer,

Winger, Ruthrauff, Gehr, Bowers, Suesserot, Zacharias, Ludwig, Omwake, &c., &c.

We state these things simply as historical facts and not in the way of invidious comparison. Our people, we can say without boasting, belong to the most substantial part of our population. With a fair proportion of professional men, they are, as a rule, farmers, mechanics and merchants, who form the bone and sinew of every prosperous community. Few of them are now so ignorant or ignoble as to be ashamed of their German-Swiss origin or the church of their Reformation forefathers.

EDUCATIONAL AND PUBLICATION RELATIONS—MERCERSBURG THEOLOGY.

Some of the most important educational and publication interests of the Reformed church have had an eventful history within the borders of Franklin county. For 18 years, from 1835 to 1853, the chief college (Marshall) of the church was located at Mercersburg, where some of the most prominent and useful men of both church and state were educated.

The Theological Seminary of the Reformed church remained at Mercersburg 17 years longer. Mercersburg Christological Theology, with the corresponding philosophical mode of thought, became famous all over the civilized world.

It makes the Person of Christ central in the Christian system, even more really than the sun is central in the planetary system to which our globe belongs. He is the central sun of the moral universe. Not any abstract theory of predestination, any form of church polity, mode of administering sacraments, or mode of eucharistic presence, or theory of conversion is the central controlling principle of Christianity, but Christ Jesus Himself is the principle of principles. He is the Alpha and Omega, the beginning and the end of Divine revelation—the centre and source of all true history, the object of all saving faith and genuine adoration. In Him the decrees and promises of God are yea and in Him Amen, living, historical, everlasting realities. The best thought of Europe, Great Britain and the

United States has come to a substantial agreement on this point, which is after all the citadel of our holy religion. The names of Rauch, Nevin, Schaff and Harbaugh are revered among all liberal-minded, large-hearted Christian scholars. The college and seminary have long since been removed to Lancaster, where the good work of training our Reformed pastors goes on, but the fragrance of their memory still lingers around the old Mountain Home. Mercersburg College rendered important service to the cause of education during its fitful career of a dozen years or more, and now seems to have a promising future before it as a collegiate institution, under the judicious management of Dr. Aughenbaugh.

The printing establishment of the church had a long and successful career at Chambersburg, under the faithful management of Dr. S. R. Fisher, until it was finally destroyed in 1864 by Southern invaders.

Illustrious men are the noblest heritage of a community or nation. The contemplation of their characters and achievements is full of inspiration and instruction. Of these Franklin county has furnished an unusual number; more, it has been successfully maintained, than any other county in the Union. But time and space will not allow me even to name the roll of honor. This will probably be done by the historian in his address next Tuesday afternoon.

THE DEBT OF GRATITUDE TO GOD AND THE PIONEERS.

It is a great privilege to live in such a favored part of such a goodly land in such a period of the world's history. " Better fifty years of Europe than a cycle of Cathay !" exclaims the laureate poet of England. Better a generation of vigorous progressive life in this garden spot of the great Republic than a thousand years among the stagnant despotisms of the Old World. But great privileges being corresponding duties and responsibilities, American Christians should excel all others in the line of Christian activity and especially of missionary enterprise.

They ought to be the salt of the earth and the light of the world in a pre-eminent degree by bearing the gospel to the benighted heathen. Thank God they are doing great things in the blessed work of evangelizing the nations. A large proportion of the 6,000 missionaries at work in heathen lands and the $10,000,000 annually expended for the foreign mission cause comes from these United States.

With thankful hearts we should engage in these memorial centennial services which have been fitly inaugurated by suitable religious observances in the churches of the county. We dare never forget the toils, the dangers and privations of our pioneer ancestors. They turned the wilderness into a fruitful field and made the desert blossom as the rose. Cultivating friendly relations with the Indians they had multiplied and prospered in the region west of the Susquehanna, so that already in 1755 there were 3,000 men able to bear arms. Then came the blunders and horrors of the French and Indian wars, culminating in Braddock's disgraceful and disastrous defeat. A year later, in the fall of 1756, scarcely one hundred were left in all the great Cumberland Valley. 18 forts were erected to protect them against Indian forays. On every side the pioneer settlers and their families were waylaid and massacred, or borne into barbarous captivity by prowling bands of savages. McCord's Fort,. near the foot of Mount Parnell, was captured, and 27 men, women and children met a horrible fate. In my hand I now hold the MSS. journal (140 years old) of James McCullough, which contains page after page of entries reciting massacre after massacre of the pioneer settlers and their families. Those were dark and trying days indeed, and had not their hearts been stout as oak, and their sinews strong as steel, they could never have withstood the fearful strain of body and mind which the anxious suspense must have caused even for those who escaped the tomahawk and scalping-knife of the merciless savages. All honor to the brave men and women of those pioneer days ! Base and ignoble are those who fail to cherish the memory of such an heroic ancestry.

CULTIVATE THE HOME FEELING.

This is a sacred memorial season, a hallowed jubilee year full of inspiring associations. It is a time to visit the old homestead, to trace up and record genealogical tables, to hold family re-unions and revive the fond memories of the olden time.

Such is the spirit and sentiment of our text, "ye shall hallow the 50th year and proclaim liberty throughout all the land, unto all the inhabitants thereof. It shall be a jubilee unto you, and we shall return every man unto his possession, and we shall return every man unto his family."

Happy are they who can do this with gratitude to the God of their sainted forefathers! Happy are they who can thus return to the home of their childhood! Happy are they who remain in the honorable possession of the patrimony of their pioneer ancestors! The love of liberty, of home and of fatherland will be strong and abiding in the hearts of such a people.

A CONTRAST BETWEEN THE PAST AND PRESENT.

Great and marvelous have been the changes and improvements of the century just ended. The pack-horse and the lumbering Conestoga wagon have given place to the traction engine and to the locomotive and railroad trains which daily pass through our streets from New York to New Orleans. The express rider, galloping over the mountains and through the wilderness on panting steed, at the peril of his life, has been superseded by the electric telegraph, which conveys messages of love and light in the twinkle of an eye to the remotest part of the Republic, yea underneath old ocean's briny waves to all parts of the habitable globe. The flail and the sickle of our fathers have given place to the steam separator and the four-horse reaper. The thirteen colonies along the Atlantic coast, with three or four million people, a large number of them negro slaves, have increased to thirty-eight States, reaching from ocean to ocean, with a population of fifty odd millions and territory enough for twenty States more. "The Lord hath done great things for us as a nation, whereof we have reason to be glad and to bless His holy name." And with the Psalmist we may exclaim: "Bless the Lord, O my soul, and all that is within me, bless His holy name. Bless the Lord, O my soul, and forget not all His benefits."

The blood-thirsty savages no longer skulk about our dwellings as they did in the days of our pioneer ancestors, when young and old were ruthlessly slaughtered regardless of sex, age or condition.

In our valley hundreds of Indian youths are now receiving instruction in the elements of education and Christian civilization within the precincts of Carlisle Barracks, whence the heroic Bouquet marched to punish their race for their atrocities, 120 years ago. The same work is going on at Hampton Institute, Virginia, where I addressed a large number of them through an interpreter, a few weeks ago, and told them of the universal Fatherhood of God and Brotherhood of man. No longer do our children go to school, and our people to church and to their daily toil at the peril of their lives, as did our pioneer ancestors. Peace and plenty, prosperity and safety is the portion of our inheritance in this goodly land.

OUR DUTY TO CHERISH THE ANCIENT LANDMARKS.

The blessings of constitutional liberty, the principles of representative self-government for which our Reformation forefathers suffered in Switzerland, Germany, Holland, France and Great Britain, have become a fundamental part of the institutions of our land.

Let us cherish these as something more precious than silver or gold. Above all let us cherish the principles of Christian faith and piety, so dear to the hearts of our sainted forefathers. For the sake of religious principle, our Scotch-Irish and German-Swiss ancestors endured the dangers and hardships of pioneer life, and only by imitating their fidelity to the Lord Jesus Christ can we preserve and perpetuate the blessings of civil and religious liberty enshrined in our constitutional form of government. It is true now as in the days of old "righteousness exalteth a nation, and sin is a reproach to any people." We have made great progress in the arts and sciences, in agriculture and the mechanic pursuits, but the old-fashioned principles and habits of honest industry, frugality and piety remain the enduring basis of all true prosperity and power. In these respects let us gratefully "remember the days of old." Thus shall we "honor father and mother,'' and inherit the divine promise that our days shall be long in the land which the Lord our God, hath given us. Let us walk in the good old paths of truth and righteousness and keep in view the ancient landmarks.

CONCLUSION.

And, finally, my Christian friends, let us remember that all these earthly jubilees are but faint shadows of the grand reality, the Jubilee of glorified humanity, when the ransomed of the Lord, from every land and nation, shall enter the home of the blest with songs and everlasting joy upon their heads. That we may all stand accepted in the Beloved and be numbered among the saints in glory everlasting, in that great and notable day, should be our hope, our prayer and our supreme endeavor. Amen. And, Amen.

CENTENNIAL SERMON OF REV. J. HASSLER,

OF MERCERSBURG, PREACHED IN ST. PETER'S REFORMED CHURCH, IN FORT LOUDON, PA., ON SUNDAY EVENING, SEPTEMBER 7, 1884, AND IN THE TOWN HALL, IN FANNETTS-BURG, PA., SEPTEMBER 14, 1884.

DEUT. 32:7—"*Remember the days of old,* consider the *years of many genera-tions;* ask thy father and he will show thee ; thy elders and they will tell thee."

Three thoughts are before us: 1. Thanksgiving and praise for our *grand old mountains,* and the *rich* and *fertile valleys* that characterize the *geography* of our county.

2. Thanksgiving for the *moral integrity* and *upright, religious life* of our *pioneer settlers.*

3. *Civilization* and *National Freedom, the price of blood.*

I. SCENERY AND FERTILITY OF SOIL.

The words of our text constitute an extract from the plaintive song of a dying man. The great drama of a great life is at an end. The greatest commander that ever lived— the greatest moral hero that ever stepped on the stage of history—he, who is the most honored of all human beings, who talked with God "face to face"—whose hand met the fingers of Jehovah in receiving the Law—this great man, whose whole moral life is the greatest miracle of the greatest age that ever characterized the inhabitants of earth ; whose life, and deeds, and death challenge infidelity, and will ever scatter to the winds of heaven all doubt or uncertainty as to the truth of inspiration—this great man is called upon to die, to pass away from the scenes of earth! His death song is contained in this chapter, the import of which is : *Obedience to God secures independence, personal and national prosperity. Disobedience brings ruin, loss, captivity, death !* So *to-day.* It is meet and right for us, as a religious community, to look back a *hundred years* and consider the many trials, hardships and cruel captivities our fathers endured, to give us this beauteous land of freedom ; and these grand and fertile valleys, that surround these lofty mountains of beauty and power! And thus, by this review of a *century past,* generate in our hearts *praise, thanksgiving* and *obedience* to our fathers' God.

In 1682 William Penn came from England to this country and founded a colony, which he called Pennsylvania— the *forest land,* or *land of Penn.* The whole country was inhabited by rude and untutored Indians, who lived in wigwams and subsisted on hunting. Penn desired his people to live in peace with these wild and savage tribes, hence his "Treaty of Peace," on the very spot where now stands the City of Philadelphia, on the banks of the Delaware.

But oh! what changes! Instead of wild game, Indian huts and camp-fires you now see hundreds and thousands of houses, built high, three, six and eight stories; of brown stone, brick and marble; and thousands upon thousands of white people, all with busy step and hurried tread, eager in business, trade and commerce—buying, selling and getting gain!

Where is the old "*Elm Tree,*" under whose wide spreading branches, late in autumn 1682, the treaty was made? Alas! the sacred spot is now covered by a large, populous city; and the place itself is only marked by a *marble monument,* to perpetuate its memory. The *tree itself* stood till 1810, when it was blown down by a storm at the age of 283 years, being 155 at the time of Penn's treaty. When the

British troops occupied the city, during the Revolution, it was guarded by a band of soldiers. It was held in great veneration, and its sacred wood is yet preserved under the form of *ornaments* for the *parlor table?* But, oh! the changes it witnessed !

So, too, similar changes belong to the fertile vales and growing towns in our own county, in the 100 years that are past! Could some old Indian chief, who once roamed these hills and drank at the beautiful spring below our town, where old Ft. Loudon stood, revisit this land, he would be *completely lost*—his mind would be filled with *wondrous surprise!* So, too, at a later date—from 1790 to 1830—if some of the McCulloughs, Smiths, McFarlands, Bards, McDowels, Crawfords, Dickeys, Pattons, Lanes, Scotts, and others, who lived amid these hills and tilled these lands, could return to earth, oh! how spell-bound with surprise !

The old line of *"pack horses,"* traveling with steady step up the rugged steeps of *yonder mountain gorge*—the Cove Gap—where are they? The old " *Conestoga wagons,*" high and long and deep, with canvas top, that lined this western turnpike, heavy laden with merchants' goods from Baltimore to Pittsburg, where are they? Not one to be seen. The line of *"four-horse stages,"* too, six and eight a day, crowded with Western merchants and others, eagerly bound for the Eastern cities, every hour feeling for *their money*, hid in the *lining of their coat*, or *in their boots*, or *some secret place*, lest the Robber Lewis and others, who lurked in these hills, would rob both traveler and driver alike—these, alas! all gone !

The days of military parade, militia muster—"review days"—with shrill fife and noisy drum, and gaudy soldiers, and galloping troopers—these, too, have all disappeared; together with the gleaming sickle; sowing wheat broadcast; cutting the broad acres with a hand-cradle, four and six in a row; tramping the wheat in the winter months, a six weeks' work; all these have disappeared, and we now have railroad cars, horse-rakes, phosphate grain drills, the sulky plough, the road traction engine, and a dozen or more of other farming implements.

But in the school-room and in the school-house, oh!

what changes! "Cobb's Spelling Book," with the picture
of the boy on the apple tree, pelted with stones by the
honest farmer for his first theft; the "New Testament,"
with Matthew, Mark, Luke, and John, all to the Book of
Revelation—this the scholars' "*only reader*," and then even
skipping the *hard names*—all these have disappeared.

So, too, in church building, and in the familiar scenes of
the home circle; oh! the changes!

The high-backed pews, wine glass pulpit, or as the poet
has it—

"Their pews of unpainted pine, straight-backed and tall;
    Their gal'ries mounted high, three sides around;
    Their pulpits, goblet shaped, half up the wall,
    With sounding board above, with acorn crowned."

These are now no more. So, too, the old Franklin stove,
the open fire-place, with "brass fender," and back-log
burning brightly; "the oaken bucket, the moss-covered
bucket, that hung in the well,"—all, all have given place
to the "radiant home," "the gas burner," the "cast iron
pump." Thus, too, instead of the "*old lard lamp*," and
"*tallow candle*," and "*snuffers*," you have coal oil, gas
and electric light!

But, oh! the changes in the spheres of *human life!* The
inquiry is, where are the great men who laid out these
towns, built these mills and subdued these forests? Echo
answers, *where?* Franklin county, to its credit be it said,
has furnished "more men of mark," both in Church and
State, for the Judge's bench, the Governor's chair, and
Halls of Legislation, than any other part of the State.

The greatest railroad king that America ever furnished,
Col. Thomas A. Scott, was born in this village, under the
shade of these mountains, in yonder "*public mansion;*" and
he who sat in the President's chair, the 15th President,
James Buchanan, received the light of day in yonder
mountain gorge (Cove Gap); and when a little boy his fond
mother placed a "bell around his neck," lest she would
lose her Irish boy amid the rocks of the impending forest.

But these reminiscences carry us too far.

On the 9th of September, 1784, an Act of the Assembly
was passed erecting the county of Franklin, out of the

southwestern part of Cumberland, thus bearing the name of our own honored natural philosopher, Benjamin Franklin. Its greatest extent from north to south is 38 miles, and from east to west 34 miles, containing an area of 49,740 square miles. In 1870 the population was 45,365. In 1880, 49,855. The greatest part of the county consists of an extensive valley of fertile land, well watered, well cultivated, and highly improved. The product of wheat alone in 1880 was 1,033,824 bushels—other grains, such as rye, oats, Indian corn and barley, in equal proportions.

On the east you have the range of hills called the South Mountain, reaching an elevation of 600 to 900 feet. On the west and northwest a more elevated and rugged range, called the North or Blue Mountain, running in almost an unbroken line from the Delaware southwestward and abruptly terminating in Mt. Parnell and Mt. Jordan's Knob.

Path Valley lies between these lofty peaks and the Tuscorora Mountain, which stretches southwest, on to the waters of the Potamac. Some of these lofty peaks range from 1,500 to 1,600 feet above the level of the sea. Oh! the grandeur of this mountain scenery—its health-giving power. With the homesick Swiss soldier, when far from his native Alps, we can say, "Geb mir Berge oder Ich Sterbe." The eye of the traveler is never wearied in looking upon the rugged brow of old Parnell and Mt. Jordan, joined together in one perpetual brotherhood of beauty and power, and looking down in quiet majesty upon the peaceful village of Ft. Loudon, nestling quietly amid the shade of these lofty peaks; or, casting our view six miles beyond, over to our neighboring town of Mercersburg, far-famed both in Europe and America for schools of learning and theological power; and then, still farther on toward the south you see "Casey's Knob," "Two-top," and the grand and beautiful chain of vast blue mountains on to "Penn-Mar" and the Potomac, forming "one vast amphitheatre" or "crescent" of beauty and mountain scenery hardly eclipsed by any other in the whole State. Strangers never cease to admire the beauty of *our mountain homes*. Yes, these grand old mountains are the finger-boards of nature that point the weary pilgrim up to heaven—to God—to our eternal home!

The purity of air that encircles their top, the green clad plains and fertile vales that lie at their base, the laughing rivulet and the towering oak that dwell upon their haggard sides, all serve to give health and tone to the body, invigorate the mind, and inspire within the breast of man feelings of awe, reverence and devotion! God himself built these lofty hills. He laid them deep; He made them broad; He shaped their conical form, their broad foundations, their haggard sides. He built them for himself, to point upward, to heaven, to our home above!

The Saviour loved the mountain. He prayed there; He preached there; He wept there; upon the mountain he died; at its base he was buried; from its top He ascended to heaven! Oh! the mountain! the mountain!! ' What Christian born in Franklin county but loves the mountain? Especially as these lofty hills remind him of Tabor, Carmel, Lebanon, Pisgah, Calvary, and above all Mt. Zion, the city of the living God, a truthful type of the Christian church!

Never can we gaze upon these rugged hills, or travel over their haggard sides, or look upon their lofty peaks, without thinking of the hill-country of Judea, and the mountains of Galilee, consecrated to the holy purposes of our holy religion, by the prayers and tears, and deeds, and awful sufferings and holy blood of our blessed Redeemer! Yes,

> "To Zion's hill I lift mine eyes,
> From thence expecting aid;
> From Zion's hill and Zion's God,
> Who heaven and earth has made."

II. But we must take up our *second point: Praise and thanksgiving for the moral integrity aud upright, religious life of our pioneer settlers.*

Living in the midst of such beautiful scenery, dwelling under the shade of such lofty mountains, what else could our fathers be than *devout, honest, religious ?*

In Path Valley, tradition has it, a man borrowed a hundred dollars from his neighbor. After the money was paid and the note written his neighbor said :

> "John, you keep *this paper too,*
> Then *you'll know when the note is due.*"

E

The man had both money and note. This story is a noble tribute of praise to primitive virtue, neighborly confidence and Christian love.

The character of Enoch Brown, the noble, heroic schoolteacher, murdered by the Indians, with his *ten scholars*, (one only making his escape,) on the 26th of July, 1764, in Antrim township, three miles from Greencastle, is only a *moral type* of the good and religious character of our pioneer settlers. This teacher is said "to be a man of liberal culture, particularly noted and respected for his *truthfulness, integrity and Christian character.*" His courage was *praiseworthy*, as it is said he offered himself first as a martyr, to save the lives of the innocent children.

It is to perpetuate the memory of this terrible sacrifice to the cause of freedom and education that our offerings *to-day* are to be devoted. To erect, at moderate cost, a *granite monument* to mark the *resting place* of this noble teacher and his murdered scholars.

The first settlers in our county were of Scotch-Irish descent. Religious persecution and a desire for freedom in religious worship drove them from Ireland and Scotland to this Western world. The rich valleys of the Conococheague settlement were objects of interest and attraction. These settlers were moral, honest, religious and devout. The Sabbath was strictly observed. The ten commandments committed to memory; next to the Bible, the shorter catechism was daily studied; grace at the table, and evening and morning prayers, a usual occurrence in their religious life.

Many of this noble race and of their descendants still reside in our county, but the German population of a later date is fast gaining the ascendency, both in numbers and in way of possessing homes and lands once occupied by this noble ancestry of the Scotch-Irish race.

The Rev. Michael Schatter, a Reformed minister, one of our first missionaries, who came to America in 1746, and who visited· Conococheague settlement in r748, uses these words: "The first inhabitants, as already stated, were from Ireland and Scotland, and a few from Germany and Switzerland. Benjamin Chambers, the first settler, induced others of his countrymen to immigrate to the Conococheague settlement. Soon afterwards some German and Swiss descendents, principally from the lower part of Lancaster county, found their way to this settlement; since then they constitute a great proportion of the present population. They speak the language of their fathers, but of late years the English has the preference with many whose grandparents immi-. grated from Germany,''

For the benefit of .these Germans, who soon intermarried and united their religious worship and social life with their Scotch-Irish neighbors, for their good Rev. Jacob Weymer and others, Reformed ministers, visited Chambersburg, Greencastle, Grindstone Hill and other places, where Reformed churches were established as early as 1784. A Reformed church stood on Stenger's hill, below town, as early as 1790. The old brick church, to the east of town, much of the material of which also is used in the erection of the new church edifice (1876) was built in 1819, by the Presbyterians and Reformed united. Thus, in point of morals, religion and true piety, the inhabitants of this county can boast of a noble ancestry.

Of course there are many exceptions to this estimate of moral character. Theft, robbery, horse-racing, intemperance and other vices were also known in those days. The old stone jail in Chambersburg, built two stories high in 1798, was often *"filled to overflowing"* with criminals *confined for debt.* This punishment many regarded as the fruit of indolence and intemperance. This may be all true enough. Evil is hereditary. Sin goes with the race. Wherever the foot of man treads their evil and sin keep apace, if not with a *faster* at least with an *equal step* with the march of virtue. And yet history generally credits this noble ancestry as being exemplary in moral integrity and the practice of the Christian graces—education and religion. The school and the church—these were the two cardinal marks of *the primitive settlements of these hills* by our pioneer fathers.

Rev. Dr. M. Brown, for a long time President of Jefferson College, who studied theology under old Dr. King, of Mercersburg, pastor of that church from 1769 to 1813, has this testimony, "that in all his extensive travels in the United States he found no population equal in virtue and intelligence to the people of the Cumberland valley."

So, too, Rev. Dr. James Brownson, of Washington, Pa.,

whose maternal grandfather laid out the town of Mercersburg, expressing his regret in not being able to be present
at *this centennial celebration*, uses these words: "Not for
silver or gold would I barter away my lineal descent from
such a race." "So noble a planting in one of the best and
most beautiful regions in our county, by a race unsurpassed
in intelligence, culture, patriotism and piety, and such a
development and progress, extending over 150 years since
the first white settlement, are worthy of being held up to
the grateful admiration of the descendents of a matchless
ancestry."

Such testimony, in favor of integrity and true morality,
is worthy of special regard.

Patriotism, too, was a crowning virtue. McCauley, in his
history of '76, says: "Not a Tory was to be found in the
whole Conococheague settlement."

No one present to-day need be ashamed of his Scotch-
Irish ancestry.

But these early settlers experienced all the sad consequences common to *frontier life*. Homes were hardly
secured, the land tilled, or barns built, till these homes
were burnt by savage Indians, the grain destroyed, cattle
killed, and wife and children carried into cruel captivity.

"For eight or ten years after General Braddock's defeat,
July, 1755, the whole frontier of your county was exposed
to the incursions of Indian war parties," who would *secretly
surprise* the inhabitants; shoot down the cattle, massacre
the men, women and children, or carry them away into the
horrors of cruel captivity. Here Border Life, and the narra-
tives of Col. James Smith, John McCullough, Col. Crawford, and others, are full of most thrilling interest. These
noble patriots gave their lives for our good and for our
homes. This leads us to our last point.

III. *Civilization and national freedom the price of blood.*
On the Fourth of July, 1876, eight years ago, we celebrated the *centennial* of our National Independence. It
was right and proper on that joyous occasion that we should
have poems, orations, historical readings, Declaration of
Independence recited, the highest forms of mechanical
art that genius could invent; all this, along with military

processions, bands of music, banners afloat, flags waving, national toasts, responses and firing of guns—all this joyous festivity to impress upon the mind and heart of every man, woman and child in the land that our National Freedom *is a reality*, and this reality the *price of blood. Citizen sovereignty* is a problem in civil government the old monarchies of Europe can't solve; but our Pilgrim Fathers solved it; but they did it with *treasure, bloodshed, death !*

So these fertile hills and these grand old homesteads in this fertile county are ours only by the toil, hardships, labor, and fearful sufferings and bloodshed of our Germanic, Scotch-Irish ancestry.

This great truth, human perfection and true religious freedom, are *the price of blood*, history, redemption and science all clearly proclaim. The Apostles died for the truth they preached. The reformers bled and suffered for the truth of the Gospel. "The blood of martyrs is the seed of the church." The idea of spiritual freedom from sin and death is a plant too celestial, too heaven born to grow on the soil of the human heart without the watering of blood to ensure its growth. The Disciples felt this, they knew this. They were willing every one of them to suffer martyrdom for the cause of Christ. They knew that righteousness, truth and eternal life are ours only by the death and crucifixion of their Master. Christ crucified contained the seed of a new creation. Sin and pride were the cruel monsters that drove the spear into His side. The Saviour's truth and purity were too holy and divine to germinate in the dead stock of humanity without the shedding of blood to ensure its growth. Christ's death is the germ of life. "If I be lifted up I will draw all men unto Me." *Via Crucis, via Lucis.*

So, too, in the sphere of intellect. No freedom from this darkness of ignorance and superstition except by toil, hardship, and even self-sacrifice and death. Robert Fulton, in 1807, was hissed at, laughed at and mocked when he sought to launch forth his first steamboat on the waters of the Hudson. Columbus is called the madman because he seeks the discovery of another world. Galileo, in Italy, is imprisoned because he seeks the improvement of astronomy.

E*

And even that holy man, Paul, as he stood on Mar's Hill, is called a Jewish babbler because he reasoned of "the resurrection and the life to come."

History, too, is full of the same truth. States perish, nations die, all the forms of life are mutable, only that the living spirit of humanity may go forward with new energy and create out of these smouldering ruins *new forms* of life and activity. The decay of Greece is the life of Rome, and the eruption of the northern barbarians, who lay all Roman civilization in the dust, gives life to the Germanic nations and the Anglo-Saxon race. Death is the condition of life. So in the history of civilization and in the progress of civil freedom. The wars of George III., the long years of cruel Indian warfare and the hardships of border life, all prove that our peaceful homes and these fertile valleys which we now so richly enjoy are the price of blood ! They are redeemed for us from savage rule and the cruel tomahawk, only by toil, hardship and sacrifices the most horrible, such as only true courage, martyr-heroism and earnest piety could endure.

Mark well, therefore, the *resting place* of the man who fell a sacrifice to education and offered his life a ransom for the lives of innocent children ! Keep green the graves of our patriot fathers, who spent their treasure and shed their blood to secure to us the fertile fields of this *rich old county*, whose history *to-day* reaches up to the *hoary foot-prints* of a *hundred years !*

Follow closely in the steps and pathway of a *most worthy ancestry*, who loved God, studied His word, kept the commandments, believed in His Son, confessed His name, and everywhere dotted this whole county with the church and the school-house ; and then God will be honored, our children blessed and freedom perpetuated.

Our mountain homes, the fruit of their blood and the scalps of their children !

Oh ! sing to-day as you never sang before—

> " My country ! 'tis of thee,   -
> Sweet land of liberty,
>   *Of thee I sing.*
> Land where my *Fathers died*,
> Land of the *patriot's pride*,
> From every *mountain side*,
>   *Let Freedom ring.*

SERMON OF REV. J. W. KNAPPENBERGER, A. M.,

PREACHED IN TRINITY REFORMED CHURCH, MERCERSBURG, PA.,
SEPTEMBER 7, 1884.

PSALM 90. Last clause of the 9th verse. "We spend our years as a tale that is told."

After speaking of the antiquity of the psalm, its beauty and sublimity and rich meaning, of the custom of telling tales among Eastern people and when all were told how short they would seem in thinking of them, we spoke as follows:

And just so in many respects is it with our lives. They are like tales that have been told. How short they seem! How quickly do they pass away! Three score years and ten roll into eternity, before we are aware of it. As we think of our past history, the oldest among us, how dim and indistinct, do the most prominent facts in our lives stand out in memory! You, whose hair has been silvered with the weight of years, and even those of you, who have only reached the middle mile stone of your life, try to recall the scenes and incidents and experiences of your early years,—those which happened under the parental roof, when father, mother, brothers and sisters were with you, when you gathered together, it may be, around the family altar, when you ate, drank, laughed and talked, played and toiled with one another,—when you rejoiced together on some notable interesting occasion, or wept with them over some great sorrow; or when with bowed head and sorrowing hearts, you stood together around an open grave, which received one after another of those, who were to you most dear. How you mourned their departure! How you missed them when you got back home; how sad you all were then and how time gradually healed the wound, which death had made!

Or think, if you please, of the companions and associates of your early years, of those who went to school with you,— of the lessons, which you studied and recited together, of incidents that happened, indeed of all the things connected with those early, interesting days, and as you dwell in meditation upon them does not your whole past life,—all the facts, incidents and experiences,—seem very much like a

tale that is told? You know it was real, actual and yet
how dim and shadowy, how like a tale it all appears now !
    But all their experiences, every early impression, as well
as everything, that has happened to us or which we have
done, have had an effect upon our lives, an influence which
we cannot even now overcome. All these things have been
worked up into the very texture of our being, and made us
what we are. Had it not been for all these associations
and influences we would not be what we are to-day. Our
characters are the rich ripe fruit of all these complex forces.
    And as it is with the history of our individual lives, so is
it with the history of a community or of a country. As we
think of the early, history of this country, the bloody scenes
which marks its pages, the struggles, hardships, dangers, and
sacrifices of the early settlers,—of the condition in which
this country was at that time, the valleys covered with tall
prairie grass, the rivers and creeks lined with forest trees
and the whole overrun with the Red Man, and the wild
animals peculiar to this district of territory at that time—how
difficult is it for us to throw ourselves back into the spirit of
these trying days, and make the conditions, which actually
existed, and the things which really took place, seem real to
us now ! We can read the facts connected with the massacre of Enoch Brown and his ten scholars, but we can't make
them as real to us as they were to those who found their
mangled bodies, and buried them together in one large box in
one great grave. And so it is with the story of John McCullough, the burning of Ft. McCord, the killing of men and
women, and the taking of prisoners. All these facts and
incidents, as well as hundreds of others connected with the
early settlement of this county, seem now very much like
tales that have been told. And yet the history of those
early days is a true account of the struggles and conflicts
and dangers of *real* men and women, who labored to get a
foothold in this new district of country. Had they not endured, toiled, fought and bled as they did, our country
to-day would not be what it is. They did a grand, noble
work, in times, too, which tried the mettle of which men
and women are made. In the midst of peace, prosperity
and plenty, we should not forget the pioneer settlers who
helped to secure the blessings which we now enjoy. Their

labors of love and sacrifice should still be held in fond remembrance.

As we think of the condition of this county and its people
one hundred years ago, and their situation to-day, what a
contrast ! If we take a position on the top of one of our
high mountains, and cast our eyes over the surface of
Franklin county, we can see hundreds of beautiful farms,
in a high state of cultivation, yielding rich harvests of
almost every kind of grain, vegetables and fruits. The
whole number of farms in this county, according to the
census of 1880, is 3,602, and their estimated value, with
their improvements, is in the neighborhood of twenty (20)
millions of dollars. Upon these farms are comfortable
dwellings, large barns, good fences and every machine
to lighten labor, and make the soil fertile and fruitful.
Why, the value of the farming implements and machinery
alone is to-day in the neighborhood of nearly one million of
dollars. All these facts indicate a prosperous condition of
affairs in this county to-day.

But look back one hundred years, or more and what do
you see ? These same acres were covered with stones, bushes,
briars and trees, and it was only with hardest labors that
the inhabitants could secure enough from them to satisfy
their necessary wants. It required the honest labor of
hundreds, yea, thousands of persons, extending through a
hundred years or more, to make their farms what they are
to-day. If all the persons that worked on these farms for
the past one hundred years, or more, to make them what
they are,—were to assemble in one place, what an army
would there be ; what labors and patience and sacrifices
and sorrow would they represent ! In the enjoyment of
present blessings how prone are we to forget what others
did to secure them to us !

To-day there are roads and lanes running East and
West, North and South, intersecting one another at almost
every angle, so that we can travel anywhere and everywhere in perfect safety, feeling assured that the law which
rules and reigns in Franklin county is no dead letter, but
that it is powerful to protect her citizens, and terrible in its
punishment of the transgressor. *One hundred years ago*
these roads did not exist in the condition in which they are

at present, and men had to travel from place to place as best they could, and with that feeling of insecurity which belongs to first settlers in a savage, barbarous country. The contrast in this respect is very great.

One hundred years ago, there was not a post-office in the county, nor was there one in it until about six years after its organization. Letters on business, letters on friendship or love, had to be sent, if sent at all, by some traveller. News from parents at home, or from friends and lovers on the other side of the great waters, or even in this country, could be secured only at long intervals, and in the most unlooked for and unexpected manner. The facilities, therefore, for communication in those early days were very poor and irregular, indeed. When we think of all these things, we cannot help but exclaim, what a deprivation! what an inconvenience! Why, we feel terribly disappointed and chagrined if our mail does not come twice every day, and even if it is an hour behind time, as it has been so frequently of late, it annoys us not a little. And if it were not to put in an appearance some day at all, we should almost consider it a personal bereavement. In that case we fear the third commandment would be violated by not a few.

There are now within the county about 60 post-offices, and the facilities for communicating with one another are getting better every year. We get our daily newspapers, weeklies, monthlies, quarterlies, so regularly and promptly, that we are liable to make light of the blessing and advantages which we enjoy over and above those who lived one hundred years ago. We can receive news from the Old World by telegraph every day, know all that is going on in civilized countries, aye, by putting one ear to the telephone and listening, we can hear the pulsative throbs of the world's great heart. In our complacency and self-satisfaction in thinking over the deprivations of the early settlers, we are apt to make light of them and say, ''O they wouldn't have enjoyed these advantages and benefits anyway. ' They would not have had the time, nor the inclination.'' But we should remember that they were *men and women*, just as we are, with the same feelings, sympathies, infirmities, hopes. They had hearts, too. They loved the Fatherland, the dear ones at home just as tenderly and truly as we love our nearest and best friends. News from them would rejoice and cheer their hearts, and give them as much satisfaction as news from our friends and relatives do us. The tears which they shed over their deprivations in this particular, and the sorrows which they experienced are known only to themselves and to God. And we do not refer to them to magnify them, but that we may see how much more highly favored we are than they were, and to show what wonderful progress has been made in this one respect, not only in this county, but in this country and throughout the world during the last one hundred years. The contrast in this particular is as great, if not greater, than any other.

But then think of the schools in those days. They must have been primitive, indeed. The merest elements of an education only could be secured, and many of the children, on account of bad roads, the distance to be travelled, and the dangers incident to a new country, would be deprived almost altogether of the privileges and blessings of the most limited education. The number of schools must have been very small. The school buildings were anything but inviting or comfortable. But what a change has taken place! There are to-day about 290 schools in this county, and there is spent annually in the payment of teachers' salaries near- ly sixty thousand dollars. The estimated value of school property is nearly three hundred thousand dollars, so that no boy or girl can have any excuse whatever for growing up in ignorance in such a favored county as this one is. Would to God that every parent might appreciate the privileges and benefits of the public school system, and show their appreciation and good sense by sending their children regularly and daily to school during its sessions.

We have yet to speak of the influence of religion in moulding and shaping the history of this county. It has always been, and always will be, the conserving, preserving power among any people. It has been so in this county. The majority of the men who settled in this county belonged to some branch of the Christian church. They sought to practice the principles of God's word in daily life. It is true, their characters are not models of human perfection. They did many things which would not meet our approval. But we cannot be too thankful for what they did in advancing the cause of the dear Redeemer. They organized congregations, they built churches, they united their voices and their hearts in the worship of the triune God on the Sabbath Day. Many pure, noble, righteous characters stand out prominent in the history of this county. Hundreds of men and women, noted for their love of righteousness and abhorence of evil, have gone out from this county, and have been a power for good in other communities, who owed all their influence to the splendid moral and religious training which they received under the parental roof. And while we have no statistics to verify the statement, we venture the assertion that the Christian religion has a stronger hold upon the people of this county to-day than it ever had before. There are churches enough to accommodate all its people, and would to God that every soul within its borders would bow at this time in submission to the dear Redeemer, so that the rejoicings on this centennial occasion may cause rejoicings among the the angels in heaven, over the sinners saved in the blood of Jesus.

One hundred years have passed away—one hundred years of mingled joys and sorrows, of labor and blessings.

When we think of the hundreds of families that were organized and then broken up by the hand of death—when we think of the great army of persons who walked over these hills and valleys and mountains during all that time—of the plans which they laid, of the pleasure which they enjoyed, of the trials through which they passed, of the work which they performed, of the emotions which filled their souls, as they looked upon the very scenes which meet us on every side, and then think that their souls have been called back to the spirit world, and their bodies are moulding away in the silent cities of the dead, does not the whole history seem like a tale that has been told? Yet, how *real* was it all.

One hundred years ago you and I were not. One hundred years hence we shall not be. As God has vouched to us a favored land, with so many privileges, blessings, advantages, let us live to some purpose. Let us live to God's glory, that our lives may reflect His principles, that heaven may be our eternal home. *And to God be all the praise.* Amen.

www.ingramcontent.com/pod-product-compliance
Lightning Source LLC
Chambersburg PA
CBHW030635030726

47497CB00006B/1794